THE UNDEAD CHRONICLES VOLUME 1

Home and Back Again

PATRICK J. O'BRIAN

ISBN: 978-1-60414-983-8

Cover by John Herrick.

Published by

Fideli Publishing, Inc.
119 W. Morgan St.
Martinsville, IN 46151

www.FideliPublishing.com

Special thanks to Brad Wiemer, Korby Sommers,
Jason Chafin, Christie Sommers,

Andy McKnight, Jobina Wiemer, Mike Mueller,
Matthew Grindstaff, Tom Green,

Kevin Sommers, Jeff Groves, Dave Blackford,
Kendrick Shadoan, and Pride Inman.

*This one is for all members of the Armed Forces out there,
both active and retired.*

*Thank you for your service,
and as this world grows crazier by the day,
may you all remain safe while allowing the rest of us to rest easier.*

Other novels by
Patrick J. O'Brian include:

The Fallen

Reaper
(Book 1 of the West Baden Murders Series)

The Brotherhood

Retribution
(Book 2 of the West Baden Murders Series)

Stolen Time

Sins of the Father
(Book 3 of the West Baden Murders Series)

Six Days

Dysfunction
(Book 1 of the Terry Levine Detective Series)

The Sleeping Phoenix

Snowbound
(Book 4 of the West Baden Murders Series)

Sawmill Road
(Book 2 of the Terry Levine Detective Series)

Ghosts of West Baden
(Book 5 of the West Baden Murders Series)

Red Rain
(Book 3 of the Terry Levine Detective Series)

Sin Killer
(Book 4 of the Terry Levine Detective Series)

The Doomsday Clock
(Book 6 of the West Baden Murders Series)

Hallowed Grounds

Non-fiction works by Patrick J. O'Brian include:
Risen from the Ashes: The History of the West Baden Springs Hotel
Pluto in the Valley: The History of the French Lick Springs Hotel

Learn more about Patrick and his projects at:
www.pjobooks.com

One

The end of the world arrived so covertly, subtly, and quickly, that people literally awoke to find their everyday lives gone forever.

Wherever he went, Dan Metzger smelled death in the form of rotting corpses, only the corpses weren't decaying inside buildings, or lying in roadside ditches. Instead, they pursued people like Metzger who remained among the living, fighting to stay that way. Death took on an entirely new meaning when corpses reanimated to seek sustenance from the living.

During those initial days when the dead returned to life, the media referred to movies and television shows for terms. They called the attackers zombies, the undead, walkers, and a plethora of other names that stuck with those who survived long enough to speak them. Like everything else in the world, live news broadcasts soon succumbed to the plague and the effects left in its wake.

Now in late September, nearly a month after the world went batshit crazy, he finally neared his hometown of Tonawanda, New York. A sizeable suburb of Buffalo, the large town held two of the few things left in the world that still mattered to him.

His parents.

Reaching the outskirts of the city on a Harley-Davidson Softail that moved through gridlocked vehicles rather easily, but attracted the undead, Metzger spied a gas station convenience store that looked like an ideal stopping point. Many stores and shops were already looted, indicating the one percent of the human population that survived the contamination and its lasting results were resourceful.

For the most part, he stayed to himself during his travels because he needed definitive answers before forming a long-term survival plan. Besides, he couldn't trust the living, especially when they traveled in numbers, because many of them viewed other people as prey with something to offer. On six different occasions Metzger had witnessed the demise of other people who were swarmed and attacked by the undead, or murdered in cold blood by the living. Whenever he encountered other survivors he tended to keep his distance, warily monitoring their activities until they were out of sight. If he was on foot, he often saw other human beings first and sought a hiding place until they passed.

While not every other person might prove to be an enemy, he dared not take a chance. Besides, meeting people provided him with other options, and he didn't want anything, or anyone, sidetracking him until he made it home.

He parked the motorcycle along the building's side, noticing the main front window was already smashed. Glass shards clung to their frames like icicles, ready to fall at any moment. A thin dusty coating peppered the remaining glass of the store, indicating the complete neglect that befell the world when the contamination wiped out much of the human race.

Stopping to look in the last remaining glass shard of any significance, hanging down from the top of the large window, he saw his reflection that included dark brown hair and a full beard. His brown eyes almost matched the dust obscuring a clear view of his face, and at thirty-three years of age, he never expected to look so haggard.

In his previous life Metzger taught grade school near Cincinnati after moving there for a relationship that eventually fell apart. Using what basic survival skills he possessed, he quickly honed his abilities and learned as he went. Unlike horror movies where everyone dressed skimpily, he often wore layers of thick clothes, even during warm daylight hours, to prevent any bites from penetrating his skin. He chose to grow a beard as fall arrived and razors seldom topped his survival scavenging list.

Riding a motorcycle along city streets provided a completely different experience than before. He casually rode an old Yamaha on weekends before the world changed, but now riding skillfully ensured his survival. The Harley once belonged to someone else, as did practically all of Metzger's belongings. Former owners weren't going to lodge any complaints, because most of them were among the dead, and no one remained to enforce the law.

Standing beside his motorcycle momentarily, Metzger waited to make certain no surprises awaited him. None of the undead exactly sprinted, although a few reached powerwalking speeds if their bodies weren't deteriorated too badly. Most tended to stumble and crawl when mobile, so they weren't incredibly dangerous except in herds. Patting the .357 Magnum at his side, already certain it was loaded with six rounds, he looked to make certain his survival knife was sheathed along his belt. Quiet kills, if one could call finishing off a dead person a kill, proved best for not getting mobbed by nearby undead denizens. Any object that reached the brain, whether bullet or blade, put them down for good. Unfortunately, guns drew the attention of both undead and survivors alike, and Metzger knew stealth was the best defense in the new world.

He knew that cities provided the best chance of finding supplies, but they offered the gravest danger as well. Zombies served as unwitting guards to the remaining canned goods, water, and ammunition survivors craved. Traveling alone within city limits certainly wasn't wise, but Metzger knew his hometown well enough to avoid certain areas with denser populations.

While he didn't consider himself armed to the teeth by any means, Metzger possessed a shotgun and two swords that he briefly considered leaving with the Harley. The two swords came from a higher end pawn shop during his travels, and with a little sharpening, made for very useful weapons. One was full length, and excellent for attacks that required a little distance, but he liked the short sword for taking off heads from behind, and during the few occasions he found himself backed into a corner.

Knowing the store wouldn't be entirely easy to navigate with shelves knocked over and goods spread across the floor, he opted to take the short sword with him. Already dressed for combat with the undead, Metzger wore steel-toed biker boots and leather chaps that protected his calf muscles from ground-level bites. Sweat formed along his face and neck, trickling cool droplets down his shirt beneath the nylon jacket he wore while riding. Despite the late September date, the weather on this day felt more like summer, so he chanced wearing some lighter gear to remain comfortable. Passing out from dehydration would certainly leave him in a vulnerable state regardless of what clothing he donned.

Hearing a throaty growl as he neared the shattered window, Metzger stepped carefully around a toppled Hostess display as he pulled a folded black trash bag from a pocket. Holding the trash bag in one hand and the short sword in the other, he stepped inside after a quick inspection revealed only one obvious threat.

When the end of the world first came about and he understood the danger around him, Metzger studied the undead and finished off every single one he could to make the world a less dangerous place for fellow survivors. He soon realized what an exhausting goal he set for himself, and the attitude of most of the living left him less concerned about their welfare over time. The zombie a few steps away from him wore distressed blue jeans and a ripped New York Yankees jersey that contained streaks of dirt and dried blood. Part of the zombie's upper lip was missing, giving it a permanent sneer of sorts to accompany its lifeless eyes.

He certainly didn't expect to find the undead wearing suits in this part of town, nor did he plan on spotting a luxury car. With winter on the way he certainly wanted to move on from the Harley, however, and into something that could get around and make it through the winter months. A hybrid car sounded perfect for the short term, but he was going to wait until he completed his personal quest before switching vehicles.

After the apocalypse occurred, every attack from even a single zombie left Metzger fearful for his life. Adrenaline kept him moving, and he remembered being incredibly nervous and tense whenever an upright dead person drew near. What felt like life or death, sometimes pure murder in the beginning, became as casual an event as removing the top from a mayonnaise jar.

Being prudent, he stabbed the nearby zombie through the skull as silently as possible, watching it drop to the ground in a heap as he flipped the garbage bag wide open. The noise of rustling plastic failed to attract more danger, so he cautiously walked through the store, picking up canned goods and wrapped perishables. He also snagged a bottle of motor oil for the Harley and a few items to keep it running smoothly. Knowing the day would come when soft drinks would expire and taste flat, he grabbed a few bottles of Coke from the cooler since it was still running.

Some communities still had electricity and utilities, but those few places were falling into darkness as resources dried up and no one replenished them.

Even as he gathered the last of the useful items, Metzger wondered if he really wanted to make the last leg of his journey. In his heart he already knew what he was going to find at the home his parents purchased when they chose to downsize. In the month it took him to recover from the shock of the world's drastic change, and navigate impassible roads while avoiding anything upright, he imagined hundreds of scenarios awaiting him when he walked through that front door.

For weeks he tried calling his parents on both their landline and their cell phones, reaching voicemail every time. He thought about skipping the perilous trek to his native state altogether, but there wasn't anywhere else to go, and he received a phone call that provided him with hope about a week after the world fell apart.

Taking a look around, he saw a few old factories in the distance, knowing Lake Erie was once a major port for businesses. Those days passed even before the end of the normal world, but strangely only a few undead stragglers stumbled down the road in his direction. He knew better than to assume the road ahead was equally uninhabited. His journey home required careful navigation because carelessness meant potentially being downed and devoured like a gazelle in the African safari. Any trip required numerous stops, and sometimes hiding for hours on end, to avoid herds of undead walkers, or their living, marauding counterparts.

He missed simple pleasures like hot showers and carefree rides on his old motorcycle, and if not for his pressing need to reach a familiar house before dark he might have risked cleaning up at the convenience store.

Answers about the disaster that claimed billions of lives certainly weren't forthcoming. The undead were just that, because shooting them anywhere except the head didn't faze them one bit. They didn't even flinch from conventional gunshots. Blood barely emerged from wounds after people died and came back, and it always appeared somewhat coagulated.

Metzger wondered if any scientists remained who might be able to identify the problem, but if *they* were dead any possible cure died with them. The news was little help before radio and television stations signed off for good. Most of the breaking news after the onset showed gruesome and confusing images of staggering walkers attacking people. Later they reported where survivors might find shelter and food because the military was setting up secure camps in metropolitan areas. Eventually every television station went dead, mirroring the human population.

He wondered what kind of devious mind created something that did *this* to humankind. Little doubt remained that the ground zero event, or events in this case, occurred with deliberate malice. Answers never really came from the media, because everyone was busy running for their lives, and the military provided little information other than safety tips. The apocalypse wasn't some sort of trick-or-treat night where people needed warnings to wear reflective clothing and make certain their candy was wrapped. Avoiding strangers might have proven to be a solid tip, but telling the living from the undead wasn't much of a challenge for survivors or animals.

In general, the disaster only affected human beings, not nature or its creatures. For their part, fall leaves continued to change colors to brilliant yellow, red, and orange variations. Plant life and what animals appeared unaffected by whatever airborne pathogen or disease wiped out most of mankind. Metzger hadn't figured out a reason for his own survival, whether it was immunity or some action on his part that kept the contagion from infecting him.

Either way he needed to get back on the road if he planned to make it into his old neighborhood before dusk. After dividing his newfound goods into the two saddlebags he swung one leg over the bike before hitting the ignition switch. The Harley roared to life and Metzger took a sweeping look at the disarray around him, including dead vehicles, and garbage randomly strewn across the road and vacant lots.

A dingy look overtook the world, like a sepia lens used in apocalyptic movies. He supposed those movie directors had it right after all, though he never expected to see such an odd, dusty sight personally. He knew that dust in this case came from flakes of dead skin, and there was certainly enough of that to go around. Rural areas still appeared natural, but the city, with so many smooth surfaces, attracted dust like magnets pull in metal shavings.

Perpetual stench lingered in the air everywhere he went, though he hoped to find rural surroundings again someday for safety and a sense of normality.

Of course such a plan didn't sound feasible for a loner, because supplies eventually ran out and Metzger wasn't skilled in farming.

Booting the kickstand upward, he started down the road toward the more populated areas of town along the highway. He thought about one particular call he'd received from his brother about a week after the plague wiped out mankind and any hope Metzger held of finding his loved ones alive. After taking steps, sometimes risky ones at that, to ensure his smart phone remained charged, Metzger received a call one afternoon from his brother who served in the United States Navy aboard the destroyer *USS Ross*. The *Ross* was on a NATO exercise with a Japanese ship near the Middle East when all hell broke loose. Initially the ship was ordered to stay at sea until the government got a handle on the plague sweeping the nation, but it didn't take long for the destroyer to get ordered back to the States.

Metzger learned little else from his brother except the ship's intended destination, the place he planned to travel as soon as he discovered the fate of his parents. He promised his brother he'd check in on Donald and Connie Metzger, even though it put him behind the expected date for the *Ross* to reach the East Coast.

He pondered momentarily whether to wear a helmet or not during his short trip, thinking he'd like to feel the wind in his hair, unrestricted because there were no longer helmet laws. He often wore it because riding a motorcycle meant constantly dodging stalled vehicles or undead that might lurch toward him at any given second. Putting a bike down suddenly felt a lot more possible with even more dangers than moving vehicles in the new world.

Deciding that acting safely had saved his life in the past, he donned the full-face helmet and fastened the strap beneath his chin. A few minutes later he weaved through stalled cars, some with undead drivers and passengers still trapped by their seatbelts. They groaned and groped as he passed, their discolored fingers refusing to curl as they reached at him hungrily.

Metzger couldn't help but feel some indifference towards the world around him. His emotions hit peaks and valleys the first few weeks after the world changed, and during that time he contemplated ending it all when no realistic options presented themselves. It quickly became apparent that his daily life had gone from shaping young minds to following the routine of a rat, scavenging whatever he could find to survive. Never again would he sleep a full night in comfort, never again would he walk into a restaurant and eat conventional food or worry about how large of a tip to leave, and the chances of discovering anyone he knew alive felt slim.

He expected to find a horrifying scene at the home of his parents, but if he failed to locate his brother, Metzger wasn't sure how much longer he could carry on.

As he took to the side of the road to avoid a cluster of vehicles, his eyes narrowed when he spotted a thin plume of smoke rising in the distance. Immediately thinking it was a burn barrel, his mind scrambled for a plan of action to avoid any potential survivors. Most everything that caught fire after the end of the world extinguished itself within a few weeks of the disaster. Metzger quickly learned the difference between apocalypse fallout and manmade destruction, and this individual plume of smoke wasn't the least bit hidden.

He sensed a trap, and anyone ahead had likely already heard the sound of the Harley approaching. Turning around at this point meant wasting additional time, along with the possibility of being stuck outdoors without shelter at dusk. At a second glance the smoke appeared to be originating from a residential area, but Metzger refused to be complacent. Being cautious and pessimistic about other people had kept him alive among an ever dwindling population.

Desperate people gravitated towards hope and large groups, sometimes with the opposite result of their desires.

A few miles passed in a blur, though Metzger took note of fewer and fewer undead the further into town he traveled. Experience taught him that urban areas were more densely populated with survivors and undead, so his concerns heightened. He entered a business district that once included numerous gas stations and restaurants, finally spying more dead walkers among fewer vehicles. It looked as though someone had made an effort to move many of the vehicles to the side of the streets, so business parking lots all looked like used car lots, packed from end to end.

Figuring he had a vast choice of options when he wanted to ditch the Harley, Metzger didn't take time to study the makes and models just yet. He wanted to get through the business district and closer to home, his stomach still aching because his mind was plagued with the idea of finding an image at home that would haunt him forever. When he finally neared a residential neighborhood a few minutes later he spotted a pickup truck approaching an intersection with a driver, passenger, and someone standing in the truck bed toting a shotgun.

Metzger drew to a complete stop at a non-functioning stop light, watching the truck as it passed. It seemed impossible that everyone in the truck failed to notice him, but even the person in the back glanced with brief indifference at the man on the large motorcycle. Hesitating only a few seconds, Metzger rode forward, shifting into second gear quickly before the truck crew changed their minds and turned around.

He wondered who had taken the time to clear so many streets in the suburb, and why, when his motorcycle entered a rather barren stretch of road. A cluster of storage barrels were located on both sides of the road ahead of him, causing his survival instinct to kick in again because they certainly didn't belong there. His body tensed the second he noticed a chain lying across the road, and as it rose to a taut position about the height of the barrels he prepared for emergency measures.

In an action movie he simply would have laid down the Harley and popped up, uninjured, to draw his weapon and gun down his assailants one by one as the bike skidded down the road with an unrealistic amount of sparks shooting upward.

In the real world he wasn't a thoroughly accomplished motorcycle rider, though he knew how to lay down a bike well enough to skid beneath the chain and avoid damage to his torso or throat altogether. Beyond the chain is where things went wrong, however, as part of the Harley clipped the blacktop and sent the bike into a double flip. Everything happened so quickly that Metzger only saw the Harley hovering over him for the briefest of moments before the top of the seat landed on his shoulder, possibly breaking his left collarbone as pain shot through that area of his body.

The bike landed behind him and teetered on two wheels briefly as though it might fall his way. Figuring his chances were fifty percent with the Harley landing on him, Metzger reached for the sidearm with his right hand, prepared to defend himself against the four men he'd already spied emerging from behind the barrels.

Likely weighted down with concrete, the barrels had secured the chain to ensure the bike's momentum couldn't plow through the crude barricade. Two of the men held baseball bats, and the other two were armed with shotguns, making Metzger's choice of whom to take out first rather easy. Inside the helmet he could only hear his heavy breathing as he pulled the .357 from its holster while cocking the hammer. He typically used the single action mode for accuracy when shooting the undead one at a time, but in a tactical situation it wasn't very prudent.

This was not a negotiation scenario because they hadn't said a word and immediately set to stalking him. He opened fire immediately on the shotgun goon to the right, winging him enough to floor him. The second shotgun carrier brought his gun up immediately, prepared to end Metzger's life when something behind him drew his attention. From the corner of his helmet visor Metzger spied the truck from earlier making a hard stop behind the group of thugs, likely ready to start a turf war for whatever supplies he carried.

Metzger raised the revolver as he pulled the hammer a second time, prepared to dispatch the second shotgun thug when a large shadow eclipsed the sun and he realized the bike wasn't going to fall safely away from him.

"Oh, fuck," Metzger muttered to himself before the Harley came crashing down on his helmet, sending him into blackness.

Two

Metzger immediately sensed a completely different environment when he awoke from unconsciousness. He wondered if he might be dreaming, because his surroundings felt safe, almost peaceful in fact. There wasn't any wind blowing terrible odors into his nostrils, and in fact he thought he smelled a scented candle of some kind. It took him back to his grandmother's house as a child, thinking of the handmade soap bars and their floral aromas on the farm outside of city limits.

Images of furniture began to materialize around him, letting him know he was indoors, but not necessarily safe because his hands were handcuffed to bedposts. If not for the fact that he was restrained, Metzger might have enjoyed the feeling of tranquility that lying atop a bed in a clean house provided. He tested the sturdiness of the handcuffs by tugging on them a few times, finding they were less likely to give than the wooden bedposts they were wrapped around.

His left shoulder hurt like hell, but he felt confident the collarbone wasn't broken. It wasn't until he turned his head to look at a nearby window that he realized a pounding pressurized sensation like two large hands were clamping both sides of his skull and pushing inward. Thinking he might have sustained a concussion from the crash and his motorcycle landing atop his helmet, Metzger discovered a purple sky that indicated dusk was upon his home city.

He certainly wasn't reaching his objective on this day, and he wondered if living to see morning would pan out. If the people who set the snare simply wanted to loot his belongings, there wasn't any need to abduct him. They simply could have killed him or left him in the middle of the road for zombies to feast on before he ever regained consciousness. He couldn't reach any *good* conclusion about why someone might want to hold him captive.

Although he couldn't see much, Metzger figured he was inside a multi-level house, possibly built during the Victorian era. Objects on the ground outside of the window appeared lower, and the skyline was clearly visible, meaning the house likely had two or three stories. As for the room, aside from the bed he saw a dresser complete with mirror, a rocking chair a few feet from the bed, an end table with a lamp that seemed to be functioning properly, and three large boxes stacked in one corner. For a change there weren't streaks of blood, litter, grime, or dead bodies within his line of sight.

Only his jacket had been removed, leading him to believe he hadn't been abducted by looters who wanted his belongings or his life. His chaps and boots remained below his torso, which proved a bit uncomfortable when he wasn't riding where the breeze and the weather kept him cool. Although curious about his captors, he didn't want to yell out and make a bad first impression. The positioning of his body made any kind of relaxation impossible, even if he suddenly adopted a philosophy of letting the chips fall where they may.

His questions were answered in part when a young girl, probably around eight years of age, stepped to the bedroom door and stopped at the threshold for a look at him. Metzger tried to avoid staring at her, and he definitely didn't want to talk to her because adults were certainly nearby. The last thing he wanted to do was present himself as a manipulator of children or some kind of evil bastard. Appearing somewhat sheepish to him, she deflected her looks from him to the floor, causing him to wonder how much, or how little, she had seen of this harsh new world.

Her olive skin made him question her ethnicity, not that such a fact mattered much considering his predicament.

Metzger didn't have to decide his next move because a pair of hands came to rest on the girl's shoulders, gently ushering her away from the door. A slightly overweight man just over forty years in age came into view at the doorway, staring at Metzger through trendy eyeglasses. The man's dirty blond hair seemed thick and well-groomed, and a trimmed beard with blond and gray hairs covered much of his lower jaw. He wore blue jeans and a flannel shirt, both clean as though the apocalypse hadn't yet struck this part of the city.

Leaning against the doorway, he folded his arms and continued to scrutinize Metzger as though he wanted the handcuffed man to initiate a conversation.

"Are the cuffs for my protection or yours?" Metzger finally asked in a neutral tone, not wanting to anger this man until he understood his motives.

"They're for ours," the man answered with a slight lisp.

"I'm not dangerous. I was attacked out on the highway."

"We know," the man answered. "Just because someone wanted your things doesn't mean *you* aren't dangerous, too."

Metzger groaned, really not having a reasonable way to explain his innocence in the entire ordeal since this man didn't seem inclined to believe him.

"Luke, what are you doing?" another man's voice called from behind the first.

When the second man came into view, he appeared about twenty years older than the first, with gray, thinning hair shaved close to his scalp. A five o'clock shadow adorned the lower half of his face, but his piercing blue eyes immediately looked to Metzger with concern and surprise. He apparently hadn't expected to see him awake quite so soon.

"Luke, this is no way to treat the man," he said, gently caressing the first man's shoulders a few seconds before stepping inside the room.

Metzger quickly assessed that the two men were more than just friends, though he questioned how the girl fit into their living situation.

He tensed as the older man drew closer until he realized the man was holding a key in one hand, as opposed to a knife.

"A little jumpy?" the man asked as he undid the handcuffs, much to the chagrin of his partner standing with folded arms at the doorway.

"Everything about this world makes me a little jumpy," Metzger answered, rubbing his wrists once free of the handcuffs.

"You took quite a spill on the road," the man said. "We didn't want to take any chances in case you had a head injury."

"It hurts, but I don't think I'm a danger to anyone."

"I'll be the judge of that," the man at the doorway said.

"Luke! That's enough!"

The older man provided an apologetic look as Metzger swung his feet to the side of the bed to try regaining full circulation.

"I'm Albert," he said as he shook hands with Metzger. "Before all of this happened I was an ER nurse in Buffalo."

Metzger stood, trying to stretch his appendages and assess any damage to his body from the motorcycle fall.

"Why are you trusting me?" he asked.

"Because you're alone. Those pricks wouldn't have targeted you if you were a real threat."

Supposing that made sense, Metzger shrugged.

"My bike?"

"We think the bastards took it. But we managed to fend them off long enough to get most of your weapons and supplies."

"Thank you," Metzger said. "I'm Dan, and I was a teacher in Cincinnati when the world fell apart."

"And what brings you back here?" the husky man asked suspiciously.

"I'm from the area and I never found out what happened to my parents. They live a few miles from here. Well, assuming *here* is close to where I was ambushed."

"You'll have to forgive my partner," Albert said. "He thinks everyone is the enemy."

"It's probably not the worst credo to stand by these days."

Metzger felt like a third wheel in their cozy setup, knowing it was too dangerous to step outside at night, although he felt uncomfortable staying. He wanted to trust two gay men and their adopted daughter, but he knew some people posed a far greater threat than the undead. Until his weapons were returned to him and he saw daylight outside, Metzger couldn't fathom feeling remotely comfortable.

"Luke, why don't you go check on Samantha?" Albert suggested.

Without so much as a word, the younger man provided a sour look before doing an about face and leaving the doorway.

"He's probably a little bit sensitive with another man in the house."

"Have the three of you been alone since this began?"

Albert took a seat in the rocking chair to get comfortable before continuing their conversation.

"I was with Luke before all of this began. He's always felt a bit insecure because for the longest time I made most of the money. Just before the world fell apart he received a promotion to technology director at one of the local museums. It finally offered him some influence and a hefty raise. Just when he thought we were on equal footing the world went and pulled the rug out from under him."

"The world doesn't care about money these days," Metzger stated the obvious.

"Yes. And with a complete lack of survival skills, Luke is now forced to rely upon me once again. I'm teaching him what I know, like how to shoot and scavenge for food, but it's tough when we're forced to take care of a young one."

"Was she orphaned when everything went down?"

"Yes. Samantha lived a few doors down and the poor thing came to us covered in blood, in complete shock, the morning everything went crazy. Like a lot of people her parents were torn to shreds before they had a grasp of what was going on around them. Her father was a black lawyer in the area, and her mother a nice white lady who tutored and did taxes during the spring. They made Luke and me feel like we weren't the only odd ducks on the block."

Metzger rubbed his wrists, trying to regain full circulation and lose the red circles that the handcuffs created.

"I might as well give you the nickel tour," Albert said, standing from the chair as Metzger slowly rose from the bed to follow him.

For the first time Metzger noticed the man had a holstered pistol tucked into his backside, which proved he wasn't entirely trusting of his guest after all.

"So you two lived here before everything went down and you're *still* here?"

Albert nodded without turning around as they exited the bedroom.

"So far we've found everything we need in the Tonawanda area, and the house is pretty secure most of the time."

"Most of the time?"

Albert shrugged, flipping on the light to a nearby bathroom to begin the tour.

"We still have power, but we try to keep light and noises to a minimum to avoid attracting undesirables. There's no telling how long that's going to last, so we stock up on candles and firewood."

Metzger took a look inside the bathroom, which looked practically immaculate considering three people resided within the house. It featured a sink, a full bathtub with shower, toilet, and some white cabinets for storage.

"We still have hot water," Albert noted.

"Nice."

"So what's your story?" Albert inquired as he showed Metzger room by room what the old Victorian house held, including two more bedrooms on the second level.

"I'm from this area, but I moved near Cincinnati to be with a girl I met during my college years. We reconnected on one of those online friend sites and started dating over the internet. I moved there when I got a job, but things didn't work out between us."

"Did she make it?" Albert asked as they descended the old wooden stairway.

"I don't know. Things ended badly between us, so I never really checked."

Metzger pictured more details of her in his mind, but he wasn't going to tell his entire backstory and love life to a complete stranger. In truth, he knew a little more than he let on, but he wanted to push that first day of tragic circumstances out of his mind.

"Where do you hope to end up?" Albert asked, showing him the immense kitchen with an island for preparing food and dining.

A rack full of pots and pans hung over the island, while the opposite side contained three stools with backrests for convenient dining.

"I'm trying to get east because my brother's ship is heading to their base in Virginia."

Albert shot him a strange look.

"He's in the Navy," Metzger explained. "I'm trying to figure out what happened to our parents before I meet up with him. I figure it's a lot safer being around military guys with food and rations if I can make it there."

"Makes sense."

"I've gotta ask. How do you guys keep from getting overrun in this place?"

"Like I said, low profile for one," Albert said as he walked toward the front door, opening it for them to look outside. "And the other reason is that."

Metzger stared at a wooden gate that stood close to eight feet high, blocking the view of the street outside. He glanced left and right, finding that the gate surrounded the entire house, though the yard wasn't very large because the neighborhood houses appeared very close in proximity.

He considered the structure an impending deathtrap because the neighborhood appeared dense with houses, which meant plenty of undead lurking in the area.

"Do you clear the area?" he asked.

"When we go out for supplies I usually clear the block. We don't get many surprises since we keep things quiet."

"You're not going to be able to stay here forever," Metzger noted. "There's just as much danger from the living if they find out you have a safe haven with food and supplies."

He realized what a colossal chance the trio took in saving him from certain death. Even if the people who stole his motorcycle didn't kill him, they certainly would have left him for the undead to devour.

"I want to thank you for taking a chance on me out there."

"You're quite welcome," Albert said with a nod. "I'm just glad you didn't turn out to be some psychopath loner."

"I'm no psychopath, and I'm hoping to meet up with family and ditch the loner tag soon enough."

Albert chuckled.

"Well, you shouldn't have to-"

Before the older man finished his sentence, both were startled by the sound of a loud truck roaring just up the street from them. Sucking in a deep breath to listen intently, Metzger felt certain it was growing closer, and in a hurry.

"The lights!" he warned Albert in a hushed, frantic whisper, thinking of the few candles they still had burning inside.

To survivors, any artificial lighting indicated living people huddled within a house, and he suspected this truck was somehow tied in with the highway incident from earlier.

Metzger followed Albert inside, peering out the window closest to the door through a slit in the closed blinds. He quietly shut the door beside him, tracking the truck's movements through the window, finding a single street lamp outside that refused to shut down, making it difficult to follow the headlights. The sound of the truck's loud engine and lack of proper exhaust drew closer, and suddenly the lights went off, causing Metzger's heart to skip a beat. He felt positive this truck was looking specifically for survivors or places to raid. He wanted to believe that these people outside had nothing to do with Albert and Luke, but didn't dare rule anything out just yet. For all he knew this could be a stage in an even larger, more elaborate trap.

He turned around, finding no one behind him.

Although he couldn't see the two men or the girl, Metzger heard voices in one of the nearby rooms. For some reason Albert hadn't snuffed any of the candles within the house, probably because Luke caught his ear first. It sounded as though the two were arguing about something, and Metzger knew that any delays jeopardized all of them if the people inside the truck were aiming to cause trouble.

"We need to make this house dark," he said as he stepped into the next doorway, startling both men. "Do either of you know who these people are?"

"No," Albert said, quickly brushing past him and darting up the stairs.

"Has anyone come around here like this before?" Metzger pressed, following him.

Albert stepped into the first bedroom and blew out a candle before answering.

"Not before we stopped to pick you up."

The tone in the man's voice seemed to imply he wasn't entirely trusting of his guest.

Both stopped in their tracks as they heard the truck brake loudly almost directly in front of the house.

"You're not equipped to fend off multiple attackers," Metzger noted. "Especially with a child in the house."

"What are you suggesting?" Albert retorted, picking up the pace as he headed for the second bedroom and cut off the oil supply to a small lantern, darkening it immediately.

Metzger made his way toward a window that faced out front, wanting an overhead look at the person or people who had the audacity to travel at night and seek out supplies from the living. He saw a burly man in the driver's seat, and the person beside him seemed to be aiming some kind of device in a semicircular pattern. As Albert assumed the other side of the window, Metzger stared at the device, initially thinking it might be some sort of tracker, or camera, still functional despite most technological devices proving useless as power dwindled.

"Son-of-a-bitch," Metzger muttered, finally realizing what the man in the front passenger's seat was holding. "They've got a thermal camera."

Numbers of trips with school kids to fire stations provided Metzger with the ability to distinguish what a thermal camera looked like and how it worked.

These thugs were likely looking for heat signatures from people or recently used vehicles.

He looked to Albert.

"Where did you park your truck?"

"We leave it on the street because we don't have anywhere to hide it."

Metzger groaned, closing his eyes momentarily. He knew these people couldn't possibly prove friendly, and he suspected they were members of the group that tried to take his head off earlier in the night with a chain.

"I need my weapons," Metzger said sternly.

"You can't fight them," Albert insisted, turning back after a glimpse out the window. "I saw at least four."

Metzger counted four as well, now that the men were all exiting the truck and beginning to explore the area. All four appeared armed with pistols or rifles, each of them wearing dark clothing to conceal them in the impending darkness. They didn't move like police officers or former military personnel, nor did their garb look anything like uniforms. Perhaps they were just stragglers who found one another over time, not possessing much experience with tactics or firearms.

He looked to Albert, finding apprehension in the man's face like he dared not take an extra step beyond freeing his guest from handcuffs.

"Your best case scenario is I can distract these guys away from you, and keep them from finding your girl. The worst case is that I'm with these guys and it becomes a five-on-three situation for you. But I think you already know that's not the case."

Albert looked out the window to the four men now scouring the area, then back to his guest with a poker face.

"Time is ticking away," Metzger pressed.

"Fine," Albert said, walking briskly to the stairs with his guest close behind.

They descended the stairs before heading into a family room with several custom book shelves built into the walls, a large wooden desk, and a gun safe in one corner. Metzger was actually surprised when Albert bypassed the safe entirely for a hallway that was hidden in plain sight, painted in such a way that the naked eye couldn't even tell it led to another room until only a few feet away.

Following Albert inside, Metzger found the man grabbing a few pistols for himself, along with a shotgun, simply nodding toward a small pile of weaponry that Metzger recognized immediately. He took up the pack that held his two swords, getting his arms through the straps with practiced ease. The weight of the .357 felt good as he strapped the gun belt around his waist, taking up a survival knife immediately after that. He wasn't sure he wanted the burden of a rifle while trying to sneak around outside, but after spying the MP5 he often kept in the Harley's saddlebags, he decided a strapped weapon he could throw around his shoulder wasn't too cumbersome.

"You're leaving the rest?" Albert asked with a hint of surprise.

"I plan on coming back," Metzger said, speaking the truth. "If that's okay with you."

Running off into the night was one of the most reckless and rash things any sane person could do, and he couldn't remember the last time he slept a full, restful night without fear of being ripped apart by the undead, or freezing to death in the gradually cooling overnights.

"If you can get rid of them, we'll be in your debt," Albert admitted. "And if not..."

He racked the slide on the semi-automatic pistol he had just picked up to indicate he wouldn't go down without a fight if any of the four men dared enter the house.

Metzger gave an understanding nod, knowing there wasn't any time to waste. "How can I get out of here unseen?"

"This way," Albert said, leading him to the back of the house.

A few sounds reached their ears from outside the front door, causing Metzger to believe the four men were battling some of the undead that heard the ruckus.

Albert showed him to a well-secured backdoor that featured several brackets with wood laid across them and a metal panic bar that forked directly beneath the doorknob. Albert pulled away the panic bar and Metzger assisted him with removing the timber nestled in the brackets, which allowed them to open the backdoor. He gave his weapons one last check as Albert pulled the door open.

"You didn't unload them, did you?" Metzger asked, drawing a thin smile from the older man.

"You're good to go."

"Wish me luck," Metzger said before stepping into the darkness and cold outside, wishing he'd asked where his jacket went while gathering his other belongings.

It might have provided protection against the cold and against bites from anything that wasn't warm-blooded.

Because the house wasn't very bright inside, Metzger required very little time for his eyes to adjust to the darkness outside. His hearing felt incredibly acute as well because he heard zombies, the four men, and their running truck simultaneously. Unfortunately he found himself surrounded by the wooden fence that encompassed the house and the property. Getting on the other side of the fence wasn't going to be easy because numerous objects like trash cans and vehicles were placed against the rails to act as secondary barricades.

"Great," Metzger muttered, heading straight to the back end where a gate might normally be found.

He walked less than twenty paces to find the gate completely blocked by a smart car that might be easy to move if he possessed the means to start it. Instead of searching for alternatives, he decided to climb the vehicle to jump the fence. After scaling the vehicle's small hood, he peered over the fence to find a safe landing awaiting him, free of booby-traps and anything with teeth. Grabbing hold of the top, he propelled his body over with ease, completely lacking the style of a gymnast.

Metzger immediately headed for the narrow space between the fence and the house next door to find a vantage point to see how the four men were faring against what few undead populated the neighborhood. As quickly and quietly as he could manage, Metzger tiptoed along the side yard until he reached the end of the gap near the front of the house. All noise except for the running truck motor had ceased since he jumped the fence, so he cautiously peered over the junk lined up near the end of the makeshift alley, hoping to find the four men giving up their search and moving onward.

Instead he discovered they were splitting up and beginning to search each nearby yard, including the house Metzger exited less than a minute ago. Keeping himself hidden from view, Metzger decided not to act unless one of the men barged into the Victorian house. It remained unclear what drew these strangers to the neighborhood, or exactly what they expected to find. He had a feeling the four belonged to the group that attacked him earlier, which meant they would receive no quarter in any kind of skirmish.

Because he focused so intently on the four armed men, Metzger forgot to check behind him. Less than two feet separated the wooden fence from the neighboring house, so when he heard the low growl of a zombie behind him, Metzger quickly turned around, accidentally kicking a few aluminum cans on the ground. Immediately cursing under his breath, he saw the undead straggler about ten feet away, but the bigger threat came from the attention he drew.

"Hey!" he heard the nearest man yell to his group as he began walking from the porch of a nearby house toward Metzger's location.

About to enter the fight of his life, Metzger checked the MP5 to ensure it was ready to fire and set to fully automatic. He took a deep breath, hunkered down behind the trash heap, and waited to see which form of potential death would reach him first.

Three

Hidden from view where the four men had exited the truck, Metzger listened for the one gun-toting man to draw closer as he watched the growling undead walker stumble toward him in the starlit space between two houses. Feeling certain he was about to get bitten, shot, or both, he heard footsteps draw closer by the second, only able to monitor the zombie. If he dared peek over the piled trash that blocked any direct view into the street, he placed himself in the line of fire. Considering the single gunman had called for his friends, Metzger had no idea whether the man was alone or drawing three friends to his side.

He hadn't heard any other voices, but that didn't mean they weren't using some kind of sign language to encircle him.

Hearing footsteps on the other side of the trash wall, Metzger was forced to focus on the female zombie drawing closer to him. Tattered remains of a blouse with blood and dirt stains barely clung to her torso and a bite mark was evident in her neck. A lot of people were caught off-guard those first few days, falling victim to what everyone initially believed was a sickness sweeping through their cities. He imagined this woman came home to a husband or child already turned from a death state, assaulted before she comprehended the danger.

Metzger knew none of the undead possessed very much strength in their arms and legs. Their power came from herding together, and in their teeth, which snapped shut with quickness and ferocity seen only in wild predators. He wondered if their other senses were dulled, or might fade over time. The fact that their brains still operated on some rudimentary level gave him the impression it might be years before the danger truly dissipated.

Hoping he didn't get shot for his efforts, Metzger dared reach toward the zombie, grabbing some of its clothing near the waistline before pulling it near him. Keeping low in a seated position, he was able to use momentum to yank the zombie toward the opening behind him. The armed man reached the opening at just the right moment, receiving a zombie attack for his curiosity as the undead creature immediately snapped at his throat, finding the mark. His howls filled the air, and although Metzger couldn't see the attack very well, he heard the sound of skin splitting as the zombie fed on the tissue and blood like a child slurping a juice box. The screams lasted only a few seconds, and by then Metzger was halfway down the narrow walkway between the two houses, knowing full well the sound would attract trouble in the form of the remaining three men and more undead.

Sounds of noisy eating, like a family dog scarfing down moist food, continued to reach his ears as he neared safety.

Needing to know how the remaining men would respond, he found a fairly safe spot near the end of the grassy path. Turning around, he watched the zombie fall over the makeshift garbage barrier to finish devouring its victim. He hoped the men might believe their colleague was careless, falling victim to a random zombie while he scoured the area. Somehow he doubted such luck was on his side, but it only took a few seconds for the three men to emerge and convene on the area. From his position, Metzger was able to hear virtually everything around him, so he caught what few words they spoke.

"Fuck," the first muttered, standing in the center with a scowl.

"He got careless," the man on the left stated as the zombie continued to feed on the fourth man without another care in the world.

His brown hair was slicked back in a disheveled ponytail, and Metzger judged him as the muscle, maybe even a decent shot, but someone who followed orders. Perhaps he wanted to be accepted as an intellectual contributor to the group, but his forensic analysis of this particular situation wasn't accurate.

"Like hell he did," the man on the right growled. "Mike knew better than that."

Metzger sensed this man was the brains behind the operation, whatever their membership and mission statement might be. Slender, strong, and well-spoken, this man seemed to have a handle on their situation, even with danger surrounding them.

"What now?" the center man asked.

"We keep looking. Those pricks came this way after stealing our shit."

With no visible empathy for his fallen comrade, the same man removed a knife from its sheath on his belt and stabbed the distracted zombie in the head, downing it permanently while not giving away his location to living or dead alike.

Feeling utterly bewildered, Metzger wondered what he missed during his state of unconsciousness on the highway. He knew his hosts picked him up from what seemed to be certain death along the road, but how on earth had they found time to steal anything from anyone?

"Those sons-of-bitches loot our stash and expect us to take it?" one of them grumbled aloud.

To Metzger the three men seemed furious, though consistently so and not simply pissed off about this one particular incident. He wondered if his new hosts had indeed invaded someone else's stash or perhaps another party was guilty. Of course no one else could have retrieved loot and happened to return to *this* particular area he surmised, shaking his head. Albert didn't seem like the type to mastermind the theft of someone else's goods, particularly with a partner who waffled about virtually everything, and a young girl to protect.

Something didn't add up.

He watched as the three men returned to their original plan of splitting up and searching for whatever they sought. For some reason they had left the thermal imaging camera in their truck, probably because they found a vehicle with a warm engine just down the street. For a fleeting second as he watched all three walk in different directions at the end of the narrow walkway, Metzger considered leaving the property altogether. Getting into a turf war over supplies wasn't part of his plan, and he no longer felt confident his hosts were trustworthy people.

At this point he dared tiptoe to the end of the path once again, stopping to view the remains of the fourth man and the zombie that ripped his neck and internal organs apart. Blood and intestines rested next to both bodies, and it occurred to Metzger that the trio hadn't stabbed their buddy in the head. If he was going by movie and television lore, considering this man had been bitten by an infected zombie, he was due to turn into one sooner or later.

Personally, Metzger hadn't witnessed this notion being proven or disproven in the month since the world as he knew it ended. Of course he hadn't been around other people long enough to experience much of anything.

Although it was an unnecessary risk, he decided to leave the body behind and see what happened. His eyes followed the directions the three remaining men took, noticing one of them had headed to the right, directly toward the front gate of Albert's house. Giving a glance in each direction, Metzger made certain no one spotted him before stepping over the two bodies and moving toward the porch under the cover of darkness. No street lights worked directly overhead, moonlight was currently obscured by clouds, and the truck the four men drove in was pointed in the opposite direction.

He wasn't certain if Albert might have taken steps to defend the house or not, so he decided not to jump the fence and walk up to the residence. Stepping past a window might cause a startled reaction that sent buckshot his way through a front window.

Metzger had spent the past month surviving on instinct and avoiding people virtually altogether. Now he found himself stalking one of three remaining dangerous individuals along a dark residential street. Trying to stay along the sidewalk and out of any moonlight, he crept along without a sound, drawing a nervous breath because the man wasn't visible, and he didn't know where the armed individuals disappeared to on their individual routes.

Unable to watch his own back as he looked to his right for the man closest to Albert's house, Metzger spied the man undoing the tall, wooden gate's latch to let himself inside. A safe distance away, he was able to step atop a trash can and observe the man over the fence top.

In what he assumed was an attempt to avoid drawing attention to the residence, the porch looked reasonably unmodified except for a few staged items blocking the stairs to the front porch. A plastic trash tote, a trash bag that appeared full of aluminum cans, and a few toddler plastic push toys barricaded the way enough that an undead walker might stumble over them and create noise and provide some warning of nearby danger.

In this case the armed man eyed the items suspiciously as though thinking they were conveniently placed there by the living and not indiscriminately thrown away. Metzger crouched, staring at the man for what felt like an eternity as his heart thumped in his chest. He nervously prayed he wouldn't need to act, and wasn't certain of what he planned to do if the man started up the wooden stairs.

Don't do it, he thought to himself, trying to psychically dissuade the man from carrying out an act that might end in someone's death.

Stepping over the black trash bag, the man cautiously stepped on the first wooden stair, causing it to squeak. He looked down, as though making certain he didn't trigger any kind of trap before lifting his leg toward the second step. Metzger prayed for intervention, and just before the man's foot reached the second stair, a static-filled squawk came through the radio at his side, startling him enough that he fell backwards, barely catching the weight of his body and staggering upright instead of crashing against the littered ground.

Feeling certain his breathing could be heard around the city block after being equally shocked, Metzger sucked in a breath and held it while a transmission came across the man's portable radio, less than twenty feet from his position.

"We found the assholes who took our shit," the voice said. "Get back here and help round up the rest of them and our loot."

Metzger didn't know who the culprits were, or how many of these armed men camped in the greater Buffalo area, but he wouldn't have wanted to be the one guilty of stealing from them. He waited and watched as all three men emerged from the shadows and returned to their truck, talking about putting a hurting on some motherfuckers when they got back to their camp. Metzger now knew Albert and Luke weren't the guilty party, which left them in the clear for now. His heart sunk at the fact that the men had traveled to this area to find the thieves, which possibly put the two men and their adopted daughter in mortal danger if the group returned.

Tracing his path between the two houses back to the rear entrance, Metzger stepped over the two bodies, able to think more clearly about ending a man's life in the name of self-defense. Certainly no murderer by nature, even in the current circumstances, he felt bad for using a zombie as a weapon. He wondered if the man's buddies felt any remorse for leaving his body behind like discarded trash.

Within a few minutes Metzger found a pile of debris that helped him scale the tall fence along the backyard and return to the backdoor of the house. He decided to knock, hoping Albert knew the men had left the area and didn't blast him with a shotgun from the other side. Being cautious, he stepped to the side of the door, waiting patiently a moment for the door to open or the scuffling noise of someone approaching it from inside. Waiting in silence, Metzger listened carefully but heard nothing as he debated whether to knock again or simply leave the premises with his life and most of his belongings.

He was just about to turn away when he heard the deadbolt sliding from the inside and several items being moved away from the door. When it opened he was surprised to find Luke on the other side with a rather sheepish look, as though admitting without words that he misjudged Metzger initially.

"Come in," he said, waving his arm quickly toward the house's interior.

Metzger hesitated, wondering if they had set some kind of trap for him just inside the door. Between the way the world operated now, and this man's mistrust of him less than an hour prior, he couldn't help but feel suspicious. Taking too much time to process information or reach a decision often proved deadly in a world where the undead ruled and the living scoured the earth for what precious few commodities remained for the taking.

Stepping inside, he looked around rather cautiously, finding no one except Luke standing beside the door. The man closed it rather quickly as Albert and Samantha finally made their presence felt by coming down the main stairway. Their footsteps sounded hurried, as though they were anxious to hear what Metzger had to report. Perhaps they hadn't seen or heard a single thing that transpired just outside their house, but Metzger had a feeling they weren't yet safe based on the way the group of men tracked a warm vehicle to their neighborhood.

"What happened?" Albert asked with a relieved look, openly excited about escaping the jaws of death so easily.

It required only a few minutes for Metzger to provide the group with his harrowing tale. He skimmed over the part where he used a zombie as a murder weapon with Samantha present, and refused to tell the trio how much trouble they might be in because the three remaining men suspected their friend wasn't simply attacked by the undead. He did inform them that the armed men were contacted by others via portable radios, and only left so quickly because their missing goods were located.

"You need rest," Albert said after a visual examination of his guest. "You're spending the night."

"I don't want to impose."

"We aren't sending you on your way in the dark. It's too dangerous out there."

Metzger didn't sense any ulterior motive from any of his three hosts. They all appeared thankful he went outside to confront the intruders, even if he didn't really contribute to the reason for their departure.

He wasn't sure he'd be able to sleep after everything that transpired outdoors, coupled with the snare that knocked him from his motorcycle earlier. Adrenaline once kept him involuntarily awake for hours, but his body shut down quickly due to fatigue, injury, and the overwhelming guilt that accompanied him from basically taking his first human life.

It required only a few minutes lying in bed for him to decide that he wanted to take a chance on a full night's rest. If his hosts meant him harm, his death would likely come swiftly and he would never know it. No matter where he normally crashed for a night, impending danger always lurked in the form of the undead, or worse, the living who wanted the space or supplies for themselves.

When he awoke, it wasn't due to some strange noise or a nightmare, it was actually because his face grew warm from sunlight striking it. Squinting, he discovered the curtain covering most of the bedroom window didn't cover one edge, and when the sun positioned itself just right the curtain let the morning light inside. He supposed technically the planet rotated, giving the appearance of the sun moving overhead, but Metzger wasn't a science major and decided not to think too hard on the subject. Instead he rolled over and attempted to capture a few more minutes of sleep.

His attempt failed when the aroma of cooked bacon and eggs reached his nostrils from the distant kitchen. In a world of perishable food, Metzger considered anything fresh a delicacy, wondering how much longer such eatables were going to last. Most animals were being needlessly slaughtered by creatures that likely didn't need to eat for any real sustenance, and unfortunately the undead outnumbered absolutely everything else on the planet.

At least in what little bit of the world Metzger had seen, this particular theory held true.

He walked downstairs to find Albert cooking in the kitchen with Samantha seated on a barstool behind the island. Incredibly well-behaved, she barely said a word, though she wasn't shy or intimidated by strangers. After years of teaching, he expected any kid who hadn't reached puberty to be bouncing off the walls wanting to dash outside.

Being confined to a house felt like prison, but stepping outside meant a death sentence to those who weren't prepared for what awaited them.

"Want some breakfast?" Albert asked as Metzger stretched his arms, surprisingly fulfilled by a full night's slumber.

"Smells great."

"Go take a shower and I'll cook you something when you're ready."

"Shower?" Metzger questioned, immediately realizing he barely managed to contain his excitement over the prospect of a hot shower.

"God knows how long, but we still have hot water."

Metzger nodded before returning upstairs to lock himself in the bathroom for twenty minutes until the hot water began to dwindle. Perhaps circumstances toyed with his senses, but he felt certain the shower was the most refreshing he'd ever taken. Feeling like a terrible houseguest, Metzger used shampoo, body wash, and even a fresh bar of soap to remove the dirt and grime from every crevice and pore along his body. He got dressed and decided to step outside the front door before eating breakfast, wondering if he was just putting off leaving a safe and secure place, or delaying what answers awaited him down the road.

Moans and groans from the undead wandering nearby immediately reached his ears from beyond the front gate, hurling him back to any reality the smells of breakfast and the comforts of hot water provided. He considered walking inside to grab one of his swords when a voice called down to him from above.

"Beautiful morning."

Turning around, he found Luke sitting on the flat porch roof above him, smoking the last of a cigarette. Deciding not to be rude, Metzger climbed a nearby metal ladder that provided access to the roof, taking a seat next to the man a moment later.

"There aren't many of these left in the world," Luke said, taking a final drag from the cigarette before snuffing it out along the roof tiles. "They're going to be a hotter commodity in this world than they ever were in prisons."

Metzger chuckled.

"Might be a good time to quit."

Both sat silently on the porch roof a moment, hearing the sounds of the undead and smelling the unpleasant stench that coated the urban world. Occasionally Metzger took roads less traveled during his journey north and escaped the odors, only to be slammed with them when he drew near cities or towns once again. Death provided its own nauseating scent, but urine and fecal release accompanied death, providing a toxic trio of stenches that lingered in the air.

Taking notice that Luke had completely clean shaven, Metzger considered doing the same, but it would simply grow back during his travels. A beard was easier to trim than to take down to stubble or skin, so he opted not to touch a single hair just yet.

Luke took off his glasses momentarily, cleaning them with his button-up shirt.

"I really don't even need these," he commented, placing them back above his nose. "They were more of a fashion statement before all of this, and no one really gives a shit anymore."

"So you have twenty-twenty vision?"

"No, but I'd see well enough if I were to lose them."

Both sat in awkward silence a moment as the undead sauntered by, just outside the fence on an otherwise, warm, sunny day.

"I want to apologize," Luke finally said, still staring at the suburb before them.

"For what?"

"I don't want to trust anyone, and I'm so afraid of losing Albert."

"Losing him? To those?"

Metzger nodded toward the staggering undead that bumped into cars and fences without feeling any pain.

"No. I'm afraid someone better is going to come along and replace me."

"That's not going to happen," Metzger said confidently.

Luke looked at him with a level of uncertainty.

"I know you don't feel built for this world," Metzger said with a light shrug. "Truth be told, I don't bring any skills to the table. I'm not an engineer, a soldier, or even a very good mechanic. Fuck, I'm just trying to survive long enough to find my brother and some of his military buddies."

"This house is the last thing we have from the old world. It's crushing us to think about leaving it behind."

"Does that mean you *are* thinking about it?"

"We talk about it, but we don't know where we'd go. These things are sure to freeze during the winter, aren't they?"

Metzger shook his head, wishing he knew how undead anatomy responded to freezing temperatures.

"You have to leave here eventually," he warned before even thinking about his words and putting them more tactfully. "It just isn't safe with so many survivors around here. Last night was a close call, and I have a feeling those assholes will be back."

Luke nervously fingered his chin momentarily. He seemed to understand Metzger's advice was sound, but something about his situation held him back.

"Albert doesn't want to leave. He thinks we can fortify this place and keep Samantha safe with us."

"You can fortify it, but that draws attention to you. Hell, being on the road isn't much better. I haven't been able to trust anyone I've come across."

"Until last night I felt the same way."

Metzger wanted to help the trio since they took a major risk saving his life, but they weren't willing to travel, and he wasn't willing to stick around the Buffalo area with them, even if he received an official invitation. Before deciding anything long-term, he needed closure about his parents, and to see his military brother alive and well.

"We have several vehicles we've collected," Luke said after a moment of silence between them. "There isn't much else left to fill our days, so we scavenge what we can. You're welcome to take one of the cars if you want, since you lost your mode of transportation."

"It was never really mine," Metzger admitted with a grin. "I can probably find another one, but the bikes just announce your presence to the world."

"I think we have a hybrid that'll be a lot quieter. You're welcome to it."

"I appreciate that."

Luke laughed momentarily.

"It's not like you can't grab one of the millions of cars lining the roads out there, but we can save you a few minutes."

"I just can't believe I'm finally this close," Metzger admitted.

"You're in an unenviable position. After Albert and I came out, most of our families turned on us, so we didn't have many people left to worry about. I tried to contact what few friends and cousins I still cared about, but when I got no answer I just assumed the worst."

Metzger suspected about ninety percent of the population was roaming the world without life, which meant suddenly many people were the sole remainder of their bloodlines. His brother had a wife and son that neither of them had been able to reach since the mystery plague killed many of the living. Considering they were living near the military base in Norfolk, Virginia, where Metzger was heading after this adventure, that didn't bode well for what he expected to find there.

"I'm not getting my hopes up," he said with defeat in his voice. "It's just closure for me and my brother knowing one way or the other."

"Did you talk to them after everything went crazy?"

"I talked to Mom a few times, but things didn't sound good. She was afraid to look outside the window and I heard Dad keep telling her to get back. We got disconnected the last time and that was the last I ever heard from either one of them."

"That's terrible," Luke said, his eyes falling to the roof beneath them before he slowly glared at the undead milling around the street just beyond the fence. "Damn whoever started all of this."

Metzger went inside after a few minutes to accept some breakfast. In the kitchen he found Albert giving pointers to Samantha about how to fire a pistol. Standing at the threshold momentarily, he felt somewhat taken aback to see a child holding a firearm and pointing it straight ahead. Admittedly, her form looked good enough to take down a few of the undead if she didn't hesitate from fright. Albert stood behind her, adjusting her stance and giving her some pointers as she aimed the pistol at what appeared to be a paper plate on the refrigerator.

"It's okay," Albert said with a nod as he glanced Metzger's way. "It's not loaded."

"That's a relief," Metzger replied.

"Luke can't stand that I teach her how to use a firearm, but the dead ones don't discriminate, and Samantha needs to know how to defend herself."

"It's dangerous," Luke chimed in, crossing through the kitchen to another room.

He didn't even bother trying to tame his lisp this time as he had much of the time Metzger spent in their presence.

Samantha went to hand the gun back to Albert, aiming the barrel straight at him.

"What did I say about handing the gun to someone?" Albert asked, raising his voice to a slightly higher pitch as he went into teaching mode.

"Always treat it like it's loaded," Samantha answered quietly, still too shy to speak out loud in front of their guest.

She flipped the gun around, careful not to aim the barrel at herself as well, and handed it over to her caregiver. Metzger had to admit that Albert had taught her well, and he agreed that everyone in the new world needed to know how to use weapons. Samantha couldn't count on adults to defend her forever, and kids were like sponges when it came to learning.

He sat at the kitchen island after Samantha ran off to play, watching Luke and Albert fuss over who did what chores, just like an old married couple. He felt thankful for human interaction, able to temporarily forget what smells and sights awaited him just outside the walls of the old house. Even as he ate breakfast and savored the taste of foods he once placed at the bottom of his fine dining list, he thought about the journey ahead. He hoped the two men before him would choose wisely when it came to deciding when to leave their home and where to go next.

On a full stomach he gathered his belongings, received a set of keys from Luke, and said farewell to all three of them on the front porch. He thanked the men for their hospitality, and for saving him, and openly wished they could stay in touch. Before turning to leave, he gave Luke a look with a nod, indicating he wanted him to talk Albert into the right course of action before more marauders came to the neighborhood. They lacked the skills and the numbers to make a stand on their property, particularly with a child involved.

During one of the last warm days in the fall, the sun shined from a virtually cloudless sky, giving the impression all was well in the world until Albert opened the front gate and Metzger spied five undead in the vicinity. Unwilling to leave them there for the residents to deal with, he drew his short sword and made his way to each of the walkers before they could surround him. He wasn't going to give them the opportunity to claw at him or use their teeth, so he dropped his excess gear and went to each one of them individually, slicing through the center of their craniums with precision swings.

Blood spewed from the fresh wounds, but it didn't gush or spurt. On some rudimentary level the undead still lived, though they did not appear to breathe. Their senses of hearing, smell, and sight all seemed to function at an almost normal human level, and blood remained a liquid in their systems, whether it flowed or not.

Metzger felt less out of breath each time he confronted the undead and did battle with them. He attributed this to both calmer nerves and getting into better physical condition over the course of the past month. They weren't exactly adept at silent attacks, often groaning and hissing with excitement when they spotted potential prey. And while he didn't procrastinate when dispatching any zombies, Metzger did study how his attacks affected them and their overall condition.

The first four zombies had headed directly for him, inadvertently making a semicircle which allowed him to slice through their heads with relative ease, dropping them all immediately to the ground. When the fifth one approached him he stabbed it several times in the chest, legs, and arms, backing away each time as he did so because the wounds failed to faze the zombie in the slightest. Only when it started gnashing its teeth and chomping repeatedly did he finally kick it in the knee hard enough to break the joint and topple the attacker to the ground. Feeling no pain whatsoever, the zombie struggled to regain any footing for its next attack and Metzger decided to cut through its skull with the sword before it discovered it still had one good leg for footing.

He watched the top half of the skull fall to the pavement, looking something like an upended turtle with the rounded portion seesawing on the ground, part of the graying brain still inside. Taking a quick look around, he heard and saw nothing, so he gathered up his belongings and headed toward the gray Toyota Prius Luke told him was parked in a driveway three houses down. Careful as ever, Metzger checked the alley where it was parked for any danger, which included looking beneath the car.

From experience, he knew zombies sometimes preferred to lie around in a dormant state until something came their way.

Satisfied no immediate danger surrounded him, he opened the car and threw his belongings inside the trunk and backseat. He slid into the driver's seat, and pushed the button on the dashboard to start the vehicle, pausing a moment in thought. His objective, the only objective that mattered in this moment, awaited him mere city blocks away.

Mere minutes, in fact.

A wave of hesitation crashed over him, because not traveling there meant the possibility of his parents alive and well would always exist in his mind. He didn't want to see them in a walking state of rot, and if he found such a horrific sight, Metzger didn't know if he could finish the job. Closing his eyes, he knew his parents wouldn't want to walk around like monsters, endangering people and animals still among the living.

The fact also remained that he'd promised his brother he would find out the truth so they could move forward to the next hurdle, or hurdles, before them.

Opening his eyes as he exhaled through his nose, Metzger decided to visit his old neighborhood one last time and discover what was certain to be a painful truth.

Four

Driving to the familiar home he had visited for years when staying with his folks wasn't very difficult to reach. Unlike the highways and interstates, the city streets weren't completely littered with vehicles. Of course the undead staggered here and there, sometimes in packs and often times in solo fashion. Metzger avoided them whenever possible, not stopping to deal with any of them individually because he still wondered if looters remained in the area.

Very few houses he passed retained any sort of natural appearance. Most of their yards were strewn with debris, household items, and occasionally a dead body that didn't move. Metzger wondered why some bodies failed to reanimate, because some of them didn't have obvious head trauma. He tried to drive carefully, but quickly, because while the hybrid car traveled rather quietly the undead still spied it and heard debris crunching beneath its tires, which drew them to it.

Luckily for him they didn't move very quickly, and he was able to lose them around a left turn before pulling onto the street he barely found familiar. Metzger's heart sunk when he found the street in worse disrepair than the others he'd traveled to get there. Residential windows were smashed, doors kicked open, and patches of grass were barely visible through the items discarded on every yard. Because the street was part of an isolated neighborhood, with limited ways in and out, the houses were likely targeted because the undead couldn't easily navigate the few streets, fences, and shrubs surrounding the houses there.

While that likely held true a month ago, time allowed them to find their way everywhere, including this particular neighborhood. Metzger didn't care, so long as he didn't have to deal with more assholes like the ones who tried to be-head him on the Harley. He couldn't believe the world had become so cutthroat in just a month's time, when survivors could further their cause by banding together. Groups were essential to surviving the apocalypse long-term, but Metzger hadn't found a pack worth joining, and he still hadn't completed his two personal missions.

He stopped down the street from the familiar house, in part because debris blocked the road, but also because he wanted time to approach the house and gauge exactly what awaited him. Once again the nagging doubt hung over him like a dark cloud, even as he stepped from the car and quietly shut the door without looking at it. His eyes scanned the street ahead for any lurking danger before he turned in place to take in the remainder of his surroundings. Seeing nothing dangerous, he let his mind slip back in time when his parents awaited his arrival on the porch, or neighbors said hello whenever he came and went.

Now those people probably wandered the streets in a strange purgatory, craving flesh while they shuffled aimlessly along.

Metzger began moving towards the house, feeling unsettled by the complete lack of noise around him. Once the sound of industry echoed through the Buffalo area, and even after the ships stopped traveling Lake Erie the city survived by other means. A wind farm replaced one of the major rail and boatyards, and even the whoosh of the giant propellers no longer reached the suburbs. Only the sound of his motorcycle boots clopping against the concrete reached his ears, and he looked through the windows of each house as he passed.

In the green house immediately before his parents' residence he stopped in his tracks to look at the haunting view in the front picture window. He spotted what appeared to be a mannequin in the blood-spotted window with tattered curtains. The figure wore clothes soiled with various maroon and brown colors, and it slowly turned his way due to a complete lack of anything else to occupy its time. When the faded brown eyes spied him, the figure put its hands against the window, trying in vain to venture outside, like a hamster trapped in a plastic cage.

"Mr. Garvey," Metzger muttered under his breath, recognizing the familiar neighbor, even in a deteriorated state.

He wanted to walk up the front stairs and put the poor soul out of his misery, but stepping inside the house might present other unseen dangers. Sighing to himself, Metzger planned to move on when another figure walked to the window beside Charles Garvey. Wearing a floral print dress, the man's granddaughter was frozen in time as a five-year-old child, her attire also stained, and her face a twisted snarl when she turned and saw a living person standing outside. Like her grandfather she clawed at the window, causing a tear to form in Metzger's right eye. He hadn't stuck around Ohio long enough to see loved ones and colleagues transform into monsters, but this scene made him face the awful truth for the first time.

After a moment of standing in place, stunned by what he saw, Metzger continued toward the more familiar yellow house. Only a month into the apocalypse, it wasn't obscured by overgrown shrubs, faded from the sun, or coated in dust. Except for the messy front yard, it looked much as it had the last time he paid a visit.

The moment he stepped around some empty cans, a backpack, and a few trash bags Metzger turned to see a highly disheartening scene at the front door.

Although the porch appeared mostly intact, a bloody handprint stained the paint along the jam. Even the mailbox hanging beside the door had fell victim to bloody graffiti, a few junk mail letters still jutting upward past the open metal flap. Memories of the last conversation with his parents haunted him because it felt completely unfinished, much like the scene before him. He suspected all along that things hadn't ended well for his folks, but the front door, open a few inches as though inviting everyone inside to impending doom, concerned him.

Wincing, he drew a large knife from the sheath along his belt as his right foot hit the bottom step. He heard the clop of his boot against the wood, wondering if the noise might attract any nearby undead. His knuckles gripped the handle a bit more tightly as he reached the landing, pausing momentarily at the threshold. Hearing and seeing nothing unusual after a few seconds, Metzger quieted his breathing before slowly extending his fingers and pushing the door open.

He stepped inside, closing the door behind him without turning around. Surprised it still latched, and hadn't been damaged or kicked in, Metzger stood perfectly still a moment. He wanted to see if anything came for him while he breathed in what he suspected was his final trip to the old homestead. If he failed to find his parents, he thought of no reason to ever return to the house, or the Buffalo area for that matter.

Despite the ominous exterior of the house, Metzger felt a rush of shock and relief to see the inside of the residence very much intact. Just beyond the small foyer he found the living room complete with chairs, a sofa, and a coffee table that all remained untouched. The hardwood floors barely displayed a coating of dust, leading directly into the kitchen and the stairway that led to the spare bedrooms and bathroom on the second story.

A mantel held several family photographs of Metzger, his brother and his family, and a few old framed photos of the entire family. A painting of a farmer at work in his barn around dawn hung above the couch, still untouched by vandals or the effects of time. Several throw pillows still lined the couch, a few of them turned sideways, but not necessarily victims of a struggle. His mother loved candles with floral scents, and he thought he detected lilac and rose pedals from somewhere in the house.

Although the entire house only contained seven distinct rooms, Metzger felt a bit overwhelmed because each one he searched might hold no answers for him. And as the number dwindled, so did any hope Metzger held for finding his parents alive and safe. He didn't want to face complete disappointment, but he couldn't put off the inevitable, so he slowly walked to the kitchen to cross it off his list.

Continuing to check around him for any silent undead that might silently approach, Metzger stepped into the kitchen and looked at the table, which still had a plate and a stained empty glass, long since deprived of any contents they held. Vermin likely stole what morsels remained atop the plate, if any, before seeking refuge somewhere else. He opened the refrigerator, finding it stocked with the usual condiments and some containers with moldy leftovers. Fearing his parents met an agonizing end, he opened the pantry, finding a good number of canned goods lining the shelves. Unless they were forced from the house in a hurry and dared not return, his folks would have taken what food and supplies they could have carried.

In a cupboard he found the one item he absolutely needed to find if he couldn't locate his parents, in the form of a satellite phone. His father insisted upon buying the expensive phone just in case their oldest son couldn't communicate with them through conventional means. Although Metzger's father wasn't a prepper, he often took precautions to make certain his family could communicate even if power and utilities crashed.

At this point absolutely everything had failed, or soon would, making his father appear wiser than ever.

Working on low-Earth orbiting satellites, or sometimes the geosynchronous types, the phones lacked the clarity and transmission speed of cell phones, and sometimes required the user to be outdoors or poised beneath a satellite at the right point in its orbit. Metzger looked at the phone as an insurance policy, simply another way for his brother to reach him if all else failed.

He scooped up the phone and the charger, feeling fortunate the phone already possessed a full charge. His brother knew cell phones were due to become little more than paperweights once their towers lost power, so he informed Metzger about the sat phone, figuring it was the one sure way for them to stay in touch.

Knowing that lingering in one spot might leave him vulnerable, Metzger checked the enclosed back porch, finding both entrance doors locked and secured. Returning inside, he checked the master bedroom on the ground level. His parents had chosen this space to avoid climbing stairs any more than necessary. He found it eerie how orderly everything appeared, as though they had packed and left for vacation rather than experienced the end of the world. The green and white comforter was made and tucked atop the bed, and the pillows looked freshly fluffed.

He checked under the bed, inside both closets, and the attached bathroom, finding nothing living or dead. Both of the closets appeared fully stocked with clothes, as though his parents hadn't packed a thing for travel, which left him thinking they didn't leave voluntarily, or left hurriedly. Part of him considered grabbing a few of his father's clean clothes for the road, but doing so felt insensitive. His parents would heed such an act no mind, but Metzger felt as though claiming their belongings meant he'd given up hope of finding them. He wasn't ready to throw in the towel quite yet, though he felt reasonably certain they weren't in the house, or even nearby.

With the ground floor inspected he ascended the stairway, seeing nothing in the common area upstairs. Immediately he noticed all three bedrooms and the shared bathroom had their doors closed, which disturbed him. Closed doors were always a mystery, sometimes with gnashing teeth and decaying flesh on the other side.

Atop the stairway a bedroom awaited him on the right, so he rapped on the door with his knuckles, waiting a few seconds for any noise from the other side. Nothing audible reached his ears, so he slowly cracked the door open, looking inside before he dared enter. Much like the downstairs, the room appeared very neat and tidy, as though his parents had decided to give it a thorough cleaning before fleeing for their lives. He checked every nook and cranny, finding no undead and no clues about what might have happened to his parents.

He checked the other two bedrooms next, finding them equally tidy and free of hazards. Growing frustrated, Metzger simply wanted some answers because he expected to hear from his brother in the near future. As upside-down as the world was turned, he planned on finding something inside the house. He'd mentally prepared himself to see bodies torn apart, or blood stains on every wall, but it looked more like his parents carefully packed their belongings and crossed the border into Canada.

He knew better, because what few news reports he saw before network television crashed revealed that no country provided safe haven.

Without much regard for his own safety he opened the bathroom door before knocking, finding only a spotless bathtub and vanity inside. The small window on the other side of the room provided some natural light, and for a moment the restroom looked like heaven within a dream it was so white. His father had won that battle, giving the guest bathroom a sterile look after his mother splashed the master bedroom and bathroom with color schemes.

Metzger checked behind the shower curtain, finding nothing mobile waiting for him. He whisked the curtain back to its original position, sighing to himself at the thought of only one area within the house left to check. Instinctively he checked that all of his usual weapons remained holstered and sheathed along his belt before descending the main staircase. His footsteps echoed through the empty house that used to be full of life as he skipped down the first few steps like he did in his younger days in their previous residence. Quickly feeling guilty for reminiscing in such dark times, he slowed his pace to a somber walk the remainder of the way down.

When he reached the bottom he looked to the front door, finding it closed the way he left it with no flesh-munching undead clawing at it from the other side. He couldn't get over how quiet the neighborhood remained, as though inviting him to drop everything and simply make a go of it in familiar territory. Too many unresolved issues stood in his way, so he couldn't fathom making a decision about where to call home quite yet. Nowhere felt safe, and too many questions remained about his parents, his extended family, and whether anything other than head trauma could stop the undead, particularly in mass quantities.

Each day that passed left him with less hope that the government and scientists would intervene and cure the plague that created such a mess. He couldn't imagine enough humanity remained within the undead to bring them back to life. At some rudimentary level they functioned like creatures with only one purpose to their existence.

To feed.

Standing on the ground floor, Metzger gave the house a look from one end to the other before slowly making his way to the basement. He saved the basement area for last with good reason, somewhat apprehensive about opening the wooden door. Placing his hand atop the sidearm on his right hip, he took a deep breath and exhaled before slowly turning the knob, figuring zombies weren't going to naturally clamor to the top of the old creaky stairs. Pulling the door outward, Metzger fingered the gun's grip, prepared to find answers downstairs or leave the property completely disappointed.

As luck would have it, he found nothing waiting for him on the other side of the door, but the basement offered only darkness and a damp, musty smell that immediately permeated his nostrils. He took one step down and immediately came to a halt as a throaty groan reached his ears. Feeling certain his heart stopped as well, Metzger knew that visually confirming nothing left him with a lingering hope that finding undead parents did not. He wanted hope, and he didn't want to tell his brother the worst possible discovery if and when they spoke again.

Making a fist, Metzger tapped the wood beside him, hoping to reveal any additional zombies, or draw the first one to him. The first walker grumbled and groaned again, shuffling several steps closer to the stairs, creating a dramatic moment as Metzger waited to see if it looked familiar to him. He didn't want it to be one of his parents, still roaming freely after devouring his other parent to the point that he or she couldn't even reanimate. The thought of shooting his mother or father in the head, whether they were technically dead or not, haunted him.

"No," he muttered to himself as his heart raced, unable to confront such a major revelation just yet.

He walked to the top of the stairs and closed the door behind him, unwilling to face the truth. Sucking in deep breaths, he leaned against the door momentarily, hearing the zombie clop against the stairway behind him before tripping and falling. Metzger walked into the kitchen to search for a flashlight inside the cupboards, using the search as an excuse to prolong discovering the harsh truth. He felt certain he was about to confront what nearly every offspring confronted sometime during their lives, although this was far from a traditional method of finding one's parent deceased.

Knowing he was simply delaying the inevitable, Metzger wandered aimlessly around the kitchen, trying to decide whether he wanted to vomit or collect his wits and confront whatever lurked in the basement. His breathing came in heaves as he placed both hands on the countertop, attempting to calm himself and make a decision. Already knowing he couldn't leave the house without knowing one way or the other, he began opening cupboards until the third one revealed a flashlight. He pushed the button, finding the batteries still provided light to the durable device with a beam that lit up the kitchen, even with natural light entering from several angles.

He made a snap decision to take care of the matter swiftly and deal with the consequences afterwards because he simply needed to get moving if he wanted to meet up with his brother. Holding the flashlight in his left hand, Metzger drew the .357 with his right hand and returned to the door. He managed to turn the knob awkwardly with both hands before stepping back as the door swung open. Immediately detecting the zombie at the bottom of the stairs, Metzger shined the light downward, saw the yellow of its eyes, and shot between them rather effectively before any details burned themselves in his memory.

Immediately the zombie fell limp and the head smacked against the wooden stairs leaving a blood stain. Although he tried to avoid seeing any details, Metzger got a glimpse of the undead walker and felt reasonably certain it wasn't anyone he knew. Considering the undead were roughly a month into a state of decay they still looked very much like their former selves.

Refusing to waste time, he bounded down the stairs and examined the fully dead zombie, finding the clothing to be fairly young in taste, like something a college student might wear. When he reached the concrete beyond the last step Metzger lifted the head, finding the face unfamiliar with a red spot in the center of the forehead where his bullet found its mark. He released the hair, allowing the head to smack soundly against the stairway as he turned to examine the remainder of the basement.

Mostly storage for holiday decorations, and where laundry got done during the week, the basement harbored no other secrets upon exploration. It smelled terrible, thanks in part to the corpse lying at the foot of the stairs, though a second pantry offered more canned goods when Metzger opened it. He felt surprised that no one had raided area houses, but scavengers likely wanted to hit retail stores and local markets first. Eventually desperation would drive the living to the houses where rotting surprises awaited them. Clearing a house wasn't incredibly dangerous if done correctly, and choosing to invade residences over stores might have kept Metzger alive to this point.

Depressed and disappointed, Metzger trudged up the stairs to the first floor, wondering what forced his parents from their home and why absolutely no clues presented themselves. His mother was the master of leaving messages, whether on a notepad or Post-it notes placed on the kitchen table or refrigerator. Metzger plucked the hard line telephone off the receiver along the kitchen wall to verify that it indeed produced no dial tone. Knowing the phone wasn't a viable option for his parents, he wondered why his mother hadn't left any kind of message behind. Casual searches of the cupboards and any drawers throughout the house hadn't produced anything useful.

He spent nearly fifteen minutes going through the remainder of the house, searching for anywhere notes or clues might have been left. A fruitless, exhaustive search left him more frustrated than before, so when he returned to the foyer and spied movement outside the house he decided to extend his detective work to the outdoors.

Grabbing the shorter of his two swords, which he had set on the living room floor between exploratory stints, he opened the door and stepped outside to the brisk, fresh air. The air never really smelled fresh with thousands of undead wandering aimlessly, but Metzger barely noticed any foul odors in the old neighborhood. Clutching the sword with a death grip, he stalked directly toward the zombie with a purpose, determined to put down every single undead walker he found until he discovered something about his parents.

Ordinarily he might have immediately regretted his decision, considering he lacked protective clothing at the moment, but his anger and a need to vent overtook any collective reasoning at the moment.

As the lone zombie stumbled over to him, Metzger clutched the sword handle with one hand and used the other with an open palm to shove the tip of the blade through the zombie's eye socket like a skewer. It dropped instantly, and he was careful to let the sword fall with it before pulling it out for fear of snapping the thin blade. Shaking any blood and brain matter off the blade, he held it at his side and waited to see if any other undead appeared to confront him.

"Come on!" he shouted at the top of his lungs. "Come and get me!"

He waited impatiently for about a minute before some of the undead that roamed the streets during his initial approach began filing through some shrubs and stumble across the curbs at the neighborhood entrance. Half a dozen drew closer to him, staggered in intervals that didn't cause him concern for his safety. He sliced directly through the skull of a black female zombie that showed its teeth when it drew within striking distance. Before it even hit the ground Metzger charged the next member of the undead, kicking it in the chest with his boot, which knocked it to the ground, allowing him to stab the sword through its skull to finish the job.

Metzger studied each face as the undead approached, looking for anyone familiar, desperate to piece together the mystery that plagued him. He recognized none of them, though they appeared to come from a variety of occupations and walks of life. His sword finished a deceased gas station mechanic, a businessman wearing a tattered tan suit, a woman wearing blue jeans, a flannel shirt, and dirty gardening gloves, and finally a teenager wearing kneepads and a helmet who appeared to be out skating when the inevitable happened. Saving him for last, Metzger noticed a bite mark along the young man's shoulder that could very well have ended his vibrant young life and transformed him into a flesh-eating monster.

A combination of a growl and a hiss emulated from its throat as it drew near Metzger, beginning to extend its arms upward to grab at his potential victim. Instead of simply utilizing the sword for a quick execution like the others, Metzger walked backwards, switching the sword to his left hand so he could draw the .357 Magnum. The lack of answers left him furious, and though he knew his emotional state, combined with his irrational actions, might get him killed, he no longer cared. Waiting only a few seconds because he didn't want to regain his senses and back down, Metzger fired a bullet into the center of the zombie's head, certain to attract more of its kind in short order.

"Come and get me, motherfuckers!" Metzger screamed, his blood now boiling because he wanted every single one of the undead eradicated for disrupting his life and his family.

Staring at the bodies lying around him momentarily, he waited for additional takers, but nothing stumbled his way over the next few minutes. He began to calm down slightly shortly after that with nothing to strike at or shoot. Feeling somewhat like a transformed monster returning to his far less angry human form, Metzger began to control his breathing, nearly coming to terms with his careless behavior. He holstered the .357 once he found no need to use it around him, holding the sword at his side until he verified no danger remained.

About to rationally contemplate his next move for survival and gathering answers, he turned around to find Charles Garvey staring at him with blank, brownish eyes, clawing at the window he once could have easily opened if he chose to.

Now windows, doors, and child-proof gates might as well have been hardened prison bars to the primitive undead behind them. Occasionally they broke through, or accidentally opened them through random movements of their hands and fingers, but for the most part any barriers kept them at bay.

Somewhere in the recesses of Metzger's brain a faint red glow became a fiery ember that quickly caught fire and sent him charging the front door. He wanted to know why the neighbors hadn't acted to help his parents, wondering how they were so careless that they became undead themselves. Without so much as a split-second of indecision, he tromped up the front stairs onto the short concrete landing, kicked in the door near the doorknob, and waited with his short sword drawn for any undead inside to come his way.

Because the door broke away from its top two hinges it fell awkwardly inside at an angle, likely to trip anything that crossed its path. Still barely attached to the bottom hinge, the door was left mostly horizontal at knee level except for the one corner that touched the ground. Metzger heard footsteps before any of the undead came into view, and as the footsteps drew closer they sounded something like a herd of elephants and Metzger wondered just how many people sought refuge with the Garvey family when everything went bad.

"Shit," he muttered dejectedly when several undead rounded the corner and began tripping over the door and one another.

Once their pale, dead eyes locked onto his form, they crawled, walked, and stumbled in his direction as quickly as their decaying forms allowed.

Although it required more concentration this time because more than half a dozen charged Metzger in a formation of sorts, he tried to study their faces before swinging away with the sword. It occurred to him that his parents might have gone next door to stay with the Garvey clan for safety, because strength certainly came with larger groups. If a single person among their group became infected, however, the disease could have easily become airborne or transmitted through a bite. Metzger wished he understood the science behind how the apocalypse began so he knew any additional precautions to take, but he wasn't around many dying or diseased people the past month.

Apparently children zombies moved more quickly because of their size and the fact that they decayed somewhat slower for some reason. The granddaughter and grandson reached him first, even more ominous than adult zombies because their growls were more like defensive hisses than throaty groans. Both eyed him like he was the pizza they had ordered hours ago, warm and delicious to their palates. Unfazed by their age and appearance, Metzger waited until they were close enough to taste the blade of his sword as he swung through their necks, beheading both in a single swipe.

He knew from experience that removing the cranium from the body didn't entirely kill the zombie because the head remained animated with a biting jaw and eyes that continued to scan the area. Impending danger kept him from finishing the job as four zombies closed on him and more reached the front door of the house. Knowing adrenaline could sustain him for only so long, Metzger opted to continue using the sword, rather than firing a second shot that might attract additional undead.

Within a minute he took down Charles Garvey, the man's wife, and two other adults he didn't recognize. He required only a few more seconds to stab through any craniums left on the ground that continued to move, looking down to find blood droplets on his blue jeans and shirt. He felt terrible for finishing off the Garvey family because for the first time he essentially killed people he knew, who once conversed with him and spent many a neighborly evening with his parents. His mother spoke of times the couples made dinner for one another or sat around a fire pit in the backyard during fall evenings.

Looking at the carnage around him, Metzger felt the anger ebb from his body, replaced by a feeling of complete solitude and emptiness. After all of the travel, risking his life from one town to another, he arrived home to find no one he knew among the living, and no answers. He suddenly wished he'd found his parents, even if they were undead, so he wouldn't feel trapped in his home state. As much as he wanted to reunite with his brother and move on to whatever life awaited him, Metzger felt compelled to find something, *anything* about his parents.

When the urge struck him to move along before more undead stumbled his way, Metzger stole a glance toward the front door, seeing one final zombie fill the threshold, catching him by surprise. Positive he recognized this particular walker, he fell to his knees and continued to stare forward, feeling a tear come to one eye. Perhaps he wished too soon for answers at any cost, because his heart fluttered momentarily at the shock of the zombie standing before him.

"Mom?" he questioned as his fingers released the grip on his sword, allowing it to fall beside him.

Five

etzger never felt his knees hit the concrete of the sidewalk because the onset of shock left him staring blankly at the front door of the Garvey household where he felt certain his mother died. His initial awe lasted only a few seconds as the female zombie came into clearer view from the doorway.

Although she was clearly of senior citizen age when she died, this woman drew closer, looking at him simply as dinner, and looking less like his mother with each step. The undead straggler wore only two facial expressions, one being completely and utterly neutral and the other a feral, gnashing of the teeth attack mode. Too mentally and physically exhausted to grow angry again, Metzger stood as he scooped up the sword, barely finding the energy to take a swing at the zombie's skull. Fortunately the blade did most of the work, severing flesh and bone, dropping the attacker immediately.

Wondering if the house was free of undead, Metzger trudged to the front door, waiting to see if any other enemies appeared in the doorway. He didn't feel much like clearing the house, but felt it was necessary in case his parents had sought refuge with their neighbors as so many others apparently had done. The house had no front porch, and a set of three steps led into the house, which immediately provided a different atmosphere than the more familiar residence next door.

Bowls, plates, food cartons, plastic containers, and silverware appeared randomly strewn across tables, chairs, and the floor as though survivors had confined themselves to the house for a period of time before the group turned. Metzger sheathed his sword, opting to pull the .357 in case he was surprised around a corner or doorway. He immediately found it impossible to move silently, because every step emitted a clop from his steel-toed boots or the crunch of something discarded along the floor as he stepped on it.

Feeling reasonably certain every zombie had already stumbled outside to greet him, Metzger made his way through the living room and kitchen rather quickly, finding nothing hazardous awaiting him. A bathroom and one small bedroom also revealed nothing except more clutter and some dirty clothes. Metzger made it a point to look for evidence of what happened within the house, or any notes left by the group while they were alive. He surmised the house maintained power through at least a few weeks, providing safe haven for the group until something drastically changed.

"It must have been swift," he figured aloud, following the same path he had in his parents' house since this place also had an upstairs and a basement.

He walked up the wooden stairs to the second story, immediately hearing some kind of noise from the other side of the bannister. Hesitantly climbing the last few stairs, Metzger found the upstairs rather dark because windows were covered with quilts and blankets, allowing minimal daylight to peek through. Much like the neighboring house, all of the upstairs doors remained closed, and one of the rooms presented some noise as thin shadows swayed back and forth beneath the wooden door. Instead of four, there were three doors this time, but he immediately disliked the idea of examining the room with groans and moans.

Considering the door was the furthest from him, Metzger started with the nearest door, finding a fairly well-lit bedroom with nothing dangerous inside. Clothes lay strewn across the twin bed, and several black trash bags were lying beside the bed with their tops ripped open, revealing more clothes inside. He wondered if the group scavenged some local stores and houses to find food and clothing when the outbreak first began.

Nerves crept into Metzger as he carefully opened the door of the middle room, discovering a spacious bathroom that appeared to be the only clean room in the entire house. He stepped inside only to whisk the shower curtain aside, finding nothing except a white tub and shower combination within the otherwise blue-toned room. With nothing else left to examine, he swallowed hard, prepared to see what horrors awaited him in the room that continued to emit groans and thumps that sounded through the walls.

Now thinking more rationally, he decided to slide the gun into its holster and draw the shorter sword once more. Short of a bedroom packed with zombies that could overrun him, he figured the sword would be enough to help him euthanize any undead that stumbled forward. Studying the door as he walked across the upstairs floor, Metzger accidentally made a board creak along the wooden floor, which seemed to draw the interest of whatever awaited him inside the room. He sincerely knew *what* awaited him, but the question of how many bothered him a little bit. Several times during his travels he avoided large packs of undead that simply roamed highways and city streets together. Although their primitive mindset likely failed to comprehend that their strength came in numbers, Metzger knew all too well.

Licking his bottom lip in anticipation, he opened the door and immediately backed away, holding the sword in a ready position to stab or slice, depending on how the undead approached him. When the door opened fully, two zombies presented themselves, backlit by the daylight from the window. Unable to see details, he prayed the duo wasn't his parents, but he couldn't make out any details except that they both appeared thin as they headed toward their new freedom beyond the threshold.

He spent a few precious seconds trying to study their faces, but the entire upper floor was too dark, save what little daylight pierced the covered windows. Metzger wanted to try identifying them before going to work with the blade, but once through the doorway, they both ambled in his direction without hesitation.

Groaning outwardly, he kicked the one on the right side away from him, which he believed to be female, allowing him to swing the sword smoothly at the head of the taller one, flooring it instantly once the top half of its skull tumbled to the ground. By this time the second zombie grabbed for him after recovering from a complete fall, but Metzger used both hands to grab it by the sides of the head and study its face. Even in the dark he knew it wasn't his mother, and this woman wasn't older than forty in life. Without hesitation he thrust her head into his raised knee, which didn't finish off the undead assailant, so he did so repeatedly, losing count after the sixth escalating violent reaction.

"Fuck you!" he shouted repeatedly with each knee thrust, his anger once again boiling to a dangerous level that might be considered temporary insanity by a psychiatrist.

If any shrinks even remained on the planet to analyze him.

Throwing the zombie to the ground by the hair, he took up the sword and stabbed her through the already caved in skull for reassurance, his breaths coming in heaves.

After waiting a few seconds to make certain neither of them moved, he knelt down beside the deceased male and plucked his wallet, finding the name and license photo both unfamiliar. Tossing the wallet aside, he wondered how many people Charles Garvey put up when the world went berserk, and why so many folks flocked to this particular house. Upset, but calming down more quickly than before, Metzger walked down the stairs and gave the house a final glance before stepping outside.

No new surprises awaited him in the great outdoors, though the sky transformed from blue and partly cloudy to deeply overcast during his short stint inside.

Taking a moment to observe his surroundings, Metzger began walking back to his parents' house without even meaning to. Perhaps a sense of safety and serenity drew him back to the familiar house as he made certain all of his weapons were sheathed. He took notice of how strangely quiet the cul-de-sac became without anything trudging across the colorful fallen leaves. The seasons failed to take notice that the human population declined by better than ninety percent as the days grew colder and the weather carried on like always.

When he reached the driveway this time he paid more attention to the detached garage at the end of the blacktop. His father waited several years to cover their gravel driveway with concrete when he received a promotion at work, eventually coating it with blacktop to protect it from the elements. No longer supporting either of his sons, he began upgrading his new, downsized house a little bit each year. A longtime engineer for the railroad, he happened to be home between runs when the world fell apart. Part of Metzger felt glad his parents were together when the dead began roaming the streets, but he wanted more closure than a disconnected phone call from them.

Answers continued to plague him, even as he stood at the end of the blacktop, staring at the garage, wondering why he bypassed it so quickly before.

Naturally the house and the mysteries awaiting him inside distracted him the first time through, but now he wondered if the small one-car garage held any answers or useful items. Fingering the gun at his side, Metzger slowly walked to the yellow garage that matched the house. For some unknown reason his father painted the house and garage in the same shade of yellow as their old residence. Most of the houses in the neighborhood seemed to keep their original vintage tints, giving the area some character, particularly since mostly older residents resided within them.

His father's pickup truck remained parked in front of the garage door, which led him to initially believe his parents might still be in the area. When he approached it for a glance inside, he found no keys, and no evidence that anyone had tampered with the four-wheel-drive vehicle. Harsh Buffalo winters made durable vehicles a must, and owning a personal snowplow was a perk that a number of residents, including his father, rather enjoyed. Not only did owning a plow guarantee one made it to work, but it also provided extra income from neighbors who gladly paid to have their driveways cleared.

Passing the truck after a cursory examination of the contents, Metzger walked to the side door of the garage, stopping briefly to examine it. The door appeared locked, but he pounded it with a closed fist anyway, hearing nothing from inside after he waited several seconds. He tried the knob, finding the door locked, as his father often left it due to all of the tools and seasonal decorations left inside. Metzger remembered springtime when his father dragged out his push mower for the first time, changing the oil and filter before knocking any clumps of grass from the underside of the mowing deck. The smell of freshly-cut grass filled the air surrounding the garage before the yard was even ready for mowing. Most years the yards remained tan and muddy for what seemed like months after the snow finally disappeared. Summer was often a two-month season with only a few warm months for swimming and outdoor activities before school and football season rolled around again.

As Metzger raised his foot and kicked in the door to the garage he thought of how much he missed simple childhood years and throwing baseballs and footballs to his brother.

A single window within the garage provided little illumination because dust covered the single pane that his father refused to replace for some reason. The garage wasn't heated, but the window endured a misfired tennis ball that produced a crack, and a piece in the corner fell out completely a year later for reasons unknown. Donald Metzger refused to replace the window, even at that point, despite his sons telling him it compromised security to his precious garage.

Dust floated through the air like miniature snowflakes once the door flew open to disturb it from otherwise eternal rest on the car and across the work-benches. Metzger blew into the air to keep from breathing excessive amounts of the dust, but it couldn't be helped as he stepped into the center of the dusty snow globe. It looked exactly as he remembered with tools hanging everywhere and his mother's car perfectly centered. His father hung tennis balls from the ceiling as markers to help park the vehicle correctly each time so enough room was left for the lawn mower, his snowplow, and a few other seasonal items.

Cracking a grin as he panned the garage, seeing childhood items like his old baseball mitt and a box of old comic books Bryce left behind when he joined the Navy, Metzger walked directly to the workbench that held those items. Even after his parents sold their house and downsized, they brought items that belonged to their sons with them.

Strangely, Metzger didn't remember his father leaving anything on his bench, much less sentimental items. He kept the garage organized in such a way that only he knew the layout, and when he finished any project his tools all went back to their respective areas.

After his folks sold his childhood home, Metzger stayed in the new house when he visited, but he never gained complete familiarity with the place. New surroundings truly made him feel more like a guest than a family member, although his parents never treated him any differently. His mother still cooked him breakfast each morning, and he helped his father with chores and repairs around the property.

He wondered if his father took a stroll down memory lane after things went bad, or if he came to his garage with one last purpose in mind. Metzger walked over to the car, hoping his parents hadn't decided to gas themselves as a way out of the madness that likely consumed their little corner of the world.

Wiping a thin layer of dust away from one of the side windows, he peered inside, seeing nothing unusual. He breathed a sigh of relief, knowing his parents hadn't committed suicide together as a final act. With the property fully explored he felt a little bit better knowing they might always be alive in the possibility, if not reality.

It occurred to him that he hadn't found a few items around the property that he expected to locate at some point. His mother's purse was missing, along with her cell phone and a few family photos he felt certain he remembered seeing on the refrigerator the last time he visited. As for his father, there was no wallet, no cell phone, and a few knives and guns were missing from the collection. The weapons were all things that could be carried during a quick escape because they weighed little, and extra rounds were plentiful. But if they left, why hadn't they taken one of their vehicles?

Perhaps they found someone to carpool with, which might have been a best case scenario. One of the train engines his father worked on would certainly provide a safe haven from the undead, considering their construction and the fact that virtually nothing could stop them once they gained momentum. Modern engines lacked the exaggerated cow catchers of their ancestors, but they still had enough solid metal up front to turn most zombies into fleshy goo upon impact.

Numerous times Metzger tried calling both of his parents on their cell phones but each time after his last conversation with them he received generic operator messages about cell phone service being disrupted. Cell phone coverage proved spotty at best, and it was certain to fail completely over time when all forms of power to cell phone towers came to an end. Unfortunately utilities required maintenance, replacement parts, and manpower to continue functioning, and all of those were jeopardized now.

Walking over to the main workbench beyond the car, he picked up the baseball glove, surprised his father kept it after both of his sons moved out. He used the extra bedrooms as specialty rooms and storage areas, but seemed to find room for keepsakes that stirred good memories. The trinket reminded Metzger that he wanted to gather some photographs and familiar items from the house before moving along. Traveling light proved a must in the new world, but Metzger wasn't sure he'd ever see his parents or the last home that still held memories for him again, so he decided to take the risk.

As he went to set the glove down a piece of paper fell from it all the way to the ground. He felt a hint of excitement, thinking it might be a note from his father about their whereabouts, hidden where only he might find it. His hopes were quickly dashed, however, when he unfolded it to find a list of things to do from his mother to his father that apparently got stuck to the underside of the glove at some point.

Deciding he wanted to search the house more thoroughly a second time, Metzger headed for the door, about to step through when a zombie surprised him from the other side. Because it made no noise while approaching, it caught him completely off-guard, causing him to stumble backwards and trip. Landing hard on the ground, Metzger immediately felt some pain in his lower back just before the back of his skull struck the rear fender of the car, causing him to see stars as the zombie dropped to its knees for the kill.

Adrenalin and instinct took over almost immediately because he drew his left leg back before letting loose with a kick that struck the undead walker squarely in the forehead. Far from a killing blow, the kick hurled the zombie outside the door, buying Metzger some time to evaluate his ailments and draw his short sword simultaneously. His back hurt because he landed on a small rock along his backbone, and his head, despite the earlier injury from falling off the motorcycle, wasn't about to send him spiraling into unconsciousness.

During his first attempt to pull the short sword from the pouch along his back, Metzger found the weapon stuck due to his weight pinning it to the ground. Performing half of a sit-up, he forcefully pulled the sword from the pack as the zombie began crawling in his direction. Exercising caution at the last possible second, Metzger kept from cutting into his own flesh by turning to one side so the sword cleared the sheath as it pulled out cleanly.

Metzger provided his assailant with a second swift kick to the skull, buying him enough time to regain his footing and walk over to stab the sword downward through the footprint he created on the skull of his attacker. Suddenly realizing he was breathing hard again, he no longer wanted to attract every zombie within earshot, so he looked around the area cautiously before walking toward the house. He hoped to search the house one last time and move on before dark to find the one last immediate relative in his life. Of course cousins, aunts, uncles, and even a few of his grandparents might still be out there, but he couldn't exactly contact them with social media or phone calls.

When he walked into the house he made certain to shut and lock the front door behind him, a bit worried that his earlier actions might have attracted more than the undead. With a makeshift plan in mind, he searched drawers and cupboards thoroughly, looking for any notes and family belongings he wanted to take with him. As he went, he boxed up every canned good he could find, whether the items were to his liking or not. He figured desperate times lay ahead when food became scarce, so he would either eat to survive or trade canned goods for other items.

He visited the gray Prius a few times, loading boxes of food and gear into the trunk. In a world where vehicles became disposable transportation and occasional lodging when danger came along, Metzger made certain to keep the important items within an arm's reach in the front passenger's seat. With each piece of furniture and each room he cleared, Metzger felt a bit more depressed because his parents hadn't left him anything.

No note.

No e-mail.

No voicemail message.

Before technology began faltering, he checked every outlet possible, but no reassurances ever reached him.

After another two hours of scouring the house he felt his shirt drenched with sweat, and no closer to any answers about his parents. Four boxes of perishable goods remained secure in the trunk, and a smaller box of family items for Metzger and his brother sat up front with his weapons. Wiping the perspiration from his forehead onto the shoulder area of his shirt, he walked outside and stared at the front of the house, taking in the sight of it one last time. As desperately as he wanted to know what happened to Donald and Connie Metzger, he wasn't going to search all of Tonawanda, staring at every undead face that crossed his path. Either his father was healthy and intelligent enough to get them to safety, or the worst possible scenario came to pass.

If his parents were stumbling around his hometown with graying skin and pale, yellowed eyes, he decided he really didn't want to see them again. He firmly believed in an afterlife, and though he questioned some of his maker's recent decisions, Metzger hoped to find them again when his heart stopped beating in his earthly husk.

Leaving the door as he found it, ajar just a few inches, he shuffled slowly to the Prius without looking back, afraid he might change his mind and stay the night. Already a tear formed in one eye when he slumped into the driver's seat as another small hoard of the undead made their way onto the street. He couldn't muster enough rage to exit the car and do battle again as his weapons sat in the seat beside him, already in storage for all intents and purposes. Instead, he shut the car door, glancing at the house momentarily as he closed the chapter on finding his parents, feeling lost.

He hadn't heard from his brother in days, and though he knew use of the satellite phone aboard the *USS Ross* was limited, he expected an officer to find a way to use it more often. In this case no news was bad news, because if the commander decided to take the ship somewhere other than their base in Norfolk, Virginia, Metzger might lose contact with Bryce completely. He wasn't sure his brother might call his father's sat phone again, although the phone indicated three missed calls during the past few weeks from the same number.

Time slipped away from Metzger as he shed a few tears, trying to sever the emotional bond with the house where he last saw his parents. A few of the zombies began clawing at the Prius, knowing fresh meat awaited them on the other side of the window. Their tapping and pounding on the car didn't faze him because for a moment he just simply *did not* care. Such mindless creatures no longer remembered their childhoods, or throwing baseballs with their fathers. The parts of their brains that once conjured images of Thanksgiving and Christmas surrounded by family, or childhood birthday parties, likely rotted soon after they fell over dead. Metzger closed his eyes, drew a deep breath, and realized he hadn't put one foot in the grave just yet. He still cared for others, remembered what made him a decent human being, and never forgot where he came from, even if the neighborhood changed in degrees he never thought possible.

He pushed the button on the dashboard to start the car and slowly backed out of the driveway, and over one of the zombies, in his attempt to leave. A speed-bump and a crunch later the car was on the road, and Metzger instinctively drove in the direction of the sole friendly confines he'd found since becoming a weary traveler. He didn't want to overstay his welcome, or give them the wrong impression about his intentions, but the nearby raid the night before concerned him. Finding them safe and sound would ease his conscience before he headed east, and their neighborhood wasn't far.

By the time he pulled onto their street, Metzger had pulled himself together, passing numerous zombies without stopping. He didn't exactly feel at peace, just mentally and physically exhausted after so much effort failed to convey a payoff. Ignoring a few straggling undead, he pulled up in front of the house where Albert and Luke provided safe haven for a girl they never knew before the world fell apart.

Immediately something felt wrong to him when he pulled up to the front gate, finding it wide open. A sense of panic shot through him because he felt certain his instincts were one-hundred percent correct, despite him wishing he were wrong. Throwing open the door and grabbing both the short sword and his .357, he headed for the gate, noticing the man he purposely threw into a zombie the night before continued to lie on the ground. He didn't know why he gave the man a second glance, but he felt positive he saw a few fingers twitch. Much of the man's abdomen area was eaten away, along with small chunks of his arms and one leg, but apparently enough of him remained for him to reanimate.

"Fucker," Metzger muttered, making a beeline for the newly undead man, stabbing him in the head with the short sword so he couldn't surprise anyone from behind later.

Returning his attention to the larger problem at hand, he walked toward the front gate, which made their house look a bit like a fort behind the tall wooden fence. He suddenly thought it unrealistic to believe any wooden fence, even one approximately eight feet in height, would deter many people from scaling it. Short of a guard posted continuously within the house, the fence couldn't be defended, and it truly offered minimal defense. He walked past several sections of fencing until he reached the open front gate, finding it kicked in with enough force that the latch was broken on the door, and the wood splintered around it.

His eyes slowly moved from the shattered pieces of wood up the concrete path to the front porch and the house's front door. Exactly like he found where his parents once lived, the front door was open just a few inches, indicating something terrible happened to the three people living within the old walls. Clutching his sword in one hand and his gun in the other, Metzger began taking a step forward to investigate when the sound of a branch snapping behind him brought him to a complete stop.

"They're gone," a raspy female voice said as Metzger turned to find a brunette holding a rifle of some sort with another woman and four men standing behind her. "And you can either wait to join them, or you can join us."

Six

"And just who the hell are all of you?" Metzger asked, not liking the idea of being given an ultimatum after the day he'd endured.

"We're the ones with the numbers on our side," the woman answered, though she still hadn't aimed the rifle at Metzger.

"I don't have much in the way of supplies, if that's what you want," Metzger told a fib, considering four boxes of canned and dried goods sat in the trunk of the car he drove to his current location.

Most groups wanted weapons, food, and occasionally clothing. Knowing he wasn't going to win a battle against these people, or survive if they wanted him dead, he decided to negotiate rather than fight or flee.

"We aren't interested in anything you have," the woman said. "The people who lived here, did you know them?"

"Yes," Metzger answered, seeing no point in denying the fact considering all three of them appeared to be gone.

Now the entire group seemed to be put at ease, lowering all of their weapons during an odd few seconds of silence.

"They were kind enough to put me up for a night after some assholes tried to kill me," he added, hoping the group before him wasn't the group in question.

Something told him they weren't.

"Sounds like the same assholes we're after," one of the men spoke up. "They've kidnapped friends and family from each of our groups."

"Why would anyone do that?" Metzger questioned aloud.

"Because they have a camp and they want cheap labor to fortify where they're staying," the woman answered. "My name is Molly by the way."

"Dan," Metzger said, shaking her hand. "So why are you all here and not following these pricks?"

"We're not *all* here," another of the men said. "Some of our people are following them back to their base so they can radio us with exact coordinates once they scout the place."

A number of questions ran through his mind, but Metzger believed he already knew the answer to the most important inquiry.

"We followed them here last night and saw you," Molly elaborated from her earlier statement. "Got here too late to save your friends from being taken, but we knew they only abducted three people, so we stayed to look for you."

"You found me," Metzger said. "And I take it you want me to join your merry band and go after these punks?"

"The more the merrier," Molly said with a sly grin. "We plan on catching them off-guard and getting our people back. So what do you say?"

"I have somewhere I need to be in a bad way," Metzger replied, "but considering they tried to decapitate me, I can spare another day for some revenge."

Metzger knew the worst that might happen was their entire group getting wiped out by a more organized force and his brother would never see him again. At this point he wasn't even certain his brother would make it back to port, or contact him with details. He wasn't ready to throw in the towel, but Metzger thought the idea of sticking with other people made a lot more sense than striking out on his own again. Besides, he owed Luke and Albert because they risked their lives to save him from being kidnapped or killed a day earlier.

Refusing to leave the car behind, even though he was told the drive was just a few miles away, Metzger followed the group in a few of their vehicles to a church parking lot. Everyone got out of their vehicles to form a circle around Molly, who accepted a large rolled up sheet of paper that Metzger thought might be a poster. She knelt down, unrolling the paper atop the blacktop, revealing a hand-drawn map of a large building and its surrounding grounds. Metzger recognized a few new faces in the group, which meant the people who conducted surveillance drew a detailed map by sight alone.

Something about the layout and scale of the building drawn on the large sheet of paper felt familiar to Metzger.

"Is that a school?" he asked.

"It is," one of the new men answered. "The entire area is fenced in, and they had some of their prisoners reinforcing their fences with wood and steel."

Not wasting any time, Metzger thought, wondering how on earth this group planned to break people free from such a large area. Schools were secure by nature, and when the fences were entirely closed, it made silent infiltration nearly impossible. He hoped these people knew more about the jerks within the school confines than they let on, because going against a large group on their own turf was almost guaranteed suicide.

"What do we know?" Molly asked the two new faces.

"We counted at least six with firearms who were supervising the outdoor work, and there's probably more going on inside," one of them answered. "They don't have anything tall enough to serve as a tower, so they can't see us coming from a high vantage point, or snipe us."

Metzger couldn't believe they were seriously talking about invading the property in a straightforward manner.

"We could wait until nightfall and cut a hole in the fence along the back where there aren't many windows," the second scout suggested.

"And how do we get into the locked school?" Molly questioned, pleasing Metzger who was thinking the same thing.

"For all we know these guys killed a janitor and took his keys, or one of them *is* the janitor and knows this school top to bottom," he added before anyone could disagree with Molly. "These guys go out to kidnap people and scavenge for supplies, don't they? Why don't we knock down a few of their numbers that way?"

A few members of the group glared at Metzger for speaking as the 'new guy' but the others seemed to agree with his suggestion.

"They sent a truck out about an hour ago," the first of the two scouts noted. "It hadn't returned last we saw."

"Covered truck?" Metzger asked.

"It was full-size with a cab on the back."

Everyone looked to every other set of eyes in the group, all knowing they might have a way into the makeshift prison. Getting in wasn't necessarily the difficult part of their plan, because they all knew the risks of getting into a firefight with the group inside an unknown floorplan. There was absolutely no way of knowing how many overseers existed, how many weapons they held, or how they managed to keep so many prisoners at bay. Personally, Metzger didn't like the odds at all, though the element of surprise might benefit his new allies significantly.

"I apologize that I'm new to all of this, but what else do we know about these douchebag kidnappers?" he asked.

"We know a few are former military," Molly answered. "All of us came together while trying to track them, so we know a few of their travelers by sight. What we have is fragmented, but we've been watching them without them knowing it for a while now. It wasn't until they abducted your friends last night that we discovered their location."

"So my friends were bait?" Metzger inquired somewhat angrily.

"Not exactly," one of the other group members answered.

"It sounds like they were," he pressed. "You could've just as easily captured one of these assholes and made them talk."

"That was the plan," Molly said, "but we lost track of them near the neighborhood. When we finally caught up we saw you out there with three or four of them, and we didn't dare make a move. And then they scattered after you took out one of them with a zombie. We were a little too late again this morning when we went to speak with your friends, but Brian and Will were able to spot them and follow them to the school."

"How far is the school?" Metzger asked.

"Less than a mile," one of the scouts answered. "There's only one good road in and out of there, so if we wanted to set up an ambush for their driver it wouldn't be too hard."

While the group had been discussing their plan of action a few straggler zombies wandered into the church parking lot, now making their presence felt with growls and snarls. Before any of the others rose to deal with the problem, Metzger drew the survival knife from his side and walked over to stab each of them in the skull as silently as possible. He grew concerned, because if he was the warrior of this group with practically no survival or fighting experience, he didn't like their chances inside the confines of the school grounds.

"Can I have a word with you a minute?" he asked Molly.

She eyed him momentarily and he worried she was going to give him the standard line about anything he wanted to say to her he could say in front of the group. But she stood from the map after a few seconds and followed him behind of the vehicles.

"I want my friends back as much as all of you, but I'm a little concerned we're rushing into this without much of a plan."

"Something tells me you've been swept into all of this without much warning, so maybe you're a little overwhelmed at the thought of working with a group."

She appeared completely serious as she spoke, with an even tone that made her a strong leader. Metzger thought of her as determined, confident, and courageous, though not recklessly fearless. Something about her instilled confidence in her group, and to an extent within him, but he still felt unconvinced about her course of action.

"Those two walkers back there," she said, nodding in the direction of the two zombies with head wounds, "were a test for you to see if you could handle yourself. We may look ragtag, like we don't have a plan, but when the shit hits the fan we handle our business. There will probably be casualties no matter how we try getting our people back, and we accept that, but we're willing to risk our lives because we all have people we care about inside there. Do you care about your friends?"

"Of course. They saved my life."

"Then you're welcome to contribute as you have been, because Lord knows we can use some good ideas, but at the end of the day we are going to make the first move to get our loved ones back whether you're with us or not."

I guess that's settled, Metzger thought to himself, feeling a bit more confident about the group and their ability to handle a fight. As he followed Molly back to the group he noticed some smirks, understanding why they felt a need to test him. To them he was a complete stranger, and they needed to know what he brought to the table, and if he would be a liability who might endanger their lives.

"I do think he's right," one of the men in the group stated, nodding towards Metzger, "we're better off trying a Trojan horse and sneaking in, rather than some kind of frontal assault."

Metzger felt vindicated for bringing a good idea to the table, but he still didn't love their chances. Battles by invading forces seldom ended well for such groups because they didn't know the lay of the land, or where the weapons were located.

"We have radios," Molly stated. "Even if a few of us get inside perhaps they could get some extra recon done before finding a way to let everyone else in."

"Do you have any firepower beyond guns?" Metzger questioned.

"Like what?" one of the group asked.

"Like something that can blow a door off its hinges if we get compromised and stuck in a bad place."

One of the scouts looked at him with a sly grin.

"You'd be surprised exactly what we have in our arsenal. And hopefully the assholes at the school won't be expecting the kind of party we're bringing them."

***

Refusing to leave his car behind once more, Metzger ended up following the convoy of vehicles a short distance down the road where they took them into a grove, ensuring they were out of sight from the nearby road. Dangerously close to the school, but not within viewing distance, the group broke into pairs and smaller clans to take up positions along a ditch where they were invisible to any-one driving their way until it was too late.

Metzger ended up with Will, one of the scouts who appeared to be only a few years older than a high school senior. With a thin frame, shaggy brown hair that hung near his eyes from lack of a recent haircut, and remnants of acne, the young man was denied a normal adulthood already. They hunkered down in the ditch, which thankfully proved to be dry in the fall weather while tall, tan grass provided them with adequate cover.

"This still seems insane," Metzger admitted to the younger man.

"I felt the same way when I first met some of these guys, but they are capable. We've taken down entire swarms of zombies together."

Metzger decided against starting an argument, but taking down a group of shuffling zombies wasn't the same as dealing with live ammunition from people who knew how to efficiently fire it. Their best bet, and perhaps their only hope of minimal casualties, was a minimal number of people controlling the prison, using guns and intimidation to keep their workforce at bay.

Personally, Metzger had left some of his larger firearms inside the vehicle, opting to travel somewhat lighter so he could move quickly and avoid making noise. He often tried choosing the best weapons for the immediate future, because too many guns and blades weighed him down, making travel cumbersome. Sometimes when he located new guns, he took whichever suited him better and hid any others where they could be retrieved later. Available ammunition, or lack thereof, often made his choices easier.

"How long have you guys been planning this?" he asked Will.

"About two weeks."

Metzger gave him a quizzical stare.

"Well, it was just a few of us in the beginning," Will admitted. "A few of us banded together for survival and after we found a few more our stories started sounding similar about seeing loved ones killed or kidnapped. It wasn't long after that we decided to find these dickheads and do something about them."

"And you just waited for the numbers to be on your side."

"That, and to find out where they were taking everyone. A school was *one* of my guesses, but I wasn't sure why they wanted to kidnap people, so the whole slave labor thing came as a surprise to me."

"Why else would they want people?"

"Intel, perhaps. Or maybe to eat them."

Metzger couldn't fathom cannibalism, particularly since the food supply wasn't completely drained. Scores of retail stores, factories, schools, food pantries, and individual homes still provided adequate food and supplies, even for large groups.

"How exactly do you know it's the same people kidnapping everyone?"

"They drive the same two vehicles all the time. One is the truck with the cab on top, and the other is a van that has some kind of cage in it. We spotted them individually a number of times when they took people we knew, or tried to take us. Once we banded together and started talking, we knew these were the same ass wipes and we had to do something about them."

Shifting his position, considering they were basically lying diagonally within the ditch, Metzger looked to both sides, seeing the other small groups basically waiting in silence or making small talk to pass the time. No one appeared to be visible to oncoming traffic, and thus far the undead weren't even a factor. He wondered if the group at the school cleared them out regularly, meaning they might have another major vulnerability if they left the safety of the mesh wire gates.

"Do you worry about what we're going to find in there?" Metzger asked.

"*If* we make it inside. Some of these guys are phenomenal shots, but if we're outnumbered we won't make it far."

Metzger wondered if any of the prisoners were left in a position to assist them during the attack. They would be unarmed, putting them completely in harm's way, but even distractions might be enough for the gatekeepers to let down their guard and for Metzger's new group to push forward. Everything within his mind was a hypothetical daydream, thinking back to the schools where he worked, and how they were laid out, to get an idea of what they might find inside. Ideally the school interior would be completely lit, and every living person would be confined to one specific area. Schools were like caves with their multiple hiding places, and Metzger knew the more areas that required clearing meant more danger along the way.

"So who did they take from you?" he inquired.

"My cousin Jeff."

"Your cousin? Where's the rest of your family?"

Will shook his head negatively.

"None of them made it. And Jeff was always like a brother to me growing up. We were close in age and did everything together. Baseball, videogames, treehouse adventures all through childhood, and we were inseparable. Jeff learned to be a great mechanic from his father at a young age. Could've had his own shop, but he kept working for some old dude for a lot less money."

Metzger imagined cash flow became the least of Jeff's worries when the dead began walking around, biting everyone in sight. Perhaps the people running the unofficial prison at the school tricked survivors into joining them in the beginning, or lured them in using other creative means. He doubted they were subtle with Albert, Luke, and Samantha, trying to avoid envisioning the terror on their faces when armed men barged into their beautiful home, ripping them away from their little paradise in the center of a wasteland.

He hoped it never crossed their minds that he threw in with such heathens to enslave them.

"What about your family?" Will inquired.

"That's actually why I'm here. But the answer to your question is a big question mark thus far."

"Being alone in this world is a scary prospect. Guess that's why I'm willing to risk so much to get Jeff back."

"How did they get him?"

"They swept the neighborhood where we were crashing, looking for food and supplies I guess. Jeff knew they were going to find us, so he went out to try reasoning with them. Those pricks just beat him down and took what supplies we worked so hard to find. I hid the entire time he confronted them, and he bought me enough time to escape. They never even knew I was there."

"I'm sorry," Metzger offered as silence fell between them momentarily.

"I felt like such a coward," Will said almost blankly. "Jeff told me to hide in case things went badly and I just did what he said."

"If you came out they would've taken you, too. And we'd have one less person helping us now. They're the cowards, Will, treating people like they're slaves. When we get inside we'll get our people back. You did the right thing."

Metzger wished he felt as confident as he sounded. He wanted to think the people in charge of the makeshift prison were lazy and cowardly, but in truth they were probably bullies with guns. He never tolerated bullies during his school years, or when he taught school, so he wasn't going to feel badly harming any of them.

Every successive part of their plan relied upon the first step going flawlessly, capturing the vehicle and driver without anyone inside the schoolyard being alerted. Metzger was about to perk up like a prairie dog for a look down the road to see if they were missing anything, but remained still a moment longer. Although each group possessed a portable radio, Molly suggested they not use them if possible once near the school to ensure their radio traffic wasn't overheard. Metzger inched his way up toward the road for a look, seeing no other heads peering up from the ditch in either direction. Knowing he would hear a vehicle when it came, and knowing at least two other groups were further down the row from them, he thought of the plan and settled down into his position.

A throaty growl sounded behind him, and he recalled an open field beyond the ditch when they observed it from the road. He motioned to Will that he planned to deal with whatever zombie issue awaited them from behind, carefully switching sides in the large ditch. Before giving little more than a glance into the open field, he began pulling himself up before he noticed more than a single zombie awaited him. Witnessing a perilous situation, he saw a zombie closing on their location, but staggered anywhere between five feet and five-hundred yards he found dozens of undead wandering aimlessly.

Although the field appeared clear when they first arrived, the group had been waiting in the ditch for close to an hour now, giving the undead plenty of time to migrate.

Feeling certain karma hadn't kicked him hard enough just yet, he heard the sound of a vehicle traveling quickly in their direction along the road behind him. Metzger had barely hoisted his body to sternum level over the top of the ditch, so he slowly lowered himself down before any undead took notice. His new allies were about to follow through with their plan to stop the truck by clever means, but a herd of undead stumbled their way. If none of them were spotted or heard, the group stood an excellent chance of pulling off their plan before many undead reached them, but if the plan went astray they might be overrun before they knew what happened, *and* the schoolyard people would be amply warned of an impending attack.

"What is it?" Will asked, reading the distressed look on his face.

"We have a problem in the field behind us."

Will nodded, immediately understanding the situation, having heard the growls growing closer.

"There's no time," he said, concurring with Metzger's assessment. "We take the truck quickly and deal with everything else after that."

Holding his position in the ditch, Metzger heard the truck come to a stop, exactly like their plan called for, but he also heard the sounds of the undead stepping dangerously close to their position.

Closing his eyes, he picked up the shotgun he had set down when he originally entered the ditch and clutched it tightly, waiting for the plan to unfold. He prayed it went smoothly with no glitches.

Or deaths.

Seven

According to the plan, the second, and younger, female in the group, Jillian, needed to put on an acting clinic, crawling and fighting to stand up alongside the road when the truck drew near. Warned not to behave like a zombie, the group coached her into acting like she was weak and wounded, enough so that the truck driver would stop to see if she held potential for their schoolyard prison.

Planning practically every detail, they found her some dirty, tattered clothes, rubbed dirt on her face and arms, and worked with her on her movements before they retreated to several hiding spots. The signal they waited for was a single scream to indicate a driver only, or the signal they actually anticipated, two screams to indicate two or more men in the truck. Jillian understood that she might have to scream during a moment that seemed out of place to the people trying to assess her, knowing it was more important to warn her group about what they faced.

Trying to drown out the sounds of zombies drawing closer in the field behind him, Metzger looked to Will without a word. Both heard different sounds in front of them, like feet hitting the ground when two people exited the truck after it came to a stop with slightly squealing brakes. Immediately Metzger knew the answer to their most pressing question without Jillian needing to use her vocal cords. If there were only two men, and both exited the truck, overtaking them might be easier than originally imagined.

Suddenly the sound of crunching grass behind them caused both he and Will to turn, finding a zombie standing at the edge of the ditch, close to falling over and right on top of them. Like a cheetah, Will zipped across the ditch, clutched the zombie by the leather belt holding its pants up, and yanked it into the ditch with them. It couldn't react quickly enough before Will stabbed it in the head, silencing it as two screams reached their ears from the other side. Entering the final phase of their plan that now seemed layered with hidden dangers, the two sprung out of the ditch simultaneously with the other six members of their group.

With eight guns trained on them, the two men appeared shocked when they whirled around. Jillian, not wanting to be an impromptu hostage, quickly left the vicinity, circling around the truck to join her people. Metzger noticed the two men were near her when he reached the top of the ditch, but it looked as though they hadn't gotten a chance to lay hands on her. Both wore incredulous expressions as one of the group members grabbed the keys from the ignition and walked to the rear of the truck to unlock the camper shell. With minimal prompting, three people filed out of the makeshift cell and stood by, unsure of what to do or think.

"Give me one reason I should let you two live," Molly said, aiming her gun at the one on the right.

"We can get you inside," the man on the left volunteered immediately.

"We're just transporting these three people to our camp," the other man said.

"Against their wills," Molly stated. "We know who you are and what you do, so let's dispense with the pleasantries and excuses. We all have people inside your walls that we want back. You call yourselves the Wardens, but you're nothing but bullies and thugs, no better than Hitler the way you treat people."

Metzger looked to Will for an explanation of Molly's last statement.

"We've heard them refer to themselves as Wardens when we spied on them," Will whispered. "They bragged about it, like they were proud of coming up with the name."

Both captured men exchanged concerned glances, as though something more than the obvious awaited everyone beyond the protective fencing. Neither seemed interested in offering any further words, as though entering the grounds meant a death sentence for them as well as any strangers.

"There are dozens of zombies behind us," Metzger said, nodding toward the open field across the ditch. "We can just as easily leave you two for them and take our chances getting inside. Whichever you prefer."

As though prompted upon request, the groans and moans of the undead crossed the ditch and reached the ears of everyone present. Even the minimal noise from the standoff around the truck was enough to attract them to the area. Metzger glanced at the three released prisoners, who stood nearby, openly confused and shaking with fear. A woman, a young man who appeared to be her son, and an older woman with graying hair might have been housed together when the two men abducted them, but now they were caught in the middle of a deadly situation.

"We need to get them to safety," he said aside to Molly.

"They're safer with us," she replied just above a whisper, her expression indicating she didn't want an argument about the topic.

"They didn't ask for this," Metzger pressed.

"What kind of chance do you think they have walking down this road without transportation or weapons?" Molly fired back. "If you're afraid we're going to use them as bait, or get them killed, feel free to keep them with you."

Metzger wasn't a soldier or mercenary capable of protecting multiple people at once, but he agreed with Molly that sending them hobbling down the paved open road wasn't the best idea. He didn't want to prolong the argument, knowing all too well danger was closing in from behind and the two men could easily call for help. The school was just barely out of sight beyond some buildings and a few trees, but sound would travel far enough for their friends to hear.

"They're with me," Metzger agreed. "Let's get moving before we lose the element of surprise."

He motioned for the three newcomers to join him, and they reluctantly did so, the confusion evident on their faces. Although he wanted to give them an explanation, or at least some reassurance, time didn't permit for either.

"We don't need both of you alive," Molly said to the men from the schoolyard. "Just one of you can get us past any guards. "Who's it going to be?"

Both of them looked terrified at the prospect of dying, but to their credit neither tried to indicate they were willing to see the other sacrificed.

"You," she said to the one on the right. "You were driving, so we're going to leave it that way. "Tie the other one up and throw him in the back," she added, giving orders to a member of her own group.

A wave of relief crashed over Metzger, who didn't particularly want to see cold-blooded murder in front of his three new charges. The group quickly readied themselves for entry into the schoolyard, realizing only a handful of them were going to fit in the back of the truck unless they wanted to be crammed like sardines. If everyone sat Indian style they could all fit, but if shooting started unexpectedly they would be trapped inside the cab with no backup. It was quickly decided that four of them would ride in back and one up front with the driver to make certain he didn't give away their plan to any guards at the gate.

Metzger was left behind with the three innocent bystanders, Jillian, and Will, who openly admitted he was far better with a knife and blunt weapons than firearms. Jillian possessed a holstered firearm, but Metzger suspected she wasn't expertly trained in how to use it. They watched the truck drive in the direction of the school, slowly following on the side of the road closer to the open field to keep hidden by the trees and shrubs behind them. Metzger and Will kept vigil for any undead that made it through the ditch and came anywhere near them.

"Keep walking," he encouraged the three newcomers, who appeared hesitant to commit to any action.

He imagined they were still shell-shocked by the events of the past hour.

"Why are you doing this?" the older woman asked, seeming far less afraid, probably because she had seen enough life that the apocalypse and abduction didn't seem quite as foreign.

"You're safer with us," Metzger replied, keeping his voice down.

"But you're taking us to their camp, just like they were."

"I don't plan on taking you in there," he replied. "There are too many undead out here to just let you go wandering by yourself."

All six kept a regular pace at this point, and the school slowly came into view over the next horizon. They stayed close to the trees, still too far away for anyone to spot them unless they had elevation and a rifle scope or binoculars.

"I hate to say it, but we should probably walk in the ditch," Will suggested.

The group climbed down into the ditch, which became less like a trench the closer they drew to the school. Still, it provided better cover than walking along the pavement, and just a few minutes later they received a message on their radio from Molly.

"We're in," she said. "We'll be at the gate waiting for you."

All six picked up the pace, and soon found themselves alongside the school looking for an open gate. Metzger had seen schools with fencing around portions of the parking lot and sporting areas, but never encircled around the main building like some kind of compound. He noticed some of the fencing was new and not professionally installed, though it appeared solid enough to repel small numbers of stragglers or the undead. It reached about fifteen feet in height, making it difficult to scale without drawing attention, and portions of it were wrapped in barbed wire along the top.

Metzger saw no one along the roofline spying for intruders, and strangely, he found no one working outside as Molly and her group had reported seeing. The weather was overcast, but not particularly cold, and certainly not rainy. He wondered why these purported slave drivers didn't have people outside securing the facility unless they had turned their attention to the interior. If that were the case, rescuing loved ones without putting them in harm's way just became exponentially difficult.

A few zombies stumbled into the ditch from the field, allowing Will to make short work of them with his knife. The group barely lost a step in the process as Metzger considered the young man a very useful ally to whatever folks acquired his services. Personally, Metzger didn't plan to join any groups or recruit anyone to head east with him. He feared being slowed down on the journey to see his brother, though he didn't necessarily see himself turning down company if anyone wanted to tag along.

First things first, he thought, knowing he needed to free three allies from the clutches of kidnappers before anything particularly bad happened to them. What felt like forever actually took them mere minutes to reach the open gate, finding the other members of their group standing cautiously inside. Metzger passed through the sliding gate with his three wards near him, finding a body immediately to his left on the ground. He tried not to stare, but the man who was likely guarding the fence and letting people inside was face-down with a bullet in the back of his skull.

Metzger said nothing, but shot Molly a glance to ask if murder was really necessary. She replied with only a stern look that indicated nothing was more important to her than the people they risked so much to rescue.

"I'm not going to ask any of you to come any further," he informed the three unarmed victims. "You have no weapons, and it's not safe out there. It's probably safer for you to stay right here until we get back, but if you leave please don't let anyone see you. We need the element of surprise if we're going to rescue our friends."

"What is this place?" the young man asked with a perplexed stare.

"It's a makeshift prison where they kidnap people and put them to work."

Something seemed to click with all three of them, transforming them from victims to advocates based on their expressions.

"I want to come with you," the young man said. "I'll help if I can."

Both of the women seemed to object momentarily, but quickly realized their limited options weren't good in any sense, and protection from an armed group might not be a bad thing.

"We'll stick with you," the older woman said, indicating Metzger personally.

He realized he had missed some of the instructions being provided by Molly, but he didn't exactly plan on leading the charge with three unarmed people in his care. Trying to take in the setting, he noticed a few access doors along this particular side of the school and fewer windows than the other sides of the building. He hoped no one had seen them enter with a group, because murdering a sentry wasn't going to bode well if one of the schoolyard Wardens witnessed it.

"Do we have keys?" he heard one of the group members ask Molly after she finished going over a very brief plan of action.

She jingled them for everyone to see. Metzger figured she lifted them from the bound man in the back of the truck, and when he took a look inside he found the man still bound, lying with his face atop the rubber mat. Blood oozed from somewhere along his upper body, pooling atop the mat, and his eyes remained wide open as though he never saw his death coming.

"Shit," Metzger muttered, thinking he was only here for three people he barely knew because they saved his life.

Pressing forward, he glanced inside the truck's cab, finding the driver slumped over the wheel, killed under similar circumstances. Blood still dripped from his skull, which remained pressed against the top of the wheel beside both of his hands. Metzger couldn't help but think keeping one of them alive as a tour guide of sorts certainly might have helped his group's cause. Growing angrier by the second, he wondered if Molly kept him behind and saddled him with the three kidnap victims to keep him from objecting to their senseless brutality. The group had plenty of time to subdue the three men at gunpoint without putting bullets in their heads.

He understood that perhaps the rest of the group saw unthinkable things during their surveillance that he hadn't, but they had yet to justify murder to him.

"Don't look," he said to his three wards as they passed the truck behind him.

He wasn't sure three murders would faze them much considering two of the three deceased men had just abducted them from their normal lives. A normal life wasn't anything like before, but people still deserved the right to freedom, and not being scooped up by tyrants.

Possessing only a shotgun and his .357, Metzger wasn't as well-armed as the others in the group ahead of him. Some of them sported automatic weapons and combat shotguns that held more shells and fired without being pumped each time. He harbored concerns about all of them entering the same exact door and becoming targets for anyone inside.

Molly already seemed extremely agitated with him, so Metzger said nothing, but let everyone else in the group enter the building, hesitating momentarily before he followed. When he stepped through the door he found both directions open with his group heading to the right side. Although not completely dark, the hallway in either direction appeared dim due to the lack of windows. No overhead lights were turned on, assuming the school even had any electricity or generators to power lights and appliances.

Without saying a word to his three wards, Metzger pointed to the left, and they silently followed him down the hallway as the others went right. Although he worked as a teacher, Metzger never considered himself much of a natural leader, yet here he was leading three strangers away from the jaws of certain death.

He hoped.

From what he actually did hear of Molly's plan, the group was going to get inside and split up, taking different hallways to conduct some reconnaissance of the school's layout. From there they wanted to draw up a more thorough plan, deciding exactly where they wanted to attack, and how.

Metzger found it difficult to believe that in a month's time a large number of people jumped on board with the concept of imprisoning fellow human beings like slaves. He didn't expect the number of Wardens to be especially high, and if more than a dozen roamed the grounds he felt the chances of success for his group weren't very high. Of course three members of the enemy force lie dead at the gate, reducing the number of potential lethal encounters, but he could not condone murder. In this world where the living were by far the minority, he considered people the world's greatest resource. Not food, not supplies, and certainly not luxury items people once took for granted.

Taking the lead, Metzger came to the first corner, which only went to the right because the left and ahead were both exterior walls. Where they entered appeared to be an area where the gymnasium and locker rooms were located nearby, but after a short walk he entered an area filled with classrooms and possible danger.

None of the classrooms had lights on, and blinds or blankets covered all of the windows. Ahead, Metzger saw wooden barricades blocking the hallway like those used by police along roads to limit traffic access. Painted white with orange striping, they blocked an intersection that turned back to the right or went directly ahead. The hallway directly ahead was the blocked portion, so Metzger approached cautiously, looking to the right and finding only more classrooms. Ahead, the hallway grew darker, and after about fifty feet became pitch black. He wondered if the area was cut off to prisoners, the Wardens, or everyone in general.

Without lighting or some kind of night vision he wouldn't be able to get far, but he decided to head that way anyway. He patted down his pockets and belt for the stubby flashlight he carried, but couldn't locate it within the darkness. Ensured his three charges followed, he quietly walked down the hallway, looking for a light switch or some means to illuminate the hallway beyond the darkness. About halfway down he detected an odor that immediately alerted him to death, whether it came in the form of the undead or recently deceased people lying nearby. The undead didn't usually stink too badly unless they were in herds because their flesh decayed at a far reduced rate due to the reanimation.

"Something's wrong," Metzger whispered to the three people with him. "Smell that?"

All three nodded affirmatively, which he saw only because their silhouettes were backlit by the minimal light behind them.

He thumbed for them to head back toward the intersection but all three stopped short when the noise of footsteps reached their ears. At first, Metzger believed it might be Molly and the others circling around the hallways, finally reaching this area, but he doubted they could cover that much ground so quickly. He motioned for his three companions to take a few steps back, into the darkness, before shoving his hand downward repeatedly. Following his command, they all hunkered to the floor, surrounded by darkness, watching as three unfamiliar men rounded the corner, running in the direction of the door where Metzger and the others entered.

All three were dressed in dark clothes that appeared tactical in nature, and each carried some sort of firearm. Metzger's heart sunk because he needed to carry out the last act he wanted to, and he needed to do it alone.

"Stay here," he whispered to the three people with him. "I'll be back."

"Are you sure?" the young man asked with questioning eyes, barely visible in the darkness.

"No."

Metzger didn't waste time with another word, dashing in the direction of the three men, hoping to intercept them before they found Molly and the others. He didn't know if they discovered the bodies outside, had some form of security system within the school, or spotted some of the group members within the hallways. And though he knew his steel-toed boots made an awful sound clopping against the ground with each step, the three men made at least as much noise during their militaristic sprints.

Fighting to catch up to them, Metzger wasn't accustomed to sprinting for very long distances, despite having to escape the undead on a few occasions. Of course they shambled at a snail's pace compared to normal people.

Reacting a little too quickly from a tactical perspective, Metzger barely realized he possessed a shotgun and his faithful six-shooter against potentially militaristic weaponry. Not until he reached the blind corner did he begin to slow down and think, barely coming to a complete stop before he dropped to one knee for a glance around the corner. A shotgun shell splintered the wall just above his head immediately, leaving him thankful he didn't provide them with a full target. He ducked back, feeling his face, having noticed only one of the three men stayed behind to fire at him from the brief glance.

His other two buddies had run ahead, but hopefully the gunfire alerted Molly and the others to their presence. Despite placing himself in grave danger, Metzger felt he had done his allies a service by alerting them the best way possible, given the circumstances.

"Why don't you come around that corner and play, boy?" the man who shot at him asked as though he were a character from *Deliverance* with a Louisiana accent that sounded exaggerated and fake.

Knowing his options were limited, Metzger could retreat and put his three wards in danger, advance and likely get himself killed, or figure out a different approach before more Wardens came down the hallway behind him. He wondered why only three men were sent, unless they didn't know the number of people intruding in their sanctuary, or they didn't have many people in their camp. Wishing he possessed a grenade, Metzger scooted away from the corner, looking to the ceiling, and then the classroom across the hall from him.

Too high to reach, the ceiling offered no sneaky way to hide or ambush anyone, and unless the classroom was unlocked, he'd make too much noise trying to enter it and give away his position. The door to one classroom across the hallway made him an easy target, but the one almost diagonally behind him presented an opportunity so he scrambled across the tile floor to try the door.

Finding it locked, he darted across the hallway to the lit, open corridor where the three men had emerged. He immediately found some rooms accessed by solid doors, with no windows, indicating they might be janitorial closets or the mechanical room where heating and cooling components were stored. The first was unlocked, revealing a utility closet with nothing immediately useful when Metzger opened the door and flipped the light switch, illuminating the small room to his surprise. He started to pull the door closed when he spied something useful on the wall in the form of an extension cord. Grimacing, he wondered if he had enough time to manufacture what he considered an ideal weapon from the bright orange cord.

A few minutes later he heard the man coming around the corner, being a complete jackass by continuing to call out. For some reason he seemed to think Metzger was cowering in terror, intimidated by a single gunman. In truth, as Metzger crouched within the closet, looking to the extension cord, now plugged in just above him, he worried more for the three people he left in the darkness with a foul odor surrounding them.

Metzger opted to leave the light on because he didn't believe it was visible beneath the door. Even if someone saw it, the idea was to attract the lone gunman his way. Somewhat cramped within the small room, Metzger felt the metal shelving against his back that held a number of cleaners, spare mop heads, and a few small tools. To his front was a small washbasin on the ground for filling mop buckets and dumping the dirty water, and across from that was another storage shelf with lightbulbs, instruction manuals, and a few old computers.

As quietly as possible he dumped a chemical agent from a spray bottle into the washbasin and used one of the rubber hose lines to fill the bottle with water. He didn't bother to cap it as he heard the man draw closer, still speaking taunting lines. Metzger wondered why the other two hadn't come back with this particular man, deciding they probably didn't care much whether he lived or died based on his demeanor. He debated whether or not to make a sound when he heard footsteps draw closer to lure the man to the door, but he decided that might be too obvious and give away his plan.

With the electrical cord stripped at one end thanks to his pocket knife, and the exposed wiring wrapped around the doorknob, Metzger held the bottle of water in one hand, fully prepared to electrocute the man and end this ordeal quickly when the footsteps stopped. Complete silence overtook the hallways momentarily, and he could hear only the sound of inhalation through his nose as he waited a few seconds, and then a few more. He felt certain the man was on the other side of the door, debating whether to play it safe and study the door or recklessly turn the knob and yank it open. Their stalemate soon became a moot point when the sound of a sneeze, brief and completely unintended, echoed throughout the hallway.

Hearing the footsteps begin to walk away from the room in the direction of his three charges, Metzger reached up slowly to unplug the extension cord from the wall with a gentle tug, his eyes never moving from the door. Quietly collecting the shotgun beside him, he slowly stood, set the water bottle in the basin, and placed his hand on the doorknob.

He decided he wanted maximum effectiveness from the shotgun, so he opted not to wait until the gunman reached the darkness and three helpless victims before taking action. Even though it left him completely exposed because the door swung the opposite way from the man's location, Metzger threw the door open, racked the shotgun for effect, and cupped the weapon along his right side. He watched the man whirl around in complete surprise upon hearing the rack slide back and forth. Perhaps he thought one of his allies had caught up to him, or realized too late he wasn't following the sound of an armed man sneezing, but his jaw had just begun to drop when Metzger pulled the trigger, unleashing dozens of pellets into his torso.

Unlike the movies, the man didn't go flying back into a wall some unrealistic distance away, or even leave his feet. In the middle of trying to raise his own weapon, he accidentally blocked some of the buckshot with his arms. Even so, enough caught his chest from Metzger's vantage point that blood immediately spurted outward and he stumbled backwards, landing hard on his back after a few steps.

Metzger possessed a variety of shells for the shotgun, which held five at a time. The 12 Gauge used a variety of shells from the BB type, to birdshot, to buckshot that included single to triple-aught. With plenty of each type in reserve, he left the birdshot and BB shot shells in storage, knowing he wasn't going to be hunting when he stepped outside. In this case the double-aught shells appeared to have done their job, so he picked up the shell discarded from the gun when he pumped it and slid it down his right pants pocket. The man continued to groan and gasp as Metzger approached him, no longer the arrogant ass who thought he had easy prey cornered when he separated from his two buddies.

Immediately questioning how the man was even breathing after taking fire from close to twenty yards, Metzger began to contemplate why the men all wore tactical clothing.

"Body armor," he muttered to himself as the man sat up like some kind of killer robot from a movie and grasped for his shotgun.

His face and arms both drizzled blood, and fortunately for Metzger the man's arms weren't functioning correctly because he failed to grasp his rifle and hold onto it. Already halfway closer than the distance he shot from, Metzger moved swiftly after the man dropped the rifle the first time. Caught in the open, he had little choice but to move toward the man, readying the shotgun with pump action before aiming it closer to the man's head this time. Considering the man appeared dazed, entering a state of shock perhaps, Metzger didn't shout any commands, but simply stepped closer until he was able to kick the automatic weapon away from the man's side.

Drawing the man's friends to their location wasn't a good idea, so he didn't want additional gunfire echoing through the halls.

Looking up, Metzger noticed his three wards peering around the corner with concerned expressions. Once they saw he had the situation under control they cautiously stepped closer as Metzger debated what to do with the subdued man who lacked sufficient use of both arms but wore some kind of body armor that protected his torso from receiving major damage. Body armor stopped any kind of shotgun blast, even from close range, except for a slug. The man's face received only a few punctures from the buckshot, and Metzger couldn't determine the extent of his injuries. At the moment he needed to get the man out of sight, regardless of whether he chose to end his life or somehow subdue him.

Kneeling down, he removed the semi-automatic sidearm from a holster along the man's side as the former assailant continued to sputter and spit, as though his brain had somehow been scrambled. Metzger quickly patted the rest of the man's body down with one hand, keeping hold of the shotgun, and finding a rather large knife along the man's belt. Knowing time wasn't on his side regarding the other two armed men, and who knew how many others, he tossed the young man the sidearm.

"Get him out of sight and subdue him," Metzger said, looking between the young man and the two women. "If you even *think* he's going to make a move, shoot him. And keep yourselves out of sight. There are several rooms down this hall where you can hide."

"And what about you?" the older woman asked with concern.

"The other two will get the jump on my group if they haven't already."

He scooped up the automatic rifle, grinning a bit as he looked at it.

"I'm going to see if I can even the odds."

Eight

Back to square one, Metzger rounded two corners just to get back to where he last got stonewalled. This time no one waited to ambush him around the left turn, but he slowed his pace and made certain to walk quietly. Having heard nothing, especially any gunfire, he wondered where the two men had gotten to. They seemed to have an idea someone was trespassing within their school when they ran purposefully that way. Either they were tracking Molly and the others, or they had stepped outside to examine how trespassers entered their domain so easily.

Part of him wished he'd stuck with the main group, but now he suspected their presence was detected and he might be the only one from his group who knew that fact. Soon he reached the area where his group originally entered, peering outside of the door to see if both armed men were outside. Considering the door was already open, resting against the frame with a thin strip of daylight coming through the opening, Metzger figured they at least opened it for a look.

Daring to put his eye up to the slit of daylight, Metzger saw the two men returning from the main gate where they surely discovered the slaughter of their three allies. From the second or two he dared peer that way he noticed they looked exceptionally angry and concerned. One lifted a radio to communicate with someone, reminding Metzger that he also possessed a radio and the means to contact Molly and the others. With the ruckus down the hallway he temporarily forgot about establishing contact with them, but now he faced a major decision.

He could radio the others and risk being caught by the two men about to reenter the building, or attempt to subdue both of them himself. Realistically the only way to overtake two armed men was to murder them with the automatic weapon he now possessed, giving them no opportunity to return fire.

With only seconds left to make a decision, he looked to the floor, prepared to scoot down the hall to find a secure place to radio Molly when he spotted something useful.

Plucking the orange security latch from its resting spot against the wall, Metzger pulled both doors closed and dropped the latch into place, making them both impossible to open from the outside. Both men immediately rushed to the doors, yanking on the handles to no avail as Metzger walked away, pulling out the portable radio from his pocket. Hammering noises continued behind him as he pushed the button to transmit after making certain the radio remained on the correct channel.

"Molly, this is Dan. I've subdued one armed man and two others are now locked outside."

Only a few seconds passed before the reply came.

"Where the hell *are* you?"

"I'm at the doors where we entered."

"Okay. I'm coming back to you."

Molly sounded less than thrilled, and he assumed only she and her designated partner were coming back to him, since everyone was split into teams. In the meantime, the pounding behind him ceased at the double doors, leaving Metzger to wonder where the two men went. Numerous doors and windows offered access, and the two men knew the grounds better than anyone entering the school for the first time. He considered radioing a warning to the others that the two might reenter the school through another area, but decided to check in with Molly first.

Metzger walked back to the area where he'd been, where his three wards hopefully dealt with their problem, to look into the rooms. He wanted to peer through the windows in the classrooms, but they were mostly covered, offering very little observation of the outdoors. Disappointed and upset with himself for letting the two men off so easily, Metzger briefly considered checking on his three charges but thought better of it. Having already disrupted whatever plans the group formed, he didn't want to incur the wrath of Molly and the others.

When Molly finally emerged from the opposite hallway she appeared infuriated as one of the group members trailed behind, warily looking in every direction for attackers. Metzger couldn't remember his name, remaining mostly focused on Molly, who pointed a finger directly into his chest.

"What the hell do you think you're doing?"

"I'm protecting three defenseless people and keeping them away from whatever war you're about to start."

"It sounds like you're the one starting the war. We hadn't found a single person in our direction when you let them all know we were here."

"They were running through the halls, tracking all of *you*. They would've shot you in the backs if I hadn't stopped them."

"Stopped them? Then where are they?"

Metzger hesitated before answering, knowing the double-edged sword his words presented, no matter how he crafted them.

"I shot one. The other two are outside."

"Perfect. And where are your three *defenseless* people?"

"Back the other way keeping the one I shot subdued."

Molly shot him a look of absolute disgust and disbelief.

"Why did I ever stop for you? You've yet to do one thing right, and you undermine every aspect of my plans."

Their argument was quickly cut short when someone fired an automatic weapon from the direction Molly and the other man came from, hitting the man in the back with every single bullet. Dead before he even began falling to the ground, he provided just enough shielding for Metzger to grab Molly by the arm and pull her to safety around the next bend.

"Jerry!" Molly shouted, though her ally wasn't ever going to hear an earthly word again.

"He's gone," Metzger said, forcing Molly to look him in the eyes. "We need to retreat and get to cover."

Not inclined to disagree, Molly followed him to the strangely dark area of the school before Metzger turned toward the janitorial areas where he hoped to find his three wards and an unconscious troublemaker.

"Is this your other two assholes?" Molly asked while they retreated, possibly wanting to place blame on Metzger for not claiming their lives.

"They couldn't have gotten inside this quickly," he surmised aloud. "They had radios, like us, so they probably called for help."

"You could have shot them," Molly said fiercely, eyeballing the automatic weapon he now held, along with the shotgun strapped around his shoulder.

"And you *didn't* have to murder those three at the gate."

Rounding the corner, Metzger darted for the same room he hid in before, hearing footsteps clop to a halt behind them. Their pursuer, or pursuers, stopped at the corner, fearing firearms being aimed their way. Metzger made use of the borrowed time as he and Molly crammed into the closet by unraveling the extension cord with the stripped end and plugging it into the wall.

"Grab that water bottle behind you and dump half of it along the bottom of the door," he ordered her.

Although she didn't appear the least bit happy about following his orders, she quickly understood what he wanted to accomplish and carefully lined the water along the bottom so it wasn't exceedingly visible on the other side.

"They can shoot us through the door," she hissed just above a whisper.

"They certainly will if you keep talking," Metzger replied in a low growl.

"And how can you blame us for killing any of these bastards, knowing what they do to people? Do you think they keep adding to their workforce because they want a community?" she asked with a fire burning in her eyes, still keeping her voice down. "No, they do it because their workers are expendable. We're a month into the end of the world and these select few think they're some kind of superior regime above the rest of us. People like that don't deserve to live and claim this world."

Metzger couldn't entirely disagree with her logic, though he wanted more proof than a few eyewitness statements from outside the school before he started shooting people in their brains. Perhaps too much of the old world remained within him, but he certainly wasn't going to allow himself to be a victim either. He wrapped the exposed end of the extension cord around the metal doorknob before making certain the wires directly touched the metal. Plugging in the extension cord, he heard hesitant footsteps coming down the hallway in their direction.

He wondered where his three wards had gotten to with the subdued assailant, hoping they found adequate cover.

Both he and Molly stepped away from the new puddle, waiting to see what happened if and when their unseen enemy touched the doorknob. Metzger wasn't foolish enough to expect the man to grab the knob and stand there receiving an electrical shock until his body fried from the inside out like the movies. He did fully expect the man to receive a shock large enough to knock him back, possibly rendering him unconscious in the process. A large enough jolt might deal damage to his heart, possibly causing it to lose its regular rhythm, or stop it altogether. He felt reasonably certain only power lines possessed guaranteed amperage enough to kill a human being, but at this point he simply wanted to walk out of a janitorial closet alive.

Halfway expecting the man to bypass the room altogether and foil his plan, Metzger jumped back half a step when he heard the man's hand wrap around the doorknob and a brief painful cry from the other side of the thick door. It took several seconds, and he actually thought he saw an arcing light from beneath the door, but a thump finally reached his ears when the man fell back from his painful encounter. The overhead lights flickered, and he felt fairly certain the outlet's breaker kicked a few seconds after the man grabbed the doorknob, but Metzger unplugged the extension cord anyway.

Looking to Molly to make certain she was ready for their next move, he received a nod as she raised her gun. Metzger pushed the door open, letting her take the first step as she surveyed the hallway. He quickly stepped out behind her, observing the man who chased them this far, finding him on the ground unconscious. Metzger stepped on the assault rifle to ensure it wasn't used against them suddenly, but the man still didn't flinch.

"Is he alive?" Molly asked.

Like a car sputtering to start, the man exhaled a gasp that provided an answer. Molly started to aim her gun at him to finish the job but Metzger intervened.

"No," he said, pointing the barrel of her shotgun toward the ground. "We might need one for information, or at least a hostage."

"Don't your people have one of them?"

"If they kept him alive."

Molly didn't argue as he patted the man down for extra weapons, finding a few before they dragged him inside the janitorial closet and used nearby zip ties to bind his hands and feet. Metzger also stuffed a used rag inside the man's mouth to keep him quiet in case he regained all of his faculties.

Once in the main hallway again, Molly radioed her people for an update and no word came back as she waited about thirty seconds. Metzger continued to hold the automatic weapon in a ready position because he wasn't certain the subdued man came after them on his own. She started to raise the radio again but Metzger stopped her by grabbing her forearm.

"They could be pinned down somewhere where radio traffic might get them killed."

"They might also be dead *already*," Molly replied with a stone-cold stare, causing him to question her occupation before the regular world ceased to exist.

She could have been a cop, a CEO, or perhaps a nun that taught at a Catholic school for all he knew. Independent, capable, and strong-willed, Molly knew how to handle herself, but she appeared reluctant to listen to ideas or deviate from her plans. Metzger thought maybe it was him in particular she took issue with, but he figured she viewed herself as weak in front of her people if she wavered about any decision.

"I want to double back," she said, hesitating as though waiting for Metzger to volunteer to join her.

Deciding his wards were likely fine on their own, and anyone traveling the hallways alone was a terrible idea, Metzger nodded affirmatively and let her lead the way. For what seemed like the sixth time he went back the way he originally came, following her lead. Both kept their firearms aimed upward as they navigated each corner, finding no enemies in their path. Even as they reached the doors where everyone entered, the metal yolk remained in place, keeping both doors secured from the inside.

He and Molly looked from the doors to one another before continuing. Now reaching unfamiliar territory, he followed her down the hallway as they looked ahead for trouble. A few independent lights clung high on the walls, providing intermittent light along the otherwise dark hallway. Metzger followed her lead because she knew the hallways ahead, hoping they found the rest of her people alive.

Now treading on dangerous ground, they didn't know where their enemies were located, how many remained, or what to expect around the next few corners. Familiar with several schools over his career, Metzger felt reasonably certain they were in the portion of the school where teaching did not occur. Barely removed from the janitorial area, he believed the football field and track were out back, which meant they were likely closing in on the gymnasium. They passed two more corners before his beliefs were confirmed in the form of two sets of interior double doors that remained closed.

He silently motioned for Molly to stand beside the doors as he silently stepped toward another entrance around the side. Traveling down a darkened hallway, Metzger located a single door that remained locked when he gave it a gentle tug. Feeling rather certain that something of interest remained behind this door, he made his way back to Molly. Without a word she gave him a questioning look and he shook his head negatively. He started reaching for the door when both of their radios squawked with traffic, startling them both.

Knowing what awaited them on the other side of the door might be dangerous, they both scurried several feet away to listen. A member of Molly's original group reported that they had shot the two men that Metzger locked outside. She quietly inquired whether or not they were alive and the reply came that they were still checking. A moment later they provided an update that both men were dead after initially opening fire on the group. Metzger questioned how many potential enemies were left inside the school, but focused his attention on the gymnasium.

"That side door is locked," he told Molly, continuing to keep his voice down. "I need you to make some noise at that door and distract anyone who might be inside. That way I'm not a ready target when I try to open these doors."

"For all we know there might be scores of undead in there," Molly argued.

"Why the hell would they keep undead around?"

"Because they aren't normal, sane people. Do you have a plan for escaping a herd of staggering undead when you open those doors?"

"Yeah. Run like hell."

Metzger didn't truly believe the Wardens would keep undead locked inside the gymnasium. Disposing of them was easy enough, and if someone wanted to use them for defense it would be much wiser to keep them outside in plain sight. He wasn't sure the other two doors were locked, but they didn't have keyholes like the side door, which meant they needed to be latched from the inside or unlocked.

"This is insane," Molly said, putting forth one last bit of resistance.

"I have yet to see one living prisoner in this place," Metzger countered. "They have to be somewhere. And if these doors open, and *if* there are zombies behind them I'll shut them lickety-split. I'm doing the dangerous part."

Molly couldn't argue with any of his logic, so she went down the hallway to the side door. Waiting until he heard her trying to open it, and making sufficient noise in the process, Metzger tried the door on the left, finding it secured. Deciding to proceed with caution, he slung the strap of the rifle over his shoulder to pull out the .357 and the stubby flashlight he sometimes held up with it to light darkened areas now that he had located it. Able to maneuver both objects between both hands, he tried the door on the right, finding it unsecured as it swung outward.

Ducking down to make his body a smaller target, Metzger shined the light inside the gymnasium, finding no one visible inside the large area. The flashlight came from the corpse of a police officer somewhere in Pennsylvania during Metzger's travels and acted like a small floodlight in any area. Molly approached him from behind, following the beam as he spanned it across the gymnasium.

"Empty?" she thought aloud.

"Looks that way, but there might be a locker room or two across the way."

More radio traffic came across that the others were pressing forward and checking more of the school. Molly appeared concerned about something upon hearing the transmission.

"Go check on them if you're worried," Metzger offered. "I can handle this and I'll let you know if I find anything."

"We've already lost someone, and I don't want the others walking into something they aren't prepared for."

"I'm going to check this out and find my three castaways," Metzger said. "After that we'll meet up with the rest of you."

Molly nodded before darting down the hallway to reunite with her smaller group. Barely waiting for her to round the first corner, Metzger stepped inside the gymnasium, finding it clear of debris and foul odors. The bleachers on each side were folded and compressed against their respective walls. He couldn't help but walk across the glossy hardwood finish despite the thunderous echo it created within the assembly area. Not since high school had he stepped foot on a basketball court, and that was in physical education class. Metzger played football and baseball all four years of high school, skipping basketball, soccer, and track altogether.

Straight ahead he spied three sets of double doors that led to the outdoors, likely meaning the football field and running track. To his left he saw a number of dark streaks atop the court, indicating the path was heavily traveled. He wondered if people were shuttled from the locker room area to other parts of the school, or if supplies were kept in the locker room ahead. He reached a set of permanent stairs that led to the second level and more fold-out bleachers when they were activated. Beside the railed stairs Metzger found an alcove with a door further inward that he figured had to be a locker room.

Using his flashlight as it grew darker on this end of the gym, he found two heavy braces on the outside of the door which almost certainly got added after the Wardens took over the school. Both braces were secured by locks that Metzger couldn't break through without heavy equipment or the keys to unlock them. Refusing to give up so easily, he shined the flashlight beam along the wall, finding dirt and scuffed paint that indicated people accessed the area frequently. Finally, above his head, he spotted a set of keys hanging on a large hook that he was only able to reach by standing on the tips of his toes.

He pulled them down and stared at them momentarily, wondering exactly what he was about to unlock. Considering it was locked from the outside, it had to be something the Wardens didn't want loose, which meant prisoners or undead. Metzger undid the upper lock first, which was larger than his fist in circumference, letting it fall to the floor. As he put the key into the second lock he heard a noise from the other end of the gym which caused him to freeze, sucking in a quick breath and holding it because someone had opened a door and stepped inside. Every noise within the empty gymnasium caused an echo, so Metzger dared not make any sudden movements.

What started as a single set of footsteps soon turned into several, although they sounded hesitant, rather than marching directly his way. Metzger knew he couldn't scramble without being seen, so he quietly stepped to the end of the alcove for a glance at the people who had just entered the gym while he still had some cover. Holding his gun and flashlight closer to his waistline, Metzger peered around the edge of the short tunnel, finding three people pushing another person along. He couldn't see very well, but he sensed based on their shapes and heights that they were his wards coming to find him, or some new cover.

He decided to reveal his presence to them before they rounded the corner and opened fire at the first thing they spotted.

"It's me," he said, walking around the edge of the walkway, holding his firearm and flashlight in the air.

The young man instinctively aimed the sidearm at him until he recognized Metzger. As he lowered the firearm, Metzger noticed their prisoner was bound with some kind of rope behind his back, appearing very miserable about the tables being turned.

"Where have you been?" the older woman asked as though they'd reached the conclusion that Metzger had abandoned them.

"I've been trying to avoid this guy's friends. I met up with some of the people I came here with and one of them was killed."

All three wards appeared shocked, as though they hadn't expected a casualty report. He couldn't blame them, considering they were minding their own business before cruel people abducted them for selfish reasons.

"I found a locked room back here that I was about to open."

Metzger led the way around the alcove entrance, shining his light on the last remaining lock as he prepared to turn the key.

"I wouldn't do that," the prisoner said as Metzger's fingers grasped the lock and key.

"And why is that?"

"We keep the dead back there."

Speaking with a somewhat arrogant tone, as though he still had the upper hand somehow, or expected a rescue at any moment, the prisoner didn't sound genuine or believable to Metzger. Deciding to exercise caution nonetheless, he banged on the door three times with a closed fist to see if the noise drew any undead. Hearing no groans or moans from the other side, and smelling no particularly offensive odors from the gap beneath the door, Metzger was about to open it when he heard a voice from inside.

"Help us!"

Furious, Metzger turned to the prisoner and shoved the barrel of his .357 against the bottom of the man's jaw.

"You lying sack of shit," he muttered angrily. "What have you done to these people?"

Providing a sneer, the man said nothing, so Metzger went about undoing the second lock and removing it from the hasp mechanism. He aimed the flashlight inside the door as it swung open, finding more than a dozen men, women, and one child huddled against various walls, seated on the floor amongst their own filth. They all looked pale, gaunt, and sickly as though they hadn't been fed or rested in days. He immediately felt flush with anger, wondering how any civilized human being could do this to another person. Turning to make certain the young man wasn't right beside the prisoner as he holstered the .357, Metzger unleashed a quick fist into the restrained man's jaw, knocking him to the floor.

He suddenly understood why Molly felt no sympathy for the Wardens because he wanted to hunt every last one of them down and make them pay for their sins.

Nine

Realizing he'd knocked the man unconscious, Metzger turned his attention to the sick and injured prisoners within the locker room instead of going on the warpath. His three wards followed him inside, assisting people away from the stench of the locker room, into the gymnasium. Metzger felt certain that opening the locker room door broke some kind of invisible seal, allowing such foul odors to waft into the open.

He radioed Molly to inform her of his find, but couldn't get a response from her or anyone in her group after three attempts. Perhaps they shut their radios off or silenced them to keep safe while exploring the hallways, so he stopped trying for the time being.

Within a few minutes all of the abducted slaves were seated in the gymnasium, openly thrilled about being free. Metzger didn't want to crush their high or provide false hope by revealing that their ordeal wasn't necessarily concluded, so he didn't elaborate. As he looked them over, some of the prisoners appeared in better condition than others. Perhaps they were more recently taken and hadn't succumbed to the rigors of hard labor quite yet. Looking at their faces, it occurred to him that none of them looked familiar, so he found it necessary to ask questions.

"Are you the only prisoners here?"

He received confused looks in response, as though he should already know.

"Three of my friends were abducted today. Two white men and a young black girl."

Only confused faces looked his way.

"They keep us in different places throughout the school," one woman offered. "And they *process* us first. Perhaps your friends are in that area."

"Process?" the younger of Metzger's two female wards asked.

"We're told what is expected of us and beaten when we first arrive. Those who don't comply don't last very long."

One of the men glanced across the finished wooden floor toward the area where Metzger encountered a locked door from the outside.

"Sometimes they take people to the other locker room," he said. "But those people don't never come back."

Sighing aloud, Metzger started walking to the other locker room, located within another alcove he ignored when he first entered the gym. Thoughts of what awaited Molly and the others throughout the school overwhelmed him, spinning his mind into a frenzy, so having the simple task of investigating the second locker room helped keep him grounded. Hearing footsteps behind him, he turned to find the young man still holding the sidearm, obviously wanting to help.

"If you're going to come with me, leave the gun with one of them so they can shoot that asshole if he tries to run."

Metzger hoped one of the women would forbid him to face more peril, but both simply stared at Metzger with trust he felt was misplaced. As a school teacher, he once felt like a papa bear in regards to his students, willing to do anything to keep them safe. They practiced terrorism drills in the schools, and he planned on sacrificing himself to keep them safe if such measures were ever required. In the new world, however, he wasn't sure how to keep *himself* safe half of the time.

After delivering the firearm to the younger of the two women the lad returned to Metzger, openly happy about the opportunity to help.

"Is that your mom?" Metzger inquired, receiving an affirmative nod in response.

Now closer to the door, he began to detect some kind of foul odor that didn't present itself when he first entered the gymnasium.

"What's your name anyway, kid?" Metzger asked, happy to find a moment where he could converse without bullets flying in his direction.

"Ryan. Ryan Kreig."

"Good to meet you, Ryan. I'm Dan."

The two shook hands before Metzger reached for the nine millimeter pistol stuffed in the back of his belt. He handed it to Ryan as they walked cautiously into the second alcove.

"Know how to use that?"

"Pretty much like any other handgun."

Ryan examined it, finding the safety along the side.

"Good to go."

Metzger approached the door, which he found modified to the specifications of the other locker room. Again, keys hung above him along the wall, so Metzger reached for them and brought them down. This time, however, a familiar stench hammered his nostrils as he slowly fingered the keyring.

"What's wrong?" Ryan asked, seeing his hesitation.

"Everything in there is dead."

Befuddled, Ryan looked Metzger up and down as though he might be possessed.

"How do you know that?"

"The smell."

Before Ryan followed with more questions, Metzger banged on the door with his fist several times. Unlike before, the throaty groans of at least two undead crossed the threshold, providing proof that no one within that dark sanctum ahead of them remained alive. Unfortunately knowing no one on the other side of the door possessed a heartbeat didn't answer one burning question for Metzger.

He wondered if the already rescued people had missing loved ones, or if the undead behind the door once knew Molly or some of her new group. Metzger hated being insensitive, but he had his own acquaintances to find and the threat of more Wardens lingering throughout the school made him a bit edgy.

"You going to open that or what?" Ryan pressed when Metzger didn't immediately pop the door open to release the undead.

"This could be dangerous for these people if there are a lot of walkers in there. Better to wait until we know the school is secure first."

"That's bullshit," Ryan complained.

"No it's not, kid. We could have any one of those assholes bust through these doors with automatic weapons any second. This school isn't safe yet."

Contemplating the situation further, he wanted to check on things outside of the gymnasium now that some of the hostages were free. Glancing at the group huddled within the large space, he didn't see anyone ready to take charge of the situation, making him feel figuratively handcuffed to them.

Even so, he didn't want to open the door directly before him and risk any number of undead sauntering into the gym. Trusting Ryan with a gun was one thing, but he couldn't leave the young man in charge of a group, even for a minute. Some of the group started walking in his direction, causing Metzger to feel a bit uneasy. He knew they likely felt antsy about remaining inside the school, so he decided to corral them and explain things before anyone tried anything rash.

"Why aren't we leaving this place?" an older man in tattered clothes that looked like blue jeans and a hospital gown asked.

Upon closer examination most of the imprisoned people wore clothing combinations that made little sense in the previous world. Perhaps their captors took clothes from the dead, or provided discovered leftovers to their captured workforce.

"It isn't secure," Metzger stated. "Everyone please have a seat along the bleachers and I'll explain what's going on."

Some eyes stared at him as though he represented another form of authority arriving to further imprison them. He wasn't sure where to begin his explanation, considering he didn't know a thing about this school, or Molly's makeshift militia determined to retrieve their loved ones. Metzger knew he could easily be selfish and leave these battered folks to find the only three people familiar to him, but it wasn't in his nature.

Everyone complied, sitting on the uncomfortable floor or opting to stand while Metzger took a reluctant center stage. He slung the automatic weapon around to his backside, with the strap already around his shoulder, to avoid appearing aggressive like the Wardens surely did.

"Look, I'm here with a group of people who may know some of you," he began, immediately drawing requests for specific names of loved ones.

Everyone clung to the hope that friends and family remained in the aftermath of the apocalypse. Some of these people may have been trapped since the beginning, wondering if *anyone* they knew survived.

"Whoa," he said firmly. "I literally met these people this morning so I don't know all of their names. You'll meet them soon enough."

He hoped he wasn't giving them false hope, and that Molly and the others indeed survived their sweep of the grounds. His mind wandered to the body of the one man who gave his life, accidental as it may have been, for him and Molly to escape gunfire.

"We're trapped in here," one woman said. "If they come back they could lock us up or pick us off one by one."

"The doors are locked," Metzger said, pointing to the metal yolks holding them in place. "I can't guarantee your safety if you go into the halls."

"You can't guarantee it in here," Ryan noted with earnest sincerity in his eyes.

"We want to help," one man offered, "even if we're just a distraction. You've already freed us from a death sentence."

Metzger looked from left to right, seeing no one look away from him with reluctance or fear. These people had already reached the conclusion that their lives were measured in days. Even as ragtag as they appeared, they wanted to ensure their freedom through personal participation. Curiosity ate at him, so Metzger couldn't afford to turn down their offer if it meant discovering what happened to the other prisoners and Molly's group.

He could deal with the undead locked mere feet away from him later and lead the way with an automatic rifle down the hallway. These people likely knew the school exceptionally well, so he decided to use them to his advantage.

Cautiously.

"Fine. But stay behind me."

Ryan, who remained beside him, gave a look of concern.

"What about him?" he inquired, looking to the still unconscious man lying on the floor who would just as soon have all of them dead as to look at them.

"Lock him up where we found these folks. You can either stay here with your family and watch him, catch up with us, or get the hell out of this place. Just don't do anything stupid."

"We owe you for saving us from their fate," Ryan said, looking to the ragged people awaiting orders from Metzger. "I'll stay here and keep an eye on things."

"And stay out of that room until you have backup," Metzger said, looking to the locked room containing several undead.

Metzger began walking toward the double doors, turning as he walked backwards to face the herd of people now following him.

"Who knows the school layout?"

"We all do," one young woman answered. "I can guide you if you want."

Metzger nodded affirmatively as she took his side.

"Stay close," he insisted as he released the latch from the door, allowing the group to pour into the hallway behind him.

Unfortunately the group proved anything but quiet as their footsteps thundered on the tile floors like soldiers carrying out a poorly executed formation. Metzger pressed forward with a pace just short of a casual jog, clearing each corner before making the turn. Before he knew it they reached the darkened area where an odd stench carried throughout the nearby halls. He recalled having Ryan and his family hide within the darkness before finding little more than a dead end to the right.

"Why is it dark?" he asked his volunteer guide as they approached it, deciding to save his flashlight's battery unless he absolutely needed to use it.

He also didn't want to give away their position by shining the beam ahead to any potential enemies.

"I don't know," she answered, "but they keep the dead inside a nearby room before they bury them. We have to go up and to the left to continue deeper into the school."

Metzger soon discovered why the corner ahead was incredibly dark as everyone carefully followed him into the pitch black void. After almost two dozen steps he finally saw a sliver of light ahead, noticing that several classrooms on either side were boarded up with black paper on every single window and door so that no light escaped into the hallway. Metzger picked up his pace as the hallway gradually grew lighter, leading to a normal setting a few classrooms later. He wondered if something truly horrific was hidden in the darkness, but didn't have time to ponder the situation too deeply.

Ahead the hallway branched into several choices and he had yet to see or hear anything that compelled him to pick one direction over another.

"The next two right turns are just more classrooms and the halls will deadend," the woman informed him. "And there's still the upstairs."

Metzger sighed inwardly. From the outside he noticed a second level while approaching the school, but had yet to find a flight of stairs inside the building. He stopped and turned to the rest of the group.

"Can someone quietly check the upstairs to see if anyone is up there?" he asked, panning the group for volunteers.

"I can," a young man of about twenty said.

"Stop at the top of the stairs and peek," Metzger said. "You can't let anyone see you because even my new allies may be trigger happy."

Metzger hated putting others at risk, but he hadn't exactly asked to be a leader of men inside a dangerous, unsecured school. Coupled with the fact these people wanted to expedite their escape, he understood all of them risked *something*, so he didn't dwell upon the danger for long. Instead he pressed forward, giving each hallway to the right a thorough look before crossing the intersections.

He watched the young man dart down the first intersection they reached, obviously knowing exactly where the stairs were located.

"What's ahead?" he asked his guide just above a whisper.

"Science labs, a few more classrooms, and the cafeteria at the end. That's where they keep a lot of the other prisoners. And process us when we come here."

Metzger felt a hint of excitement at being reunited with the only three people he felt a real connection with in the Buffalo area. Granted, he stayed one night at their house and hadn't even gone a full day without seeing them, but the thought of them being ripped from their own home angered him. Simply trying to live normal lives, naïve as that may have been, they didn't deserve mistreatment from anyone.

In the back of his mind he wondered why they hadn't crossed paths with anyone, either from Molly's group or the Wardens. Every hallway looked pristine, as though the prisoners were forced to clean them between their duties outside. Any foul odors were confined to the dark area of the halls behind them and the secured room within the gymnasium. A faded aroma of cleaning supplies lingered around him as Metzger began pushing forward, hoping for an answer about the upstairs before getting too far.

"Where are the other stairs that lead to the second floor?" he asked his guide.

"There's a set behind us," she answered. "It's beyond the dark area."

Metzger wondered how he missed a set of stairs, but he'd spent most of his time in the school either hurried or running for his life.

"There's another set further up this hallway."

He pressed forward to the next stairwell, finding the front office nearby, along with a large area used for shop class. Beyond that, the hallway went on for quite a while, lined with a mix of opened and closed lockers. Stopping just short of the stairs, he decided to wait for the young man to return with news, which took less than two minutes before he dashed ahead of the group to inform Metzger directly.

"I did what you said and didn't see anyone up there in either direction."

"Good," Metzger replied. "We're going to press forward. Can you stay at the end of the line and shout at me if you see anyone coming behind us?"

"Done," the young man said without another word before darting to the rear.

Metzger rather liked him. He followed orders without question and didn't waste time.

Knowing silence wasn't possible, Metzger decided to move quickly with his elephant herd in tow. Heading straightforward just short of a jog in terms of speed, he passed the lockers rather quickly before a sharp right turn led them down a short hallway directly to a set of closed and secured double doors. Motioning for everyone to stay put, he walked to the doors, finding no keys along the wall like he had within the gym. Every cafeteria he ever entered was filled with natural light, even in hospitals, so he knew either the cafeteria area was secured somehow, or someone guarded the prisoners inside the confinement. Windows provided too easy an escape route if captives were left to wander within the cafeteria walls.

He returned to the group without even touching the door, looking to the woman who guided him most of the way there.

"Who's in there besides the prisoners?"

"There's usually one or two of the Wardens," a man beside her answered. "They have some secret knock they use to let one another in."

"Does anyone remember it?"

A woman in the middle of the line raised her hand reluctantly.

"I think I can do it."

Metzger nodded, concerned that portions of the enemy group had already radioed one another, revealing the fact that their sanctum wasn't safe. He also didn't want to cause an unnecessary hostage situation if they didn't simply open the door after the knock, but the secret knock seemed like his best option at the moment.

With no one else in the group armed, he ordered everyone to stay back, at the end of the hallway and around the corner, until the coast was clear. Only he and the woman who thought she knew the sequence approached the door, standing there momentarily to collect their thoughts. Swallowing hard, she looked to Metzger and nodded, indicating she felt ready to give the knock a try.

Each of them stood to the side of one door, and the woman carried out a series of knocks with a particular rhythm and varied numbers between the silent breaks. Once she finished, Metzger motioned for her to step back a little bit further as they waited. Seconds passed with no sound from inside the cafeteria, and he wondered if the knocks weren't right, everyone inside was already dead, or perhaps the prisoners overtook their captors, simply waiting for more Wardens to step inside for target practice.

In essence, he felt centered in a stalemate.

Both doors had single-grip handles with a thumb latch that opened them once a key unlocked them along the side. He wondered if any of the imprisoned or killed Wardens possessed keys to the doors throughout the school. The thought of sending someone back to look at the bodies and the captured men occurred to him, but the sound of footsteps from behind the door caught his attention before he reached a decision.

He realized only a few steps separated him from the person coming toward the door, leaving him with a fight or flight decision. Knowing he didn't have enough time to retreat, Metzger slid his back against the wall beside the left side door, hoping the person opened the opposite door. His luck held as the man on the other side did just that, appearing confused when he stuck his head out just long enough for Metzger to strike before the man could react. Using the butt of the automatic weapon, Metzger struck the man in the side of the skull, sending him falling into the cafeteria.

Catching the door before it closed completely, Metzger ducked down for a look inside, seeing no one else awaiting his arrival. The scene before him, however, gave him pause because he couldn't believe the cruelty that existed within the human race.

Before he could examine the cage centered within the large cafeteria, he needed to deal with the lone guardian who tried sitting up after the stunning blow to his head. Metzger took a swift soccer kick at the man's head, sending him into an unconscious state this time before peering around the entry door at the woman who assisted him.

"Stay with the others back there," he said, pointing to the corner. "I'll clear this place and let you all know when it's safe to come inside."

Much of the square footage where kids once ate lunch was now cleared, with tables and chairs stacked in every corner of the common area. Like much of the school, the windows remained covered with cloth, paper, and whatever other spare materials the Wardens found that could do the job. Although it remained dim inside the cafeteria, Metzger was able to immediately see the payoff he so desperately wanted to find. Confined within a large custom-built cage centered in the room, people looked desperately in his direction, beginning to realize that he wasn't one of their captors, and he might be their opportunity for freedom.

Constructed from wood beams, iron bars, and chicken wire that provided the outer layer for the entire structure, it looked something like an octagon used in cage fighting, only a little bit larger. Without concern for the floor, the people who constructed it drilled into the floor and used concrete or some kind of mix to hold the iron bars in place. Enough metal bore down into the foundation, all the way around, that no one was pushing the structure over, or escaping, particularly with someone standing guard at all times.

"Dan?" someone called out from inside the cage, catching his attention.

He walked toward the sound, recognizing Albert immediately from within the cell as the man pressed his face between two iron poles against the chicken wire.

"Good to see you, Albert," Metzger said, smiling for the first time the entire day. "Where the hell is the door to this thing?"

"Over there," Albert said, pointing as best he could from the confines as Luke and Samantha stood just behind him, assuring Metzger they were all safe. "I think that asshole you clocked has a key."

Thinking the makeshift cell might be repurposed in short order, Metzger decided to check the man for a key rather than shoot the door or began tearing apart the structure. He didn't have the tools or the time to dismantle the cell anyway, so he frisked the man, removing two firearms and a knife in the process before finding the key.

He also stuck his head out the door momentarily after finding the key.

"It's safe in here," he called to the other group of former prisoners, a few of which peeked around the corner to see what happened. "Come on in."

As the group from the gymnasium entered the cafeteria they immediately ran over, some overjoyed at seeing former prisoners, friends, or family about to discover the freedom they recently came to know. Metzger turned the key, releasing at least two dozen people from the cage, feeling how incredibly sturdy the cage was built when he cupped his hand around the doorway and tried to push on it.

He felt certain his efforts failed to move it even a single millimeter. Someone among the Wardens, or one of the prisoners forced to build the structure, knew a little something about construction and engineering. Standing back to let everyone outside, Metzger received a group hug when his trio finally emerged, feeling a wave of relief and accomplishment crash over him. He reciprocated the hug, wanting the moment to last forever at this point. Seldom did he find more than a few seconds of happiness in the modern world on any given day, but he definitely felt as though he won a battle today.

The war, however, remained heavily in the favor of the undead.

Seeing a few angry ex-prisoners storm toward the unconscious Warden, Metzger quickly broke away from his group, running to intercept them before they mobbed and killed him.

"You can't," he said, blocking the path of a few infuriated men.

"Why not?" one of them demanded angrily.

"We don't know that the school is clear yet, and we may need leverage," he explained, holding up his right hand, indicating for them to stop in their tracks. "Let's lock him up for now and deal with him once we know something more."

Both conceded, probably because they felt they owed Metzger some kind of debt, which they didn't in his eyes. Still trying to be the voice of reason, he wanted to make smart plays until the entire group knew exactly where they stood.

Albert had made his way through the suddenly crowded cafeteria to take Metzger's side in case the situation went south. Having suffered with these people, brief as the experience may have been, he could influence them with his words and wisdom.

"We need to get him locked up until we know the whole situation," Albert said, echoing the words Metzger spoke.

"There are other people clearing the school as we speak," Metzger added. "We've killed a few of them and taken a few captive, but I haven't heard from the group I came in with in almost fifteen minutes."

"Fine," one of the men said as they teamed up to hoist the unconscious man off the ground only to carry him over to the cage and toss him inside unceremoniously.

Metzger followed them to ensure they followed through on their verbal promise, and to lock the door after they threw him inside. Turning around, he tried to regroup with Albert, Luke, and Samantha, but instead found himself surrounded by people who wanted to thank him for his efforts.

He tried to shrug it off as though he hadn't done much of anything, wanting to stay close to his familiar people, but everyone wanted to shake his hand or hug him. It took several minutes to break away from the group, but when he did, he used his radio to attempt reaching Molly or the others, figuring something either very good or exceptionally bad happened to her and the others by now.

Hearing no replies, Metzger found a spot just outside the door where his former hosts came to join him.

"How the hell did you find us so quickly?" Luke asked, shaking his head in genuine surprise.

Metzger spent a few minutes telling them the tale of his entire day, including how he returned to their house only to get recruited by Molly, refraining from gory details with a child present. From there the entire rescue felt like a whirlwind to him, and he imagined any daylight was fading outside as the afternoon waned. All of the sudden dozens of people were free, but Metzger questioned how many options any of them really possessed. He apologized to the trio because he kept looking to the corner, wondering if someone was going to come around the bend with guns blazing, or if some of Molly's allies might join them.

"We thought we were goners," Albert admitted.

"I hope you didn't think I was behind any of this."

"Not for a second. We took a chance on you, and you've more than returned the favor. Say, did you find anything out about your folks?"

Metzger shook his head negatively, beginning to think traveling to Buffalo took up valuable time he could have spent heading directly to Virginia. He wanted to head that way immediately, but felt a need to ensure the trio before him made it out of the school safely, whether they returned home or not.

"Did they hurt any of you?" he inquired, looking between all three.

"No," Albert answered. "But we heard some terrible stories. These guys didn't waste any time after things went bad. They were treating these poor people like a disposable commodity."

Metzger figured that was one way to ration food, but incredibly inhumane. He knew such atrocities had occurred since the beginnings of human life, but thought the modern world cured much of it. Americans lived good lives, often ignoring the suffering and oppression in other parts of the world as though it didn't exist. Now the entire planet didn't discriminate against wealth, race, or social status.

The sound of running footsteps reached Metzger's ears from the hallway around the bend. He stood, holding the automatic weapon in a ready position until he saw Ryan round the corner with a broad smile upon seeing the prisoners freed from their bonds.

"It's over," he announced to Metzger in particular. "The entire school was searched and all of the Wardens are captured, dead, or gone. We tried to reach you on the radio but you didn't respond, so we were beginning to fear the worst."

Metzger looked down at his radio's screen, finding no LED writing, which indicated the device lost power at some point.

"Did everyone from Molly's group survive?" he asked Ryan.

"Everyone but the one guy who got shot earlier."

Metzger nodded, feeling complete relief knowing that everyone had refuge for the night without fear of attack from the undead or evil human beings.

"She asked for you to come back," Ryan added. "And there's something Molly wants you to see."

Metzger turned to Albert.

"I want you three to come with me," he said, not wishing to leave them alone for a minute after so much effort and risk was expended to free them.

"We're coming," Albert said as they began following Metzger and Ryan toward the other end of the school.

Many of the released prisoners were already making their way through the halls as though trying to assure themselves they weren't inside a dream. Metzger figured some of Molly's group would meet up with them soon enough while searching for their friends and family. He wondered what ends remained for him to tie up before he headed east with hopes of finding his brother.

Ten

Ryan led the foursome all the way back to the gymnasium where they found Molly standing over a bound prisoner. While Metzger felt a little surprised to see the man alive, seated on the ground with his hands tied behind him, he wasn't shocked to see bloody streaks and bruises along his face. Already they had begun torturing him for information, or for payment of his sins.

"Glad to see you're alive," Molly said, breaking away from the bound prisoner momentarily.

"Likewise," Metzger answered. "I see you're leaving one alive for your own amusement."

Molly gave a cagy grin.

"Actually he's being rather cooperative. It seems there are a few of his buddies unaccounted for, but they're not anywhere in the school. A few of the guys saw your efforts in the cafeteria and hurried back to tell me, so we've covered every inch of this place."

"They could've stayed to help."

"They said you had everything under control."

Metzger wouldn't have minded some assistance with the excitable freed prisoners, but he was never in any real danger from them.

"There's a very solid cell in the cafeteria if you need somewhere to keep prisoners until you sort everything out."

Molly looked at him inquisitively.

"You sound like you're not staying long."

"I've accomplished what I needed to, and I'll be heading east shortly."

He introduced her to Albert, Luke, and Samantha, who'd all been standing patiently behind him. Only a few other people remained within the gymnasium, and with a glance to his left he spied a few bodies beside the locker room door closer to the main entrance.

"We cleared out that room just in case," Molly said. "A few of the dead were known to a few of my group."

"I'm sorry to hear that," Metzger said sincerely.

"Thank you."

"Ryan told me you said there was something I should see?"

"I know you think I've been merciless about this entire expedition," Molly said, motioning for the group to follow her to the main door, "but there's something you should see that confirms the depravity of the Wardens."

A few minutes later they arrived at the formerly darkened area where a few hallways intersected, still smelling of death. At least it appeared somewhat brighter after coverings were removed from nearby windows inside classrooms. Metzger found a single door that led into a sizeable classroom at the far end of where the darkness once ruled the hallway. Stepping closer, he peered inside the only window uncovered to the room itself, seeing beakers, test tubes, and solid epoxy resin countertops complete with sinks. He knew immediately the former lab found later use in a far more disturbing way.

"They kept their dead in here until they could bury them," Molly said, opening the door for them to enter. "There wasn't anything in here when we searched the place, but we suspected as much, even before that asshole in the gym told us."

Stains lined the tile floor on the left as Metzger stepped inside, finding the smell a bit more pungent. Dust floated through the air like pixie dust, and only one window was now uncovered to the right, illuminating the room just enough to see details when one drew close to solid objects. Slowly stepping through the room, Metzger wondered what on earth he was supposed to see that was so life-altering.

His eyes finally went from the floors to the countertops before landing on the back wall, which held a mammoth mounted activity board with lots of little white rectangles pinned to it. Above it was a mounted fluorescent light that maintained power like the rest of the school, and it created a trophy case appearance for the wall that would have shone like a beacon in the darkened room.

"What is that?" he asked Molly, who took his side as though waiting for him to reach some realization.

"Those are the drivers licenses of everyone the Wardens killed or let die."

Metzger tried mentally assessing a rough estimate, seeing more than three dozen licenses easily lining the wall. A single month had passed, a *single* month, and these evil fuckers had snuffed out that many human lives needlessly to protect themselves and hold out in their makeshift fortress.

"Bastards," he muttered, shaking his head. "Which one of those pricks was the ringleader? Please tell me he's already dead."

"We're still trying to sort that out," Molly answered. "I already found my loved one on that back wall, but I'm trying to get answers for the others."

Metzger admired her restraint, looking behind him to see people from all of the groups finding one another in the hallway, embracing with joy. He wanted that for everyone, including himself when he reached Virginia, but as his gaze returned to the back wall he knew some people were destined for heartache very soon.

Unable to help himself, Metzger walked to the back wall, wanting to study the faces of the men and women who were needlessly sacrificed. He couldn't help but wonder if children were murdered or left to die as well, having no memorial because they weren't old enough to ever drive. Of course this was no memorial he stared at, knowing it was more like a trophy case in the eyes of the people who created it.

"Oh my," Luke said as he and Albert laid eyes on the everyday normal people pictured on the dozens of licenses. "That could've been us."

Metzger studied each of the faces, unable to help wondering what they did in their normal lives before they spent every day scrambling to survive, only to succumb to a group that treated them as disposable slaves. He wondered if these were the same people who knocked him off his bike, and if they planned to use him for labor or simply kill him for his goods.

Examining each of them individually quickly became too painful, so he looked at the pictures in a more general sense, trying to honor the people he wished he could have saved. It wasn't until he reached the middle of the licenses toward the right side of the board that he stopped and stared, feeling numbness overtake his body when he saw a familiar face.

And then a second face he knew and loved.

He remembered visiting Donald and Connie Metzger in August, just before the school year started for him in the Cincinnati area. Spending a week back home, he visited old friends, drank at a few familiar bars, attended a local Triple-A baseball game, and returned home, feeling certain he would see them again soon.

Now he stared at their state issued licenses where they both provided the same neutral stares that practically everyone did for passports and licenses. He gave an audible gasp that turned into a groan, unsure of what to think or believe. Falling to his knees and giving up on life sounded like a perfectly viable option for a few fleeting seconds, but in the back of his mind the montage might have contained some mistakes. Perhaps, just perhaps, not everyone on the wall was already dead. Maybe they were held somewhere awaiting execution, or Molly made a grievous error when she assumed what the licenses meant.

"What's wrong?" Albert asked before his eyes fell to the exact same spot Metzger found.

He asked nothing more, immediately understanding the find, what it meant, and how devastated Metzger suddenly felt.

Needing certainty, but hoping for a miracle, Metzger darted past the laboratory tables into the hall to find a few of the freed prisoners, asking them who'd been there the longest.

"Amy has been here since the beginning," one of them answered. "They made her do a lot of their cooking."

"Where is she?"

They pointed just behind Metzger to a woman in her thirties who appeared ever so slightly better off than most of the prisoners because she hadn't been subjected to the outside labor quite as often.

"Can you help me with something?" he asked as he ran over to her, catching her by surprise, unable to mask the desperation in his eyes.

"Sure," she answered. "What do you need?"

Metzger barely heard voices asking what was going on, or Albert explaining to a confused Molly what they had just spotted on the wall as he led the girl by the hand through the former science lab.

"You've been here since the beginning?" Metzger asked as they weaved through the tables to the back.

"Nearly. What's the matter?"

When he reached the back of the room he felt a little vomit reach his throat from trepidation of the truth about to strike him.

"These people," he said, pointing to the licenses of his parents. "What happened to them?"

Amy looked down to the stained tile floor without a word, immediately realizing *exactly* what he asked of her.

"Oh my God, I didn't even know his last name," Metzger heard Molly whisper to Albert as he realized everyone else was leaving the room.

Suddenly he felt all alone in the room with poor Amy, who carried the burden of seeing so many people needlessly die in a month's time. Even worse, Metzger felt alone in the world again, experiencing the crushing realization that his parents were no longer among the living. He felt content to think, even *hope* that they made it to safety and only the complete lack of communication kept them from reaching him or his brother.

Amy helped Metzger sit down on the floor before his knees completely gave out on him, sitting Indian style across from him. She waited a few seconds as the door to the room audibly closed, giving them complete privacy.

"Are they your parents?" she asked.

Metzger nodded, creating a few seconds of awkward silence between them.

"They were brought here a few days after I arrived," she began. "We didn't get to talk very much, but your mother told me she was on the phone with her son when three men barged into their home and took them away. She thought they had spotted your father when he was scouting the railroad yard, hoping to get them out of town safely that way."

Never suspecting that hearing the truth might hurt so much, Metzger found the details matching his timeline perfectly, feeling numb because he wanted to block his mind from reaching the end of the story.

"From the beginning your parents fought these people," Amy said, trying to be compassionate, though each loss obviously took a toll on her psyche. "They wouldn't cooperate with the Wardens, and your father started formulating plans to escape this place and overtake them. I think they got word of this, so they worked him harder and kept an eye on him all the time."

"How did they die?" Metzger asked, not sure he wanted to hear every single detail just yet.

Part of him just wanted the horrible ordeal over with so he could begin to process life without the people who raised him.

"Towards the end they threatened Connie to get Donald to comply," Amy said slowly. "They thought that would keep your father in line."

"But it didn't," Metzger said, knowing the strong will of his parents, particularly his father.

"No. It didn't."

She looked away, almost vacantly at a wall before gathering the courage to continue with the story.

"We all knew that life in here was no life at all, which is why the Wardens' plan could never ultimately work. There was no light at the end of the tunnel for us that contained food and safety, with all of us singing Kumbaya. They wanted everything to themselves, and when the time drew near for your father to attempt to overthrow them with some help, the Wardens made an example of him."

Amy hesitated, as though indicating Metzger might want to avoid hearing the details. Metzger gave her a somber look without blinking before he nodded for her to continue.

"Your dad wanted one of the work groups to attack a guard outside and take a gun, knowing none of the guards could probably shoot everyone before they got to him. I think most everyone was onboard, but somehow the Wardens got wind of his plan. One morning they called all of us into the gym before the work began. It was the first time I ever saw all of us, and all of *them*, gathered in one place at the same time."

A tear began to form in Amy's eyes as the images of that morning came more vividly to her after weeks of trying to suppress them.

"Your mother was in the center of the gym, tied to a chair, unable to move. The Wardens warned us that they'd heard of an uprising, and what was about to happen was a warning to the rest of us not to defy their commands."

Metzger closed his eyes momentarily, knowing his mother meant the world to his father. Their marriage lasted almost four decades with good reason, and both of them were contemplating full retirement and enjoying the good life together. They owned a smaller home with good neighbors like Charles Garvey, took vacations in warm locations, and minded their own business. He envisioned their sanctuary being invaded, and them being stolen from an already altered, worsening life with the undead roaming free, and he saw red.

"Who leads this group?" he asked Amy. "The Wardens."

"They all did," she answered, "but the one named Xavier was their mouthpiece. He was the one who addressed us the day your parents died."

Although he utterly feared knowing the details, Metzger asked his next question with hesitation.

"How exactly did they die?"

"Your mother was tied to a chair in the center of the gymnasium," Amy answered, picking up where she left off. "The chair was chained to some metal pull tabs on the bleachers in both directions, so she couldn't move more than a few inches in any direction. Xavier ordered some of his people to bring your father out to the center of the floor where he carefully explained that both of them were troublemakers, and to ensure none of the rest of us got any ideas in the future, he was going to make an example out of them. I think if he'd simply shot them it would've gotten the point across, but most of us would have considered an uprising somewhere down the road."

Metzger hated that his father couldn't have held out for a few more weeks and simply endured the shitty treatment the Wardens dished out. He also knew his father wasn't one to take orders from bullies or buffoons, so the outcome played out the only way it could have, he supposed.

"Your father was bound when they dragged him out. His hands were tied behind his back, but he struggled the entire way, knowing they planned something terrible for him and Connie. Xavier ordered them to cut him loose, but as they slit the rope, Xavier drew a knife and stabbed your father in the stomach."

Amy's expression grew pained as she hated spilling the details, remembering one of the most painful events of her stay at the school. Being imprisoned was horrific, but seeing the one glimmer of hope brutally murdered crushed any notions of escape or a better life.

"I need to hear it," Metzger encouraged her, just in case she wanted to skim over the gorier parts of the tale.

"Your father fell to the ground, and he didn't die right away," Amy said, obviously transported to the time when it happened. "He bled, and he struggled to breathe, and he even tried to attack Xavier once, but he couldn't get to his feet. They weren't certain if he'd turn or not once he died, so they got a syringe full of blood from some zombie and injected it into your father's arm while they pinned him down. They wanted him to know that he would become a monster when he died, because he didn't want to hurt innocent people, or have them see him like that."

Amy found it difficult to suppress her sobs at this point, forced to wipe her eyes just to see past the tears. She sniffled to keep from crying outright.

"Your father fought to the very end, maybe as a way to inspire us to never give up," she added. "And while all of this was happening, Xavier gave Donald this speech about how he brought this upon himself, and soon he was going to die. And not only was he going to die, but he was going to take Connie, and only Connie with him as he tore her apart piece by piece, when he finally turned."

"Dear God," Metzger muttered, knowing his father died with the knowledge that he was destined to mindlessly murder the one person who'd stayed by his side since their late teenage years.

"Xavier could have let us out of there," Amy continued. "He could have done a lot of things, but he made all of us stay to watch your father pass away. It took about twenty minutes for him to bleed out, and Donald suffered the entire time. Your mother started crying, not for what she knew was coming, but for him. They really loved one another, didn't they?"

Metzger nodded, fighting back tears and emotions as well.

His parents weren't the kind of people who simply stayed together because divorce was too expensive, they wanted to keep the kids happy, or they were just set in their ways. Although they didn't spend every waking moment together, Donald and Connie Metzger shared the same bed and made their time with one another count.

"I'm not sure I can finish," Amy said, dipping her head into her hands, trying to remain composed despite telling a stranger the gruesome details of his parents' demise.

Metzger felt an anger beginning to boil inside of him, unlike anything he recalled feeling since the world ended. Desperate times forced people to carry out some heinous acts, but nothing like killing a man, leaving him with the knowledge that he was going to rip the flesh from his wife and, in essence, murder her as well.

"They made you watch all of it?" he inquired, gently taking hold of her hands to pry them from her covered face.

"Yes."

"Please continue," he virtually pleaded. "Please."

"It took about another hour for your father to turn," Amy said, tears beginning to slide down her cheeks. "Your mother already knew better, but she tried to reason with him when he stood up from the floor. No one in the room said a word, and I think Connie was trying to deflect any harm from us, but she begged your father to come back to her like things were before."

"But he was a monster now," Metzger said quietly, envisioning his father with lifeless eyes and a gnarly scowl as he slowly stood from the gym floor, clotted blood lining his stomach from the knife wound.

"Yes," Amy confirmed with a simple word. "Until the day I die I'll remember the look in your mother's eyes as he went for her throat. She went from wide-eyed surprise to a look of relief when his teeth sunk in, as though she knew they would be together. I think she was ready to escape this hell, but felt bad for leaving the rest of us behind."

Metzger took a breath through his nose, not saying another word because he now felt a sense of closure.

"They're buried in the football field with the others," Amy said. "The Wardens have always burned those who turned as a precaution before burial."

Painfully closing his eyes, Metzger shoved the pain and anger further down to the point that it was about to explode like a jack-in-the-box. The final indignity of his folks being burned like concentration camp prisoners sent him over the edge as he stood without a word, snatched up the automatic rifle, and stormed into the hallway.

By now the halls had thinned out, and no one dared speak to or approach a man walking with a purpose to the cafeteria where none of them wanted to be anyway. Most of them viewed him as the hero who rescued them, likely fine with whatever actions he took in the near future. A set of footsteps quickened behind him, and Metzger suspected that Albert, who was still talking to Molly when he departed the science lab, wanted a word with him.

"Don't do anything rash," Albert encouraged, obviously taking note of the rage building within Metzger as Amy's story unfolded.

"*Not* the time, Albert," Metzger warned, continuing to trudge forward without slowing.

"You're not a murderer, Dan. Think before you do something you can't take back."

Now Metzger stopped to point a finger directly at the man he respected, but didn't want advice from at the moment.

"You were here less than a day, Albert," he said heatedly. "They kidnapped my parents and *murdered* both of them. And for what? So they could live in a fucking school the rest of their lives? None of these motherfuckers deserve to live."

At a loss for words, accepting that he wasn't going to sway Metzger's opinion, Albert simply sighed through his nose and stood in the center of the hallway as Metzger turned to finish what he started.

Less than a minute later Metzger reached the cafeteria, finding it completely empty as most of the prisoners never wanted to see the confining octagon again. Reaching into his pocket, he produced the key as he slowly walked toward the door, trying to find a speck of rationality in a mind consumed with wrath. He wanted to lock up the surviving Wardens within the octagon, kill one of them, and let it attack the others. A group could survive and take down one zombie, however, so he knew his ideal plan was already flawed.

He stopped at the manmade prison's door momentarily, looking between the key in his left hand, the firearm in his right hand, and the door. The realization that the Wardens were complete monsters washed over him, causing him to rethink his earlier mercy and the following justification to Molly. He believed Amy's account of what happened to his parents, he knew why Molly hated the group so vehemently, and Metzger knew he wasn't going to see the people who raised him ever again.

Still, he needed to see the man locked inside the octagon to understand if the Wardens were truly evil, or brainwashed by Xavier, the mouthpiece.

When he unlocked the door and stepped inside holding the automatic rifle in front of him, he found the man smiling on the other side of the cage, thinking he'd been rescued. His look quickly soured when he saw the man responsible for putting him there standing on the other side.

"Do you recognize me?" Metzger asked, using the strap attached to the automatic weapon to sling it over his shoulder.

"Should I?" the man asked, his expression stopping just short of a sneer.

"I'm related to some of the people you brutally murdered a few weeks back," Metzger elaborated as he undid the leather strap holding the .357 security in its holster.

"You're going to have to be more specific," the man replied as Metzger thumbed the hammer, readying the gun for immediate use with a hair trigger.

Perhaps because of the low lighting, the man took a few seconds to study Metzger's features without daring step forward. A brief flicker of realization showed in his eyes, as though he suspected what troubled souls Metzger entered the school to free.

"The older couple," the man finally said, maintaining a neutral expression. "Taking them was a mistake."

"Why's that?"

"Because they were nothing but a giant pain in the ass until we put them out of their misery," the prisoner replied, taking a step forward as though daring Metzger to shoot him.

In one swift motion, Metzger pulled the firearm from his holster as the man began charging him, remembering videos about how people could avoid being fatally shot if they had twenty-one steps when charging police officers. Making certain he didn't miss, Metzger aimed at the man's chest, pulling the trigger.

Falling as though his feet had been swept from under him when the bullet impacted his torso, the man hit the ground with a thud, writhing in pain from the bullet wound to the right of his heart. Both men knew exactly why they were standing in the octagon prison, and both possessed the mindset that only one was going to leave the structure still breathing.

Sputtering blood as his breaths came in heaves, the man rolled slightly from one side to the other, knowing he wasn't going to recover. He seemed to sense the man holding the .357 wasn't going to let him leave the octagon alive, even if Metzger himself wasn't entirely convinced of his endgame.

"You'll be with them soon enough," the man said defiantly between labored breaths. "They were pussies, and so are you."

Without another word, Metzger pulled back the hammer one more time, aimed the .357 at the man's forehead and pulled the trigger, ending their brief skirmish. He wasn't anxious to take a human life, but the man was mortally wounded, and needed head trauma to ensure he didn't turn and harm someone later.

"Two birds, one stone," Metzger muttered, holstering the firearm.

Minimal blood spurted from the wound, and even as the man lay perfectly still, unable to return as a zombie and seek human flesh, Metzger didn't feel much relief from his anguish. He received what he considered justification, if not provocation, from the dead Warden, but his task still felt incomplete.

"Now you understand," Molly's voice said from behind him, not judging his actions, but sounding somewhat relieved that he finally came to terms with truth the rest of the group realized weeks ago.

He slowly turned to her, surprised to see empathy from her for the first time that day.

"I suppose I do."

Eleven

Metzger found himself transported back in time as he stood in the classroom where his fourth graders met daily at Blue Ash Elementary School. The community of Blue Ash rested about fifteen miles northeast of Cincinnati, and the last published census of living townsfolk stated the community contained just over twelve-thousand residents.

Despite a major factory fire along the outskirts of Cincinnati that morning, the kids all made it into school the last week of August. Everything began normally as Metzger transitioned from reading to math by the time music class came around. After ushering the kids down the hall to the music room, Metzger decided to eat an early lunch in the teachers' lounge. When he stepped inside with a brown bag lunch that consisted of potato chips and a turkey sandwich on rye, he found half a dozen teachers glued to the television.

"What's going on?" he asked, sensing some uneasiness throughout the room.

"The whole country is going crazy," Tami Hollinsworth answered without looking from the television, which showed a large building on fire.

"Is that the factory fire?"

"No. It's somewhere in Chicago. There are fires in almost every state."

Metzger watched the television, unwrapping his sandwich without looking while aerial footage covered numerous buildings from every major city that might as well have been constructed by the same company.

"They all look the same," Metzger noted, discovering that all of the buildings possessed the characteristics of factories, employing hundreds or thousands, and all caught fire before noon.

"It's terrorism," Ted Kirkpatrick said with assurance. "We let all of those towel heads into our country and they bring their Jihad ways with them."

Metzger remembered 9/11, even though it occurred during his teenage years, and these events felt reminiscent of that day. All of them sat transfixed, watching the footage shot across the country play out without definitive answers. Masked hoodlums didn't claim responsibility, no one reported suicide bombers entering the factories, and for some reason the employees weren't being interviewed on the news.

Feeling on edge when the principal announced early departure for students and staff, and even while he helped monitor the bus loading, Metzger couldn't shake the suspicion that the events were something history books would record. He stopped for a sub on the way home, knowing he wasn't going to leave the house again that day. He spent the remainder of the afternoon fixated to the television in the basement of the nine-hundred square foot home he rented.

His plans of marriage, owning a home outside of any city, and having some kids of his own had fallen apart during the last school year when his girlfriend of three years opted out of their relationship.

To think he went through the trouble of obtaining an Ohio teaching license, moved two states away, and committed to her home state still ate away at him. She hadn't given a reason for the breakup at first, simply saying she wanted a break, but through the grapevine Metzger heard rumors that she wasn't faithful to him. He reached a point that he didn't know what to believe, but his love for the job and his school kept him in Ohio another year to see if his relationship with Deidre could be resolved.

After placing the sub in the refrigerator, Metzger spent the afternoon and evening in the finished basement watching the news. He switched between local and national coverage, unable to fathom what caused such havoc across the nation. Reports eventually surfaced that explosions caused the factory fires, and that employees near the blast areas complained of an unexplained illness. Many of them were taken to area hospitals for examination while the government scurried to find answers.

Metzger ended up falling asleep in his recliner, never making it upstairs to eat or properly get into bed. When he awoke at the break of dawn the news showed a much bleaker version of the world if that even seemed possible. Tuned in to one of the local Cincinnati affiliates, Metzger watched as a reporter and her cameraman attempted to film what looked like chaos in the streets of the city. Most people were running, and in some cases were savagely attacked by slower-moving people who walked stiffly and groped after anything that went past them.

He watched in stunned silence for several minutes, wondering if the events before him were some kind of elaborate hoax, or perhaps some reality show that went too far for ratings. It wasn't until he heard a man's scream on the television, followed by the camera dropping to the ground, that he began to believe. From a sideways perspective the reporter ran down the street in her high heels, making it less than twenty steps before she was tackled by one of the sluggish attackers and bitten repeatedly before a few more slow assailants dropped to their knees to join in the biting frenzy.

Her screams haunted Metzger immediately, so he decided to separate himself from the unraveling world on television by walking upstairs.

Shaking his head as he reached the main level of the house, he felt some comfort just seeing the everyday items in his life undisturbed. He strolled to the front door, taking a look outside and seeing the start of a sunny day as he heard the central air kick on to cool the house. Somewhere between wanting more sleep and fully awake, Metzger decided to brew some coffee to ensure he stayed conscious. A minute later, the coffee maker gurgled and began its daily job as he walked to the front door for a second peek, finding a virtually cloudless sky that allowed for immediate daylight just after dawn.

Located in a fairly isolated area, chosen with intent when he shopped for housing, the dwelling offered peace and quiet for Metzger and many of his senior citizen neighbors. Rain hadn't fallen in over a week, leaving the area muggy and hot as schools started classes and parents and students alike adapted. At first glance his street appeared completely unaffected by the crazy events overtaking the rest of the world, and Metzger felt thankful to be away from those dense, urban settings.

After pouring himself a cup of coffee, he decided it might be a good day to call in sick if school hadn't already been canceled. He dialed the number reserved for teachers and staff, listening to it ring before it went to a generic voicemail. Someone always manned the phone line a few hours prior to the school's daily opening, so he grunted and looked at the time.

6:14 a.m.

"Shit," he muttered, realizing he might be cutting it close if he didn't live just minutes from the school.

He called a second time, receiving the voicemail again, perplexing him. Surely the strange uprising in the cities hadn't affected everyday life in every other community, he thought. Dressed in only his sweatpants and a T-shirt from the previous evening, Metzger opened the front door and stepped onto the landing to look for his newspaper. Looking down, he saw nothing along the sidewalk, and no evidence on either side of him that the neighbors received their papers.

Fully prepared to walk down the street to survey the neighborhood, his home phone rang inside, distracting him. Without closing the door he jogged inside to swipe the phone off its charger, expecting an automated message from the school announcing cancelation, or one of his fellow teachers calling to pass along some news. He hit the talk button, surprised to hear the voice on the other end of the phone before he uttered a word.

"Dan, is everything crazy there too?" Connie Metzger asked him from the Buffalo suburb where his parents resided.

"Mom? What's going on?"

"There was an explosion in Buffalo yesterday and everything fell apart after that."

"What do you mean?"

"People are running through the streets attacking each other like they've all gone crazy."

Metzger thought back to the news report, realizing the chaos wasn't just in Cincinnati. It spread all over the country, just like the factory fires, meaning the terror continued to wash across the nation like a tsunami.

"Mom, stay indoors, whatever you do."

"A few of them have come up to the door, but we aren't letting anyone inside. Your father went and loaded his shotgun just in case they broke down the door."

"How many of these people are there, Mom?"

"Oh, dozens. They're everywhere."

Metzger felt a growing panic, wondering if his parents were capable of holding off a large number of invaders, knowing he wasn't nearly close enough to assist them.

"Daniel, your brother is calling. Let me call you back in a little while."

"Mom, be careful, and don't let *anyone* inside."

"Will do. Love you."

"Love you, too."

She sounded almost a little too nonchalant to provide Metzger with any comfort, but as he set down the phone he heard a footstep at the threshold of his front door, providing him with his own major problem.

Whirling as quickly as his body allowed, Metzger came face-to-face with his first gnashing assailant in the form of a burly highway worker, complete with dirty blue jeans and an orange vest. Finding little time to focus on the details, Metzger dodged snapping teeth, noticing the man already had blood across his face and throat. The attacker lunged forward, forcing the school teacher to parry by stepping aside and letting him fall into the backside of the kitchen counter.

Not the least bit fazed by the tumble, the man growled and immediately regained his footing, charging towards Metzger with the balance of an intoxicated bar patron. Uncertain of exactly what he was dealing with, Metzger backed up to the door and headed outside with the grating teeth and the strangely yellowed eyes of the man tracking his every move. The impaired highway employee seemed to have his head slightly tilted to the right side at all times, indicating either an injury or some kind of physical defect.

"Stop, buddy," Metzger said, still backpedaling down the stairs and into the front yard, hoping to put distance enough between him and the man to rush inside to safety.

His plan quickly came unhinged, however, when an elderly woman wearing a light blue nightgown with floral prints came stumbling across the grass, baring teeth as she headed directly for him with bad intentions.

"Oh, fuck," Metzger said to himself because no one within his vicinity could understand his words.

Heading away from the woman, and around the man, he dashed into the house and shut the door behind him, turning both the doorknob and the deadbolt locks. His heart thumped within his chest at the thought of being chomped at and ripped apart by mindless freaks. He ran into his bedroom, searching under the bed for the .357 Magnum his father bought him for high school graduation to keep for protection. Of course gun laws in New York State went crazy after terrorism changed the face of New York City and people weren't allowed to carry, much less transport, firearms throughout the state.

Ohio proved a bit more practical with their gun laws, but Metzger never joined the unofficial conceal and carry club.

Secured in a small plastic case he bought to keep the gun and its six-inch barrel from collecting dirt and particles, the gun remained beneath his bed. He reached in, sliding the entire case to him before grabbing a small shoebox behind it containing at least a few hundred rounds of ammunition. He planned to shoot target practice occasionally at one of the indoor ranges, not to fire at anything alive short of a home invasion.

As he pulled the gun from its case and a box of ammunition from the shoebox, Metzger ran downstairs to get the latest on the news. He switched channels, finding that some cities were slower than others to catch on to the happenings, and in a few cities the strange assailants were virtually taking over the streets because of their sheer numbers. A few videos showed police forced to fire at the attackers, unable to bring them down, or even slow them, with slugs to the limbs or chest. Reporters who spoke to one police official said the man wished not to be identified, but stated that only trauma to the head was capable of subduing the staggering aggressors permanently. The reporter added that gunshots, baseball bats, even larger sharp objects would do the trick.

"This is fucked up," Metzger muttered, returning upstairs to look out his front door where he noticed a third unwelcome visitor had joined the other two in clawing at his door.

He stood there somewhat stunned a few minutes until his phone rang, bringing him back to the present. Thinking his mother might be calling him back, he dashed over to answer it, finding the number somewhat foreign to him.

"Hello?" he answered, deciding the risk of a telemarketer calling was the least of his worries at the moment.

"Dan, it's Bryce. Don't talk, just listen."

"Okay," Metzger said quickly, sensing urgency in his older brother's voice.

Deployed halfway across the world, Metzger recalled, his brother wasn't due back to the States for at least another month.

"They're keeping us out to sea while they sort out what's going on every-where. This thing is worldwide, little brother. You've got to get to Mom and Dad and protect them."

"But I have a job and responsibilities, Bryce."

"You don't get it. The world as we know it is over, Dan. These *things* are ev-erywhere, and this is literally the apocalypse. If one of those things attacks you, shoot it in the fucking head. Look, I've got to go. Things are pretty tense on the ship because word has already gotten out."

Metzger started to say something but the call ended with a lack of any voices or background noise at all. Still holding the phone, he looked to the front door, which contained just enough frosted glass in the center of its solid wood frame to let him see daylight being blocked by a number of trespassers. He virtually dragged himself down to the basement, unable to process the unraveling world around him. Listening to the news, he loaded the .357 and stuffed several addi-tional rounds into his right pocket.

Updates indicated that anyone who was bitten and died seemed to return to life in some rudimentary sense. Words like 'undead' and 'zombie' were tossed around, but Metzger wondered how much time the living possessed before every-one stumbled around the streets looking for anything living to prey upon.

Beginning to formulate a plan of escape, he thought about his neighbors, realizing he didn't really know them personally. He didn't want to be selfish, but getting to his parents took precedence, and if he got killed trying to save the neighborhood he didn't do them a lick of good. He drove a black Chevy Colo-rado to work most days, and it sat in the short driveway providing amble oppor-tunity for him to escape if he could reach it.

He trusted Bryce implicitly, so he decided to pack light, bringing only what clothing and supplies he needed. Snatching his cell phone, some food and a can opener, he began tossing smaller items into a backpack he had taken from the lost and found at school after months of no one claiming it. He originally thought it might be handy for packing extra items for weekend motorcycle rides, but cur-rently he wanted to drive the truck to bring more items, and for security.

Metzger triple-checked that he'd packed everything necessary for a trip to Tonawanda, trying to envision the number of stationary vehicles on the highways and interstates. Cities were a complete mess, but he wondered if people were fleeing, jamming the roads, or if many of them stayed in shelter, hoping for the best. Metzger didn't expect the police and military to come save everyone, because they were battling just to survive the swarm of newly undead attackers on the streets. They couldn't be expected to outlast an army that continued to grow with every fresh death.

He left a small pile of goods, and the backpack, next to the front door, knowing he needed to deal with the unwelcome visitors outside before loading up to leave Blue Ash behind. Carefully checking the backdoor, he found the open backyard clear of any activity, so he stepped outside. Immediately the sound of gunfire reached his ears from a distance, intermittent and desperate in nature. Pulling the hammer back on the revolver, he quickly and cautiously made his way around the house, finding the undead still pawing at his door because nothing else had come along to attract their attention.

Only seconds passed when he reached the corner before the female zombie noticed him, beginning to amble his way from the front steps. With the neighboring house only a few feet behind him, Metzger didn't have anywhere to run except to the backdoor or into the street. He held up the gun defensively, hoping he wasn't about to commit murder.

"If you can hear me, please stop," he said to the woman, who continued to gnash her teeth and look at him ravenously.

Dead less than twenty-four hours, she might as well have been in the ground for a year from the looks of her. The irises of her eyes looked a vacant brown, with the former whites of her eyes yellow in appearance. Her skin was already beginning to turn dry and flaky, and even her clothing possessed an earth tone about it, as though she had been kneaded in dirt like a baker might work dough through flour. She showed absolutely no indication his words reached her ears, or her brain, and her new allies followed, showing equally aggressive tendencies. Metzger simply couldn't believe that someone who walked on two feet and made noise, even in the form of a growl, wasn't still alive somehow.

He shook his head negatively as he raised the gun, firing directly into her forehead, downing her immediately. Much to his surprise, the gunshots didn't faze the other two one bit as they stumbled toward him, walking over their fellow zombie on the ground. Their eyes never left Metzger, continually studying their quarry, unaware of anything else around them.

Metzger provided each of them with a bullet to the forehead in short order, looking around to see no one living or dead appearing on his street. He spent the next five minutes loading his truck with the boxes, bags, and the backpack, thankful he put a hardtop over the truck's bed that past spring. He shut everything off and locked the house in case his brother wasn't accurate and he might return to Ohio someday. As he walked out to the truck from the closed front door, Metzger looked down the street, spying a lone member of the undead shuffling along because it hadn't noticed him yet. He thought about taking action, but decided to head northeast, hoping to arrive within a few days if luck was on his side.

It turned out nothing went right for Metzger over the course of the following three days. He immediately found gridlock on the interstate and ended up abandoning the truck in lieu of an abandoned smart car, which weaved through traffic a little better for part of a day until it died. His travels felt like they took him feet per day instead of miles, and he grew disheartened after a second conversation with his mother ended up interrupted or severed. Attempts to call his parents were met with their voicemail after five rings or entirely disrupted phone service as power and cell phone towers began to fail in certain areas.

Bryce was right, he decided, and told his brother that when he received a second call from the Navy lieutenant commander. He also told him about the interrupted phone call with his mother, only to have his brother press him to get to Tonawanda more quickly. Bryce promised to call again, and about a week later, before the generators running local cell phone towers finally gave out, the Navy officer spoke with him several minutes.

"It's starting to get rough out here," Bryce stated. "Most of the guys can't reach anyone from their families and they're freaking out. We've been rationing supplies, but we're running out, and most of us have lost contact with our families. The captain can't reach any of our people on the mainland, so he said we're heading home. We haven't received orders from the Fleet in three days, and he says he's worried about his wife and kids like the rest of us."

"How the hell do I find you?" Metzger asked.

"I have to believe the base in Norfolk is secure," Bryce said. "Head there once you find Mom and Dad. I'm going to round up Isabella and Nathan when I get back, but it's going to be a few weeks. We're halfway around the world right now, and I don't think we're the only ship heading home. I just hope we can make it with what supplies and fuel we have."

Metzger didn't like the idea of completely losing contact with his brother. Aside from sat phones and smoke rings, very few reliable methods of communication remained.

"I won't have any way to contact you if something goes wrong."

"Dad has a sat phone at the house. When you get there, get it from him. I'll find some way to call you."

"Bryce, I hope they're still okay when I get there," Metzger confessed, his concerns genuine, and growing by the day. "It's going to be slow going all the way. The highways are jammed with cars and the undead."

"Stay tough, Dan. I'll see you soon, I promise. Gotta go."

"Take care."

"You, too."

During the next few weeks following the phone call, Metzger traveled during the day, changing vehicles often when he was able to navigate the roads with them. He began taking state highways and county roads to avoid the inadvertent blockades. Some people abandoned their vehicles when it became clear no one was getting anywhere quickly, but even more died in their vehicles, or nearby. Each time he took a new car, truck, or motorcycle, Metzger left more and more belongings behind. He discovered food wasn't difficult to replace early on, so he held on to weapons and what few photographs and important personal items he brought from Ohio.

He witnessed fellow travelers getting mauled and killed by the undead, which fueled his eventual desire to take out as many of the murderous, mindless monsters as possible. It didn't take long for him to see some of the living prey upon travelers as well, holding them at gunpoint to steal their supplies. A person left without food or weapons wasn't long for the world, and Metzger felt for them, but he also couldn't take on groups by himself.

Often thinking of the kids in his school, he wondered if some of them survived, or ran around as little discolored zombies, chasing people and animals to feed a hunger that could never be satisfied. He hadn't gotten to know the kids in his class very well during the first few weeks of school, and thought maybe that helped him avoid dwelling upon them and their families so much. Eventually he reached the outskirts of Buffalo on Highway 5, making a final switch from a Ford Escape to a motorcycle he spied lying along the side of the road.

Closer to the city, he found vehicles crowding the road in all of the lanes. For as many people who wanted to flee the city and likely never made it, thousands wanted entrance into the second largest city in New York to find loved ones. Already possessing riding items that fit from previous vehicle changes, Metzger put on the chaps, a thick shirt, and a leather jacket to protect him from the undead and any accidents. He also grabbed the helmet from the back of the Escape, keeping it because so many clothing items he found were stained with blood or brain chunks from their former owners.

Drawing closer to the Harley-Davidson Softail he spied near the side of the road, he noticed a body near the bike also clad from head to toe in leather. Not until he stepped only a few feet from the motorcycle did he notice the body moving a little from its prone position along the edge of the highway. Still wearing a helmet, the man near the Harley wasn't among the living as his head shifted to spy Metzger and a throaty growl emitted in muffled form through the full-face helmet. Both legs appeared shattered, preventing him from standing, and he hadn't learned to crawl by using his elbows or hands. Based on the way the neck and the helmet didn't quite align, Metzger wondered if the man snapped his neck during a riding accident, killing him instantly.

Drawing the shorter of the two swords from his pack in the Escape, Metzger jabbed the tip of the blade up through the man's chin, reaching the brain immediately and putting the poor soul to rest.

Metzger began the task of transferring his items from the Ford to the Harley's saddlebags, discovering he was low on food. He knew of a few convenience stores within city limits he could visit, hoping the undead weren't too thick along the outskirts. Feeling close to his objective, he wanted to find his parents before nightfall, but wasn't sure he could weave around the traffic easily, even with a motorcycle. At that moment, hope coursed through his body, knowing he might find his mother, only to have her explain that the phones went dead across the city in the middle of their conversation.

Awaking suddenly from a dream that felt incredibly vivid, Metzger couldn't immediately place his position. Sitting up nervously as he reached for a weapon, his heartrate escalated until he remembered he was surrounded by friendly people within a safe location.

Everyone ended up spending the night at the school, though no one felt exceptionally comfortable. Three of the Wardens escaped the property because they weren't found after several thorough searches of the school grounds. One of them included the infamous Xavier, and after examining the bodies and the one remaining living prisoner, Metzger didn't see anyone who matched the man with the ponytail outside of Albert's house from the previous evening. He couldn't be one-hundred percent certain those men were part of the Wardens until he asked the survivors at the school. Several of them described the missing men to him in detail, leading him to think the events of his motorcycle incident and the two raids at Albert's house were perpetrated by the same people.

He stood, prepared to say a few goodbyes and leave the school grounds as soon as possible, knowing he still needed to travel southeast. Traveling to Norfolk, Virginia wasn't going to be any easier than heading from Blue Ash to Tonawanda. The journey required crossing through Pennsylvania and Maryland while navigating around Washington, D.C., which surely contained far more dangers than just the undead. Only once had Metzger ever driven near the nation's capital, and even then the interstates were a major hassle. He couldn't imagine what the roads looked like with abandoned vehicles everywhere, particularly since it was a target of the factory explosions.

Gathering what few items he brought with him from the Toyota, Metzger wanted to step outside to assess the landscape before heading back to the gray car. He parked it a few miles down the road, hidden from plain view, the previous day before everyone walked to the school. Most of the former prisoners continued to sleep, along with a few members of Molly's group who participated in the rescue efforts. A few were lucky enough to have sleeping bags or blankets discovered in the closets and the offices the Wardens kept for themselves. A few simply slept on the floor in their clothing, happily resting while they breathed air that felt free.

Carefully stepping around the people slumbering closest to the door in the gymnasium, Metzger thought back to the events of the previous evening, including how some of the survivors cleaned out the octagonal cell to make room for the one remaining prisoner that Molly let live. Although he hated the circumstances that made it such a fortress, Metzger knew the school provided a safe haven for anyone who stayed. He hoped Molly would take a leadership role and help the survivors thrive in a familiar environment, even if some of them struggled to forget the past.

Entertaining thoughts of simply walking down the road and never looking back crossed his mind, but as he reached the main exit that would lead him through the gate outside, he heard a voice behind him.

"Where do you think you're heading?"

Turning, he found Albert standing there with Luke and Samantha.

"I was heading to the car to make sure everything was ready to go."

"You can't leave yet."

"I can't?"

"No. Molly has something to ask of you."

Now feeling like a prisoner himself, Metzger set most of his belongings near the door, wondering what more he needed to do for this group before they felt content to let him leave.

Sighing aloud, he looked to Albert, wanting nothing more than to begin his journey south.

"Let's get this over with."

Twelve

etzger virtually stormed down the hall with the three people he actually termed *his people*, even though he hadn't actually used those words aloud.

When he arrived in the science lab where Molly stood near the back wall with Jillian and a Hispanic man about Metzger's age, he saw them removing the licenses from the wall. Immediately he believed he overreacted to Molly asking to see him, took a deep breath, and walked more calmly to the back of the room.

"I know you've had a lot on your plate since yesterday," Molly began empathetically. "First off, I want you to have these, if you want them."

She handed him the licenses of his parents, which he took before staring at them momentarily, still infuriated that his parents were buried in a shallow grave behind the school.

"We're going to do a memorial to the people we lost here at the school," she continued. "And we're going to give them each a more proper burial."

"Does the memorial involve the licenses?" he asked.

Molly nodded.

"There's nothing else to use."

"Then take these," he said, handing them back to her. "I still have some family pictures. It'll mean something to these folks if they have a complete memorial."

"I'm sorry if I was a little harsh yesterday," she added. "Things got pretty intense toward the end."

"It's understandable. Just glad I could help. And I'm sorry your person didn't make it either."

A few seconds of silence filled the room until Molly spoke.

"I know you're leaving soon, and we certainly don't want to hold you up, but I was wondering if you might be willing to take a few people with you."

Metzger felt a bit perplexed that anyone would want to tag along with him, considering he was an emotional wreck at the end of the previous evening.

"Really?" he questioned, his surprise evident.

"I think you already know Jillian Varitek," Molly said with a nod.

"That's the first time I've heard a surname since I got to Buffalo," Metzger said, realizing how little time anyone found for personal interaction after the apocalypse.

"My sister didn't make it, and I have family in Virginia, not far from the base," Jillian explained. "I'd like to go as far as I can with you if that's possible."

"Sure," Metzger replied.

Barely in her twenties, Jillian remained a stunning brunette despite the circumstances surrounding her, almost like a poster child for innocence. Her hair barely reached her shoulders, and her face was smooth, free of acne, and very pretty. Metzger assumed she didn't bother with makeup in the new world, much like other people did without hot showers and gourmet food. She had a farm girl next door quality and appearance, and a slight vulnerability that seemed intensified after learning about the fate of her sister.

"And this is Juan Vazquez," Molly said after a few seconds, introducing the Hispanic man as he and Metzger shook hands.

"Thank you for what you did yesterday," Vazquez said gratefully. "If I'm not a burden, I'd like to travel with you a while. I need to get south."

"Okay," Metzger said with a nod, feeling certain if he traveled too much further alone he might never speak to another human being again.

Vazquez appeared very physically fit, either remaining clean shaven or incapable of growing much facial hair. He wore blue jeans, tennis shoes, and a pastel green shirt a bit louder than what most people opted to wear during their travels. Metzger didn't recognize him from Molly's group, so he assumed the man was freed with the others and donned whatever clean shirt he could readily find.

"Got room for three more?" Albert asked him, catching Metzger completely off-guard.

"You want to leave your sanctuary?"

"Well, I wouldn't say we *want* to, but it seems we're better off with others than standing our ground at the house. The power isn't going to last forever, and if you're heading south, that sounds like the better bet. Luke and I talked it over, and Sam is willing to go along with it. She trusts you."

"Is that true?" Metzger asked Samantha after kneeling down to her level.

As usual, she said nothing, but bobbed her head up and down a few seconds to let him know she agreed with her two guardians.

"We have a number of cars at the house if we could head over there and grab a few of our things," Luke added.

He looked to Molly.

"You're welcome to take any of the other vehicles. We probably have about a dozen ready to go."

"Thank you," she replied.

Metzger looked to Jillian and Vazquez a moment.

"Let me run them to the house and we can return with a second vehicle before we head south. I can't promise you how far we'll get before we have to ditch the cars and start hoofing it, and it will be dangerous, so are you sure this is what you both want?"

Both nodded affirmatively.

"This is the best chance we both have to see our families again," Vazquez said.

He spoke excellent English, indicating he was likely a natural American citizen, despite his full name. Just a hint of accent lingered in his voice, however, as though he might have been raised in a home that regularly spoke Spanish.

Metzger looked to Albert with a bit of concern.

"Do you want to bring Sam along? It could get hairy out there if more undead followed the noise to your neighborhood."

"We can look after her if you want," Molly volunteered. "I think I saw a box of toys in the main office."

"Can I stay?" Samantha asked with a smile from ear to ear, jumping up and down slightly.

"Yes, you can stay," Albert assured her, openly happy to see her joy. He leaned over to quietly speak to Metzger. "I've never seen her like this. And it's a good idea to keep her out of harm's way."

"We have a little bit of a walk to the car, but it shouldn't take long after that," Metzger said.

Molly stepped forward slightly.

"We can have a few people walk with you to the car if you want. There are still three of those assholes out there."

Metzger hated to inconvenience anyone, figuring the three Wardens were likely long gone after their sanctuary was invaded by a larger force. Before he could speak, however, Albert answered for the group, likely worried about his partner's lack of fighting experience.

"That would be great. Thank you."

Close to fifteen minutes later the three men and two more men carrying automatic weapons walked down the road to the Toyota. Metzger surveyed the ditch now on his left as they walked, and the intermittent buildings to his right. On a few occasions the undead staggered their way individually, or in pairs, and he dealt with them using the short sword to avoid anyone using noisy guns.

When they reached the Prius, Metzger moved several items to the trunk to make room for his passengers while the two men assigned to them stood guard near the vehicle. He felt somewhat relieved that no one broke into the car, and more so that his family photos and other belongings remained intact. Already prepared to lose them at some point in the future, he wouldn't have been shocked or surprised to see the items gone from his life so soon.

Once the car was ready for travel the two men gave friendly nods and headed back to the school. Metzger assumed the driver's seat and began heading to the now violated house that Albert and Luke called home well before the world fell apart.

"Are you two sure you want to tag along with me, rather than stay at the school?" Metzger asked them a few minutes into their journey.

"You act like you're not sure you want company," Albert stated from the front passenger's seat. "You didn't seem altogether thrilled back there when Molly asked you."

Metzger grimaced a little, keeping his eyes on the road.

"It's not that I don't want company, but I hate feeling responsible for others. I spent a month on the road by myself dodging virtually every person I came across.

It's hard to trust other people, and when I do finally get there, I don't want to see anything bad happen to them."

"You can't control everything," Luke said. "This isn't a classroom where you're responsible for defenseless kids. Some of us are more capable than others, but we all have to live with the choices we make nowadays."

"I know," Metzger said dejectedly. "And you're all more than welcome, but life on the road isn't easy. It's somewhat easier with other people, I assume, but it's going to get worse as time goes on."

"You mentioned something about your brother and a military base in Virginia," Albert said. "That sounds pretty secure."

Metzger shook his head.

"I'm not sure what it's going to be. I haven't heard from him in over a week, and the last time we spoke he said the skipper had decided to bring the ship home because they weren't receiving any orders from the Navy."

"What's your plan?" Albert inquired.

"To get close to the base, quietly and carefully, and see if I can find him or his wife and kid. Assuming I don't hear from him first."

"You're lucky," Luke said.

Metzger evaded some unevenly parked cars in the middle of the street, making his way around some corpses and debris as well. It amazed him how some parts of the city were crystal clear, and others looked as though a war ravaged the landscape.

"How am I lucky?" he dared asked. "I just discovered my parents were rounded up like Jews into a concentration camp and murdered in just about the most horrific way possible."

"And we're very sorry about that. But at least you *still* have someone. Most of us can't say we had anyone left after things went bad."

"So far it's the hope that's kept me going," Metzger admitted, looking to some of the abandoned businesses around him.

Within urban areas, most of the businesses and apartment buildings appeared readily accessible because their doors were torn from their hinges, or the windows already smashed from looters. Civility went to the wayside like the thousands of corpses that filled ditches and open fields after people were brought down like defenseless prey. Metzger felt reasonably certain more people died as a result of attacks than from whatever chemical or disease that killed the initial wave.

Every so often the trio spotted members of the undead shuffling along the side of the road, or sometimes in the road. Unwilling to bring harm to the car unless absolutely necessary, Metzger swerved around them until he reached the outskirts of Buffalo, drawing closer to the old two-story house.

"Didn't you say you were an ER nurse?" Metzger asked Albert before they traveled much further. "You probably saw some crazy shit when everything went down."

"I worked at Mercy Hospital," Albert answered. "I was actually off that day, but they ended up calling me in for overtime after the factory explosion."

Metzger found it odd how so many major cities suffered factory fires and explosions around the same time on the same day. Americans were so accustomed to acts of terrorism being thwarted that he wondered if this time they had inside help, or worse, the terrorists were domestic.

He questioned if the end results were intentional or a horrific side effect of the fires and the strange chemicals they emitted.

"Only a few of the workers in the factory were killed by the initial blast," Albert began his tale as Metzger avoided a few more awkwardly-parked cars and stumbling undead. "I heard later on that even they reanimated. My hospital took some of the overflow from the other hospitals, so we didn't know what we were in for right away. We received three of the factory workers and they were suffering from some kind of respiratory distress because they breathed the chemical involved in the explosion."

Based on what he saw on the news before his untimely departure from Ohio, Metzger questioned whether every factory contained the same chemicals involved in the explosions because they all seemed to produce the same illnesses.

"By the time they arrived, all three were beginning to turn ashen from the chemical," Albert continued. "We gave them oxygen and monitored their vitals, but they continued to decline. With all three, we ended up putting them out to help slow their breathing because they couldn't remain still, and we knew we were going to have to intubate them to keep their airways open."

"What exactly does intubate mean?" Metzger asked, having never been one to watch medical dramas on television.

"Basically sticking plastic tubes down their throats to keep airflow possible. But all three faded fast, and when they expired, we tried CPR along with oxygen therapy, but nothing was bringing them back."

Albert appeared a bit somber about the situation, which seemed a bit out of place for someone who dealt with death and sickness on a daily basis.

"Things went from bad to worse pretty quickly. Two of the bodies were left in place while the first was wheeled down to the morgue. All three of them started moving about the same time, and when people first saw these factory workers all covered in dirt, grime, and soot walking down the hall they made the mistake of rushing to help them instead of studying the details first."

Metzger looked in the rearview mirror, noticing from Luke's expression that he already knew this tale and wasn't particularly thrilled about hearing the details all over again. He kept looking away, out the side window, at something, anything to distract him from the harrowing story.

"People were bitten," Albert said with a pained wince. "At first we all thought we screwed up and misdiagnosed one or two of them, but our own started dying and coming back. The hallway floors became rivers of blood, and we tried saving the ones who didn't die right away. Hospital security and the police ended up shooting some of the attackers, and that's when I realized something *really* wasn't right about the people returning from the dead. They weren't people in any sense of the word anymore because they didn't feel a thing. I think the cops thought they were sick, because they tried shooting them in the legs, and eventually the chest, but nothing worked until they aimed for their heads."

Albert stared out the windshield at a zombie with the lower part of its jaw hanging onto the deceased man's face by just a shred of flesh. Its eyes continued to glare with a predatory stare at the car as it passed, turning the heads of every undead straggler.

"It's hard to believe how quickly things escalated," Albert said with a numbness that mimicked shock. "People just kept coming to the hospital to check on the loved ones, which just made it worse. More and more people just kept becoming *them*, whatever they were. I don't know how I didn't get bitten. We were trying to help the living, so when they expired I just simply moved to another table and went back to work. Things got so bad that within a few hours they were talking quarantine, and military, and a lockdown of the hospital until order was restored. Word spread, and now we had patients who were already bitten running into the streets, dying and biting. I left before they closed off the hospital to outsiders. Told them I was going to grab a few supplies down the hall, but I just walked out, got into my car, and somehow made it home."

Shaking his head, Albert openly continued feeling shameful about his actions.

"You couldn't have done anything more," Metzger said sympathetically, knowing he planned on missing work the day after everything fell apart.

"I just think of all the people I saw daily," Albert confessed. "Now they're probably locked inside that building, condemned to shuffling around the halls for eternity."

Silence filled the car during the last few minutes it took Metzger to reach their home, finding the neighborhood and their house much the way it looked the previous morning. Sunlight provided ample light for them to spot any danger as all three emerged from the Toyota. Metzger offered to conduct a quick search of the area and stand guard while they gathered what essentials they needed for the trip south.

Finding no undead roaming the streets within eyeshot, Metzger passed through the front gate and took the stairs leading into the front door, closing it behind him. Holding the MP5 he retrieved from the Prius once he returned to the car from the school, he observed the house from the center of the downstairs, keeping his finger just outside the trigger guard. Although his father initially taught him how to use guns, his brother later taught him a few additional things about gun safety that stemmed from his military training.

Metzger learned some valuable lessons from Bryce, wishing he'd taken more time to soak in knowledge like a sponge. Learning on the fly was a good way to get killed, and thus far only sheer luck kept him from dying or getting captured a few different times. He saw very little of his brother, a committed lifer in the Navy, except when Bryce came home from deployments during seemingly random times. Christmas was never actually in December with the family, Thanksgiving was often a conference call, and most other holidays didn't even count when he was halfway around the globe.

Bryce passed up several opportunities to remain stateside where he could instruct at a base, or take an assignment that kept him closer to his wife and son. Metzger wasn't sure if his brother was pursuing higher aspirations, or if another reason kept him far away from family. Their brotherly discussions never got too deep, as though Bryce felt certain his sibling couldn't possibly understand the motivations of a military man.

Taking in the simple beauty of an organized house around him, Metzger heard a few thumps from upstairs as the two men packed their essentials. In a world of chaos, with death literally everywhere around him, he appreciated any setting that reminded him of the old days, even if those times were only a month behind him.

His eyes wandered to the front door where he spotted a shadow crossing the frosted glass centered within the upper portion of the door. Slowly walking toward the door, Metzger refused to blink, much less let his eyes wander from the door. He never felt completely safe, knowing he couldn't let his guard down for one second or dismiss any activity around him as coincidence.

Tapping his finger against the trigger guard, Metzger prepared to shoot anything on the other side of the door that didn't belong. After his experience at the school, where his parents were murdered, he didn't possess nearly the amount of patience or mercy when it came to strangers.

When he reached the door, Metzger peered outside of the frosted side panels, seeing no one standing on the porch. Although the door window components prevented him from making out details, he was able to distinguish a human shape from anything else if he spied someone outside. Just because he didn't see anyone outside didn't mean they hadn't passed by the front door and moved to the side of the house. Growing more paranoid by the second, he decided to head upstairs to check on Albert and Luke.

"Albert!" he called with a repressed yell to avoid anyone who might be lingering outside from overhearing.

"What's wrong?" Albert asked as he reached the door of the room where he and Luke had been packing.

"I saw a shadow cross the front door," he answered in a hushed voice. "When I looked through the window I didn't see anyone out there."

"So?" Albert asked with a confused look, unsure of what Metzger wanted.

"So hurry. I don't want the wrong people paying us a visit."

Understanding completely, Albert gave an affirmative nod before hurrying into the room to redouble his efforts.

Metzger returned to the front door, peering out of each available frosted window before carefully looking out of the larger picture window along one side. He saw no people, no undead, and no unfamiliar vehicles sitting through the open front gate. Not entirely willing to believe what he saw at a glance to hold true, he darted to the backdoor for a look in that direction. Less cautious, he walked from window to window, seeing no intruders.

Less than a minute later Luke reached the first floor, holding a black trash bag with Albert close behind. Albert carried a small suitcase with him, clutching it as though it held items far more important than clothing and toiletries. Metzger looked from the suitcase to Albert, knowing all too well the importance of clinging to memories of the old world. A select few remained inside the Toyota for him, reminding him of his parents, and his brother. Metzger felt certain if he lost all of those items he might disconnect from the world and numbly walk into a deadly trap.

"Out back," Metzger said, pointing to the backdoor, motioning for them to exit the house that way in case someone was lying in wait for them at the front gate.

As the only one of them openly holding a firearm, Metzger opened the door, peered outside from side to side, and took a step after seeing no movement. He chose to round the corner, circling the house around to the front with Albert and Luke behind him. When he reached the inside of the front gate, Metzger motioned for them to stop as he looked outside, hoping a sniper rifle wasn't aimed at his head from afar.

Seeing no danger outside of the wooden fence, he led the way to the Toyota, which hadn't been parked very far away. Albert and Luke quickly jumped into their respective seats, getting their luggage situated as Metzger assumed the driver's seat. Starting the car hurriedly, he pulled out of the neighborhood, taking a look back as he spied someone in the center of the road looking ominously at the back of his car. Like some fictional horror movie killer, the person wanted to make certain he was seen, standing erect and perfectly still.

"What the hell?" Metzger dared ask aloud, fixated on the rearview mirror.

"Look out!" Luke yelled from the backseat, causing Metzger to return his eyes to the road ahead, seeing a different form of danger awaiting them.

A small barricade of cars cut off their return path, with two men standing ominously behind them. Metzger immediately recognized one of them as the man with the ponytail a few nights back in the darkness. If that man was present, that certainly meant the infamous Xavier was either the man beside him, or the threatening figure staring from behind the car. He also knew these men followed them to the house, a second time no less, leaving little doubt they meant to harm the trio inside the Toyota.

Though they presented no weapons as of yet, Metzger felt certain these men were armed. Left with the option of ramming their barricade, or veering to the right where a shallow ditch stood between them and a small city park, he didn't foresee either move ending well for the Prius. He did know that stopping the car meant certain death for him and his two passengers, because the Wardens weren't going to accept the loss of their sanctuary lightly.

Grabbing the steering wheel with both hands, he veered toward the ditch to the right, hoping the car somehow avoided crashing or getting them stuck.

Thirteen

Metzger fully expected a loud thud when he crashed the front end of the car, followed by an airbag punching him in the nose like an MMA fighter, predicating the end of his natural life. Instead, the front right tire managed to land on something solid within the ditch that kept the car level enough for him to reach solid ground at the edge of the city park on the other side. He didn't dare slow down for a second as he caught a glimpse of Luke whirling around in the backseat to assess their situation.

"Are they following us?" Metzger asked.

"No. They're just standing there with stunned looks on their faces."

Sighing a breath of relief, Metzger managed to quickly find a concrete path within the park that eventually took him back to city roads. He remained weary, picking up speed slightly once they were surrounded by buildings and street signs again, knowing it wouldn't take long for the Wardens to regroup if they wanted to pursue the Prius.

"They're going to know where we're going," Albert stated the obvious.

"We're ahead of them," Metzger said, "and unless they're on dirt bikes they aren't going to cut us off."

He detected tension from the couple, as though they hadn't experienced much peril outside of the undead staggering around their neighborhood. Metzger tried to put aside his mentoring ways when his job as a teacher was ripped away by a changed world, but if people were going to travel with him, they needed to know how to survive. By no means an expert on living off the land, he knew how to deal with the undead, and how to avoid potential living threats as well.

Even as his heartrate slowed to a normal pace, he sensed his two passengers weren't entirely at ease.

"You sure you two want to make this trip?" he asked after a minute or so. "This kind of thing isn't entirely uncommon."

"We have to," Albert said. "Our house isn't safe, and we have Samantha to worry about."

"The school is safer for all of you."

"There are at least a few dozen personalities living under that roof now. How long before tempers flare? How long before the food runs out and we're forced to go out for supply runs to places that have long since been picked over? It's a roof and walls, Daniel, but that's all it is."

Metzger couldn't argue any of Albert's points. For him, the secured school remained a painful reminder of where his parents lost their lives. With nothing else left for him in his old stomping grounds, he needed to move southeast to discover the next chapter of his life. Having company he could rely on sounded good, but he also couldn't afford to be slowed. For all he knew, the *U.S.S. Ross* had already reached the Navy base in Norfolk and his brother hadn't been able to contact him.

"I just don't want either of you surprised at what you'll see on the road," Metzger said. "None of it comes easy. Shelter, food, weapons. Trust."

"Is that why you traveled alone?" Luke asked.

"I traveled alone out of necessity at first. It just seemed easier jumping into a new vehicle, or dodging other survivors because I didn't really have a reason to speak to anyone."

Avoiding a few vehicles, Metzger realized they were drawing closer to the school. He fully planned on driving through the front gate this time instead of leaving his car a mile or two down the road.

"Truth be told, I expected to be reunited with my family, or at least some of it. Talking to them after everything went bad seemed too good to be true, especially now that I've seen what everyone else lost. When you're on the road for that long you fall into a trap where you convince yourself it's just easier to be alone."

"Why do you say it's a trap *now*?" Albert asked, giving a knowledgeable, wise glance that indicated he already knew the answer.

"Because I met some people who proved me wrong."

No one spoke again until they neared the open gate at the high school, met by a few familiar faces holding firearms.

"When did you plan on leaving?" Albert inquired.

"Possibly today."

"Possibly? I thought you were dead set on heading out."

"I was, but that was before we met up with those three assholes at your house. That's twice they've been there, and I have some concerns they're after something."

"Or *someone*," Luke added.

After the two armed men stepped aside, Metzger parked the Prius near the school, feeling a bit paranoid that the Wardens were going to seek revenge, possibly against the first available targets. Albert and Luke headed inside first to locate Samantha after Metzger assured them he wasn't going to leave without them.

After entering the school he asked the first person he found about Molly's location, discovering she was helping convert some of the rooms on the second level into sleeping quarters. It seemed things were moving along expeditiously at the school, and Metzger knew he guessed correctly that certain people were going to accept power positions. He assumed none of Molly's people acted with bad intentions, and reaching the level of evil exhibited by the Wardens felt a million miles away, but a select few with power was never a good thing.

Considering the rough few days now behind him, he hadn't given the situation much thought, but now he saw what Albert meant as he climbed a set of stairs to the second floor. With some of the windows uncovered, natural light now crept into the hallways, allowing people to see with less assistance from the few generator-powered and overhead lights. He heard clanking noises from the top of the stairwell, which led him to a rather large lab where seats and desks were being removed to make room for whatever bedding the new residents could find.

Half a dozen people actively worked to clear the room, which made him hope she sincerely cared about everyone remaining in the school. She spotted him and walked over, giving him a quick hug that felt genuine, and most welcome at the moment.

"Glad you made it back," she said with a smile, as though he'd been gone for days instead of just over an hour.

"I need to talk to you," he said, motioning his head toward the hallway.

"Okay," she said hesitantly, following him through the door.

"The Wardens set a trap for us at the house," he said without hesitation once they were alone in the hallway.

"What?" Molly asked with a shocked expression, physically ushering Metzger further away from the door.

Metzger briefly explained the circumstances of the blockade and their narrow escape from the neighborhood.

"I wanted you to know in case they have a plan to attack this place," he said. "There's a possibility they're still watching."

"They're only three in number," Molly said, sounding assured that her new group could thwart an attack from them.

"That's enough to hunt us when we leave today or tomorrow."

"You should stay another night," Molly insisted, touching his forearm. "Give us time to sort this out and find them."

Metzger shook his head negatively.

"We aren't going to *find* them. Sending anyone out there wouldn't be wise."

"I don't want them lurking in the shadows, waiting to pick us off one by one," Molly insisted. "They aren't getting this place back, no matter what they try."

"Nor should they," Metzger agreed.

Feeling frustrated, he rubbed his forehead with his palm.

"We didn't get the second car because of the attack."

"There are extra vehicles here," Molly offered. "Take whichever one you need. We'll find more."

"Thank you. We should be out of your hair within the hour."

"There's no hurry," Molly assured him. "We're going to be occupied the rest of the day converting this place from slave labor to housing."

With all of his items already loaded into the Prius, Metzger soon helped the others gather their belongings before choosing a minivan as their second vehicle. They needed something capable of carrying multiple people while providing at least moderate protection from the undead and living attackers. Holding an old comprehensive map of the country with details for each state, Metzger met everyone between the van and the Prius once the vehicles were loaded.

Everyone walked inside one last time to say their goodbyes to the people they were about to leave behind. Metzger went in to thank Molly for her assistance, and he felt the two hadn't exactly bonded, but did manage to reach an understanding. Each had experienced much different scenarios during their travels, but found common ground at the school, even if the experience proved both heart wrenching and liberating in the same day.

Neither got sappy about their departure, but Metzger did give Molly a quick hug before walking out of the school with the others immediately behind him.

"This is it," he said when they drew near the vehicles. "Last chance to bail if you don't want to drive to Virginia."

No one balked, but Vazquez bit his lip as though fighting the urge to state something that weighed on his mind.

"What is it, Juan?" Metzger asked, pressing the man for an elaboration before they departed.

He didn't want to be responsible for taking someone from the safety of the school if they weren't committed to the migration.

"I didn't want to say anything earlier, because I didn't want us to lose time in case I was wrong."

"Wrong about what?"

"There are several small airports around Buffalo," he said slowly. "Both public and private types that have commuter planes and even a few private jets."

Having no idea how to fly a plane, Metzger indeed considered the statement a complete waste of time. Attempting to fly a plane and dying in the process wasn't a productive move in the least. The more he looked at Vazquez, however, the more he realized the man hadn't yet reached his point.

"Can you fly?"

"I was only a few flights away from getting my private pilot's license."

"He's practically a pilot then," Albert said assuredly. "I took a few lessons once, and if he was *that* close he may be the best pilot left in the world."

Vazquez shrugged uneasily.

"I don't know about that."

"What can you fly?" Metzger inquired, finding the notion of reaching Virginia in hours instead of days or weeks rather inviting.

"I flew small planes like a Cessna and a Piper for the most part. My instructor owned a Cessna 421, which held half a dozen people."

Metzger hesitated before asking his next question, not sure he wanted to hear the answer.

"Where is that plane located?"

"That's the problem. It's at a small public airport in Lancaster."

Metzger knew Lancaster was east of Buffalo by only a few miles, but they weren't exactly in the heart of Buffalo at the moment. He believed Vazquez, but a lot of ifs crossed his mind, knowing exactly how many things might go wrong during the short, potentially dangerous drive to Lancaster.

"If we get there, can you fly that plane with confidence?" he asked.

"I can fly it, but I can't guarantee it's *still* there," he said before hesitating momentarily. "But even if it's gone, there are more than two dozen other aircraft stored there."

"How secure is it?" Luke asked, openly worried about undead roaming inside the fences.

"It was fenced all the way around," Vazquez answered. "It required a code to enter at the fence, which I *do* know."

Metzger weighed his options, knowing there wasn't much choice now that flying to Virginia suddenly became a viable option. Every hour he spent traveling to the military base decreased the chances of him finding his brother in a world where discovering living people was already a challenge.

"Anyone afraid of flying?" he asked aloud, seeing no one balk at the notion.

"It sounds better than sifting through thousands of zombies on the ground," Albert stated. "When can we leave?"

"Right now," Metzger said. "I'm keeping Juan with me and we'll lead the rest of you there. Be careful, because we don't know what's going to be waiting for us."

Within a few minutes Metzger assumed driving duties in the Prius while Albert drove everyone else in the van. A wave of cautiously optimistic relief washed over Metzger, thinking how flying spared them from the open road, trying to syphon fuel, dealing with the undead, and avoiding hardcore groups of the living. He remembered most of the communities surrounding Buffalo, but gave Vazquez the satisfaction of navigating their way to the airport.

"Even if this one is overrun, there are other local airports, aren't there?" he inquired about five minutes into their trip.

"Probably close to twenty that were within reasonable driving distance of Buffalo, back when you could travel with normal congested traffic."

"So what's your backstory?" Metzger asked as he avoided a small herd of undead and a school bus turned awkwardly across two lanes of traffic.

"Pardon?"

"You know, your condensed autobiography."

"Oh," Vazquez said, getting Metzger's point the second time around. "I was born and raised in New Mexico. My parents worked on a ranch out there, trying to provide for me and my sister. She moved to Washington, D.C. a few years back to work for a state senator."

"So you're hoping to find her?"

Vazquez shrugged.

"I want to, but the last we spoke they were trying to get her out of the city with some other people. It's a wild goose chase at this point."

"But you're still going to try," Metzger said, already knowing the answer.

"If all goes well, I'll get you folks to Virginia and make my way up to Washington."

"It's not entirely impossible they tried to move some of those people from Washington to the Navy base in Norfolk."

Vazquez shook his head negatively.

"I think they had something even more secure in mind from the way Maria talked. I'm not even sure where to begin."

Vazquez pointed to the right.

"Turn here."

Metzger made the turn, swerving around a few cars to discover the road ahead less cumbersome than most he'd traveled recently.

"So what brought you to Buffalo?" he asked.

"I got work installing wind turbines, and Buffalo was our latest job. They were adding half a dozen of them near the old shipping yards after clearing the area."

Metzger remembered the old shipping yards from his childhood because his father worked on the railroad. In the old days, boats and trains were the backbone of Lake Erie, shipping virtually everything under the sky before planes and tractor trailers stole their thunder. Now much of the old docks and tracks were removed in the name of progress and giant windmills took their place to generate power for the surrounding communities. He wondered if Vazquez possessed knowledge of how the power-generating devices worked, or he simply installed them.

"How did you start flying?" Metzger inquired.

"Obviously I'm not afraid of heights, and my boss owned one of a plane to get from city to city easier. He started taking me flying and offered me lessons when he needed me to preview some of our upcoming projects. He wanted some company for the flight, and I was a willing student."

"You seem to know the area fairly well."

"Installing the turbines isn't an overnight process. We worked here about five months before everything went bad. Fewer and fewer of my coworkers showed up to work each day and I finally decided I wasn't going to get paid when *no one* came to the site, so I switched over to survival mode. Things just got crazier by the day, and I guess I was a little slow on the draw when it came to watching the news. When those pricks came and nabbed me I was fighting a bunch of those *things* on the street. They pulled up in a truck and told me to jump in so they could take me to safety."

Vazquez shook his head slowly and Metzger completely understood that the sanctuary they spoke of turned out to be a sham.

"I wasn't there from the beginning," Vazquez admitted with a hint of sorrow. "A lot of those people didn't make it. We slaved for them and buried the bodies of the dead when it could've just as easily been a community from the beginning. I'm really sorry about your parents, Dan."

"Did you talk to them much?"

"There wasn't much time for conversation, but I could tell they were good people. They tried to start a revolt, but everyone was scared, just trying to stay alive long enough for help to arrive."

An awkward silence filled the vehicle momentarily as Metzger debated whether or not he could blame anyone at the school for the inaction that killed his parents. He couldn't believe that no one else possessed backbone enough to take a stand against the Wardens.

"I don't blame anyone," he decided aloud. "I wasn't there, so I can't pass judgment on what people did or didn't do."

Both of them seemed uncertain of what to say next for a moment.

"We're getting close," Vazquez finally said as he pointed left at a fork in the road created by an assortment of abandoned vehicles.

A few minutes later the group found themselves surrounded by a number of cornfields that would never be harvested. Some of the fields contained beans and other shorter crops that allowed them to spy the tall chain link fence surrounding the airport. Vazquez directed Metzger to the entrance, but both of them noticed movement within the fence once they reached the road parallel to one of the airstrips that would grant them access.

"That's not good," Metzger commented, seeing dozens of undead roaming around inside the facility.

"It got overrun," Vazquez noted, his eyes darting left and right, searching for the reason the small airport fell victim to the undead.

Both of them spied a section of the fence knocked inward at the same time. While it allowed them to bypass the front gate and a potentially dead electronic keypad, the opening provided them with additional danger. Metzger counted somewhere between two and three dozen undead roaming around the main building where they were about to enter.

"Which hangar is it?" he asked Vazquez, seeing three parallel white buildings with orange roofs, each longer than the last.

"They store it in the middle one."

Metzger didn't immediately drive to the hangars, knowing every zombie on the property would turn and follow.

"What are you doing?" Vazquez questioned with obvious concern.

"Getting to an open area so I can give Albert some instructions."

Down one of the runways he found virtually no undead staggering near the concrete, so he drew to a stop, and Albert stopped the van behind him. Metzger quickly stepped out and darted back to the van as Albert rolled down the window.

"Go near the hangars, honk your horn, and get them to follow you as far away as possible," Metzger instructed. "We'll probably need five or ten minutes to get the plane out and ready it for flight, assuming there aren't any hiccups."

"Got it," Albert said without wasting any time.

He drove the van toward the group of undead wandering around the front of the property, immediately honking the horn and driving slowly enough that they noticed and followed him without hesitation.

"I'll give him a head start before we head for the hangar," Metzger said as he slid into the driver's seat.

Both men watched as Albert led most of the undead away from the terminal and the hangars with ease. Metzger took a few seconds to examine the hangars, finding no outward damage to the buildings, and none of the doors left open. Either no one took any aircraft from the airport, or they were courteous enough to close the doors behind them.

"I'm hoping this turns out as good as it looks," Metzger said when he finally drove toward the hangars, still seeing a few undead stragglers in the area.

He planned to deal with them while Vazquez opened the middle building to see if the Cessna remained inside.

"You do what you need to, and I'll cover you," he instructed Vazquez as he pulled to the corner of the hangar in question.

Both jumped out, closing the car doors behind them out of cautionary habit. As Vazquez ran over to check the large metal door, Metzger returned to the car, pulling a Beretta semi-automatic pistol from between the seats to use on the lingering undead. Knowing the gunfire would assuredly lure the zombies to his location, he needed to make his shots count, and get rid of the problem quickly.

"It's locked!" Vazquez shouted from the smaller entrance door to the hangar.

The regular entrance door was embedded within the large, folding garage door that allowed planes to be maneuvered in and out of the hangars.

Fortunately Metzger hadn't yet fired a shot as he ran over to the door, barely hesitating before he threw his shoulder into it. Refusing to give, the door required a few more rams before it finally gave way, allowing him inside to spy the larger garage door. Its two large sections were meant to ascend and buckle before neatly folding overhead, allowing daylight for a preflight inspection or the opportunity to move the aircraft.

"Thanks," Vazquez said, stepping behind him. "I may have bigger issues getting that door open and figuring out how to move the plane outside."

Metzger stole a glance at the pristine airplane inside, deeming it flight worthy in his estimation if they could somehow move it outside. A bit larger than other planes he'd seen in small airports, it sported dual propellers, indicating a smoother, more efficient ride than he originally anticipated.

"Handle it and I'll cover you," he said before stepping through the entrance door to discover what awaited him.

He immediately patrolled the area on foot to seek out the undead and put them down permanently. He found a few around the first corner, putting a bullet into each of their skulls from close range. Staying fairly close to Vazquez so the man didn't have to worry about being attacked, Metzger waited for the undead to come to him.

A former redhead rounded the corner in a tattered party dress with a chunk of her left cheek missing. She gnashed her teeth only once before Metzger fired a bullet into her skull, downing her as two male zombies followed in her wake. He fired two more shots, dropping them before checking the opposite end of the hangar. Everything appeared clear of danger momentarily as Vazquez scrambled to hook a power tow to the plane after somehow opening the hangar door. The device looked something like an elongated snow blower with forward, neutral, and reverse options listed near the hand grips. Metzger assumed it ran on fuel, without dependency on electricity.

"I could use a hand," Vazquez stated as he tried hooking two metal prongs to the front landing gear of the Cessna.

"And I'm not looking to get bitten from behind," Metzger said as he glanced at either end of the concrete path before rushing to the machine. "How the hell did you get the door open so quickly?"

"I found the chain hoist," Vazquez answered, finally securing the metal components into place. "Got it."

Stuffing the gun along the back of his belt, Metzger prepared to assist the pilot with moving the plane, but Vazquez started the power tow on his own. He steered the machine rather easily, as though he'd done so a time or two, and the tow carried out most of the work. It sounded like a large riding lawnmower, sure to attract any lingering undead their way. Once they got it into the open, Vazquez shut down the mechanical tow and wasted no time beginning to inspect the aircraft from head to toe, front to back.

"How long do you need?" Metzger asked as he pulled the gun from behind him, ejecting the magazine to see he had at least six more shots with a quick glance.

"Give me five minutes just to make sure we don't crash as soon as we take off."

Metzger watched him grab a ladder and climb around the plane, checking the seals, the fuel levels, and glance inside to make sure the controls were in working order. Able to dart around the three hangars while Vazquez worked, Metzger took out a few more undead, seeing no immediate threats when he looked out at the runway, finding the van some distance away, leading most of the undead a safe distance away from the Cessna.

Breathing a sigh of relief, Metzger believed for a moment that they might all escape the runway without harm. He turned to check on Vazquez one last time as his ears detected the sound of a motor in the distance. Not the van, and certainly not the Cessna, the motor sounded powerful, like a muscle car, drawing closer to their location by the second. He tried waving with both hands to Albert, unsure if the older man noticed his distress signal before he ran back to Vazquez. The pilot wore a look of grave concern, having heard the roar of the motor as well.

"We need to get out of here," Metzger said firmly. "Now."

Fourteen

Immediately suspecting who had tracked them to the airport, if not stalked them in the worst possible sense of the word, Metzger grabbed the MP5 from the car and slung it around his shoulder. He also snagged the semi-automatic AK-47 the group had let him take from the school, which rather surprised him because he hadn't asked for additional firepower. It fired one round at a time, not converted to fully automatic like so many of its kind that wound up in the hands of children forced to fight for rebel causes in foreign lands.

Vazquez immediately opened the plane's hatch, jumping inside to see if he could start it under pressure. Metzger ran to the edge of the runway area, hoping to flag down Albert if no one inside the van spotted his arm signals the first time. He found the van traveling his way, but not with speed that indicated they understood the danger closing in on the airport. Metzger motioned for them to reach him more quickly by using his hands and arms, so Albert picked up speed as the motorized sound reached the opening in the fence.

Metzger watched in horror as a black car that resembled a classic Dodge Charger burst through the opening, partially covered with makeshift armor as though ripped from some apocalyptic movie, heading straight for the van. Albert saw it too, and tried to veer to the right, but the car smashed the van on the driver's side. With a push bar like police cars often had attached to their front bumpers, the modified muscle car moved the van, but failed to tip it over.

Pulling the AK-47 to a shooting position, Metzger looked down the iron sights, taking aim at the driver's side window, then the windshield, waiting for a clear shot at the driver. As though sensing the danger directly before him, the driver quickly backed away from the van, driving erratically around the parallel runways. Metzger continued to trudge forward until he reached the van, which appeared damaged, but still running. Albert looked up, his forehead dripping blood after hitting something within the van, his eyes struggling to focus on Metzger.

"Is everyone okay?" Metzger asked, drawing eye contact from everyone inside the van as most of them nodded. "Albert, see if you can make it over to the hangar. I'll cover you."

Albert nodded, punching the gas while Metzger monitored the black car as it turned to head straight for him. Metzger held his ground, taking aim at the driver's side of the front windshield until he heard the van stall behind him. It made several clacking noises that indicated it wasn't going to start again before the engine sputtered and died.

He started to look back, hoping to assess the problem, but knew he couldn't afford to lose focus for a second. Carefully staring down the iron sights, he waited until the swerving car veered back to his left before timing a shot at the driver's torso. Managing to fire a single round, Metzger saw the cobweb appear in the windshield where he hoped it would, causing the car to drag heavily to his left as though something tugged at the steering wheel, or someone slumped over it. His right ear, the one closer to the rifle when he fired it, rang incessantly from the loud shot, and Metzger could tell his hearing wouldn't recover as easily as it might with a smaller firearm.

Within a few seconds the car corrected its direction and started on a path that led directly toward Metzger and the van behind him. Unsure if the driver recovered, or the passenger took hold of the wheel, Metzger raised the AK-47, taking aim at the passenger side this time. He fired just as the vehicle swerved slightly to his right, forced to dive out of the way before he could see where his bullet struck.

Once again the car rammed into the van, but before Metzger could regain his footing and fire numerous rounds into the vehicle it took off once again, veering wildly to and fro. With limited ammunition in the gun's magazine, and no spare rounds with him, Metzger needed to make every shot count. Much to his horror, he watched the armored car head straight toward the three hangars, endangering any chance the group stood of leaving New York expediently.

Running up to the van, Metzger heard Albert's failed attempts to restart the vehicle, so he smacked the passenger side of the van twice to gain the attention of everyone inside.

"Get some weapons, get what you absolutely need, and head for the hangar!" he shouted before sprinting across the runway closest to the hangars.

He could only watch as the car slowed to search for the plane, or its potential pilot, once it crept past the first hangar. Clutching the AK-47 in his right hand, Metzger darted as fast as his legs would allow to rescue Vazquez from the impending danger. He heard the plane's engine attempt to start before it sputtered, and before a second attempt was made gunfire sliced the air. Metzger quickly closed to a distance he considered within his range of hitting sizeable targets, but as he raised the rifle the car quickly sped ahead, taking a hard right around the last of the hangars.

"Fuckers!" he muttered under his breath, picking up the pace once again in a dead sprint.

Hearing the car screech around the far edge of the hangars, Metzger felt helpless trying to deal with three fronts at once. He needed to make certain Vazquez survived the rounds volleyed in his direction, four other people were relying on him to make certain they reached the hangars, and at least two maniacs were driving around in an armored car wreaking havoc. If Xavier and his cronies had indeed stealthily followed them from the school to the small airport, Metzger suspected three attackers were after them unless the driver was indeed disabled by the AK-47.

As he reached the first hangar, Metzger took notice that the car was driving to the far edge of the fenced in airport, off to his right side. A glance behind him indicated that Luke, Samantha, an injured Albert, and Jillian were offloading what few essentials they deemed necessary from the van. He rounded the next corner, finding the plane, but no Vazquez as his eyes darted from left to right.

"Juan?" he called out.

"Over here," he heard a pained groan in return.

Metzger found his pilot inside the hangar, his right hand pressed over his left shoulder, applying pressure to a fresh bullet wound.

"Oh, God," Metzger stammered. "How bad is it?"

"It went through," Vazquez said quickly. "I'll live, but I think they might have nicked some of the plane."

Metzger turned, half expecting to find fuel dripping from one of the wings where it was stored on the plane. Seeing no leaks, and no damage in the plane's vital areas, he hoped they might still escape the airfield in one piece if he could find a way to deal with the black car.

"I was trying to start it when they zipped around the corner," Vazquez said. "I jumped out and ducked for cover."

"You did the right thing. I'm going to try and deal with them once I get everyone over here."

"Go!" Vazquez insisted. "I'll get her started."

Metzger nodded before dashing back to the edge of the hangars, seeing his four companions make their way to him, each of the adults carrying firearms and minimal luggage in the form of small backpacks or bags. He heard the roar of the armored car's engine growing louder, and as he glanced to the left, seeing it speed their way down the runway, he yelled to the four.

"Look out!"

Albert and Jillian had already spied the car as Luke protected Samantha by wrapping her in his arms and heading back to the van for cover. As though the situation wasn't already hazardous enough, undead stragglers returned from the opposite end of the airstrip while new arrivals, attracted to the various noises within the small airport, filed through the gaping hole in the front gate.

While none of the undead were dangerously close to anyone on foot, they soon would be if the group took too long getting to the hangars. Metzger knew the car was returning from his left, and he spied it from the corner of his eye heading for his companions with reckless abandon. He darted further onto the runway, hoping to draw attention to himself, but the car continued barreling toward the larger group.

With Luke already protecting Samantha closer to the van, Jillian was able to dive out of the way before the car ran her down, but Albert, already dazed from the earlier collision to the van, wasn't so fortunate.

He saw the car coming and made an evasive effort, but the car clipped his ankle while it was lifted from the ground in midstride, likely snapping it before it sent Albert into a painful spiral to the ground. Metzger saw him spin like a top several times before gravity finally brought him down. Luke started to leave the van to rush to his side, but fought his instincts and remained near Samantha as Metzger and Jillian dashed toward Albert while the car continued onward. It flew down the runway as though purposely attempting to draw more walkers in its direction.

"Albert!" Metzger cried out as he took the man's side, dropping to his knees.

"It's not so bad," Albert said, looking to his ankle where a bloody spot appeared along his sock, indicating a fractured bone was either piercing the skin or very close to doing so.

Metzger motioned for Luke and Samantha to join them while the car was a fairly safe distance away from the group. All four of them hoisted Albert to his feet hurriedly, attempting to carry him over to the hangars where at least some cover awaited them. Metzger stole a glance at the black car, seeing a growing number of undead lurking behind it as it slowly led the parade in their direction. Knowing they couldn't assist Albert *and* fight off a few dozen walkers, he broke off from the group, taking aim at the car once more as he strode purposefully straight for it.

Still a good fifty feet away, the car wasn't close enough for Metzger to shoot and feel assured he'd strike a high priority target. He continued drawing closer, waiting for the car to speed directly toward him or veer away after picking up speed. Neither occurred immediately, and Metzger finally saw the driver slumped against the side window, uncertain if the man lost consciousness a second time or died with the original shot. It felt improbable that the driver reached the pedal and steered the car so accurately the entire time, but Metzger now understood who his next target needed to be.

Shifting his aim to the passenger side of the vehicle, Metzger remained oblivious to the fate of his fellow travelers, focused on ending the skirmish before it progressed. He absolutely *needed* to find his brother, the one living relative he knew wasn't dead in the new world, and these bastards had targeted the very few people he currently trusted.

Knowing he'd used about five rounds thus far, Metzger estimated another two dozen remained within the magazine, but he decided to open up on them, firing single shots as fast as his trigger finger allowed. He repeatedly squeezed the trigger, peppering the passenger's side of the windshield with rounds as he took steady aim. He saw the man behind the windshield duck for cover as the car suddenly veered heavily to Metzger's left, safely away from his line of fire and the four people attempting to cross the runway.

Hearing the plane start and remain running behind him, Metzger encouraged the others to move quickly in the direction of the hangars with a wave. The black car rolled to a stop about the same distance away as the van, but isolated across the concrete runway. Thinking perhaps the ordeal was finally over, and the car or its passengers disabled, he started to turn and walk toward his colleagues only to hear gunfire ring out about ten seconds into his walk. Jillian turned to return fire in the car's direction, leaving only Luke to assist a struggling Albert across the path still adorned with white and yellow stripes to assist landing aircraft.

Danger crept in from every direction as the undead drew closer to the group and the two remaining men from the black car exited and took cover behind the vehicle, trying to shoot the five people left in the open. Metzger wasted little time raising his weapon, noticing one of the men wore his lengthy hair in a ponytail while the other had short, black, slicked back hair and an angry scowl.

"Xavier," Metzger muttered, feeling reasonably assured the man who murdered his parents stood before him.

He turned to the four people he was trying to protect long enough to leave his home state.

"Go! I'll cover you!"

Without monitoring their progress, he turned to fire additional shots at Xavier and the man with the ponytail, trying to conserve ammunition by shooting more selectively now. Missing completely with his first two rounds, Metzger succeeded in forcing both men to duck behind the car, buying additional time for the others to escort Albert safely across the tarmac.

Taking a good guess where the man with the ponytail might pop up next, Metzger took aim with the AK-47, keeping both eyes open for full field of vision. A few seconds later, the man stood from cover to fire his own semi-automatic weapon, only a foot or so away from Metzger's guestimate. Seeing that he dared take aim on the defenseless foursome, Metzger needed only move his gun barrel a few millimeters to the right to take aim at the man's chest. He fired, seeing the round strike the man directly in the upper torso, spurting blood as it entered, ending the man's life either immediately or shortly thereafter.

Likely seeing the last of his henchmen dead by his side, Xavier refused to rise from cover to provide Metzger with a clear shot. Taking a moment to observe the progress of his four colleagues, Metzger turned to see a dangerous number of undead nearing the labored group. Backpedaling from the armored car, he turned just long enough to take shots at the zombies closest to the group. Taking the first few down with headshots, he heard a subtle click of sorts after the last shot, indicating the magazine finally purged the last of its ammunition.

Metzger slung the AK-47 behind him with help from the sling attached to the firearm. He reached to his side, pulling the .357 from its holster, glancing to ensure Xavier didn't attempt to shoot the members of his group before taking down two more undead near Jillian. She took notice of the zombies drawing closer to them, and tried to pick up her pace, but she and Luke weren't able to move much faster than the undead while supporting Albert's arms across their shoulders.

"Leave me," he heard Albert say as danger drew closer to the group.

Samantha began backing away from her surrogate parents, threatening to undo the united core the group had maintained while dealing with the undead.

Beginning to realize the danger around them was too close, Luke dropped his partner's arm, running back toward the van while waving his arms and yelling for the undead to pursue him. They immediately responded, most of them following him and leaving the remainder of the group alone. Though she struggled to hold Albert up by herself, Jillian handed her sidearm to the injured man so he could shoot the few zombies still pursuing them.

Metzger continued to monitor the black car as he backed toward his group, ushering Samantha back to them like a sheepdog minding his herd. He helped Albert shoot a few of the nearby zombies in their skulls as Luke drew most of them into the center of the airport. Sounds of the Cessna taxiing onto the runway behind him reached Metzger's ears, and he felt for the first time they might actually be leaving the airport intact if Xavier would just play dead or voluntarily leave them alone.

Unfortunately for Luke he ran too close to the van, giving Xavier a vantage point that allowed him to take aim in that direction without exposing any part of his body to Metzger. The plane began to taxi from the staging area near the hangars to the airstrip the group was trying to cross, but as Metzger started to yell for Luke to return to them, a shot rang out. Stuck with his mouth agape, and no words emerging from his throat, Metzger watched as Luke collapsed to the ground. A bloody spot appeared just below his knee, indicating that was just as hobbled as Albert, if not worse.

Forced to deal with several unpleasant fronts, Metzger started toward Luke, knowing the man faced the most immediate danger. When he saw Luke struggle to his feet and limp around the van for cover, Metzger decided to focus on Xavier instead since he was caught between the van and the armored car, exposed to both the undead and the former leader of the school prison. Pulling the .357 to a ready position, he sidestepped to the car in a cautious military stride, able to defend himself or fire within a split-second.

Deciding he needed to eliminate the threat to avoid looking over his shoulder as the group attempted to board the plane, Metzger circled around the car, still some fifteen feet away from it. Apparently hearing his footsteps, or sensing the impending showdown, Xavier popped up from behind the car, closer to the end where the ponytail man fell. He didn't seem to have an immediate lock on Metzger's location, allowing the former school teacher to take an extra fraction of a second to aim at his skull before firing.

Minimal blood spurted from the right side of Xavier's head, indicating the bullet split some skin, but Metzger couldn't confirm whether or not it struck home and killed the man. Hearing the plane emerge from the staging area, drawing closer, he dashed to the van to retrieve Luke before the undead caught up with them.

"Come on," he encouraged Luke as he scooped him under one shoulder, guiding him away from the group of undead trying to feast on his flesh.

Both managed to elude the pack of zombies pursuing them rather quickly as they headed for the Cessna now emerging from the hangars. To their left, however, Jillian struggled to move Albert by herself as a few independent-minded undead staggered behind the pair. She managed to shoot two zombies closing in on their location, but one escaped her sight, able to walk directly behind Albert before sinking its teeth into his right shoulder, drawing a pained yowl from the former emergency room nurse.

Jillian and Metzger both noticed the zombie an instant before the deadly deed was committed, but Jillian turned and shot it in the skull first, causing Albert to raise a hand to his freshly ringing ear.

"No!" Luke cried out in horror, knowing immediately what the bite meant for any intended future he planned with his life partner.

Vazquez brought the plane as close to the group as he could without risking the wheels running into the grass. The ground wasn't necessarily solid enough to support the weight of a plane, and potentially dangerous litter was scattered throughout the airport. Once the Cessna drew to a complete stop the pilot jumped out to assist a shocked Luke inside. This freed Metzger to use his few remaining rounds on the closest undead, ensuring no one else received a fatal bite before takeoff. With the final bullet expended, he replaced the revolver to its holster, kicking a few undead to the ground to buy some time.

"Get them inside!" he yelled to Vazquez, drawing the survival knife from the other side of his belt to dispatch the remaining nearby zombies.

Fighting off a few more undead with defensive kicks, Metzger turned to see everyone now loaded into the back of the plane, Albert clasping his fresh wound with one hand. Blood soaked into his shirt, indicating the bite pierced his skin, allowing whatever virus or bacteria the undead carried to enter his system. Metzger held out the slightest hope initially that the bite didn't reach his flesh and muscles through the shirt, but now his heart sank at the thought of losing someone else who meant something to him.

He leaned into the already open side door of the plane, looking to Vazquez directly. Appearing a bit sweaty and pale after being shot, the pilot put forth a strong front without saying a word.

"I need about thirty seconds," Metzger said, pointing toward the hangars and the car he was about to leave behind.

Though obviously in pain, Vazquez nodded, allowing Metzger to sprint across the concrete to the staging area where he opened one of the rear car doors while using the remote to pop the trunk. Like a badger burrows into the ground, he quickly scavenged what ammunition and firepower he could from the Prius, along with his blades. He took an additional few seconds to grab the sat phone and its charger, along with a recent family photo of himself, Bryce, and their parents together. He couldn't afford to be selfish and grab entire family albums, but as he shut the car doors and trunk, Metzger stuffed the remote into his pocket after locking the car. He did so just in case he returned to the Buffalo area someday and found time enough to retrieve family photographs and heirlooms.

As he left the hangar area, Metzger stole a glance toward the armored car, seeing a dozen zombies stagger in the direction of the ponytail man and Xavier, glad because the group's escape was now assured. He could only hope the man who murdered his parents died a slow and painful death, ripped apart by ravenous fingers and teeth. Wishing he could have assured the job was completed by his own hand, Metzger closed his eyes for the briefest of seconds, opening them to begin the next phase of his existence.

Vazquez did him the service of pulling the plane closer, so Metzger quickly climbed into the open door on the left side of the plane behind the wing, dropping the excess gear in the center of the plane. The group left him a spot up front beside Vazquez, so he carefully walked the narrow aisle, assuming the co-pilot's seat.

"Buckle up," Vazquez warned, sweat beginning to soak through his shirt. "And put these on."

He handed Metzger a set of ear-encompassing headphones that worked, muting any sounds around them. It allowed them to converse while drowning out any panicked sounds behind them while everyone tried gathering their wits and assisting Albert.

All of them knew this was the furthest thing possible from a conventional flight.

"You going to be okay?" Metzger inquired, noticing a rotating compass embedded within the Cessna's front panel.

All kinds of dials, switches, and knobs surrounded him, leaving him extremely nervous about the prospect of taking over any flight duties.

"I'll make it," Vazquez said, though his appearance didn't back his reassuring words.

Metzger glanced behind him, checking on Albert, who was being tended to by Luke in the two rear seats. Jillian wore guilt on her face, though she did nothing wrong, and poor Samantha appeared completely upended by the experience as though she might never recover. Metzger removed his headset momentarily in case he needed to speak with the people behind him.

"You've got to pull through," Luke said in a concerned voice, trying to avoid worrying Samantha any further.

"We both know that's not going to happen," Albert replied. "I'll get you patched up when we land, but you have to make preparations for life without me."

Metzger's heart sank. He never intended for anyone to get harmed while joining him on his personal journey. While he hadn't requested anyone come along, he still felt some guilt for hurrying and not taking care of business around the school before departing.

Luke began openly crying as he and Albert embraced across their seats. As concerned as he felt for everyone aboard the Cessna, Metzger knew he needed to focus on keeping Vazquez conscious for the duration. Practically no one ended up bringing items aboard with them, meaning extra weapons were scarce, and no extra clothes were lying around for use as dressings.

Metzger had left his motorcycle gear behind, so he began tearing off the sleeves of his shirt, using them to dress both sides of the gunshot wound as he applied pressure. Vazquez winced, uttering no words as he groaned from the pain a bit.

"Sorry," Metzger said. "It's all I've got at the moment."

Albert painfully removed his button-up shirt, left with a white T-shirt as he handed the shirt forward for Metzger to use on the wound.

"Thanks," Metzger said with a nod to Albert.

"I won't be needing it," the former nurse said with a forced smile.

"Ain't we a sorry lot," Vazquez said when Metzger tore away the bloody part of Albert's shirt to avoid any possible contamination.

He used the remainder of the shirt to apply pressure to both the entrance and exit wounds as best he could.

"I suppose we are. Hope you can stay conscious, because I don't think any of us know how to fly this thing."

"I'll do my best. It's going to be a couple hours, so if anything happens, just keep the plane level and do your best to wake me up."

"That's not very reassuring."

Each side had a control wheel, and Metzger had watched enough movies to know that pushing forward sent the plane careening toward the ground and pulling back gained altitude. He didn't know how to put flaps down, use landing gears, or a host of other important steps that would keep the plane from crashing into a giant fireball.

Even while being treated, Vazquez had managed to get to one end of the runway and gained enough speed to get them into the air momentarily. For a private plane, the Cessna glided easily, taking to the sky so smoothly it felt more like a metal roller coaster ride than sitting inside a box of metal and plastic with wings. Some tilting and jockeying was required by Vazquez to get them to safe altitude and heading in the right direction.

"No sense in using the radio," the pilot muttered. "No one would hear us anyway."

Half an hour passed with Metzger looking back to check on everyone, seeing little difference in their faces. The cloth dressings had stopped the bleeding in Vazquez's shoulder for the time being, but the pilot had lost a fair amount of blood before he even boarded the plane. Despite his injury, he provided Metzger with a crash course in how to handle the Cessna in case he blacked out. In short, Metzger would need to keep the control wheel in its current position while making certain the plane continued in the same direction.

"Artificial horizon," Metzger said aloud, quizzing himself to make certain he understood the vital portions of his abbreviated lessons from Vazquez.

He pointed to a gauge with a blue top portion and a brown bottom, divided in half by a white line that would move as the plane tilted to the left or right. It kept the pilot aware of how level the plane was compared to the ground below, allowing him to adjust to keep both the wings and pitch level.

"You got it," Vazquez answered a bit more weakly than before.

His skin continued to appear pale, though the sweating had dropped off, possibly because his body required fluids.

"Altimeter," Metzger said next, pointing to a gauge that looked a bit like a clock.

In the top position, or normal twelve o'clock location, a white zero would indicate if they were on the ground. The dial contained numbers up to nine in what most would consider the eleven o'clock position on a clock, indicating ninethousand feet. At the moment, the plane was coasting closer to 3,000 feet off the ground according to the gauge. Such a height left Metzger a bit nervous, but he knew they could just as easily die from a few hundred feet off the ground. Without fear of other aircraft, or many birds at such a height, Vazquez kept them safe from easily being spotted or tracked by anyone on the ground.

"That's it," Vazquez confirmed. "You know I'm staying this high for a reason, and should something happen where you need to land, make it very gradual if at all possible. You'd basically feather the control wheel to a downward angle and get the plane level when you're very close to landing."

Metzger nodded.

"Directional gyro," he continued as he pointed to the final important gauge in his crash course. "Keeps us going in the right direction."

"Exactly," Vazquez confirmed.

Looking a bit like a safe combination dial, the directional gyro possessed numbers in intervals with hash marks marking denominations in between. Metzger didn't understand exactly what they meant, nor did he much care, because the four directions were represented by their designated letters. As long as the plane traveled south and a little bit east, that was all he needed to worry about.

"You've got the basics," Vazquez assured him. "We aren't going to run out of fuel any time soon, so it just needs to stay level."

"Just don't pass out."

Vazquez struggled to provide a grin.

"I'll do my best."

Glancing back, Metzger was reminded of the other struggle in his camp.

Naturally Luke felt heartbroken, but the man risked his own life for the betterment of the group at the airport. Metzger wondered if he did so believing he was the weakest link and it might be his one opportunity to contribute, or if he distracted the undead for the more personal reason of trying to save the man he loved.

Metzger finally looked to Albert until the man locked eyes with him.

"I hate to ask this, but how long?"

Albert immediately knew what he meant. They couldn't risk him dying and turning undead within a plane full of innocent, living people.

"It varies," he answered. "When people die it can take an hour, sometimes three or four. When I lose consciousness and don't wake up, it'll be time."

Luke looked away, so Albert made a request of Metzger directly.

"I want you to do it, so they don't have to."

Metzger nodded in understanding, a tear forming in one eye. After only knowing Albert the better part of two days he hated losing such a valuable member of the remaining civilized population, so he couldn't imagine Luke's agony. The statement also implied Albert didn't want Luke or Samantha seeing him in an altered state once he died.

He returned his attention to Vazquez who shook his head from side to side, as though trying to see straight, or rid himself of a headache. Metzger was about to say something to the pilot when the man slumped forward, straight into the control wheel, sending them into an immediate nosedive.

"Oh, shit!" Metzger exclaimed as he reached over to pull the pilot off the wheel and level the plane before all six of them plummeted into the ground below.

Fifteen

ortunately for Metzger, Vazquez had gotten them a few thousand feet off the ground, enough so that houses and businesses looked like ants below. After the initial panic where his heart skipped a few beats, Metzger collected his wits, pulling the pilot away from the control wheel, shaking him a few seconds to see if he regained consciousness.

His efforts failed, forcing him to grab hold of the identical control wheel on his side, keeping the plane steady while wondering how in the hell he was going to land the aircraft if necessary. Everyone else had taken notice of the incident, each leaning forward for a better look.

"Albert!" Metzger called to the back. "He lost consciousness. Anything we can do to remedy that?"

"We're a little limited on resources," Albert replied. "You need him out of the way?"

"It wouldn't hurt," Metzger answered, still trying to keep the plane steady with one hand, awkwardly reaching over to keep Vazquez's unconscious form from slumping forward.

From the brief lesson, Metzger knew that the twin control wheel allowed someone in either seat to fly the plane. In the movies people always moved the pilot out of the seat to assume control of a plane, and he instinctively wanted to do just that. He knew the controls necessary for takeoff were within reach of only the left seat, and either seat provided every switch or button needed for landing. Even so, he subliminally wanted the primary seat if he was about to assume control for an undetermined amount of time.

Flying the plane and landing it remained two entirely separate concepts in his mind, and he couldn't fathom bringing the Cessna in for a smooth landing on any surface.

Jillian and Luke soon reached the front, unbuckling Vazquez from his seat and dragging him into the aisle, allowing Metzger to reluctantly assume the pilot's seat since verbal instruction wasn't a substitute for flying experience. Knowing he had less than two hours of travel left ahead of him, Metzger simply needed to keep the plane steady, hoping Vazquez awoke from his unexpected slumber soon.

Despite his injury, Albert moved forward to assess the pilot, seeing if he could assist in any way.

"How is he?" Metzger inquired.

"Stable," Albert answered. "The bleeding stopped, but he lost a fair amount of blood."

"I need him awake within the next two hours, but sooner would be awesome."

"I can't exactly make any promises, Dan. He needs fluids and we don't exactly have medical supplies lying around."

Metzger looked out the windshield, seeing blue sky in front of him and the onset of fall colors below. He felt thankful for that, and the fact that the Cessna wasn't plummeting toward the colorful trees. Feeling somewhat bad for being short with Albert, a man who continued to assist others, even while fatally wounded, Metzger knew his nerves were getting the better of him.

"I appreciate anything you can do, Albert. I'll keep us steady as long as I can."

Over the course of nearly an hour, Metzger simply kept traveling in a southeasterly direction with an emphasis on the southerly. He felt certain even Vazquez wasn't going to land them exactly where they needed to be, but flying directly over the military base didn't feel like sound logic either. By taking to the air, they had turned a few days of travel, more than likely a few weeks, into a matter of hours. Knowing this, Metzger wasn't worried about driving the remainder of the way to Naval Station Norfolk.

Of course he needed to keep the Cessna in the air long enough to get close to Virginia, which felt doable thus far, but he knew the landing would be the tricky part.

Although not entirely comfortable with the plane, Metzger found himself able to keep it level and steady the entire time. He offered to let Samantha sit up front with him, hoping to keep her mind off Albert's slowly worsening condition. Without a word, she simply declined by shaking her head, openly concerned about losing yet *another* loved one in her life. Metzger couldn't imagine how any child coped after losing his or her parents, wondering how many of his school children and their parents survived the dawn of the undead.

Fever had begun to set in with Albert, along with a cold sweat throughout his body that he reported when asked.

"You've got to fight it," Luke encouraged.

"There is no fighting it," Albert replied evenly, resolved to let the toxin from the bite within his bloodstream run its course. "I'm just staying with you long enough to make sure you land, so I can see your new life."

"There isn't a life without you."

"What you did back there was so brave," Albert said, cradling his partner's face with one hand.

"If it hadn't been for you, I'm not sure I could've done it," Luke admitted, choking out the words as tears formed beneath his eyes.

At this point Albert was seated on the floor, propped against a seat, which started with him tending to Vazquez, and now because he grew too weak to move around. Time, it seemed, drew near for the former emergency room nurse to leave the living world. Luke cradled him, kissing him on the forehead as his eyes welled with tears.

Metzger turned to see more clouds and blue sky in front of them, daring to look down occasionally with the knowledge that he couldn't land the plane adequately if it began to fall out of the sky. He glanced twice out of surprise when Jillian assumed the co-pilot's seat beside him, though glad for the company. Putting on a headset, he handed her the other pair so they could speak and hear one another somewhat privately.

"I feel like we haven't had much time to talk," Metzger stated, glancing between her and the plane's console.

"It's been a hectic few days."

"You said you have family near the base? Have you talked to them recently?"

"Last week was the last time," Jillian replied. "The phones have all gone dead since then, so I don't know what to expect."

"Are they waiting for you?"

"My parents and a few cousins are trying to hold their home and forage for what food they can in the area."

Metzger sympathized with her plight, though he felt a bit guilty for carrying on a conversation, with Albert literally dying just a few feet behind him. Due to the dire circumstances, however, he needed a distraction from the perils of flying a plane. The landing gears were retracted, and he didn't have a clue how to draw them out if he needed to land. He tried studying the knobs and levers around him, but didn't dare play with any of them until absolutely necessary.

"What did you do before all this began?" Metzger asked Jillian.

"I was a student at Niagara University, studying history," she answered almost numbly, as though the thought of normal life felt abstract now.

"This is definitely a new chapter in the history of mankind. Maybe you'll end up recording it someday."

"Maybe."

"It's doubtful we'll ever find out what caused all of this," Metzger surmised.

"We heard it was terrorists."

"I just wonder what kind of terrorist creates a world in which no one can live."

"Maybe the kind that believes firmly in a life thereafter."

Looking to Jillian, he saw that she believed her statement, and knew all too well, even at her young age, what acts radicals were capable of carrying out. He understood religions in third world countries enough to know that some extremist groups preached it was acceptable to kill those who were non-believers. What he couldn't wrap his mind around was why they targeted indiscriminate groups, knowing full well some of their own fellow worshippers might be collateral damage.

"It's only been a month, and I'm already worried about the state of the world," Jillian admitted. "If people like the Wardens can take over a school and kill people for no reason, what hope is there for the rest of us?"

"There's always hope," Metzger said, sounding more optimistic than he felt. "I like to think some of us are left alive because of more than just luck."

"I'm not sure what to believe in anymore. When this all happened I was with my roommate in our basement apartment, hoping it was all just a bad dream."

"Basement apartment?"

"Yeah. Why do you ask?"

"I watched the news half the night in the basement of my house and fell asleep down there."

"It was terrible," Jillian said with a look of despondence. "We saw the news as it unfolded and my roommate left to find her family. I never saw her again."

Jillian paused momentarily.

"After seeing what was happening in the streets I didn't dare leave for a few days, even though the noises from the apartment above me were freaking me out."

"What was it?" Metzger inquired.

"At least a few people above me transformed into those things. I don't know if one bit the other, or what, but I kept hearing them thump around and growl every time some noise drew their attention. It was hard to sleep, thinking one of them or some looter might bust through my door any second."

Metzger couldn't help but think about the basement similarity, wondering if the substance that initially made people sick and turned them might have been too light to sink below ground. He always believed that the people within ground zero of the factory explosions were doomed the moment they breathed in any amount of the gaseous product, and perhaps the gas traveled further than anyone realized that fateful day.

"My sister was also attending school, so we talked for a few days when the phones were working," Jillian said. "We finally made plans to meet, knowing things weren't going to be safe in Buffalo much longer. She said she would come to me, but when she called me from outside my place to let me know she was there, that group snatched her. The kidnappers didn't spot me, but Molly and her group saw what happened and they approached me. I was scared to death until they offered me the opportunity to get my sister back."

Metzger wondered how Molly and her group were always one step behind the infamous Xavier and his Wardens, but he supposed the witnesses they talked to helped them compile facts and locations.

"I was told Deena didn't last long in their prison school, but no one really told me why. I'm guessing she bucked the system like your parents and they thought it was easier to make her disappear."

"I'm sorry to hear that," Metzger said, pausing before he continued. "You handle yourself pretty well. Did someone teach you firearms?"

"My father was in the Army. He taught me and Deena how to fish, hunt, and fire a gun. I'm not sure he ever realized we were girls, or he just didn't know any other way to raise us. We caught hell if we didn't attend church, even after we left for college."

Jillian drew a thin smile at the thought.

"Somehow he always knew when we weren't obeying his wishes."

"You make it sound like you're not expecting to find your family again."

"I'm bracing for the worst," Jillian admitted. "It's probably unrealistic to expect any shred of happiness in this world ever again."

She looked back to Albert with concern and despair.

"Don't blame yourself," Metzger said softly through the headset so only she could hear. "What happened back there could've been a lot worse."

"It could've just as easily been me," Jillian said in numbed monotone. "Is it wrong of me to think that?"

"No," Metzger muttered just above a whisper.

She provided a glance that indicated she indeed heard his reply, and appreciated him understanding. No one wanted to see someone they cared about ripped apart by the undead, but each of them appreciated the fact that they lived to see another day.

Both were disturbed by a commotion behind them that came in the form of multiple voices. Metzger immediately worried that Albert's health was failing severely, but as he turned he saw Vazquez coming to, shaking the cobwebs from his head. Jillian stepped away from her seat, allowing Metzger to move over once the pilot staggered forward to assume the left seat.

"Dear God, how long was I out?" Vazquez asked after accepting the primary headset from Metzger.

"An hour or so. Are you okay to fly?"

"I don't see how we have much of a choice. Did I pass out?"

"Yeah. Albert says you need fluids. Should we land?"

"I can keep going."

"If you black out again, I can't land this plane, and it's eventually going to run out of fuel."

Vazquez nodded.

"Not for another three or four hours. I'm feeling okay, so let's keep going. The closer we get to Virginia, the better."

"Fine."

Metzger spent the next few minutes carefully monitoring the situation around him. Albert grew more sweaty and pale, almost ashen in fact, as time passed. Vazquez continued to fly steadily, obviously reinvigorated by the rest that came with passing out for nearly an hour. He didn't say much, except to compliment Metzger on his novice flying abilities once or twice.

"Any idea where we are?" Metzger inquired, able to remain silent only so long.

"Not really," Vazquez answered. "Assuming you kept us heading in the right direction we should be somewhere over Maryland, or maybe the northern tip of Virginia. I'm just not seeing distinctive landmarks yet."

"I don't think I got us too far off course. If you're still wanting to get to Washington, you could set us down closer to your destination and we could find another ride to Virginia."

"Are you kidding?" Vazquez asked somewhat heatedly. "I got shot with all of you around me. I wouldn't make it one city block in that city by myself, so I'm sticking with all of you until I can assess the situation a little better. Besides, I'm not taking poor Albert to die in what I suspect is a warzone."

He said the last statement quietly enough that the other passengers didn't hear what might be interpreted as a callous statement.

"Hey, I was just offering an alternative," Metzger said defensively. "You've already saved me weeks of driving and walking by flying us this far, so it's the least I could do."

Vazquez lightened his expression slightly, realizing he'd overreacted.

"You've done most of the flying."

"I just kept it steady."

A few silent minutes passed before Vazquez spoke again.

"Sorry I snapped at you. If I'm being honest, I don't think I'll find my sister, even if I travel into Washington. Her only hope was safe passage with the people she worked with, and I'm not sure how long they kept the government up and running."

"I know from talking to my brother that ships can be deployed to house politicians and important people. I'm betting the President is alive somewhere on one of those ships, or in some kind of bunker."

"Lot of good he'll do if he can't communicate with anyone," Vazquez scoffed. "We're our own elected officials now, my friend."

A pop and a muffled boom from the left side of the plane ceased their conversation immediately as Vazquez looked anxiously outside the window. Metzger's mind initially believed someone from below shot at the plane, but considering their height he dismissed the thought right away.

"Our left engine just blew," Vazquez stated, and everyone could see what appeared to be smoke, or a mist, flowing from the engine as it gasped its last.

"How?" Metzger questioned, glancing to see everyone behind them staring nervously out the windows.

"It might have taken some damage at the airport from our stalker friends," the pilot answered as he tried looking over some gauges before the plane began tugging in the direction of the blown engine, forcing him to take countermeasures and pull hard against it with a grimace. "They probably hit the wing and we lost all of our fuel, or the fuckers nicked an oil line. I can get us on the ground, but it ain't gonna to be pretty."

"What can I do?" Metzger inquired nervously.

Vazquez quickly looked over the panel before him, trying to determine something specific.

"We have fuel, so they got the oil line with a lucky shot, or our shitty luck," he finally said. "Get everyone braced for landing. I'm not going to keep us up here with one engine and fight this thing in my condition."

Metzger motioned for everyone to get seated and click their seatbelts. He continued to watch as Luke assisted an agonized Albert back to his rear seat before securing his seatbelt for him. Sitting back with a pained, almost overwhelmed look about him, Albert couldn't even raise a hand to help Luke with the seatbelt. He appeared labored just moving and breathing at this point.

"How are we doing?" Metzger asked the pilot, noticing Vazquez was forced to focus most of his attention on keeping the control wheel moved to the right as he continued to compensate for the lack of one engine.

"So far, so good. Do me a favor and see if you can find us an open field or somewhere smooth to land once I get us lower."

Without a word, Metzger alternated his view between the front windshield and his side window, seeing objects on the ground grow larger with each passing second. Factories and houses showed more detail, and in time even hoards of the undead became visible. Roads and highways grew clearer, vehicles frozen in every direction atop their gray concrete and blacktop. A glance to his left showed Metzger what he thought for a split-second might be the White House, but a deeper stare revealed it was some stately government building, possibly not even in Washington, D.C.

"Focus," Vazquez said with a strained tone after catching Metzger's lengthy stare.

The control wheel fought him like a marlin on the waters of the Atlantic.

Metzger frantically looked in every direction, seeing only buildings below the group at first. Ahead of them, as the ground grew dangerously closer, he spotted what appeared to be a number of open fields. Between the speed of the plane and the distance from the ground he couldn't tell if the fields yielded corn, wheat, or any crop at all, and he certainly didn't see any better prospects further ahead.

"We've got fields straight ahead," he informed Vazquez.

"And ahead of them?"

Metzger craned his neck to see beyond the fields.

"They go on for a mile or two, and then there's a water tower, which probably means another town."

"Fields it is," Vazquez said more to himself than his co-pilot.

Vazquez fought to keep the Cessna level as he descended, and Metzger felt vibrations in the plane when the pilot maneuvered the flaps to slow their speed, and again when he lowered the landing gear. When the fields drew closer, Metzger expected to find corn stalks, wheat, or beans, the latter two obviously making for a smoother landing. Instead, orange specks began materializing on the ground.

"Shit," Metzger muttered.

"What does 'shit' mean?" Vazquez inquired, still too busy battling the plane to examine his surroundings closely.

"Pumpkin fields."

Vazquez rolled his eyes at the thought of landing atop the round, bumpy vegetables, still not changing course or pulling up.

"Too late now," he said. "Here's hoping we find a smooth patch to land on."

Metzger glanced behind him, finding a mix of apprehensive stares and eyes completely closed with death grips on the plane's interior. He remembered a commercial flight once as a teenager, where the landing felt much rougher than the takeoff, and that was under ideal conditions, on a solid runway constructed solely for planes.

He gripped the seat as they drew closer to the ground, seeing the pumpkins come into view, left to eventually decay in the field like the undead who stumbled past them. Double-checking his seatbelt quickly, Metzger found it secured before looking up to see the field coming at him like a 3-D movie.

"Brace yourselves!" Vazquez warned as the plane neared the ground at a greatly reduced speed, but still greater than the sluggish pace one desired when running over uneven ground, vines, and hard orange vegetables that might as well have been small boulders.

Looking intently for the smoothest part of the field possible, Vazquez attempted to touch down once, but the Cessna bounced like a ridable hopping ball that toddlers might use. Everyone was thrown about harshly in their seats, but Vazquez kept his hands on the controls, waiting only a few seconds for another smooth patch before setting the plane down again.

Unfortunately this section of the field had a bit of a slope that the pilot didn't notice until the wheels touched down. The front landing gear took the brunt of the damage as it struck the awkward landscape and a few pumpkins, finally snapping, which sent the Cessna nose-first into the ground. While the plane had slowed somewhat during the second landing attempt, the abrupt stop sent everyone lurching forward, providing them with minor cuts and bruises from the seatbelts and any debris hurled in their direction.

Metzger felt certain the seatbelt was going to cut him in half, but after being thrown forward he immediately felt his head and back slammed into the seat when the Cessna finally reached a state of inertia. Hearing moans and groans behind him, he turned to see everyone testing their limbs for injuries and trying to free themselves from their seatbelts. Seeing Vazquez slumped over without moving for a few seconds, Metzger placed his left hand on the pilot's shoulder, stirring the man slightly.

"Everyone okay?" he asked while trying to stir Vazquez, pondering their next move since they were in the middle of a pumpkin patch with no civilization nearby based on his last aerial view.

Vazquez finally sat back, a gash visible along the right side of his forehead where he struck the control wheel. Shaking his head, he tried to comprehend his surroundings as Metzger reached over to undo his seatbelt.

"We need to move," Metzger said. "I'm sure hundreds of undead saw and heard us flying overhead, and worse, the living might know we're here."

Like bears waking from hibernation, everyone tried their best to stand and gather their belongings, but their movements proved rather lethargic. Metzger grabbed a few of the guns and his swords, held together by the pack that he threw over his shoulder with a strap. Deciding he might not have time to return to the plane once he stepped outside, Metzger also grabbed the family photo and stuffed it into his belt along his back. The door required only a little bit of finagling before it swung down, granting Metzger access to the outside world where he was promptly greeted by half a dozen undead.

Staggering toward him from varying distances, they made for somewhat easy targets if time wasn't an issue and he could circle around them. He wanted to take them out silently with the short sword, but knew such a move was risky without backup. Drawing the .357, he fired the first two shots into the zombies closest to him, knowing the move only served to draw more danger his way. He quickly drew the sword from his pack with the remaining four attackers a safe distance away. One wore a dress as though she left church in her Sunday best and didn't make it far, and the one behind her wore greasy coveralls. His right eyeball hung halfway down his cheek, barely attached by the optic nerve, and his jaw remained covered by a five o'clock shadow that might have stayed the same length for eternity had Metzger not sliced his skull in half.

Sensing the others finally emerging from the plane, he charged the last two zombies, one of which tripped over a pumpkin vine in its hurry to eat his flesh.

Slicing the sword horizontally through the air, he beheaded the first of the two, stabbing the second one through the skull as it tried to lift itself from the ground.

Quickly checking his surroundings and seeing no danger, Metzger turned to assist everyone out of the plane, including Luke, who supported a severely ailing Albert. It felt almost ironic to Metzger that a man who aided thousands of people during his years of nursing now required assistance to walk at the end of his life. He appeared agonized, as though every step sent excruciating pain through every nerve ending in his body. Luke barely made it five steps away from the Cessna before gently laying Albert on the ground because the man couldn't continue walking.

"I can't go on," Albert said as everyone gathered around him. "My body feels like it's freezing and being prodded with a thousand hot pokers at the same time."

"We can't stay here," Metzger said as sympathetically as possible. "There are too many undead around here."

"You can leave me," Albert said, directing most of his focus on Luke.

"No," Luke said emphatically. He looked to Metzger. "We can't leave him out here."

Metzger paused only a few seconds, weighing his options.

"We're not leaving him."

"We weren't far from the road," Vazquez suggested. "It's in the open and we can defend ourselves until we find a vehicle."

"He *can't* travel," Luke said emphatically, nodding toward his lover.

"Then all of you stay put and I'll look for a vehicle. If things get hairy, just get in the plane and shut the door until I get back."

No one put an argument, and everyone in the group trusted Metzger implicitly.

"It's that way," Vazquez said, pointing behind Metzger. "I don't think it was far."

"Then I'll be right back."

Quickly finding out that the pilot was accurate in his assessment, Metzger located the road and a few vehicles parked off to one side. A newer car that resembled a station wagon was completely out of gas, much to his dismay, and a medium pickup truck held a zombie inside, which clawed at the window upon spying his approach.

Figuring the person died inside his own vehicle, Metzger assumed the truck was good to go. Seeing no other vehicles or buildings down either side of the road, he decided to report his findings to the group. Albert's injury hampered the group because none of them wanted to leave him behind, despite what he requested, and he cried out in pain whenever his body was touched or moved. Metzger hated the idea of waiting for the man to die, but didn't see any other options. Luke needed closure, and not to be wondering if the man he loved was roaming the earth in an undead state forever.

Personally owing Albert his life for saving him from the middle of an intersection, Metzger wasn't going to treat the man badly in life or death. He trudged back to the plane, listening and watching for any signs of undead, keeping the AK-47 in a ready position after loading a fresh magazine from his pack into the weapon. He threw his legs over the top of a wooden fence as he kept the Cessna in his view, seeing hundreds of pumpkins lining the slightly inclined field. He took a few steps forward before he realized no one appeared to be standing outside of the plane, still some distance away from him.

Not until he carefully rounded one side of the plane was he able to see everyone was huddled inside and two strangers were approaching the downed aircraft from the uphill portion of the field. Feeling his heart begin to race, Metzger ran directly toward the plane, prepared to deal with anyone who threatened his group in the most forceful of ways.

Sixteen

Guessing that his traveling companions had ducked into the plane for safety, Metzger approached the duo walking toward the Cessna, slowing from a sprint to a walk almost immediately. He noticed they held weapons of their own, and saw what he believed to be a dog of some sort walking close behind. Unable to move stealthily or take cover behind a crop that didn't even reach his kneecaps, Metzger simply moved straight toward the plane where they couldn't spot him until he moved to one side.

Drawing closer, he saw everyone huddled inside the Cessna, staring out the side windows facing the strangers. When he finally stepped around the left side of the plane, Metzger aimed the AK-47 at the duo, making enough noise that they had to notice him, yet a step away from cover if they opened fire.

Both the woman and the man took notice of him as the dog perked to attention, acting as though it might charge Metzger.

"Buster! No!" the husky man to Metzger's right said, ordering the dog to stay put.

Just under six feet tall and rather brawny, the man wore a camouflage jacket and tan tech pants with half a dozen pockets. Somewhere in his mid-forties, his black hair appeared to be thinning, and a thick goatee and mustache combination encircled his lips. He held an AR-15, which he refused to aim at Metzger as he ordered Buster to sit.

Beside him, a black woman closer to Metzger's age with kinky hair that barely reached her shoulders held a sidearm of some sort. She wore a rather vibrant purple sweatshirt, halfway unzipped over a blue tank top, along with black jeans.

Fashion sense mattered little in the apocalypse, and Metzger paid more attention to her reactions because she seemed to be following the lead of her companion.

"We don't mean any harm," the man said, still not raising his semi-automatic rifle. "We saw the plane and thought maybe you people needed help."

"You'll forgive me if I don't just take you at your word?" Metzger countered. "We've had some dealings with unsavory types already."

"Look, there's two of us, and a whole lot of you," the man said. "My name's Colby Sutton, and this is Gracine."

Metzger wasn't certain if Gracine's last name wasn't mentioned because the two were a couple, or because Sutton didn't know it.

"Where did you come from?" Metzger asked, wondering how they arrived so quickly at the crash site.

"We're taking shelter in a farmhouse just over the hill," Gracine said somewhat nervously, as though not expecting the encounter to take such a negative turn so quickly. "We have supplies."

"We have wounded," Metzger said, easing just enough to point his gun at the ground instead of at the duo.

Sutton clasped his own gun in the center, with his finger nowhere near the trigger, slowly putting it on the ground. Metzger noticed he possessed a sidearm which he did not offer to set aside, along with a few knives.

"We will help you if you let us," he said. "We've barely made it this far ourselves."

Metzger watched Buster with caution, seeing the dog remained on edge for some reason. He didn't seem fixated on ripping Metzger apart, which the former teacher appreciated, but something kept the pit bull agitated.

"Is he a purebred pit bull?" Metzger inquired, trying to make conversation while he decided if he trusted the pair.

"He is," Sutton answered. "Technically, he's a blue American Staffordshire Terrier. Pit bull is kind of a generic term they slap on any dog in Buster's family."

"Why's he on edge?"

"He probably smells them."

"Smells who?" Metzger asked.

"The undead."

A fully grown young adult, Buster possessed a mostly brownish coat with just a few white spots along his belly. His ears remained floppy instead of cropped and his tail wasn't clipped, indicating he hadn't been altered since birth, unless he was neutered.

Deciding Buster detected something he didn't, Metzger saw little option other than to accept help from the two strangers, hoping they weren't lying to him.

"We have someone who's been bitten," he revealed, trying to gauge their reactions to the statement.

Neither recoiled in horror, but both provided concerned expressions.

"We'll help however we can," Gracine assured him. "Can you all walk?"

"The house is about a quarter mile from here," Sutton added. "We came running outside the second we heard a plane."

"We kind of feared attracting the wrong attention once we knew we were crash landing," Metzger admitted as he knocked on the Cessna's door for his fellow travelers to open it.

Jillian emerged first, holding one of the other rifles from the stack in the middle of the Cessna. Obviously the group overheard the conversation outside, not entirely sold on whether or not they could trust the two strangers. Vazquez stepped out next, holding a pistol, while Luke assisted an agonized Albert with Samantha in tow.

"Can you walk?" Metzger asked Albert, who immediately shook his head negatively.

"You're going to have to leave me."

"I'm *not* leaving you," Metzger said, receiving a nod of appreciation from Luke. "There's a truck on the road not far from here. We can use it to take you up to the house."

Albert winced, though not from the pain and fever.

"We all know I'm not going to make it," he stated flatly. "You all need to get moving and just leave me behind."

"No," Metzger said defiantly. "I'm taking Mr. Sutton with me and we're getting that truck. None of us are in any condition to keep moving without some rest anyway."

He leaned in next to Jillian.

"If I'm not back safely with this guy in five minutes, do whatever it takes to keep everyone safe."

Jillian nodded.

Metzger looked to Sutton next.

"If you're serious about wanting to help, grab your gun. I have a feeling we'll need it."

"Now you're talking," Sutton said, scooping the AR-15 from the ground before following Metzger toward the road. He looked back at the pit bull, which looked eager to follow, despite his owner pointing at him. "Stay, Buster."

Giving the slightest of whimpers, the dog obeyed, simply heeling beside Gracine.

Once Metzger and Sutton were near the edge of the field, and closer to the road, Metzger finally spoke again.

"Why?"

"Why what?"

"Why would you want to help us? We don't have extra supplies, or food, and our group is injured as fuck."

Sutton simply looked at him with furrowed eyebrows, as though the question struck him as preposterous.

"Because it's the decent thing to do. What on earth have you seen that's got you this paranoid?"

"That's a longer story than we have time for."

Metzger put a hand on the fence, clearing it like a gymnast when he swung both legs over, while Sutton gingerly threw one leg over and planted it before virtually dragging his other leg across the top of the wooden fence.

"Are you and Gracine a thing?" Metzger inquired as they neared the two abandoned vehicles he'd already seen once.

"No," Sutton scoffed. "She seems nice, but we literally just met a few days ago in the last town."

"Where exactly is *here* anyway?" Metzger asked as he went straight for the truck, drawing interest from the zombie inside once again.

Sutton popped open the door of the truck, pulling a knife from a sheath along his waist. Still confined by a seatbelt, the zombie couldn't mount much of an attack as Sutton clutched it by the hair before swiftly stabbing it in the head.

"You're in the middle of nowhere, so to speak. This is Culpeper County, Virginia, and the closest settlement is an unincorporated town called Richardsville. Mostly family houses, some farms and such. The undead population is pretty low by default, so it seemed like a good place for me to hang out and loot for a while."

After Sutton undid the seatbelt, he yanked the zombie from inside the truck, throwing it unceremoniously on the ground. He assumed the driver's seat as Metzger went around and hopped into the passenger's side.

"No family?" he inquired of Sutton.

"None at the moment," the man answered in such an ambiguous, neutral tone that Metzger couldn't rule him out as a serial killer.

He seriously doubted Sutton was unlike most survivors who lost their families to a terrible plague and its even deadlier aftermath, but he wanted to know more about the man before trusting him.

Pushing the family issue didn't seem like a good topic of conversation at the moment, however.

"Where the hell were you guys trying to fly to anyway?" Sutton asked as he plowed through the nearby wooden fence, heading for the Cessna. "And why did you crash?"

"I'm not sure I can answer the second question, except to say an engine blew. As for the first, we're trying to reach the Navy base in Norfolk."

Sutton shot another questioning stare.

"That's about the last place I'd go."

"Why's that?"

"Sure there's strength in numbers, but that place is going to run out of supplies, and it's only a matter of time before soldiers ditch orders and logic to protect their families. And I'm not so sure they won't shoot strangers on sight, maybe thinking they're the dead heads."

"Yeah, well I have my reasons," Metzger said with more resolve than he suddenly felt.

His brother was simply a spoke in a much larger wheel known as the United States Navy. He couldn't control everything, and knowing Bryce, he would follow chain of command until the very end. For the first time since the day everything fell apart, Metzger questioned his blind ambition when it came to finding his family. He could very well walk up to the fence surrounding the military installation and get shot by someone believing he was a looter or an undead walker. Considering he hadn't heard from Bryce in well over a week, he contemplated his brother's health, or whether the *Ross* even made it to the East Coast.

When Sutton pulled beside the downed plane, Metzger climbed out to assist Albert into the truck bed. Everyone else, including Buster, jumped into the back, carrying minimal gear with them from the plane. Metzger decided to ride up front with Sutton to the farmhouse due to the crowded truck bed. Definitely one of the bumpiest rides taken during his life, Metzger felt sorrier for Albert who probably felt like a towel inside a commercial dryer.

"Was there anyone living in this place when you found it?" Metzger asked of Sutton.

"I wouldn't exactly call them living," Sutton answered. "We found an older farm couple inside stumbling around. They took their lives at some point, but didn't do it quite right. Shot themselves through the chests instead of the skulls. It looked like they each aimed a shotgun at the other and pulled the trigger."

"So you know how the reanimation thing works."

"Unless they've been living inside an underground bunker, I think everyone with a heartbeat knows how it works."

"Have you had to kill anyone yet? I mean a living someone."

"No," Sutton answered. "I've been combing rural areas, so I've barely encountered anyone the past few weeks."

Metzger felt certain the man was about to inquire whether or not *he'd* killed anyone, but they arrived at a large two-story farmhouse, complete with clothesline, a red barn on the property, and an older silo. Squirming somewhat nervously until the truck rolled to a stop, Metzger didn't want to answer the unasked question because his one slaying that wasn't self-defense wasn't exactly murder, but wasn't incredibly far from it.

Everyone exited the truck, making a group effort to carry Albert carefully from the truck bed to the house's back porch upon Sutton's recommendation. Several pieces of furniture, including a very comfortable loveseat sat within the enclosed porch. Large windows surrounded the enclosure, currently allowing warm sunlight to stream inside. Albert immediately seemed comforted by his surroundings, but Metzger questioned how many hours the man had left to breathe the country air.

Once the group had Albert settled on the loveseat, they went inside the house to explore their surroundings and mingle with their new hosts. Luke and Samantha stayed behind with Albert, and everyone respected their opportunity to say goodbye to a man they both cared deeply about. Aside from a brief respite from zombies, and allowing them to give Albert a halfway decent sendoff, staying at the farmhouse provided little else for the group.

Considering the events of the past several days, taking a little time to recuperate didn't sound entirely bad. At this point, Metzger didn't know where to find his brother, even if he reached the Norfolk city limits that very day. The last he knew, the *Ross* hadn't yet reached the docks of the base, which left several plausible scenarios floating through his mind.

His brother could be inside the base, he could have left to locate his wife and son, or the base could be overrun by the undead. Other terrible possibilities occurred to him, like the ship sinking at sea, or being stranded because it ran out of fuel. Navy ships relied on supply ships to bring them food, supplies, and fuel. If the government fell apart, or lost communication, as Bryce indicated, the men and women aboard any ship would be left to fend for themselves.

Much like it came and went during the search for his parents, Metzger began to question whether he wanted to know his brother's fate, particularly after discovering how the demise of his parents unfolded.

Much of the farmhouse appeared untouched, possibly because the two undead homeowners guarded it for so long after their incomplete suicide. A large table stained in a dark cherry color took up much of the dining room with matching chairs surrounding it. Virtually every piece of furniture in the kitchen and study was made from sturdy wood, containing either custom glass or mirrors. The living room contained a loveseat, a couch, and a few reclining chairs. What once served as a spacious area for entertaining guests now offered several places to sleep for journeyman travelers spending the night.

Now close to the middle of the afternoon, none of the people inside the house considered *not* staying the night there.

By comparison, the farmhouse felt like a safe haven to the open road or making camp with a larger group of strangers. Metzger touched a few of the antique trinkets sitting atop a desk when he passed by, realizing he seldom took time to figuratively smell the flowers and enjoy the few gifts life presented. Feeling more like a hunted wild animal these days, he often dodged the living while perpetually battling the undead. He wanted, more like *needed*, to get to a place where he could settle, both mentally and physically.

Knowing this, he couldn't afford to put off finding his brother, even if he might not like the end results.

Beyond the living room, Metzger found the master bedroom, which looked extremely appealing with a king-size bed until he noticed the two large pools of blood on the floor near the foot of the bed. A quick search of some dresser drawers provided him with a fresh, solid green T-shirt to replace his current sleeveless attire. He switched shirts, tossing the old one to the floor, regarding it as a reminder of the horrible flight and the dire events at the airport.

Hearing the floor creak behind him, Metzger whirled to find Sutton standing there.

"We buried them out near the barn, if that's what you're wondering. After we stabbed them in the skulls, of course."

"Thanks for the details," Metzger replied with sarcasm that rolled down Sutton's back like water on a duck.

"You're welcome. And I've got dibs on the bed."

Metzger nodded.

"Wasn't going to ask for it."

"There are more beds upstairs, too. And the dude on the porch was asking for you."

Metzger wondered if it was near the end for Albert. He really didn't want to be the one to plunge a blade into the man's skull, but certainly didn't want Luke to endure such an act himself.

"Thanks," he said before crossing the living room, finding the remainder of his group cautiously cheerful to be safe for the moment, enjoying their temporary surroundings without wearing their emotions on their sleeves.

He walked into the back porch, thankful to find Albert still clinging to life, looking about the same as he did during much of the plane trip. Someone had found him a shirt inside one of the farmhouse's closets, and an afghan they placed over him to keep him warm. Albert nodded at Metzger, but looked to Luke momentarily.

"Take Samantha inside, would you? I need a minute with Daniel."

Very much shaken by the events of the morning, Luke put forth a strong front and ushered their adopted daughter into the house to explore the new surroundings.

"Should I put you in for dinner tonight?" Metzger asked with a subtle grin, trying to draw a smile from the former emergency room nurse.

It worked.

"I don't have much of an appetite, I'm afraid. Look, I want to spend what time I have left with the both of them, but there was something I wanted you to know first."

"What's that?"

Albert coughed heavily a few times before speaking again, and Metzger knew whatever took hold of his body wasn't letting go. It looked like an amplified flu, quickly destroying him from the inside.

"I have no regrets about us coming with you, so don't pin any of this on yourself," Albert finally said. "Luke may think a little differently, but please take them both with you. You're going to be the only thing keeping them safe from those monsters out there. We should've left long ago, when this thing first started, but I was stubborn and thought we could make a stand at the house. I just never planned on the real monsters being other survivors."

"None of us did."

"What I'm saying is that I trust you, Daniel. Whether you know it or not, you're a natural leader. And I want you to take care of those two in there, even if Luke is an obstinate ass sometimes."

Metzger couldn't help but return a grin at the statement.

"I wouldn't be here if not for you, Albert. I'll do everything I can to protect them."

"You don't owe me. As I recall, you more than repaid the favor. The minute I saw you outnumbered by those thugs on the road I knew you were one of the good guys. A loner, maybe, but not someone out to murder and rape like some of those assholes."

Albert clasped his hand, and Metzger immediately felt his sweaty palms. His hand trembled slightly from the infection conquering his immune system.

"You'll do fine, Dan. I trust you with my family."

"I'm so sorry this happened to you," Metzger said, his emotions getting the better of him as a tear reached one eye.

"Don't be. We're all on borrowed time at this point. I'm just glad I got to spend my last few hours with the people I love. A lot of people don't get that opportunity these days."

"Is there anything else I can do?"

Albert swallowed hard before answering.

"When it's time, I don't want Luke to have to finish the job."

Metzger understood. No one wanted the unenviable task of keeping a loved one from turning after death. He certainly didn't want Luke or Samantha present for that, or them seeing Albert until whatever grave site ceremony took place.

"I'm so sorry about your parents," Albert said before another coughing fit. When it finally ended, he wiped his mouth, which was covered with mucus and a little bit of blood. "I hope you find your brother and make it work."

"Me too," Metzger said quietly. "I don't know where we'll go, but I'll do my best to keep everyone safe."

Albert clasped his hand between both of his own, squeezing with what little strength he still possessed.

"Thank you."

Metzger nodded reassuringly before standing to go find Luke and Samantha. He noticed Gracine speaking with Jillian as he walked through the house, glad people weren't being complete strangers to one another. He located Luke and Samantha on the second story, telling Luke that his partner was ready to see them again with just a subtle nod.

Once they departed, he took some time to explore the upstairs, finding two sizeable bedrooms and a bathroom. He peered out a few different windows, checking the land around the farm, seeing a few undead sauntering around one of the fields. Squinting to make certain his eyes didn't deceive him, he found Sutton walking toward the barn, carrying a shovel over one shoulder.

Already armed with the .357 and a large knife, Metzger felt comfortable stepping outside without larger firearms and the swords. Not wanting to alarm anyone else, he went out the door closest to the barn, walking across the yard to find Sutton. None of the undead had reached the yard, but they weren't far away. Metzger waited until he neared the barn before he peered inside, seeing nothing except some tools and a tractor. The sound of a shovel piercing the ground nearby reached his ears before he turned the nearest corner to find Sutton throwing dirt behind him as he dug beside two crudely marked gravesites.

"Thought I'd get a start on the grave before dark, but I didn't want to seem like a dick, so I didn't tell anyone," Sutton said without looking up from his digging.

"There was a time when that might have been considered disrespectful."

"I think some rules can be forgiven when we have pale freaks eating us."

"I wasn't going to argue," Metzger said assuredly. "There are some of those freaks in the field behind you, so I thought I'd keep watch."

Sutton nodded.

"Thanks."

Metzger watched his new potential ally dig one area almost three feet down before he shifted his focus on leveling out the rest of the grave. He couldn't fathom putting Albert in the ground, considering he'd just met the man a few days back. His luck had turned sour, completely so, when he stepped foot in Buffalo, so he hoped the change of scenery might bring some good fortune.

"You still intent on going to Norfolk?" Sutton asked a few minutes later, breaking his train of thought.

"My brother is supposed to be there with his ship soon, if he's not already. I haven't heard from him in about a week."

"So he's going to forsake his orders and take all of you in while making a stand there?"

"I'm not sure he has orders to forsake at this point. Realistically, it would be dangerous to stay there at the base. The food and weapon supply is sure to run out at some point."

"No shit," Sutton said as the growl of a zombie behind him startled both men.

Metzger drew his knife, easily stabbing the stumbling zombie in the skull as it reached forward for Sutton, focused completely on the grave digger. Two others lingered in the field, sure to walk their way once they heard the noise of the shovel unearthing soil.

"I'm going to deal with these two," Metzger said with a nod. "We don't want uninvited guests once we start the mourning process."

Metzger had to walk nearly fifty yards to reach the first straggler, which walked with its hands by its side and its head slightly tilted as though permanently stuck looking at the ground. The other wasn't very far behind, but enough so that he could deal with them individually.

Able to duck and weave with each of them, he waited until he safely got behind them or to their sides before unleashing the knife. Although they weren't incredibly hard to dispatch, he knew better than to *ever* grow complacent. Thanks to the distraction at the airport, Albert suffered the fatal bite that reduced his life to mere hours. Metzger hoped Xavier and his minions were rotting in hell for all of the misdeeds they carried out in life. He expected times to eventually get tough, but abduction and slave labor seemed like grossly inappropriate steps for a group to take immediately after civilization fell apart.

"Everything good?" Sutton asked when Metzger returned, still digging at the ground.

"So far. Hopefully they don't have friends nearby."

Metzger took a seat on the ground, crunching a few of the leaves that couldn't wait for the cooler fall weather to fall from their branches. He felt somewhat obligated to return to the house, but didn't particularly want to be around a group of people at the moment. Keeping the plane in the air drained him both physically and emotionally. His face felt flush, as though he was coming down with an illness due to the stress of the day, and being outside so much.

"So what's your story?" he decided to ask Sutton.

Sutton continued to dig momentarily, now nearly four feet deep throughout the grave. Metzger began to wonder if the man simply didn't want to answer, or had a darker reason for keeping silent.

"Why does everyone ask that nowadays, like our backstory replaces talking about the weather?" Sutton answered the question with a question.

"Maybe because trust doesn't come as easy any longer."

"It never came that easy for some of us in the first place. The world was becoming a shit pot for terrorists and people who got their feelings hurt on online forums. I spent my past few years preparing for the end, knowing it was going to come in one form or another."

"I'm sure it gets old being asked every time you meet someone," Metzger said. "Sorry I brought it up."

Both of them remained silent a moment, almost to the point that it neared awkwardness.

"Not much to tell," Sutton began without apologizing, but acting as though he felt somewhat like a jerk for his earlier statement. "I was married for the second time, but my wife didn't make it. She came home from work, already bitten, and I watched her die over the course of two days."

From what different people had said, Metzger viewed the timeline from bite to death was anywhere between a few hours and a day or two. He assumed the infection took people at different rates based on their age, overall health, and the degree of any additional injuries.

"Was Buster yours all along, or did you find him on the road?"

"He was mine. Saved me from my wife when she turned. He has a sense that tells the brain munchers apart from us."

"He doesn't attack them, does he?"

"No. He got bitten once, but survived without any issues. I think he learned a hard lesson from that little encounter."

Metzger found it interesting that animals didn't catch the disease, or suffer any ill effects from it. Of course they were far more susceptible to being ripped apart and devoured if cornered by the undead.

"I'm sorry about your wife," Metzger said later than he wished he had in the course of their conversation.

"Everyone's lost a wife, parents, kids. No need to be sorry."

Sutton stopped digging momentarily, planting the tip of the shovel into the ground so he could lean his elbow atop the handle. Sweat poured down his face, which displayed a reddish color from so much recent sun and the strenuous work of digging.

"I've been on the road almost since the beginning," Sutton confessed. "In between everything happening with my wife I spoke to my two sons, and they were going to try and make it to our old camp a few counties south of here. There's a small lake there with fresh water. Enough wild game and fish to make a go of it for a while. And the best part, no other people around."

Metzger provided a curious look, and Sutton immediately knew why.

"I know," Sutton said. "I lied about family earlier. That lack of trust thing goes both ways, you know."

"I take it they're both adults?" Metzger inquired, seeing no need to dwell on white lies.

"Yeah. One was living in Illinois with his girlfriend, and the other near Cleveland, working for a shipping company on the Great Lakes. I taught them how to take care of themselves when I had them, so they have a good chance."

"Not knowing sucks."

"Yeah," Sutton said as he jabbed the shovel into the ground. "It does."

Metzger stood, brushing dirt and leaf dust off his blue jeans.

"I know you're going there to meet your brother," Sutton said slowly, "but I'm not sure you should trust the military or any police force you come across."

"Why's that?"

"I had a few encounters with those types along the way, and they weren't interested in anything except protecting our infrastructure," Sutton answered, using air quotes when he spoke the last word. "While the rest of us were left to fend for ourselves, they were scrambling to save our politicians and military brass. Figures, the one chance we have to truly start over and they want to keep the same old tired machine running."

"You don't sound like a fan of government."

"Why would I be? They kept wanting to take our guns and have us pay for the people who were too lazy to work. I worked my whole life, paying taxes, and now I'm scrambling like a common criminal just to stay alive, rummaging through houses for food and shelter."

"Look at the bright side. We're some of the most important people in the world these days."

"There is that," Sutton said with a chuckle, tossing a clump of dirt to his side with the shovel. "Forgive me if I don't feel pampered in my new existence."

"Are you taking Gracine with you to the camp?"

Sutton gave him a slightly sour look, as though he didn't necessarily want anyone tagging along for the duration.

He stepped out of the grave, motioning for Metzger to follow him to the barn. Less than a minute later he opened the red double doors to reveal a white box truck inside. Tattooed with a few dents and at least one or two decal removals from prior service, the truck possessed the look of a survivor.

"I've been collecting supplies and food as I go," Sutton revealed. "Even dog food for Buster."

"Why are you telling me this?"

"Because I want you to take Gracine with you so I can take this truck to the camp."

"While I don't mind another person coming with us, it's not exactly up to me. I think Gracine should have a say in this."

"She will, but she can't come with me. I've got to put my family first."

Metzger understood the importance of family. After all, he was risking his own life by traveling on the road with complete strangers to find the last immediate member of his clan. And the only reason most of those people tagged along was because they shared a similar desire, or had already lost everyone important to them.

"It shouldn't be hard to cut the umbilical cord since you met just a few days ago," Metzger said, staring at the truck as Sutton eyeballed something over his shoulder. "I'm more concerned about how the hell you're going to get that truck across gridlocked highways to your camp."

Without a word, Sutton pulled his sidearm and began to raise it, leaving Metzger to wonder if something dangerous approached from behind, or the true danger stood directly in front of him, leading him into some kind of insidious trap from the beginning.

Seventeen

"**D**uck," Sutton ordered calmly, but firmly, as he aimed the sidearm just over Metzger's right shoulder.

Not wanting to suffer a bullet wound, or deal with temporary deafness, accompanied by a ringing of his ears, he dropped to his knees, plugging his ears with his forefingers.

Instead of a deafening blast, however, he heard a sound not quite like the movies where a brief high-pitched noise cut the air. This shot was definitely quieter than a firearm fired with no modifications, sounding more like a quick popping noise. Looking up almost immediately, he saw that Sutton indeed held a nine-millimeter pistol with a silencer attached to the end. Behind him, he spotted a zombie lying permanently dead on the ground, which must have crossed the road, and the yard, after hearing or spotting them opening the barn doors.

"Thanks," he said.

"Don't mention it."

"Where does one get a silenced weapon?" Metzger felt compelled to ask.

"I have several," Sutton said, replacing the weapon into a holster modified to house the weapon and its extension. "The problem is they require special ammo to keep them this quiet, and I only have so much left."

"Because you've shared it with the dead heads?"

"You could say that."

Metzger dusted off his jeans as Sutton began shutting the barn doors, securing his treasure trove once more. A bit surprised he hadn't heard the zombie's approach, Metzger figured it was far enough away that he would have put it down if Sutton hadn't.

"How long are you staying here before you move on?" he asked.

"How long are you?"

"We'll be heading out in the morning," Metzger answered.

"That was my plan as well. I was going to take Gracine a little further, but she's safer going with your group."

"When were you planning on breaking the news to her?"

"Soon. But I guess it'll have to be tonight."

Sutton walked over to the grave, resuming his digging not far from the two recent graves he provided for the couple who formerly occupied the house. Metzger couldn't fault the man for wanting to protect his remaining family, and despite his hardened exterior, Sutton exhibited mostly good morals.

Deciding few options presented themselves to keep his mind occupied, Metzger wanted to fetch the remaining items left in the Cessna before curious travelers looted the plane.

"I'm going to take the truck down to the plane to fetch the rest of our gear," he informed Sutton.

"You need any backup?" Sutton inquired, though his tone indicated that he wanted to finish his current task.

"No. I've got it."

Metzger walked to the house, first checking on Albert, finding Samantha and Luke keeping vigil over him. He could see the trio conversing, so he moved forward, seeing Jillian in the living room with Vazquez. He was lying on the couch with his head propped atop a pillow, appearing unconscious at first glance.

"How is he?"

"He's okay," Jillian answered. "Just resting."

"I'm heading down to the plane to get the rest of our stuff."

"Want company?"

"I've got it," he said assuredly.

Truth be told, Metzger wouldn't have minded some backup, but he needed the others to stay at the house. The two injured required monitoring, and he wanted to trust the two newcomers, but experience told him people could put forth trustworthy faces and be the complete opposite.

"Just keep an eye on things," he asked of Jillian. "I'll be back shortly."

She gave a nod in return.

Walking out to the truck, Metzger looked around the yard and surrounding fields, seeing no further undead as the sound of the shovel piercing dirt reached his ears. He glanced, but Sutton was focused on digging, as though he wasn't getting a paycheck until he finished. Climbing into the truck, Metzger followed the same path they took from the Cessna to the house in reverse. He reached the downed plane in a matter of minutes, finding several stragglers attracted to the scene, though none being the living variety.

He spotted three in his immediate vicinity, but he wanted to avoid making noise with gunfire. Instead of using the knife, however, Metzger climbed into the open Cessna, quickly recovering his swords. He drew the shorter of the two, his usual preference, and set to work by swinging at the skull of the female zombie closest to him.

Doing its job, the blade sliced cleanly through the skull, letting the top portion slide to the ground with gravity. A male zombie in a tattered T-shirt and badly torn blue jeans approached next, but as Metzger attempted the same maneuver, the blade caught in the side of the straggler's skull before reaching the brain.

"Fuck!" Metzger muttered to himself, trying to pry the sword loose as the zombie flailed its arms in an attempt to grab him and pull him closer for an early evening snack.

His heart began to race, and he felt like a lumberjack trying to pry his axe free from a worthy tree, needing to use some caution or risk snapping the blade. The fact that his life was in danger wasn't lost to him, but it happened so often he began to regard it as part of his daily routine. It occurred to him ever so briefly that the blade required some sharpening if the opportunity presented itself down the road.

Kicking the zombie away from him momentarily, Metzger drew his knife and pounced on it before it could regain solid footing, knocking it to the ground. Switching the blade to his left hand, he struck it in the skull opposite the side of the sword, finishing the young adult cut down in his prime.

Twice.

Standing, Metzger finally took a good look at the last undead straggler now ten feet away from him, and ambling toward him with a bloody scowl. Another young man, this one had blond hair cropped short, and a tall, solid build, appearing to have joined the ranks of the undead more recently than most.

He also wore current military fatigues like those used in the National Guard. Even as he growled and stumbled closer, Metzger didn't feel legitimate fear because his eyes fixated on the chest of the deceased soldier. A red line that looked like dried blood about three inches in length crossed the area where a living person's heart would beat within the chest cavity. It appeared this recently deceased soldier was possibly stabbed to death, leaving Metzger to wonder if an acquaintance who admitted to not trusting the military was capable of such an act.

Waiting until the zombie lurched toward him, Metzger easily dodged the mindless attacker, kicking the former soldier in the ass, knocking him to the ground. Finally able to pry his short sword from the skull of the downed zombie, Metzger quickly examined the blade, questioning the sharpness immediately. Instead of using it, he decided to use the knife on the soldier before the member of the undead made it to his feet. A swift jab through the temple left Metzger free of trouble in his immediate vicinity, but he now wondered where this soldier came from, and why he ended up stabbed through the heart.

Kneeling down, he positioned the soldier's body so he could access the torso, quickly undoing the clothes to find a stab wound near the heart. A cursory examination revealed no other wounds on the upper body until he saw some redness along the back of the neck. Flipping the body partway around, he saw three deep gouges streaming down the neck as though three fingers had slightly missed the mark and scratched the upper layers of his skin away.

He wondered if the soldier had been infected with deep scratches before his death. It made sense that infection within the bloodstream would cause someone to turn, even if they didn't die from the infection itself. Feeling left with more questions than answers, Metzger stood momentarily to look over the body.

Deciding he didn't want to wait for undead reinforcements to arrive, or leave Sutton around his people any longer than necessary, he quickly transferred every usable item from the Cessna to the truck bed. He kept his personal items aside, pocketing the sat phone after looking to find no missed calls or other activity. Mentally kicking himself for not grabbing the phone the first time around, he quickly remembered that the initial transfer from the Cessna to the truck wasn't particularly smooth.

After he placed the last pile safely into the truck bed, Metzger turned to look one last time at the soldier lying face down in the pumpkin patch, wishing he had the time and knowledge to carry out some sort of investigation. Instead, he climbed into the truck and drove uphill across the field to the farmhouse less than a mile away.

He arrived to find Sutton leaning on the shovel, taking a break from his digging now that only his upper torso was visible above the landscape. Ignoring him for the moment, Metzger walked inside, finding Gracine with Samantha on the couch, doing her best to distract the young girl from the adult problems surrounding her. They were seated on one of the living room sofas, so Metzger took a seat across from them and casually listened to Gracine teaching Samantha how to play a board game they'd found somewhere in the house. He noticed Buster sitting to the side of the couch, closest to Gracine, as though he'd taken a liking to her.

He waited until it was Samantha's move in the game before addressing Gracine directly.

"You could come with us if you want."

"I'm not sure I like the idea of walking up to a military installation," Gracine answered without looking up from the board game. "No offense."

"None taken, but you *should* come with us."

"Because Colby may not want me with him? I'm pretty sure I can convince him otherwise."

Metzger discovered she wasn't going to be easy to persuade, but he didn't want to be too forthcoming while Samantha sat within earshot.

"Have you really been with him the past few days?"

"Yes."

"Like side by side with him the entire time?"

Gracine looked up with a mildly hostile expression.

"What exactly are you getting at?"

"Nothing. I'm just concerned."

Now Gracine shot him a stare that indicated she knew there was more to his story than he dared tell.

"You'd be good for her," he said, nodding at Samantha as he swapped tactics.

"Mister, you don't even know me."

"I'm a reasonably good judge of character. If I thought you were evil, or a threat to us, we wouldn't be having this conversation."

Gracine looked as though she wanted to provide a rebuttal, but one glance at Samantha, who now paid some attention to their conversation and not the game, quickly changed her mind.

"Just think about it," Metzger said before standing and walking out of the living room before she could say anything more.

He next walked to the rear porch where he found Luke holding Albert's hand. Because it grew dark outside from graying clouds and the impending dusk, he couldn't see details very well. To him, it looked as though Albert might have lost consciousness, but the man spoke weakly a moment later. Luke took notice of Metzger standing at the doorway and stood to speak with him.

"He's getting weaker by the hour."

"When it's time, you can come get me," Metzger offered just above a whisper.

"I can't even think about it yet."

"Then spend what time you have left with him. I won't be far."

Luke appeared very apprehensive about a future without Albert, and the emptiness in his eyes gave Metzger the impression that he regretted ever leaving their humble abode. Metzger knew returning to their home would have bought them days, perhaps weeks together, but in the end someone else would have come for what they possessed.

Walking away, Metzger took the alternate route through the lower level bathroom and the master bedroom beyond it to reach the staircase. He didn't have to pass through the living room again. Starting up the stairs, he found Jillian making her way down, both stopping halfway to converse.

"I took Juan up there and helped him into bed," she said. "He drank some water, but I'm not sure he's going to be ready for travel anytime soon."

"The bullet went through, so we just need to watch for infection," Metzger suggested. "We may have to move tomorrow, regardless of whether or not we're ready."

He kept his voice down, knowing with the open stairwell Gracine might hear anything they said.

"What's wrong?" Jillian asked with concern.

"Nothing yet. I'm just not sure how long we're going to be welcome."

Metzger tilted his head slightly to his right, indicating someone might be listening below them. Jillian caught the hint and quit asking questions, providing a concerned expression.

"I'll do what I can," he assured her quietly before they both descended the stairway.

Metzger followed her through the living room and made his way to the kitchen, searching the pantry until he found some canned goods. He didn't feel particularly hungry, but decided to cook something while he had spare time, just to maintain his strength. Luckily the old farmhouse had a functioning propane gas stove in the kitchen, which required only a match or lighter to activate.

Making his way through the residence, he asked anyone readily available if they wanted anything to eat since he was going to cook. The farmhouse contained a propone tank that allowed the stove to function, providing them with easy means of cooking for the night. Gracine suggested something for Samantha, which Metzger acknowledged before frying some corned beef hash for himself, and one of the popular kid pastas from a can for Samantha. He felt like a heel preparing food with Albert not far from the kitchen, knowing nothing was going to make the situation less awkward.

Sutton returned to the house once dusk began making it difficult to see outside. By now the group had lit some candles and settled in, some even sleeping in shifts. Metzger remained at the kitchen table, not far from the back porch, waiting for any news about Albert. He wasn't convinced Luke could be trusted not to let Albert slip into the next world without informing anyone, thus endangering the entire group.

"Did you finish?" Metzger asked Sutton, his query intentionally vague.

"It'll suffice. Deeper than what the homeowners got for theirs."

"Want anything to eat?" Metzger offered, trying to strike up a conversation with Sutton, wanting to learn more about the man's motivations.

"I'm good."

Despite rejecting the offer for food, Sutton drew a chair at the kitchen table, providing Metzger with his greater objective.

"I can go with you partway through the state," Sutton said evenly, but quietly enough that no one else heard. "My camp is on the way to your suicide mission, so I'll stick with you as far as I can."

"This mean you're not going to break the news to Gracine?" Metzger inquired, keeping a calm demeanor while his brain felt as though it was melting from being idiotic and speaking out of turn.

"Oh, I'll tell her, but I'm going to convince her that her better play is to stay with you folks."

"On our suicide mission?"

"Well, I'll put it a little more politically correct than that."

Gracine entered the kitchen a few seconds later, staring both of them down as she crossed the area to look outside one of the windows.

"You two can stop deciding what's best for me," she said without turning around. "I survived this mess a full month just like the rest of y'all."

She turned around before speaking again.

"While it's better to have people, it definitely ain't a must. Not yet."

Having spoken her peace, Gracine left the room, presumably to stay with Samantha in the living room.

"Guess she told you," Metzger said after a few seconds, once he felt certain their words wouldn't be heard.

Sutton chuckled momentarily.

"I think that was directed at you."

Metzger simply nodded, indicating he didn't believe Sutton was a very good liar when it came to women. He found it difficult to fathom the man would murder a soldier in cold blood, but Metzger couldn't shake the image of the military man with a stab wound. Buster strolled into the kitchen, brushing against both men, trying to get one of them to pay some attention to him, or feed him.

"What does he eat?" Metzger asked, scratching the dog behind his ears, instantly making him Buster's best friend.

"I find dog food in different stores and houses, but in a pinch I'll cook him meat or find something in a can. It doesn't matter, because he gives off ferocious gas either way. If there's a silver lining to all of this, dog food isn't in real high demand these days."

"I'll bet," Metzger said, realizing he'd only seen a handful of wild or domesticated animals since leaving Ohio.

Both men jumped to their feet when a thumping sound against the outside of the house occurred on the other side of the kitchen wall.

"They're attracted to the light," Sutton said, looking to the candle centered on the kitchen table.

Metzger started to head for the door, but Sutton grabbed his forearm.

"It can wait 'til morning. There won't be enough of them to pose a danger overnight."

If Metzger trusted the man a bit more, he might have been touched by the show of concern, but he still wasn't convinced about Sutton's motives. Although he decided not to pursue the undead flocking to the house, he went around and made certain all of the blinds were lowered, and the curtains closed. The group didn't need every zombie within two miles attracted to the light like moths to a bug zapper.

Soon another thump joined the first, and the two bumped against the house in harmony, one right after the other, back and forth. At first it drove Metzger crazy, but eventually he grew tired sitting at the kitchen table and put his head down to rest his eyes for a moment. The rhythm of the undead striking the house's exterior began lulling him to sleep, and before he knew it he slipped into a state of unconsciousness.

***

Startled by the sound of Buster growling sometime in the middle of the night, Metzger was jolted awake, finding Sutton had fallen prey to sleep as well. Both men sat erect, stared at one another momentarily, and looked to Buster who was pointed at the back porch.

Metzger jumped from his seat, reaching the open door first, finding Luke seated beside the bed, holding Albert's hand. Looking at the clock along one of the porch's walls, Metzger discovered it was nearly five o'clock as Buster continued to make his concerns heard. Taking a cautious step toward the loveseat, Metzger stared at Albert's chest without blinking, finding that it didn't rise or fall for several seconds.

Buster already knew the cold, hard truth, and warned the others that Albert was no longer a living member of their collective group.

"Luke," Metzger said, trying to get the man's attention as he looked through teary eyes at his life partner.

It seemed Luke already knew, but wasn't letting go very easily. Metzger feared him getting bitten if the transformation happened to Albert's corpse sooner than later.

"Luke, we have to take care of it before he turns," Metzger said, trying to put the task at hand delicately.

He still didn't acknowledge Metzger, as though guilt kept him from leaving Albert's side.

Sutton eased up beside him, hand already placed on the knife at his side, but Metzger stuck a foreboding arm out to his side.

"I'll take care of it," he promised Sutton quietly.

Drawing his own knife, he took a step inside the porch, caught between respecting Luke's last few precious moments with Albert and having a potential zombie stumbling around the farmhouse and traumatizing Samantha at the very least.

"You can't let him turn, Luke. He's a danger to all of us now, and you don't want Samantha seeing him like that."

"What does it matter?" Luke retorted with an almost absent voice, still staring at Albert's body. "We're all going to end up like this."

"Look, I know it's not much consolation, but you still have us. We aren't going to let anything happen to either of you."

Luke finally turned to Metzger with tears in his eyes.

"The way you didn't let anything happen to him?"

Buster continued to emit a muffled growl, so Sutton led him to another part of the house, apparently content that Metzger had a handle on the situation.

"Luke, he made a choice for the both of you that he thought was right. Was he? I don't know. But I know this world doesn't often give second chances. Eventually your house would've been compromised, and who knows, maybe we'll get attacked heading to Norfolk. Personally, I just want to find some semblance of safety where we aren't getting attacked so we can rebuild society."

"That's a pipe dream. How can I lie to Samantha and tell her everything is going to be fine when she's seen what happens?"

"You don't have to lie. Kids aren't going to grow up like we did. They'll adapt to this world."

"Or they'll die."

"We *all* run that risk, Luke. Think of Samantha as a cub with a lot of bears around to protect her."

Luke looked to Albert, who still had yet to stir, or show indications of the transformation taking place within his body.

"It should've been me," he said. "Albert could help people. He was the rock, and I don't bring anything to the table. For anyone."

"What you did at the airport was one of the bravest things I've ever seen anyone do," Metzger confessed. "You did everything humanly possible to buy us time and lead the undead away from us."

"And it still wasn't enough."

Metzger had spent the past few minutes attempting to be reasonable and consoling, but he couldn't let Luke linger with a potential threat any longer.

"Luke, I can't say I'm sorry enough times, but we have to deal with Albert before he turns."

Luke drew a deep breath, hesitating momentarily as though he might ask to carry out the deed personally. Based on the man's erratic emotions since leaving the airport, Metzger wasn't certain he could trust Luke with a weapon at the moment.

"Just leave me with him," Luke finally muttered as though sleepwalking through the conversation at this point. "That way we can be together forever."

"Not forever," Metzger said, beginning to sound as irritated as he felt. "I wouldn't leave you both like that. And you can't just leave Samantha alone. You're the only thing she has left in this world, for better or worse, and I'm not going to let you be selfish and throw your life away."

"Selfish?" Luke questioned, his face flush with anger.

"Yes. Selfish."

Metzger finally felt angry for having to step up, because Luke had survived a full month based on Albert's actions, learning virtually no useful skills during that time.

"You don't get to check out just because you're facing a little adversity. I walked, drove, and crawled to Tonawanda to find out my parents were almost certainly dead. Did I lie down and die? No, I went ahead and did what good I could for the rest of you. Even though I barely knew the three of you, I considered it worth it to risk my own life to get you out of that school prison. You and I aren't that different. I'm not a soldier, and everything I can do I learned along the way, or from my parents while they were still around. You can learn, and contribute to the group as best you can."

Luke looked down to Albert, who appeared as though he was in a peaceful slumber atop the loveseat. Metzger also stared, thinking he saw one of the dead man's lips flinch slightly as the sound of a long, drawn out, growl-like exhale filled the room. Strangely, it could be heard just above utter silence, like the sound of a stereo with the volume control turned down to one. Metzger wondered why the man's lips didn't need to part for the sound to emerge, but he now knew that Buster wasn't indicating Albert was dead, so much as he knew he'd *been* dead and was now turning.

Metzger purposely stood behind Luke, knife in hand, ready to react if Albert's reanimated corpse made any aggressive moves in their direction. He wanted Luke to see Albert in this altered state, if only to make him understand that no part of Albert existed in the shell of a human body. As the eyelids slowly fluttered open, revealing glazed, pale eyes of a now caramel color, Luke tried to recoil and step back, but Metzger blocked his path intentionally. Albert's naturally blue eyes were transformed in death to a brown hue that looked so bright someone could have been shining a flashlight through them. From his limited science knowledge, Metzger knew the eyes stopped producing certain enzymes when death occurred, giving them a different appearance a few hours after death that lasted a limited amount of time.

For a moment the eyes focused on the ceiling, as though the body needed to adjust to the altered state before moving. Metzger questioned whether zombies simply remained motionless until something stirred their senses, causing them to rise and track down noises or track something they spotted. On numerous occasions he recalled seeing them seated in cars, or lying beside a road, simply waiting for something to activate their attention span.

Luke gasped, unintentionally drawing the attention of the newest member of the undead, who looked at him with those haunting, empty eyes. Albert no longer recognized Luke as anything except a warm meal.

"Albert?" Luke stammered, still pushing back against Metzger, who wasn't letting him off so easily, considering Albert remained a few feet away from them.

As though experiencing the body for the first time, the undead Albert tried to lurch toward the two men, falling to the ground immediately because he didn't place either foot on the ground before trying to stand. Now he began using his arms to crawl forward, before finally realizing the usefulness of his legs. It was as though it took a few minutes for muscle memory to kick in, but he began standing in a rather clumsy manner, still not making any real eye contact with either man. The throaty growl grew louder, and Metzger realized he needed to end this soon or risk the others hearing sounds of the undead inside the house.

"I can leave you two alone if you want," Metzger offered, his fingers clutching the knife in anticipation of needing to use it momentarily.

"No, I think I'm good," Luke said with an air of defeat in his voice, reacting much like Metzger anticipated.

"Go, so you don't have to see this," Metzger offered.

Luke didn't even look back as he ducked into the next room, leaving Metzger to confront the man he admired among the living, who saved his life from a group of vagabonds when anyone else might have left him to be shot or ripped apart by the undead.

"I'm sorry, Albert," he said quietly to the undead being before him, still trying to establish the simple task of standing before it attacked again.

Saving them both the wait, Metzger grabbed the zombie's right ear, holding the head steady as he jabbed the knife through Albert's skull from the other side. He barely found time to withdraw the blade before the undead Albert crumpled to the ground, no longer a threat to anyone.

He wiped both sides of the blade along the blanket left atop the loveseat to ensure he didn't accidentally contaminate anyone, himself included, with the blood left on the blade. A simple cut might infect someone with leftover blood, so he didn't take any chances, cleaning it each time he used it.

***

Leaving Luke to grieve, Metzger called upon Sutton to help him wrap Albert's body in some spare sheets. At first light, they stepped outside and dealt with the three zombies at the back of the house with knives and the silenced pistol. Almost like an undead family, the male, female, and child zombies provided some sleepless hours for some of the temporary residents inside the house overnight. By morning the undead trio had moved away from the house and separated within the yard, making them easy targets.

Both men heaved the body outside to the grave, wrapping the sheet around it as best they could before placing it within the grave. Metzger stood watch while Sutton placed the dirt over the body. Although Metzger offered to use the shovel, Sutton refused to trade roles, stating that he wanted to finish what he started.

Even though Sutton seemed peculiar and regimented, Metzger couldn't picture him murdering a soldier in cold blood. Everyone inside the house now knew of Albert's demise, simply waiting for the brief eulogy to provide some form of closure.

It didn't take long for the two men to bury Albert's body, but Metzger felt bad that they didn't have any kind of marker for the grave. Of course the past day was hectic between flying, crashing, dealing with the usual number of undead, and keeping peace between the members of his group and their temporary hosts.

Everyone else seemed to sense when they were finished as they all emerged from the house to pay their respects to a man they knew in varying degrees. Metzger listened as Vazquez spoke, noticing the man had some of his color back after a night where nothing could keep him from needed rest. The pilot said only a little, indicating he admired Albert's strength and resolve during their time as captives. Jillian offered a few kind words, though she couldn't elaborate, considering she met Albert for the first time when Molly's group took back the school.

Buster took to walking a circle around the group, sniffing the air for any undead intruders, and stopping periodically near each individual. Some of the group ignored him, remaining focused on Albert's eulogy, but occasionally he received a scratching of his head which caused a wag of his tail.

Metzger's turn to provide a eulogy arrived shortly, and although he didn't feel much like speaking, partly because he felt doing so would only irritate Luke all the more, he decided he owed it to one of the few kind people he'd met on the road.

"I wouldn't be standing here if it weren't for Albert," he began. "After a month on the road, avoiding people because I learned they couldn't be trusted, he was brave enough to save me from a group of assholes who wanted my stuff. He certainly didn't deserve what happened to him, and the same group of assholes who failed to kill me cost Albert his life."

Metzger paused a moment before speaking again.

"I owe Albert, Luke, and Samantha a debt of gratitude for taking me in when they could've left me for the zombies or that group. Albert was willing to help his fellow man, which makes him the best of us. I pray that he's found a better place than this world the rest of us are left to fix, or endure, the best we can."

Luke made brief eye contact with Metzger, giving a slight, though approving nod as he did so. From behind his back he pulled a marker of some sort, constructed from scrap wood and etched with what Metzger assumed was some kind of wood burning tool found in the house or the barn. He wasn't sure how such a tool could work without electricity unless they built a fire in the fireplace and used it unconventionally. The marker beheld no dates, or thoughtful inscription, but only the name Albert McConnell, and at that moment Metzger realized he never knew Albert's last name. For that matter, he didn't know Luke's or Samantha's either.

As Luke began a more personal eulogy than anyone else, Metzger listened as intently as he could, but his thoughts wandered occasionally to heading south and the possibility of sanctuary. He expected complications to arise from Albert's death that might separate his group, or at least cause tensions, but he needed answers sooner than later. Delaying might cost him a chance to see his brother as it had his parents, though Bryce likely had a hundred sailors around him, ready to defend whatever ship or outpost they opted to hold.

Luke was saying something about how he met Albert at the hospital after breaking his hand at work when the strangest noise reached Metzger's ears. It sounded like a corny jingle from a commercial, or an electronic game for kids, but as all eyes slowly turned in his direction, he realized the phone in his pocket was ringing with whatever ringtone his father had programed into it.

Eighteen

"Oh, God, I've got to take this!" Metzger apologized as he quickly fished the phone from his pocket, fumbling it momentarily.

He quickly overcame the urge to look at the Caller ID, because he would be willing to talk to virtually any living person at the moment, and his brother was the only person left in the world who knew the number to the sat phone.

His fingers felt like jelly as he fumbled to hit the green button to answer the call. It beeped when he finally pressed it, raising the phone to his ear in the same motion.

"Hello?" he answered, hearing only silence in return.

Pulling the phone down, he saw that the phone indicated the call was severed or failed. Instinct told him to pull up the missed call and call the number back, but he wasn't certain that sat phones worked the same as cell phones. If Bryce had indeed called, the Navy officer would find a way to call again. Metzger's hand shook as he held the phone in his palm, waiting for another call, not daring touch a single button on the sat phone.

"What happened?" Jillian asked, concern written across her face.

All eyes fell to Metzger, who could barely look up after the devastating dropped call.

"I don't know," he said quietly. "There wasn't anyone there when I answered."

He looked to Luke, who wore the same mildly shocked expression as everyone else.

"I'm sorry, Luke," he said. "I think it was my brother."

"Can you check?" Vazquez asked, looking at the phone as though volunteering to check it for him.

"I don't dare touch anything," Metzger said quickly, taking a step back from the group. "I don't want to screw it up if he tries to call back."

An awkward silence fell across the grave site momentarily until Metzger decided he wasn't getting another call anytime soon.

"Please continue, Luke," he said. "I'm so sorry."

Luke looked between a sheet of notes he'd been reading from and Metzger, as though uncertain about whether or not to move forward with his eulogy. Trying to avoid appearing disrespectful, uncertain of what the group was thinking at the moment, Metzger stuffed the phone into his pocket and stepped into the semicircle formed around the grave and Luke.

Metzger fell into his thoughts as the eulogy continued, wondering if Bryce indeed called, and if so, why the call was dropped. His brother wouldn't attempt the call if he was compromised in any way, or in the middle of danger, unless it was his last-ditch effort before communications were lost.

He felt consumed with worry, unable to concentrate on what should have been Albert's moment when those who knew him said farewell. The ceremony ended soon enough with Luke placing the natural grave marker at the head of the plot. Metzger figured within a year the marker would succumb to the elements and no one would ever know that a good man and a farming couple were buried beside the barn. Their bodies would provide food for the worms and bacteria eventually, while many of the undead denied the natural chain of decomposition by walking upright.

Lots of history was destined to be lost in the new world. Before the collapse of civilization, people could type in a few words online and discover anything about any person, or any event that history recorded. Now the world remained in fragmented colonies that would likely never meet one another.

By the time the entire eulogy ended, Metzger still hadn't received another call on his phone, which worried him greatly. Most of the group shuffled back to the house to begin gathering their belongings and what supplies they required for the next leg of their journey. Sutton had made it clear that he wanted to get moving with his supply truck toward his camp, and Metzger dared not linger, particularly if his brother landed in Norfolk only to find trouble awaiting his ship full of sailors.

Still holding the sat phone in his hands, wandering in the direction of the barn, Metzger anticipated another call, still wondering if the disconnection might have somehow been his fault.

"Watching a pot doesn't make it boil," a voice said behind him.

He turned to find Luke standing there with the folded piece of paper between two fingers, looking both somber and strengthened at the same time.

"I keep feeling like I screwed it up," Metzger admitted. "I don't even dare touch the thing in case another call comes in."

"Here," Luke said, motioning for the phone.

Metzger reluctantly handed it over, and Luke pushed a few buttons on the front before handing it back.

"It works very much like a cell phone," he said. "There's your missed call."

Metzger stared at it, finding the number familiar as one his brother had used from the *Ross* to call him previously. He felt even more disheartened for having missed the call.

"He'll call back," Luke said as though reading his mind, or at least his body language.

"I can only hope."

"I think the others are getting ready," Luke said, obviously trying to coax Metzger into taking action.

"I just hope I'm not leading all of you into some kind of deathtrap."

"None of us are in chains being dragged along, you know."

Metzger smirked.

"I know, but usually leaders have promises and guarantees. I can't offer much of anything, which makes me a pretty shitty leader."

"You've kept us alive out here in the open, and you survived an entire month on your own, which makes you stronger than most."

Metzger stepped toward the house, and Luke walked along with him.

"I was ready to let you move forward with Samantha and make a go of it here," Luke confessed. "Albert told me to stick with you, to trust in you, because I was too good to stay here, chained to a corpse."

A tear came to Luke's eye.

"I spent twelve years building a life with that man, finally in a neighborhood that didn't hate us, *finally* getting our home the way we wanted it. Things hadn't gone so well for me before Albert. He helped provide, he took care of our garden, and he was my rock who listened to me whenever I had a shitty day at work, or some gay basher gave me a hard time. Albert was the better of us. You wouldn't be alive right now if it weren't for him, because I didn't want to stop for you. Knowing what I know now, I was wrong for that. That makes me a piece of shit human being, I know."

"Then we're all pieces of shit, Luke," Metzger assured him. "We all have those momentary lapses in judgment."

"I wanted to blame you for what happened to Albert after he was bitten, for taking us out of the only happiness I've ever known, but in truth what happened to him is my fault."

"Your fault?" Metzger questioned with a raised eyebrow.

"I held him back. We stayed at that house for too long and it's because of me."

"Luke, you had an eight-year-old to care for. The open road is no place for a kid, believe me. I haven't seen many kids in my travels." He hesitated momentarily. "Not many that were breathing anyway."

Metzger hung his head after the last statement, thinking of the horrific memories that flooded his dreams on a nightly basis.

"It's my fault because this whole world scares me," Luke lamented. "Most of my arguments were with computers before, not with zombies trying to rip me apart with their teeth. The truth is, I'm scared to keep going, not for Samantha, but for me."

"You don't think I'm not scared too?"

"But you've dealt with this. It's almost second nature to you."

Metzger scoffed at the notion.

"I've been dealing with them a few at a time, careful to avoid the larger herds of them. When we get to Norfolk, I'm worried about what we're going to find there if the military hasn't cleared them out sufficiently."

Luke appeared to find a little comfort knowing he wasn't the only one gravely afraid of the undead.

Both men entered the farmhouse, finding everyone busy packing up supplies and personal belongings. Metzger discovered it was just past nine in the morning, leaving them plenty of daylight to get a start on the day. Personally, he needed to pack only a few weapons, since the remote car opener remained in one pocket, and the sat phone hadn't yet left his left hand since Luke handed it back to him. He felt a bit lost in all of the commotion, waiting for his brother to call back any second, knowing he needed to start moving southeast.

Finally snapping out of his trance, Metzger walked throughout the house to gather his items and see if anyone else required any assistance. Most everyone appeared to be making headway, so he approached Sutton in the ground floor bedroom about driving arrangements, knowing they needed to take the truck he found along the road until something roomier crossed their path.

"Does your offer still stand to travel partway through the state?"

"I don't see why not," Sutton answered. "You folks don't seem like the types to try and rob me blind."

"I think we can make do for a while with what we have."

Sutton took an armload of items and headed for the door with Metzger following, carrying his own bundle. When they reached the barn, Sutton opened the doors to reveal his box truck once more, placing his items inside the cab.

"Look, there's something I need to ask you about that's been bugging me," Metzger confessed, drawing a slightly perplexed stare from the man.

"Shoot."

"When I went down to the plane I encountered a few undead wandering around the area," Metzger said before hesitating slightly. "One of them was a soldier who'd been stabbed in the heart, and it looked like he died from that wound."

Saying nothing, Sutton turned to fidget with something inside the cab once again, as though stalling for time or avoiding the inevitable question.

"Gracine killed him if that's what you're after," Sutton said almost casually, still moving something around inside the cab.

Metzger absorbed the words, not quite sure what to ask next.

"You seem to have me pegged as some kind of bigot, sexist, homophobe who doesn't like the military," Sutton added. "So I can see why you'd jump to that conclusion. While a few of those things may be partly true, I'm no murderer."

"I wasn't judging," Metzger said. "The soldier looked recently deceased, so I wondered if you'd crossed him in your travels."

"Gracine killed him when he tried to rape her," Sutton said flatly after a few seconds of thought. "She probably wouldn't appreciate me telling you any of this, so keep it under wraps, but when we met, a band of five National Guard types were about to have their way with her."

Metzger frowned, hating that the standard practices of the old world went to the wayside with the collapse of society.

"What happened?" he dared ask.

Sutton shut the truck's door, looked toward the house, and seeing no one coming their way, began to relive the tale.

"Well, before I discovered the ol' truck here, I was in and out of vehicles, moving on foot sometimes. This happened to be one of those times, and I hear a commotion in the distance, so I'm careful, because you never know if it's going to be living douchebags or the gut eaters, so me and my M-16 quietly approach using cover only to discover five assholes about to take turns dipping their sticks in Gracine."

Metzger questioned how Sutton wasn't a writer with his colorful descriptions of absolutely everything, including the undead. He was slightly disturbed that anyone in the military or public safety realm would abandon their duty statements just because no one remained to judge them.

"I observed them a moment to see if there was any regret among the five," Sutton said slowly, crafting his words to effectively convey his meaning, and not because he harbored regrets. "There wasn't any turning back for any of them, and from what I noticed they each appeared to have a grayish-purple hue in their skin. Gracine said later she heard one of them say they'd breathed in some of the fumes near one of those factory incidents. So I guess they were on the way out, but wanted to have some fun first."

"Who does that?" Metzger questioned aloud.

"I didn't take the time to ask about their motivations. The one was already down on top of Gracine about to do his thing, and his buddies weren't keeping particularly sharp watch. I knew if I gave myself away they'd shoot me full of holes, so when the best opportunity came my way, I started shooting each of them in the head."

Sutton finally hesitated, the weight of taking human lives tugging at his conscience.

"Three of them were down by the time the fourth pulled his sidearm, but he didn't really know where to aim. He never had time to fire or take cover before I nailed him, too. This gave Gracine an opportunity to stab the last one, but she didn't get him *right* in the heart. He suffered, and she said it served him right. As I helped her up we both made the decision to leave him there to turn and rot away because he'd have time to think about his brief future."

Looking from the ground to Metzger, Sutton's face registered a bit of surprise.

"That was three days ago and about ten miles down the road," he admitted. "That dude must've been steady walking after he died, or something drew him this way."

"Maybe the sight of a plane," Metzger thought aloud.

"Maybe."

Sutton looked to the house again before patting the side of the truck a few times.

"Why are you saddling yourself down with these people?" he asked Metzger out of the blue.

"You say that like they're a burden."

"A gay dude, a kid, a girl barely out of her teens, and an injured pilot. You could blow this pop stand and stake out on your own without any worries."

"I realize you have a grand plan to see your family, and you've got all of these prepper techniques, food, and supplies ready to go, but the rest of us don't have it so easy," Metzger said, struggling to keep a calm, controlled voice, because he wasn't thrilled about the comment. "The man we just lost was an emergency room nurse, and gay or not, he was very handy in a pinch."

"Hey, I'm not judging," Sutton said, holding up his hands defensively. "I'm just wondering why you're with a group that isn't better equipped."

Metzger exhaled audibly through his nose.

"My first month on the road was hell, and when I did spot groups, they weren't usually the types I wanted to associate with. Two of these people saved me from certain death, so I returned the favor, and the others just chose to tag along. I was lucky to find a pilot, or I might not have gotten down here for another month. It feels good to finally have some people I can trust, and call me naïve, but maybe I'm looking to the future and reestablishing humanity in some fashion. I don't want to do that with a group of assholes."

"There isn't going to be humanity like we knew it," Sutton said almost bitterly. "It's going to get biblically violent before it ever gets better."

Metzger found it difficult not to agree with the man's take, already seeing murder and forms of slavery during his travels.

"Without technology to guide us," Sutton added, "we're barely better than the Stone Age, and it's going to take half a century to get people to cooperate, and another half to get groups to reverse engineer things to get the world up and running again."

Their conversation came to an abrupt end as Gracine exited the house with a pack strapped around her shoulder, walking in their direction. Samantha stood at the door momentarily before following, as though taking a liking to a strong female rather than Luke. Metzger felt bad, because he knew Luke was mourning, and probably didn't need another person turning away from him, but Luke also needed time to discover his purpose and place.

"I think everyone's ready," Gracine said, almost without turning her head, as she passed the two men to place her items in the back of the pickup truck.

Samantha stayed close on her heel, prompting Metzger to believe the girl might learn a thing or two from Gracine. Although she struggled, the girl lugged a pack with her, trying her best to help.

"You'd pass on having that around?" he asked Sutton.

"In a heartbeat," the man answered without emotion. "It'll slow you down and be the death of you. Mark my words."

Metzger shook his head, thinking no man should be an island with so much danger lurking everywhere.

Everyone loaded up within half an hour, bringing some necessary items from the farm like a chainsaw, a few heavy chains and tow straps, and some tools that might prove useful for striking the undead in their skulls. Metzger drove the pickup truck with Jillian seated beside him after Luke volunteered to ride in the back with Vazquez. Samantha and Gracine were permitted to ride with Sutton until he reached his destination further south. Buster was crammed in the cab as well, giving Samantha something to keep her occupied. The group had discovered an old road atlas in the house that covered the entire country, so Metzger asked Jillian to read the Virginia map to make certain Sutton led them in the correct direction.

Sutton already possessed maps, along with existing knowledge of some Virginia highways, but Metzger still felt leery of the man's agenda. As he steered toward the highway, following the box truck, he took one last, long glance at the Cessna, which remained surrounded by pumpkins and a few undead. He wished the plane could have taken them further down the line, but felt thankful they all survived the crash and found refuge for the evening. Having an idea what awaited them on the highways, Metzger felt his heart sink because he knew the journey to Norfolk wasn't going to be as simple as a leisurely drive over the course of a few hours.

During the first portion of their travels, rural roads and highways proved favorable and reasonably easy to navigate. Once they stopped to cut a fallen tree out of the middle of the road with the chainsaw, discovering a small truck with four-wheel-drive for Vazquez and Luke to drive. Devoid of any undead inside, the truck held a few extra supplies, and as an added bonus, didn't have blood smeared across the dash or windows like some abandoned vehicles. Both men were visibly relieved not to be traveling in the hard bed of the larger truck surrounded by gear.

Metzger kept the sat phone on the seat beside him so he didn't need to fumble for it if another call came his way. He wondered why Bryce hadn't tried contacting him again, growing worried about his brother's safety. Common sense told him his brother was a ranking officer in the Navy, surrounded by men and women who knew how to handle weapons against the living or the undead. He also suspected they were more informed than anyone in the world about the current situation, short of government leaders.

Sandwiched in the middle, Metzger followed Sutton's box truck while Luke drove behind him, allowing Vazquez to rest in the passenger's seat of the truck. The short convoy needed to drive only a few miles before they reached State Highway 17, which would take them virtually all the way to Norfolk, short of any necessary detours.

"What are the chances this goes smoothly?" Jillian asked while Metzger swerved around a few abandoned vehicles, following Sutton's lead.

"Knowing our luck, I bet we run into a dozen or so snags before we reach the shipyard."

"What about Colby's camp?"

"What about it?"

"Are we making a pit stop there?"

Metzger looked to Jillian before shaking his head.

"I don't think we're invited."

"He seemed to be coming around a little bit last night."

Metzger groaned.

"Maybe he'll come around. Why do you care if we see his camp anyway?"

Jillian shrugged.

"I guess I'm curious if it's safer than all the other places we've been."

"It's hard to think of anyplace as safe," Metzger thought aloud. "I'm thankful whenever I get a full night's sleep."

Jillian stared at the map off and on the next twenty minutes or so once the vehicles reached the highway. Metzger concentrated on every sign they passed, often asking Jillian if they were heading the right way until she gave a disgruntled sigh. Knowing to shut his mouth, because Sutton wasn't leading the group astray, Metzger wondered why brake lights remained steady on the box truck as it drew to a complete stop.

Metzger immediately jumped out of the truck to see what impeded their progress this time, figuring a cluster of vehicles required driving, or some gentle nudging, off the road. While he found a typical number of regular vehicles parked in varying positions and distances just ahead, a different sight troubled him far more.

"What the hell?" he asked, spying four tractor trailers with their loads sprawled in a straight line across the highway, which was four lanes in this area due to its proximity with Interstate 95 just ahead.

"This is a trap," Gracine said, stepping from the passenger side of the box truck, leading Samantha by the hand behind it for cover.

While the large trucks weren't parked bumper to bumper, there didn't appear to be any way getting around them without moving them. The center median was already smashed and buckled, allowing the two middle trucks to rest at slightly sloped angles in the grass. Somehow Metzger doubted the keys were waiting in their ignitions for ease of use, so he began looking around for danger.

Strangely, he didn't spy any undead wandering in their immediate vicinity.

"I might be able to move them," Gracine suggested, drawing stares from all of the men who had gotten out of the vehicles for a look. "I drove rigs across the country for a living."

"You're full of surprises," Luke commented.

"And we're sitting ducks," Metzger said, taking notice that Sutton and Buster weren't with them. "Where did Colby go?" he asked Gracine.

"I don't know. He got out of the truck just before we did."

"Can you see if one of those will start?" Metzger asked her, nodding at the trucks.

"Sure. Can you cover me?"

"We can try. Everyone grab a weapon."

Metzger didn't particularly love his choices when it came to long range shooting. He ended up grabbing the AK-47, hoping the iron sights worked accurately if they were attacked. Gracine left Samantha with Luke, carefully ducking between cars as she made her way to the big rigs blocking their path. Metzger couldn't imagine an entire group setting a trap and monitoring the trucks for hours on end each and every day. A scout, perhaps, but not a gang set on robbing travelers blind, staking their lives on surviving an attack *and* collecting booty afterwards.

Holding the rifle, Metzger continued to scan the area with his eyes, seeing no movement. He wondered if Sutton had sneaked ahead to attempt moving one of the big trucks, or to find a better vantage point. The man certainly wasn't going to abandon the group, and more importantly, his box truck full of supplies. Looking behind him, he found Luke holding a sidearm with Vazquez clutching the MP5 Metzger had used occasionally in the past. Color had returned to the pilot's cheeks, but he didn't look particularly fond of their current situation.

Jillian held an old hunting rifle found at the farmhouse with a limited number of rounds. Five or six, Metzger thought, hoping they didn't get into a shootout. Their limited resources, combined with the fact that their position made them easy targets, almost certainly ensured they wouldn't win.

Perhaps I'm just overreacting, Metzger thought, spying Gracine open the door to the rear truck. She disappeared momentarily, likely searching for keys, and as she emerged from the rig she shook her head negatively. That's when the entire group heard a bodiless voice.

"You should all throw down your weapons if you want to live," a man's voice with a bit of a twang stated.

Everyone in the group exchanged wide eyes, wondering what manner of trap they had just sprung.

Nineteen

etzger stiffened, trying to decipher the direction from which the voice originated. He thought it was near the big rigs, but all of the vehicles and no other outdoor noises created a reverberation of sorts. He motioned for everyone to duck and take cover amongst the vehicles around them, wondering what kind of threat they faced.

"We have the high ground, so we can see you," the voice continued. "These trucks were put here for our benefit, not for yours."

"Great," Metzger muttered. "A smartass."

A wooded area occupied the right side of the highway if one were facing the way the group had been traveling. To the left was an open field, which wouldn't provide a groundhog much cover, so he knew any potential attackers were either hiding behind the rigs or amongst the trees. He didn't really consider that high ground, but he supposed it beat ducking for cover within a sea of cars and trucks.

"There's nowhere to go," the charismatic voice continued. "We'd pick you off if you run into the fields, and the same is true if you tried backing your vehicles away."

Metzger now felt certain the voice originated from behind one of the rigs on their side of the highway. He wondered where the hell Sutton had gone, hoping the man didn't do something crazy to get them all shot.

"We aren't the dickhead murderer types," the voice continued. "We just want your shit, especially that nice-looking box truck. Come toward the rigs, drop your weapons, and you get to live. There are vehicles on the other side for the taking, provided you can get them started."

Gracine made it within a few car lengths of the group, knocking on one car's exterior to draw Metzger's attention.

"What are we doing?" she mouthed just above a whisper.

Before Metzger could answer a shot rang out, striking the car adjacent to Gracine, sending her sprawling closer to the ground for cover.

"My friends aren't as patient as I am," the voice stated. "See, they were hunters, but it's a lot easier getting goods this way, rather than lying in wait for animals in the woods. I guess you could say we're lying in wait for people who think they have somewhere to be."

"I want to beat this guy's smug ass," Vazquez commented, keeping his voice down. "We aren't seriously going to surrender, are we?"

"No," Metzger said firmly, though he'd been weighing every option frantically in his mind.

He didn't want them to become worker bees or murdered corpses lying in a ditch. Better to go out fighting than bend to someone else's will, Metzger figured.

Before the group could discuss strategy, or carefully search for better cover, another shot crackled through the air, but this time a groan, followed by a thud, was heard by Metzger and those around him.

It came from the wooded area. Panicked, hushed voices also now reached his ears from the same area, leading him to think someone had intervened on their behalf, or Sutton somehow gained an advantage.

Another shot rang out, then another a few seconds later, leaving everyone sandwiched between the cars looking to one another for answers. None of the bullets came their way, and after the third shot was fired, they heard a pained cry from the trees. Tense seconds turned into worrisome minutes as everyone wondered exactly what occurred. Metzger finally decided to scurry, using the cars for cover as he moved toward the rigs. No self-assured voice filled the air now, but as he drew closer he heard the same voice echoing some concern.

"Tony, talk to me," he heard the man say, possibly over a portable radio, giving away his location without meaning to. "Eric, Mike, say something."

Metzger now knew the man stood behind the truck furthest to the right, obviously trying desperately to reach his partners in crime. Getting down on all fours, he stared under the truck's trailer, seeing the man on his knees clutching some kind of radio. He didn't appear very threatening, wearing a baseball cap and tattered blue jeans with work boots. A few days of stubble remained on his face, and he wasn't especially tall or stout. Perhaps his voice was the only thing he had going for him.

Standing up, Metzger cautiously made his way around the back of the trailer, stepping around as he surprised the man, who was about thirty feet away. The man scrambled to snatch a gun on the ground, but Metzger found Sutton was already sneaking up from behind in the other direction. Sutton held a sniper rifle in his left hand, but the revolver in his right made a distinct click when he pulled back the hammer. He immediately placed it close to the man's ear, snuffing the mystery man's thoughts of grabbing the gun on the ground.

"We can renegotiate," the man said evenly as he raised his hands.

"You're lucky I don't blow your fucking head off," Sutton growled.

"We have stuff," the man said quickly, sounding more nervous now. "Take whatever you want."

"Two of your buddies are going to require medical attention," Sutton said. "The third didn't get off so lucky because I couldn't see his fat ass too well in the tree where he hid. You're going to give us the keys to at least one of these trucks, we're going to get on our merry way, and if you're lucky, we won't tie you up and leave you and your prick friends for the walking corpses."

"Sounds fair."

While Sutton secured the newly-identified voice, Metzger returned to the group to inform them of the developments. Gracine went to Sutton to see about keys, and once they retrieved the keys from the last truck in line from one of the injured men, she walked over to the semi to get it started.

Most of the group was curious, so while Luke shielded Samantha from much of the aftermath, the others walked over to the woods. All of the gunfire had taken a toll on the girl, so Luke stayed behind while Metzger walked with Jillian and Vazquez to the edge of the woods. There he saw several crude tree stands where the would-be snipers attempted to pin down any stragglers who stopped for the roadblock. One of them was indeed dead with a round through the chest, close to the heart, and one appeared to be on his way out, gasping for breath and bleeding profusely from a similar wound just slightly closer to the shoulder area. The third sniper was injured with a shoulder wound that caused him to wince whenever he moved. It bled minimally, practically guaranteeing his survival if he received no additional wounds.

Sutton picked up several pairs of handcuffs from the ground, displaying them to the others by holding them along one end. Each pair had what appeared to be dried blood on them, indicating the four men who tried to ambush them weren't benevolent captors as their voice had promised. Sutton took to handcuffing the speaker to the lesser injured man before handcuffing each of them to the dead and the dying man.

"You can't do this," the thin man with the twangy voice said as Sutton secured the last of the restraints.

"Because you were going to show us so much mercy?" Sutton countered. "There's plenty out there. You fucks were just being selfish and lazy. I'm giving you better than you deserve."

Metzger wasn't about to argue with anything Sutton deemed worthy for punishment, short of simply executing the two probable survivors. Leaving them to die with a minimal fighting chance didn't feel unreasonable, but he didn't like having murder on his conscience.

"I'm going to put these keys in one of those cars over yonder," Sutton said, holding up the handcuff keys, nodding toward the sea of vehicles parked beside the box truck. "By the time you find them we'll be long gone, and maybe the cannibalistic stiffs won't be here yet."

Knowing better than to push his luck, the man simply bit his lip and bided his time, waiting for the group to leave the area. Metzger gave one last look, seeing defeat in the lesser injured man's eyes, and perhaps some remorse for his wrongful deeds, as though he'd been talked into acting as a sniper. The more severely injured man didn't appear to be breathing at this point, making him dead weight for the two survivors. He questioned whether either or both might change their tactics or life choices if they managed to free themselves before being devoured by the undead.

Slowly, he turned and left, catching up to Sutton a moment later as the rest of the group followed their lead.

"How did you find those three guys in the woods?" Metzger inquired as they returned to their vehicles.

"With this," Sutton said, holding up the sniper rifle. "I managed to secure it from our military friends during our encounter. It has a thermal imaging scope on it, so their body heat lit them up like Christmas trees."

"Where's your dog?" Metzger asked.

"Left him in the truck. Gunfire makes him skittish sometimes, and I didn't want him running off in this mess."

Gracine required only a few minutes to move the semi, using it to ram a few cars out of the way and clear a more suitable path for them before finally parking it out of the way. Everyone kept vigilant watch for the undead or more potential attackers. The group finally climbed into their vehicles, prepared to head south to Sutton's camp, and eventually Norfolk. At this point Metzger spied several undead shuffling into the area, filtering around the numerous stranded vehicles. Sutton indeed kept his promise, hiding the handcuff keys inside a random car, not within eyesight of the bound men. As Metzger pulled away with Jillian beside him, he spied the two handcuffed survivors struggling to make their way onto the road.

He considered their chances of escaping the predicament better than fifty percent if they possessed any sort of survival instincts. Both of the living men were dragging their dead counterparts up to the road, struggling greatly with the added weight. Wondering why more people couldn't simply be cooperative in the apocalypse, Metzger appreciated the folks currently surrounding him.

Back to the grind of weaving in and out of stranded vehicles, the group didn't encounter any danger during the first several miles of driving. Metzger suspected they might have to spend the night somewhere, because driving was slow going, much like a traffic backup when the world was normal. He would've taken accidents and construction slowing traffic just to know people around him were alive, and not likely to attack him or see him as a source of nourishment.

Metzger felt certain they had only traveled about five miles within an hour's time when Sutton stepped on the brakes ahead of him and came to a complete stop once again.

"Not again," Jillian groaned.

"Let's hope not," Metzger said, stepping out of the truck immediately, finding Sutton already out of the box truck, staring skyward.

Before he laid eyes on it, Metzger heard a hum from the sky, remembering the sound of propeller aircraft during his childhood. No matter what he was doing outside, the sound of a plane or jet overhead always made him stop and look upward. What appeared to be a speck in the blue sky soon grew larger, and louder, until its details became clearer and Metzger could tell it was a sizable military aircraft. Strangely, when it drew close enough to examine, even a few thousand feet in the air, he could tell it was a transport rather than an attack aircraft.

Painted a drab gray, the aircraft certainly appeared large enough to haul troops, weapons, vehicles, or whatever the military wanted. Metzger assumed the aircraft remained under military control since he knew at least *some* portion of the armed forces remained active. He questioned why they would take a plane inland when the situation certainly had to be the same anywhere they went.

"What the hell?" he wondered aloud, questioning what or whom the military might be transporting.

And where.

"What the hell indeed?" Sutton echoed his words as the entire group exited their vehicles in stunned silence. "That was definitely military."

"What kind of operation would require transportation like that?" Jillian questioned.

"The kind that takes them halfway across the country or better," Sutton answered. "They're probably looking to bomb a bunch of the heavier populations to cover up their mistakes."

Metzger shot him an incredulous stare.

"Is everything about the military completely evil to you?"

"No. Just most of it."

"My brother is out there fighting for this country, and you would have him pegged as some mercenary about to murder men, women, and children without a conscience," Metzger said, growing angry at Sutton's intense distrust of the armed forces.

"Maybe that call was severed because they didn't want him talking to you," Sutton suggested. "For all you know they could've put a bullet in his head to silence him and set an example to the others."

"You're fucking insane," Metzger said as calmly as his nerves allowed, noticing that the rest of the group felt Sutton's words came off a bit too harsh based on their expressions.

"It's a little late for bombs and damage control," Gracine said, trying to break the growing tension. "I'm sure they have a good reason for taking their big ass plane in a westerly direction at this particular moment."

"My brother *is* going to call back and he *will* give me an update," Metzger said, pointing directly at Sutton.

"And maybe by then I'll be safe and sound at my camp where the military goon squad can't come round me up for their concentration camps."

By now the transport plane appeared the size of a fly in the distance, paying the small group no mind as it continued westward. Metzger personally harbored mixed feelings about a continued military presence. For one, he knew soldiers would protect the country's infrastructure, even if that meant rescuing and housing corrupt politicians. He also knew that his brother, like most soldiers, would continue to follow orders, which might contradict saving his wife and son, or meeting up with his brother.

Metzger prayed he would find Bryce alive and well, willing to settle for a fleeting moment, if and when they finally reached the naval base.

"If the military is still around, there is hope," Luke said, holding Samantha close to him.

"There is no hope so far as they're concerned," Sutton rebutted. "You can all call me hateful or whatever, but they aren't going to be rescuing people like us."

Shaking his head, Metzger turned away from Sutton, ready to continue their drive southeast, because he now knew navigating the roads along Virginia wasn't any easier than those between Cincinnati and Buffalo. Much to his surprise, he saw a member of the undead community silently approaching Luke and Samantha. Only a few feet behind Luke, it finally made a throaty groan, alerting everyone to its presence as Metzger drew his .357, aimed, and shot it squarely between the eyes as Luke instinctively ducked with Samantha.

Metzger would have been thrilled if that had been the end of it, but it seemed their time spent gawking at the aircraft and arguing about the trustworthiness of the military allowed a number of undead to draw dangerously close. The tattered zombies had approached from the nearby ditch, from beneath cars, and the highway behind the group where they found time to catch up to the vehicles.

"Get her inside!" Metzger yelled to Luke, speaking of Samantha.

Luke opened a door, hurrying Samantha inside just short of shoving her for her own safety. He stayed out, however, taking aim at the undead with his sidearm, waiting for them to draw nearer so he wouldn't miss.

Metzger didn't particularly want to take a stand against the undead, but several were too close that they might take a bite out of anyone trying to quickly duck into a vehicle. None were especially close to him, so he decided to cover Gracine and Vazquez while they shot a few undead, making their way around the vehicles.

"As soon as everyone's clear we need to get into the vehicles," he said, taking aim at a zombie who emerged from the ditch covered in slime and mud.

It drew near the bed of his current vehicle before Metzger shot it in the forehead. Sutton had one stumble near the front of the box truck, and as he was about to deal with it, a legless zombie grabbed his ankle from beneath the vehicle. It tried to pull his ankle closer for a meaty bite, but Sutton kicked his foot, trying to free it from the cold fingers of the zombie. Metzger was about to move forward and assist but Gracine beat him to it, blasting the standing zombie in the forehead as it drew within two feet of Sutton. By this time he had plucked his foot free of the immobile corpse, kneeling down to take aim. Metzger noticed the man drawing a strangely crooked grin as he took aim, blasting the horizontal zombie in the skull.

"Death comes for us all, my friend," he said, addressing Metzger with a broad smile when he holstered his sidearm.

"You're just not right," Metzger said, shaking his head and wondering about Sutton's overall mental stability.

Turning around to ensure everyone survived unscathed, he found Luke taking aim at one undead straggler dragging its left foot as it walked a course directly toward him. Waiting until the zombie was within his comfortable shooting proximity, Luke carefully took aim and pulled the trigger, but nothing happened. Surprise registered on Luke's face as he looked between the gun, the zombie, and the group standing too far from him to immediately assist.

Sutton raised his rifle, but Metzger halted him by putting up a hand, seeing the zombie draw dangerously close to Luke. One wrong change of direction by either might leave Luke wounded if Sutton corrected his aim on the fly. Metzger skidded across the hood of a nearby car, heading for Luke as the zombie attacked him. Instead of letting it sink its teeth into his shoulder, Luke fell backwards, taking the undead attacker down with him. The move allowed him to cup both hands beneath the jaw of the zombie to avoid getting bitten, while keeping the threat literally at an arm's length.

Gracine had also started moving to assist Luke, but Metzger arrived first, finding Luke unable to repel the assault much longer. With powerful jaws, and dead nerve endings that kept their bodies from feeling pain, the undead continued on with only one purpose. This zombie intended to make a meal out of Luke, and kept lurching forward until Metzger arrived and sunk a knife into the side of its skull, ending the struggle before any damage occurred.

"You okay?" he asked Luke, assisting him to his feet after offering his hand.

"Yeah. Thanks."

Sutton walked over, holding out his hand, silently asking for the firearm, which Luke surrendered without words. Starting with the safety, Sutton found it in the firing position, so he popped out the magazine, finding it full of ammunition. Next, he racked the slide, finding no ammunition within the chamber ready for firing. Frowning, he replaced the magazine, racked the slide again, and put the safety in the non-firing position.

"You aren't always going to have others around to save your ass," Sutton commented, virtually slapping the firearm into Luke's open hand when he returned it.

Luke hung his head, wanting to be a helpful part of the group, but his inexperience held him back.

"I just forgot to rack the thing when I reloaded it," he commented.

"Not to worry," Metzger said. "If we ever get a minute, we can give you some refresher courses."

Looking around, he found their surroundings safe enough to jump in the vehicles and embark on the next phase of their journey until something else stopped them.

Luke brought Samantha along with Vazquez in their vehicle, which Metzger considered appropriate. It wasn't fair for him to dump her off to Gracine for too long, and he needed to be there for the girl in Albert's absence. Besides, he wasn't certain how Sutton behaved around the girl, and he didn't personally trust in the man's complete sanity just yet.

Even so, Metzger followed him down the road, which appeared clear for a few miles before more clusters of abandoned vehicles slowed the convoy. Looking out his window, Metzger saw the graying faces occasionally as they clawed against windows, possibly trapped forever inside the vehicles where they died. They looked absolutely ravenous, gnashing their teeth and scratching their lengthening fingernails against the glass. Metzger wondered if they eventually faded away and stopped functioning altogether without nourishment, or their bodies worked in some minimal capacity that kept them moving along virtually forever.

He felt certain some odd scientist remained among the living that would take the time and effort to dissect them and see what made them tick, and Metzger wasn't sure he wanted to meet such a person.

It barely bothered Metzger that such intense situations failed to faze him. He did what he could to stay alive and protect others, fully expecting his life to reach an abrupt end one day. Getting bitten by the undead seemed the most probable ending, but he didn't want to suffer like Albert had for hours on end. The alternative was finding a safe haven and starting anew, or putting faith in the military to create a safe environment.

Travel became slow once again, and twice the group stopped to remove obstacles from their path, including a bus and a large felled tree. The tree felt like a trap, and perhaps it was at some point, but no one remained in the area to threaten the travelers. It took almost an hour to cut the tree into manageable chunks and move them off to the side of the road because the chainsaw required occasional maintenance.

"We need to consider shelter for the night," Sutton commented as they rested once the last chunk of wood was safely moved aside.

"Are you suggesting your camp," Gracine said, poking the bear, because everyone now understood that Sutton didn't plan on having company at his private campsite.

At least not permanently.

"My camp is about ten miles off the highway when we get to the exit," Sutton revealed. He looked up to the sun, then down to his watch, and made a sour face.

"It's about five now, and it'll be dark when we get to the exit if we keep going. I don't think any of us want to be driving on side roads or through the woods in the dark."

"Agreed," Metzger said. "We can safely travel another hour at most. Any towns in our near future?"

"We aren't far from Port Royal," Sutton said, looking at his map. "It's a little off the highway, maybe ten miles from us, and it doesn't have much aside from some scattered houses. We could spend the night and maybe scrounge up some supplies if it hasn't been looted."

"Sounds perfect," Luke said. "How long before we reach Norfolk?" he asked Metzger.

"At the rate we're going, it could be a few days. I didn't realize just *how* busy Highway 17 was."

"It was always a joy getting to my camp," Sutton scoffed. "It and Route 301were almost as bad as the interstates when it came to heavy traffic. What I find hard to believe is how this many people never made it to their destinations."

Whenever the group stepped from the vehicles it always seemed as though a line of disjointed vehicles occupied the highway for miles in either direction. Sometimes it wasn't as bad, and the heavier population of vehicles, much like the undead, appeared closer to the cities and larger towns.

Metzger considered deviating from the highway a necessary evil, because they didn't want to be traveling after dark. Navigating roads filled with undead, vehicles, and often unseen hazards proved difficult enough during daylight hours, and he didn't want to give any living aggressors an advantage in the darkness. When they exited Route 17, driving became much easier on county roads. Barely any vehicles, and only a handful of undead, were seen as they made their way into the tiny community of Port Royal.

"Did you know that John Wilkes Booth was killed by the Union Cavalry not far from here?" Jillian asked when they neared the heart of town.

"You really do know your history."

"And I read it on a sign back there," Jillian said, giving them both a momentary chuckle.

The main drag in Port Royal, if it could be called that, was literally less than a dozen buildings, mostly residences. Metzger figured there might be more to see, but the town appeared spread out, and none too populated with buildings in any area. It wasn't until they passed what may have been the only restaurant in town that Metzger grew slightly concerned.

Sutton didn't slow down for these buildings, apparently having something different in mind as he drove closer to the opposite highway intersecting the other side of the town.

In front of a restaurant and gift shop combination he noticed something odd in the tree line behind the white and yellow building. Nailed and tied to a crucifix, a zombie leaned its head forward and snapped its teeth together upon seeing the three vehicles slowly passing by. It wore tattered clothes, already faded from being outdoors in the sun so much. It was male, and part of its face appeared torn away, as though bitten in life before he died. His dark hair was matted to his head from moisture and a complete lack of hygiene that accompanied death.

Metzger considered the macabre scene a warning to stay clear of the restaurant because someone the flipside of sane had claimed stake on the property.

Ahead of them, in front of the restaurant, two more undead hung by their necks along the front sign, almost ten feet off the ground. Although the sign stood more than twenty feet tall, it possessed some horizontal posts at the base of the signage that someone had used to string up the two zombies. They swung their feet wildly, growling in protest to reach the ground and stalk the prey before them. One was female, wearing her faded Sunday best dress, and the other a male wearing coveralls, like a mechanic might don for a day in the garage, or work in a factory.

"Someone has a Halloween fetish, or they don't want strangers in these here parts," Jillian said, trying on a Southern accent.

"That's an understatement," Metzger said, figuring Sutton would lead them down the road to safe accommodations.

He soon discovered Sutton was a wildcard who couldn't always be counted on to make the rational move.

Sutton pulled over near the side of the restaurant where no windows faced the parking lot, which Metzger considered intelligent.

"Why are we pulling over here?" he questioned Sutton the moment both of them stepped out of their vehicles.

"Someone could be here."

"Isn't that reason enough for moving on down the road?"

"Normally, yes, but if someone is loony enough to put twitching zombies on display, do you really want to take a chance of them coming after us in the middle of the night?"

Metzger sighed through his nose, knowing Sutton was right once again, but not ready to admit it.

"I propose we check this place over before moving along," Sutton offered. "Maybe the crazy son-of-a-bitch is one of these braindead fuckers."

Metzger drew his .357 for protection, motioning for Sutton to lead the way since he hatched the idea.

"You want the rest of us?" Jillian asked while Metzger followed Sutton to the front door.

"No," he answered, barely turning around. "We're just going to scout it out first."

Metzger stepped carefully along the paved parking lot behind Sutton, not wanting to kick any empty cans or debris to alert someone to their presence. Something told him it might be too late for that, because the front entrance of the restaurant appeared comprised of glass from floor to ceiling when the group initially drove past. A thin dusty film covered much of it from the inside, preventing them from seeing any details or potential activity. Metzger suspected someone might have a natural security system on their hands, already alerted to the group now lingering outside the building.

On the way to the front door, the duo tried looking through the few windows along that side of the building. The windows were small and covered with dust from the inside, providing no clues about what awaited them. They were also located around shoulder height, possibly to discourage burglars from breaking in while the restaurant was operational. A set of five clerestory windows were built along a quarter-gable roof atop the main roof, impossible to reach without a ladder or a boost. Metzger sensed Sutton didn't want to waste much time casing the place as anyone inside was probably monitoring their actions.

Both men looked around cautiously at the front door when they reached it, seeing no danger outside the restaurant. The two zombies hanging from the front sign made throaty hissing noises, staring ominously at the duo as though they would be dinner if the roles were reversed. Sutton reached for the front door, and started to pull back as though being burned by an oven, due to his surprise that it was unlocked.

He pulled it open slowly, aiming the shotgun he'd brought with him inside. Metzger followed close behind, seeing the second set of dusty glass doors awaiting them, feeling something amiss. No one simply left a bountiful supply building wide-open without reason, and he didn't recall seeing any damage anywhere along the exterior to indicate a previous break-in. He and Sutton exchanged uneasy glances as Sutton reached for the metal pull handle to the second door, hearing a growl from inside too late as he pulled it open. The open door revealed a horrific sight in the gift shop area of the building, which was blocked off from the main restaurant by two closed swinging doors that appeared sealed together somehow.

Immediately the dozen zombies trapped inside the small gift shop area turned their attention to the two intruders. Before Metzger and Sutton could back out the way they came, however, a metallic snap was heard in the center of the first set of doors, and Metzger immediately knew they had sprung a trap. He threw his shoulder against the door, not budging it one inch, knowing someone had rigged it to lock only after people foolish enough to enter pulled on the second set of doors.

Something solid had locked the doors together, sealing Metzger and Sutton inside a certain deathtrap.

"Oh, fuck," Metzger muttered.

"What's that mean?" Sutton asked, personally ramming the door with his shoulder, discovering the same result. "Oh, fuck."

Twenty

Sutton immediately turned to deal with the zombies, who weren't incredibly quick to stagger their way.

"Shoot it!" he exclaimed, nodding toward the door.

Ideally, Metzger would have shot whatever dropped to lock both doors together, preventing their escape from the building, but he wasn't exactly certain where the device was located.

He used his .357 to take aim at the door below the metal push bar, finding the first shot broke through the glass, but didn't shatter the window as he expected. His peripheral vision caught Sutton trying to shove both of the interior doors shut to keep a dozen zombies at bay, but even his size and strength would give out shortly. Taking a step back, Metzger fired a second shot, which hit within an inch of the first, simply creating another hole with a cobweb surrounding it.

"Keep shooting!" Sutton exclaimed with a strained voice, trying to keep the growing mob of undead from bursting through the doors. "Same area!"

Metzger let the last four rounds fly in the same vicinity along the door, creating a much larger web of weakness, though the reinforced glass refused to simply shatter and fall.

"Shotgun," he said, receiving the weapon from Sutton a second later as the man struggled to keep the highly agitated zombies at bay.

Gunfire only made them want to burst through the door with more intensity.

Metzger used the butt of the shotgun to strike the weakened glass three times before a crack emerged from the bottom of the glass to the midway point near the push bar. He struck it one last time, shattering the lower portion of the glass, enough so that the two men could escape, just as the rest of the group came running up to the front entrance.

Crawling through the opening first, Metzger watched as Sutton held the door closed as long as he could before making a dive for the opening. The undead came pouring through the interior doors before Sutton was even halfway through the opening. They immediately grabbed for his legs and Sutton tried kicking them away. Metzger grabbed Sutton by one shoulder, virtually tugging him out of the building as Vazquez assisted along the other side. Both men might have collapsed and caught their breath momentarily, but the undead simply followed suit, dropping down to crawl through the fresh opening. A few continued in vain to push on the secured door, but quickly took notice of their undead brethren escaping the old building.

Metzger took aim with the shotgun, rather than waste time handing it back to Sutton, blasting the first undead attacker in the skull. Blood coated the glass and the yellow wooden walls behind the zombie as though someone had whipped a freshly-dipped paintbrush through the air with red paint. A second zombie forced its way through the opening and over its fallen comrade, receiving a similar fate once it reared its ugly head and yellowed teeth at Metzger. Everyone stood around in complete shock at the sight of ten more undead pushing and shoving at the doors to get outside.

"Did those people all die in there?" Jillian asked without blinking.

"Not sure," Sutton said. "But someone wanted us to be among their ranks."

"What's that mean?" Vazquez questioned.

"It means we sprung a trap and that's why we had to shoot the door," Metzger answered, feeling angered that someone guarded their stash with creatures worse than attack dogs.

Part of him wanted to blast every single one of the undead and investigate inside until he found the person responsible, but he also knew that someone capable of devising such an ingenious trap might be an engineer.

And might have more traps waiting inside.

It also explained, in part, why the person was able to rig undead props around the restaurant. Metzger knew it might take an insane person to wrangle the undead so fearlessly and create traps around and inside the building.

"Those people are varying degrees of decomposed," Luke noted, studying the undead who accidentally scrubbed the door's glass clean by rubbing against it, like flies trying to get to daylight through a window.

"Someone wanted to add us to their collection," Sutton surmised, a layer of fury bubbling beneath his calm exterior.

Metzger knew Sutton wanted to dispose of the undead, stomp inside, find whoever was responsible for the trap, and turn his head into red mush with shotgun pellets, but it wasn't the most rational play. While Metzger also felt furious that he was nearly bitten and turned into one of those monsters, he suspected more traps awaited them inside. He also doubted the insane person who created this restaurant of horrors dared go on the hunt beyond the grounds. That person likely wanted to protect something, whether it was supplies or his sick, mobile wax museum of zombies.

"I want to find the guy who did this," Sutton grumbled.

"How do you know it isn't a woman?" Gracine asked. "We can build shit, too."

"While a woman's mind is a complex labyrinth of emotions and intellect, I can't think of any female I've *ever* met capable of this kind of cruelty."

"Point taken," Gracine acknowledged, waving one hand in the air.

"We waste a lot of resources if we try taking this place," Metzger said. "And for what?"

"Some of these people were alive a few weeks, maybe a few days ago," Sutton countered. "They fell into this fucking trap just like we did, except they didn't make it out. You really want other people dying needlessly, or this fucker coming out and going on the prowl when he runs out of victims?"

Sutton appealed to Metzger's humanity, which Metzger detested. The man already knew how to push his buttons to get a desired response from him, and Metzger wasn't about to place other innocent people in danger. He knew other decent people still existed in the world, and he'd already seen how predators made short work of the unsuspecting.

"I'm not particularly interested in dying," he admitted. "I might have an idea that keeps us safe and solves our problem at the same time."

"Lay it on me," Sutton said.

***

A few minutes later, Metzger stood with Sutton near the box truck while the others guarded the door for escaping zombies, dealing with them as needed.

"I know you got some goodies from the military assholes that attacked Gracine," Metzger stated. "I'm wondering if you got some tear gas or something that might bring our mad scientist out to us, assuming he's inside and alive."

Sutton cupped his chin in thought.

"I might just have something like that. We got a few grenades, but that seems like overkill and might blow up anything useful inside."

"I'm not sure this guy has a stash worth taking," Metzger said. "I think he's just fucked up in the head."

"Or he's constantly adding to his defense system."

Sutton rummaged through a tactical backpack after opening the back of the box truck, sorting through a few guns and random items until he pulled out a small, silver canister with a pull pin. The side of the can readily indicated the contents were riot gas, and the use of such gas seemed straightforward.

Sutton clutched the tear gas grenade as the two men returned to the front, finding Vazquez carefully examining the center of the two doors.

"I think I found how this thing locked behind you," he said. "I can probably pop it if you want to deal with the undead."

"Let them come to you for now," Metzger said. "They'll be easier to deal with that way. We're about to flush any living souls from the building a different way."

Sutton held up the canister for everyone to see, so they knew not to stand beside the door and breathe in the noxious fumes about to come their way. Everyone nodded in understanding, allowing the two men to step to the front of the building where Metzger had spied the clerestory windows earlier.

"You're going to want to cover the employee entrance in back," Metzger said as Sutton prepared to give him a boost onto the roof.

"I know. I'll have a present or two waiting for our host if he comes out."

With Sutton's help, Metzger managed to pull himself up to the angled roof, ascending the pitch almost ten feet before he reached the tiny windows that provided light inside the building under optimal conditions. He waited about thirty seconds for Sutton to get positioned along the back before swiftly kicking one of the windows with the steel toe of his boot, pulling the pin, and lobbing the riot gas into the restaurant below. The sound of the canister hissing began instantly, and he was able to see a cloud of white smoke forming below, as bright as any he'd ever seen in the sky.

Not waiting around to breathe in the gas that filtered upward, Metzger climbed the roof a few feet higher before crossing the peak and descending the other side to observe Sutton. He took the time to dump the expended casings from his revolver, letting them hit the roof and roll down to the gutter. Since he didn't wear any kind of gun belt, simply using a holster that attached to his belt, he didn't have the luxury of carrying lots of extra rounds. Fishing through his right front pocket, he loaded six fresh bullets into the gun as he carefully stepped to the edge of the roof, seeing Sutton already aiming his own sidearm at the painted red metal door.

Sutton placed his index finger over his lips, indicating for Metzger to remain quiet. Standing on the edge of a roof, carefully reloading his weapon, Metzger didn't exactly have plans to yell or jump up and down. Not quite a full minute passed before the two men heard heavy coughing from inside the building, exchanging knowing glances that someone might be bursting out of the metal door at any moment.

A gunshot rang out from behind him, and Metzger wondered why the others opted to shoot the undead rather than silently take them out one at a time. When a second gunshot filled the air, he looked to Sutton, receiving a nod of approval before running up the roof and down the other side where the group was confronted by the entire group of zombies from inside the gift shop. It appeared that eight undead were left, now backing the group further into the parking lot where they were trying to make a stand. Metzger didn't dare aim down and start shooting, because if he missed, he might hit one of his allies who were just on the other side of the undead.

With the undead focused on the five survivors in front of them, Metzger decided to take advantage from behind to keep from attracting more undead, or marauders who might want their goods. Placing his hand at the edge of the roof, Metzger quickly positioned himself as close to the ground as possible before leaping down to the paved parking lot. Despite bracing his legs for impact and trying to deaden the impact, he still felt some pain in his left knee when he landed, but there wasn't time to stop.

"Someone undid the thing holding the door," Vazquez yelled to him, which didn't distract the zombies one little bit.

Metzger drew his knife from its sheath along the left side of his belt after replacing the gun, immediately stabbing the closest zombie in the skull, downing it. He barely pulled the blade free before it was dragged to the ground, potentially taking his arm and shoulder with it. Jillian moved forward, taking out another of the undead with a hatchet, leaving them with half a dozen still standing. Metzger quickly thrust the knife into another one's head without it ever spotting him. His actions attracted the attention of the zombie standing closest to it, and it turned with malicious intentions as Metzger heard a pained yell from behind the restaurant that sounded like Sutton.

Strangely, no gunfire or other sounds accompanied the cry, and as Metzger turned to look, the zombie now focused on him as a delicious meal drew dangerously close. It opened its jaws, prepared to bite into his shoulder when several panicked warnings came from his group, allowing him to spin and plant the knife into the side of its skull with practiced precision.

"You guys got this?" he asked quickly, seeing only four undead stragglers left as Gracine used some kind of blunt weapon to bash another of the undead in the skull.

"We got it," Luke promised, taking aim with a firearm to back up the others who were trying to utilize more silent techniques.

Despite the pain in his slightly injured knee, Metzger took off in a dead sprint around the first and second corners of the building, reaching a shocking sight behind the building. He found Sutton lying on the ground, his face extremely bloody and battered as his assailant stood, aiming his hateful, crazed eyes at Metzger. With gray hair and eyes that looked a strange ice-blue, the man appeared to be in his early fifties. And though he looked fairly stout, and just under six feet in height, Metzger had to question how he got the jump on an armed man and roughed him up without Sutton getting off a single shot.

A quick glance at Sutton revealed the man struggling to catch his breath, and blood sputtering from his mouth, presumably from his face as it dripped down, each time he coughed.

For some reason the older man came at Metzger without the benefit of a gun, bladed weapon, or blunt object. He could have easily snatched Sutton's gun, unless it was rendered useless for some reason, and taken several shots at Metzger. Instead he trod angrily toward Metzger with his shoulders hunched forward, never blinking as he stared with insanely wide eyes, saying nothing.

In the old world Metzger would never have dreamed about punching another human being without significant provocation because he needed to set a good example for his school kids, and he didn't particularly want to be arrested. Those restraints were certainly lifted shortly after the start of the school year, so as the man quickened his pace into a run, Metzger sidestepped him when he drew close enough. At the same time he launched a hard right fist into the man's jaw, knocking him to the ground on his side as though he were a shot carnival game target falling straight back.

His limbs appeared to go rigid, which Metzger knew was called posturing from what little first aid he learned during his teaching days. It often occurred when someone received head trauma from a blow, though it happened far more frequently in sports than everyday life. He wished the others would hurry his way, but they were probably still finishing off the last of the zombies and keeping Samantha safe. Sutton hadn't let Buster out of the box truck, which seemed to present more bad than good. The dog provided an ample distraction and warning system for humans, remaining instinctively intelligent enough not to confront the undead himself.

Metzger started to move toward Sutton to check on him, but after only a few steps turned around because he sensed something amiss. The restaurant's inhabitant exhibited a level of insanity compounded with superior intellect because he had temporarily duped Metzger into thinking he was seriously injured. Now Metzger found himself at a disadvantage because the man was already charging him, so Metzger rolled with the tackle placed upon him, keeping his arms free to land an elbow in the man's jaw before either of them hit the grassy ground.

Barely fazed by the elbow, the man mounted Metzger at mid-torso and threw a few solid punches. Metzger blocked them as best he could, but one got him in the left cheek, immediately drawing the copper taste of blood inside his mouth. Angered, he used his arms to grasp the man, and bucked him off to one side, returning the favor with a few solid punches of his own. Despite being struck in the face, the man sneered wildly as though nothing in the moment registered in his mind.

Perhaps the indignity of being chased from his rabbit hole infuriated him, but Metzger suspected the man's mental capacity for everyday conversation and life vanished with the apocalypse, or well before the world changed. The two tussled half a minute longer, exchanging punches and elbows until the man gained the upper hand. His weight pinned Metzger to the ground once again and his hands wrapped around the former teacher's throat, beginning to squeeze with the intent of cutting off his air or crushing his windpipe.

Metzger had already poised his right thumb to jab the man's Adam's apple or an eyeball, but he didn't need to because the sound of a clank reached his ears first. The older man's eyes registered surprise instead of insanity for the briefest of seconds before rolling back in his head as he slumped sideways to the ground.

In his place, backlit by the partly cloudy sky, Gracine held a shovel, offering a weak smirk before stepping over him to check on Sutton. Metzger quickly stood, glancing at the unconscious man who nearly cost them their lives, feeling more assured he wasn't getting up this time. Lacking the means to bind the man at the moment, Metzger darted over to check on Sutton's condition, while Gracine knelt beside him.

"Oh, shit," Metzger muttered, finding her dotting Sutton's face with some kind of cloth.

While the cloth absorbed some of the blood, removing it from the surface, her actions revealed the cuts and bruises occupying much of his face. He groaned, still not speaking or showing any sign that he consciously recognized them.

"How the hell could that guy have fucked him up so quickly?" Metzger questioned, checking the rest of Sutton's body for signs of injuries, finding none.

"Taser," Sutton muttered, giving both Metzger and Gracine some relief.

Metzger noticed the Taser and its expended probes and wires lying on the ground closer to the employee entrance. He envisioned the occupant opening the door, perhaps crouching low, and firing the weapon when Sutton drew closer. Only when he inspected the weapon a bit more closely did he find blood coating the cracked exterior from where it was used to bludgeon Sutton in the face. Vazquez and Jillian made their way around the corner, their faces immediately registering concern.

"We need something to secure him," Metzger said, nodding toward the un-conscious man. Vazquez started for the door. "No, no! We haven't cleared it yet. Find something in one of the vehicles."

Instead, Vazquez looked at the defenseless man with anger.

"Why shouldn't we just put a bullet in his head and be done with it?"

"Because we aren't monsters."

"This man tried to kill you. *Us.*"

"We don't know that. He was trying to defend this place, and maybe there's a good reason."

Vazquez stewed in place momentarily, debating whether he wanted to find something to subdue the man, or buck Metzger's wishes and simply kill him.

He finally chose to leave the area in search of rope, handcuffs, or some other binding material. Metzger wasn't certain he wanted to leave the man alive, out and about, if he was a threat to other travelers. He still wanted to know if the man could be reasoned with, or if something had driven him to such extremes at the diner.

Jillian hadn't moved much since finding Sutton in such bloody condition. She finally moved closer, kneeling beside Metzger to see if she could assist. By now the sky was darkening and they needed to find shelter for the night soon. Driving rural roads meant easier navigation because there weren't many stalled vehicles, but hitting a zombie was a common occurrence, more so than hitting deer in the old days.

"We need to get him to one of the vehicles," Metzger suggested, nodding at their injured colleague. "Can you stand if we help you?" he asked Sutton directly.

He received an indiscernible groan in reply, which he figured meant 'no' if Sutton couldn't even form a coherent sentence.

Vazquez returned with some handcuffs a moment later, looking extremely displeased when he rounded the corner.

"Found these in the box truck," he stated, leaning down to position the older man correctly before slapping the cuffs on his hands.

"You should probably frisk him," Metzger suggested. "We haven't had time to check him for weapons."

Vazquez groaned before patting the man's shoulders all the way down to his ankles.

"Nothing," he finally reported.

It required all four of them to basically drag Sutton all the way around the building. They placed him in the passenger's seat of the box truck, which Gracine volunteered to drive since Buster knew her pretty well. The dog immediately began licking his master's wounds, openly concerned for Sutton's well-being.

"Let's get the asshole," Vazquez said, leading the way to the back of the building.

Metzger half expected the man to have dashed off into the woods, or back inside the building, but they found him unconscious, taking shallow breaths atop the untended green grass.

"We should check this place out," Vazquez insisted.

"We will," Metzger said. "In the morning. There could be all kinds of traps in there and it's getting dark out."

Both of them grabbed the man under the shoulders and dragged him to the smaller of the two trucks, heaving him in back like a sack of grain. The group secured the front and rear entrances as best they could, given the limited materials nearby. As he walked past the main doors, now missing some of their glass, Metzger saw the row of undead bodies lining the parking lot like some kind of stone paver path to a garden. The others had taken down the threat one at a time as he wanted them to, and he felt a sense of pride that they actually followed his suggestions.

A sky of purple barely lit the way as the three vehicles exited the parking lot, continuing along the route Sutton had chosen before his sudden stop. Metzger allowed Gracine to take the lead since she had some idea what her riding partner was looking for when he deviated so far from the state highway.

Within ten minutes the vehicles pulled into the driveway of a rather large white house with an attached porch, detached greenhouse, and a small garden. A garden flag flapped mildly in the breeze when the headlights hit it, illuminating the haunting blood stains that covered the otherwise scenic artwork of a blue jay and the tree branches it rested upon. The house appeared secure, and no lights, even candlelight, shone from the inside. Such positive signs indicated it might actually be a safe haven for the evening, considering it was the only house within a mile in any direction down an isolated county road.

A separate cottage and garage weren't far from the house, and all three ve-hicles fit on the paved driveway, safely off the road. Metzger worried the vehicles were highly visible from the road, though he doubted many warm-blooded folks were going to pass by. Setting his priorities, he wanted to go through the build-ings first before worrying about the parking situation, and how to secure their unwanted guest for the night.

"Can you keep an eye on him?" he asked of Luke, who still had a pistol, re-ceiving an affirmative nod. "If he gives you any trouble, shoot him."

He knew Luke wanted more responsibility, and though leaving him with a prisoner felt somewhat risky, the man remained bound, posing little threat. The others needed to check the buildings for living or dead inhabitants, and without Sutton the task wasn't going to move quite as quickly. Metzger always knew the risk of booby-traps existed within any building they invaded, but after the inci-dent at the restaurant he felt even more uneasy.

Leaving Sutton in the box truck, the group worked together with flashlights to clear the bed and breakfast house. Metzger left Jillian and Vazquez to search every inch of the downstairs while he took Gracine with him to the upper level. It worried him that the house was so eerie and quiet throughout, without a sign of anyone having been there recently. The group met up in the living room, deciding to check on Luke and Samantha before checking the outbuildings.

"He hasn't moved," Luke reported when they approached the truck, keeping Samantha close to him.

"We're going to check the garage and the cottage," Metzger said. "We shouldn't be long."

He didn't feel as comfortable approaching the cottage for some reason. Once again, Gracine tagged along as the others tackled the garage, finding it open and shining their flashlight beams inward immediately.

"I think Colby has a concussion," Gracine mentioned as Metzger tried the cottage's main entrance, finding it locked.

Even the main house hadn't been locked, which now worried him.

"There isn't much we can do for that except let him rest and keep him out of the fray."

"I know," she said firmly. "But he's going to want to go to that cabin of his, and we can't just drop him off and leave him there."

Metzger searched the nearby area for a spare key, finding none. He walked to the closest window, adorned with country wood accents and a box planter at the window base that held flowers withering from lack of attention. Shining the light inside the window, he turned to address Gracine's concerns when a zombie struck the window from the other side, startling them both momentarily as it growled and clawed to get at them through the glass.

"Nice," Metzger muttered, sighing as he returned his attention to Gracine. "If we have to, we bring Colby with us to Norfolk. He'll be pissed, but he can always backtrack to his camp later. At least he'll be alive to do it."

"I'm worried that it could be something worse than a concussion. He didn't say a word on the drive over here."

"He got fucked up pretty bad, Gracine. It's going to take a day or two before he starts to recover from that. There was a kid a high school over from mine who took a shot to the head during a football game and it took him about thirty seconds to speak a complete sentence whenever he spoke after that."

"You're not exactly encouraging," Gracine said sharply.

"I'm a realist," Metzger said, continuing his search for a key. "I'm sure Colby will be fine, though. That douchebag got in a few lucky shots on him, is all."

"On you, too."

"I had things under control."

Gracine gave a laugh that indicated she believed otherwise.

"You just swooped in and stole my glory," Metzger said with a smirk, feeling reasonably assured he would have dealt with the crazy man personally if given the chance. "But not this time."

He pulled a key from beneath a large decorative rock at the corner of the house.

"Sure you don't want me to save you from the scary zombie?" Gracine questioned with a mocking tone.

Metzger stuck the key into the lock, giving the knob a quick turn to make certain it worked.

It did.

"After you," he said before letting the door swing inward, giving her a few seconds to arm herself before doing so.

Metzger felt reasonably certain the old woman inside the cottage might have been bitten at some point, gotten away, and locked herself in solitude. As he watched Gracine step forward with a knife to deal with her, Metzger felt badly, knowing the woman's final hours were spent alone and in pain. He witnessed Gracine putting her out of her misery with a swift stab through the temple, angled into the brain, as he stepped inside to make certain no other surprises awaited them. They quickly inspected the cottage, finding no other danger, before dragging the corpse of the older woman outside and behind the cottage.

Three bedrooms were already prepared for guests in the main house, and the cottage provided two additional bedrooms. The group provided Sutton with one of the twin beds located in one bedroom while Gracine took the other to watch over him. Luke and Samantha took one of the other rooms with a king-sized bed, and no one thought ill of the arrangement because they knew Luke had proven himself dedicated to watching over the girl. Jillian took the last of the bedrooms in the main house, leaving Metzger and Vazquez to fend for themselves.

"I'll watch over our guest," Metzger volunteered. "There are two rooms in the cottage."

"I'm going to sleep on the couch here," Vazquez said. "Unless you need a second pair of eyes."

Metzger shook his head.

"I'm a light sleeper. He'll be secured, and if he tries anything, I'll hear it."

Assured everyone was comfortable in the main house, and with a promise that they would find some canned goods and cook up some food, Metzger walked outside to find the older man in the back of the truck beginning to stir. He quickly walked into the garage, finding some twine hanging along one wall, which he used to secure the man's legs before yanking him from the bed of the truck and carrying him into the cottage.

All of Metzger's sore areas, from his face to the shoulder he injured during the motorcycle tumble, ached simultaneously. Even the night at the farmhouse hadn't proven truly restful as he dreamed of his parents, losing Albert, and confronting Xavier at the airport. Sleeping solidly felt like a thing of the past, and as he carried the man over his shoulder into the cottage, the decision to keep him alive felt like a hazardous burden. He dropped the man beside the daybed in the guest bedroom, using a second set of handcuffs from Sutton's collection to attach the chain of the first set of cuffs to the bed frame. He wasn't about to provide him with a sense of comfort by letting him lie in bed, and he wanted to hear if the diner's squatter tried to escape.

"Do you speak?" Metzger called after exiting the room, knowing the man was awake, but feigned unconsciousness, forcing him to carry his full weight into the cottage.

No answer came as Metzger checked the bed in the adjacent room, hoping the man remained quiet so he could get some rest in the overnight. The reloaded .357 remained on his right hip, easily drawn to deal with any situations arising in the overnight if Metzger was jolted awake suddenly.

After making certain the bed was to his liking, knowing clean sheets and a soft pillow were far more than he normally dared ask for, he returned to find his prisoner glaring at him from the floor.

"I'm getting ready to grab a bite to eat next door," Metzger said, trying to tempt the man into saying something. "Would you like anything to eat or drink?"

For a few seconds the man glared at him from the shadows since Metzger hadn't lit any of the available candles yet. Darkness overtook the outside, and moonlight only provided so much lighting along the isolated bed and breakfast.

"You don't really think I was the only one in that diner, do you?" the man stated with more composure and focus than Metzger expected.

"If there are more of you, we'll deal with them in the morning," Metzger answered firmly. "How you act around us will determine your immediate future."

The man slipped a thin smirk, and Metzger couldn't tell if he was now acting smug, or teetered between the realms of the sane and insane.

"You won't be going anywhere in the morning," the man answered in a low rumble of a voice. "They'll come and slit all of your throats in the middle of the night."

Twenty-One

etzger immediately punched the man in the nose, partly from anger, but also to test his mental capacity.

"You shouldn't tell lies, mister," he said. "You're lucky we've left you alive this long. If you had friends, they would have come running out to save your crazy ass back there. And we took out your undead friends."

After hearing the words a look of disappointment and shock crossed the man's face as though he'd just learned of dear family members dying. Metzger questioned how deep the layers of insanity ran with this man, and what kind of world he created that he considered zombies his friends. Perhaps he conjured up a world of imaginary friends the way little girls created identities and personalities for their dolls for tea parties. He began to question how they could leave this man alive in the world when he presented a danger to himself and everyone he encountered.

Metzger wasn't certain how much the man understood about the real world versus the one he created in his mind. Obviously he knew how to handle the undead and subdue them as moving scarecrows outside of the restaurant, meaning he might have a split personality that dealt with that aspect of danger before reverting back to his current state of mind.

"What's your name?" Metzger asked.

His inquiry wasn't answered as the man scooted back to the wall, turning his head and sheltering in as much of a fetal position as his restraints allowed. He mourned, or pouted, in his own way, leaving Metzger to wonder what snapped the man's psyche after the world ended.

Perhaps he wasn't entirely stable in the first place, and the apocalypse provided him ample opportunity to run free.

Metzger left the cottage to join the others with feelings of uncertainty weighing on his mind. He stepped inside the main house, smelling delightful odors of corned beef hash, tuna fish, and what he thought might be baked beans. He seldom consumed such food while he taught school, but now they were delicacies, like lobster or filet mignon when restaurants operated.

"Hungry?" Jillian asked as she stirred a few items atop a propane stove.

"Sure," he answered almost absently, his mind still trapped in the cottage with the insanity of the older man.

"What's wrong?"

"It's that man we found at the restaurant. He isn't right in the head."

"Obviously."

"No," Metzger said, shaking his head. "It's worse than we thought. I'm not sure he entirely understands what's going on with the world."

"Are any of us?" Jillian asked, spooning some corned beef hash, baked beans, and potatoes onto a plate for him.

Metzger took the plate, realizing he knew the current world better than he cared to. People once hated politics, taxes, and going to work, but at least the world provided a routine, safety, and some semblance of order. Now the world felt lawless, where people needed to shoot first or risk being victims. Metzger didn't like making decisions that cost others their lives, and he wasn't certain he could simply execute the older man, even if the group wanted such an act carried out.

At the moment none of them seemed openly concerned about dealing with the situation. They simply wanted some food before getting some much needed rest in the overnight.

Metzger carried his plate, forking some food into his mouth as he walked over to check on Sutton in the closest bedroom. Several candles illuminated the downstairs, allowing him to see the weary looks on the faces of his companions before he reached the room, finding Gracine at Sutton's bedside. She reluctantly ate, as though instinctively knowing she needed her strength for the days ahead.

"Any change?" he asked.

"No. He's been unconscious since we got here."

Metzger took another bite of the warm food before speaking again, basically stalling for time as he thought of the right words, or rather the reasoning behind them.

"I need you to do me a favor."

Gracine looked at him as though he might be asking a bit much at such a crucial time.

"Make sure all of the doors are locked tonight before you go to bed. Even the bedroom doors."

She shot him a knowing look, as though she knew to expect trouble.

"Okay," she said, not blinking, and refusing to look away for a few seconds, as though asking if Metzger had invited trouble by bringing the older man along.

"Just a precaution," he said, turning to head for the common area where a large table with six chairs provided ample room for the group to eat and converse.

Buster, who had spent time wandering around the house exploring, now approached everyone who possessed a plate, asking for something to eat.

"You've been fed," Jillian said, admonishing him, which he took as an invitation to walk over with a wagging tail to ask for food.

She put down a little bit of the corned beef hash for him, which he immediately devoured before lifting his head like a swimmer surfacing for air to ask for more.

"No," she said, shaking her head.

Taking the hint, he walked away, but only to Vazquez who sat closest to her.

Metzger decided to eat what he could before Buster visited him with those big, sappy eyes, trying to indicate he'd been starved for days. It only took a few seconds of Vazquez ignoring him before he did exactly that.

"You must have Sutton wrapped around your paw," Metzger commented, shaking his head negatively at the dog.

Buster protested with a groan before moving on to his next potential mark.

"How is your guest?" Vazquez asked as he ate the last morsels from his plate.

"Not saying much," Metzger answered, deciding not to comment about the overnight throat slitting the man mentioned.

Had he considered such a statement a legitimate threat he would have placed the group on high alert, but he felt certain much of the man's recent memories were fabricated within his shattered mental state.

Once everyone finished eating it seemed they all wanted to get some rest. Without proper lighting, no one typically stayed up much past dusk most nights. A majority of past entertainment went by the wayside without electricity, and after their dangerous encounter the group didn't feel much like conversing. Metzger tossed his dishes into the sink, suspecting no one would bother washing them because they weren't expecting to ever see the property again once morning arrived and they departed.

As he stepped outside, Metzger took time to walk near the road, observing it to his left before panning to his right. Except for the moonlight, complete darkness overtook the fields surrounding the bed and breakfast. He felt certain there was a time when lights from the small town or the isolated businesses would have been visible from where he stood.

All three vehicles remained in the driveway, and no one seemed motivated enough to move them. Metzger wasn't certain enough room existed between the back of the buildings and the trees to park the vehicles safely anyhow. Parking them in the grass opened up the possibility of them getting stuck, and it seemed unlikely anyone would travel the rural road in the overnight. And even if someone did pass the house and take notice, it would take a brazen group to assault the unexpected guests or attempt to steal their vehicles.

With his eyes adjusted to the minimal lighting, Metzger sauntered back to the cottage, looking inside before he opened the door as though expecting the older man to be free and prepared to ambush him. He slowly opened the door, able to see the man inside the first bedroom, still attached to the metal bedframe. The frame was solid, requiring tools to dismantle it, and the man didn't have legitimate use of his hands with them bound behind his back and the handcuffs attached to the frame.

Metzger walked to the room, leaning on the doorway a moment, staring at the man who refused to look in his direction.

Whenever the man shifted, even slightly, the handcuffs made a telltale jingle when the chains rubbed one another or the bedpost.

"What happened to you?" he asked with sympathy, not expecting to actually strike up a conversation.

Getting an idea, he knelt down beside the bed, using a flashlight to shine a beam in the direction of the man's posterior, trying to get a look at his hands. There he found the gleam of a wedding band against the potent flashlight.

"What are you doing?" the man asked, probably figuring he was about to be violated or tortured.

"You were married?" Metzger inquired, returning to his feet while wiping the dirt from his hands.

A perplexed look crossed the man's face, as though he wasn't really sure how to answer, or what the true answer might be. Metzger sensed that a traumatic event in the man's life suddenly took everything from him, and he didn't know how to cope with reality any longer. Obviously the man knew a little something about engineering, likely holding a good job when occupations were still a daily practice.

"Are you from around here?"

This time the man moved his head from staring at the floor to staring at the wall, but without a look of confusion. Perhaps, Metzger thought, he was making some headway. He wondered if there was any saving this man, bringing him back to reality over time.

Time he couldn't particularly afford at the moment.

"Look, you're going to have to talk to me if you want me to let you go, or help you," Metzger offered. "My friends aren't going to be as patient, and they really didn't want to bring you along."

"Then leave me."

Metzger paused, thinking of how to frame his next sentence without being too cold, or showing weakness.

"That's not an option, I'm afraid. Whether you meant to or not, you brought harm to a number of people back there."

"They were my family," the man said softly before staring at the far wall, likely seeing something beyond the paint and drywall.

Uncertain about what the man meant, Metzger decided he wasn't getting any answers from the basically one-sided conversation, so he opted to turn in. He walked into the other bedroom, fluffing the pillow and pulling the sheets back when he heard the man speak from the other room.

"Thank you."

Metzger wasn't certain what the statement was for, exactly, or why the man waited until he left to utter the words, but felt assured the words were meant for him. He climbed into bed, pulling the sheets and blanket tightly over his upper body, knowing the night was going to get chilly at some point. Silence filled the cottage, and as he detected no activity from the main house or the garage, which meant everyone else was likely climbing into bed after experiencing a long day.

All of his worries and cares vanished once his head hit the pillow, and he was out like a light less than a minute later.

***

During the early morning hours the cottage grew chilly, and Metzger subconsciously tucked himself into a fetal position for warmth, trying to avoid the inevitable task of getting out of bed to use the bathroom. Wishing he had searched for an extra blanket before jumping into bed, he finally threw back the covers, shuffled to the small bathroom, and urinated to the point that his body felt incredible relief.

Stepping from the bathroom, he took a second to stare out the front window, realizing a dark purple sky gave way in the distance to a sliver of orange, indicating dawn drew near. He didn't hear the clanking or jingling of the handcuffs, so he decided to check on his prisoner in the other bedroom.

Metzger didn't even reach the doorway to the room before noticing the two pairs of handcuffs still secured to one another, and to the bed's frame, but no wrists secured within their curved metal. He couldn't imagine how the man escaped the cuffs, because even the best magicians manipulated their shackles or surroundings in some fashion.

"Shit," he muttered under his breath, figuring he might be attacked out of the blue any second.

He dashed into his room, grabbing the flashlight and his .357 from under his pillow to quickly examine the rest of the cottage, finding no sign of the older man. Throwing on his clothes, he stepped outside, finding no trace of the engineer inside the garage when he shined his light through a window to light the open space.

Next he tried all of the doors along the house, finding them locked and secured as he'd requested of Gracine. All three vehicles remained in the driveway, leaving only one realistic possibility in his mind. Every facet of the man's world remained at the restaurant, even if the security measures now lied in ruins around the building. Although he couldn't justify his actions in the least, he wanted to track down the man, even if it meant driving all the way to the diner. He knew the group planned on looting the building later that morning when everyone was up, but he felt responsible for the man.

And the man's escape.

He tucked the revolver into his belt and finished dressing himself quickly as he jumped into the truck where his other weapons remained in the jump seat behind him. As quietly as possible he backed out of the driveway once the truck was started, trying to avoid waking anyone. He didn't want them to think he'd abandoned them, figuring most of them knew better if they understood him at all. Still a bit groggy, it took his mind a moment to focus on his location and remember the turns to the restaurant.

What seemed like an eternity at dusk felt a little quicker to him now as he gained focus, searching left and right for the older man on the way to the restaurant. Most of the fields yielded crops that weren't very tall, so he was able to see across them for what seemed like a mile in any direction. He spotted nothing, and began to doubt his intuition about the crazy man's agenda.

Apprehension filled his mind when he drew near the property, immediately seeing something different about the setting.

No longer did the sign bear the weight of two zombies kicking to get down from their sad lots after life, and the scarecrow zombie wasn't tied to his crucifix along the side. Instead, he saw three members of the undead knelt down in the parking lot area, greedily stuffing their mouths with something fresh and red. Even in the minimal light that dawn provided, Metzger saw a shimmering along their hands, knowing that blood appeared black in the moonlight, and crimson at this very moment.

He pulled the truck to the edge of the dozen undead killed by his group the previous evening, slowly stepping from the vehicle to find the trio paid him no attention at first. Reaching behind the seat, he pulled his short sword, sheath and all, out of the truck. Only now did one of the zombies turn to see him, the lower half of its face covered in blood and small chunks of flesh. It showed its teeth, beginning to stand, thinking in its one-track mind that new prey had arrived. Voicing a hissy growl as it drew near, the zombie that once hung from the large front sign reached for him when it was about two feet away.

Metzger swung the sword horizontally with practiced ease, severing the head cleanly in two, not even watching the top half bounce atop the blacktop before he stepped forward to dispense more damage. Neither of the other two zombies ever looked his way, allowing him to slice the female cleanly through the skull and stab the scarecrow zombie through the temple, into the brain, rendering it entirely devoid of life.

A few times Metzger had cut the heads clean off, thinking it might be a neat theatrical trick like the movies until he realized the heads remained animated, even after separation from the body. So disturbed by this revelation was he that Metzger made certain his attacks always reached the brain, causing physical trauma that shut them down for good.

With the threats out of the way, he stepped over to the body they'd been feeding on, confirming what he already suspected. Much of the man's stomach and chest had been ripped apart, exposing shiny organs like the liver and the intestines, which remained covered in blood. He couldn't help but run through the scenarios in his mind, wondering if the man released the undead on purpose, trying to tame them, or converse with them on some level. Perhaps he considered them part of his family and wanted to reach them, or maybe he saw the remains of his world lying atop the blacktop and simply wanted to be gone from the world, or join their ranks.

Suspecting he must have escaped fairly early in the morning to travel on foot to the diner, Metzger wondered why the man hadn't attacked him, or stolen a vehicle. He obviously intended malice when he made a stand at the restaurant, but something about him changed when he was removed from the setting. The last words the man spoke the previous evening still echoed through his mind.

"Thank you," he said under his breath, wondering what the hell that meant, or why this man believed Metzger deserved any sort of praise.

Taking up his flashlight, Metzger switched it on as he walked to the front door of the restaurant, still unlocked from the skirmish. He suspected the man had undone the trap latch along the outer set of doors, trying to sic the hoard of zombies upon Metzger's group in a last ditch effort to defeat the invaders. In a way, Metzger wished they hadn't stopped at the diner, looking to the man's bloodied corpse behind him, knowing Sutton might be permanently damaged from the attack.

Aspects of the new world befuddled him, and Metzger didn't always know how to act, or whom to trust in some situations.

He thought about stepping inside momentarily, but didn't dare because he knew additional traps might be awaiting trespassers. Without the benefit of natural light, such a move didn't seem prudent, so he backed away from the main entrance, hearing a throaty growl behind him, wondering how any of the three zombies could have endured his sword attack.

Turning his head to see what awaited him, Metzger discovered the undead form of the older man now attempting to stand from a horizontal position, stepping on his own intestines because they unraveled like a thread from a sweater.

If the thread from sweaters was entirely coated in clotting blood.

"No," Metzger muttered sadly, wondering if the older man who fiercely defended a building that shouldn't have held any emotional ties had finally reached his objective.

Suspecting he had freed the three zombies intentionally to let them take him down, Metzger felt sorry for the man, and disappointed at the same time. The man had shown signs of humanity the night before, along with glimpses of sanity, but his more recent actions provided Metzger with proof that the man was indeed too far gone.

Now he finally stood erect, dripping intestines and blood, gnashing his teeth like any other member of the undead community. Metzger couldn't imagine the suffering that accompanies being eaten alive, and perhaps on some level the man's lack of sanity prevented him from understanding, or even feeling the pain of fingers digging beneath the layers of his skin and into his insides.

Allowing him to draw closer, Metzger dared to examine the man's hands more closely, finding both thumbs broken or dislocated, which explained how he slipped out of the handcuffs. The self-inflicted injuries only added to the evidence that the man wasn't in his right mind, and never could be again. Somewhere deep down, perhaps he knew so, and took his own life with the only beings familiar to him.

"Why?" Metzger asked the walking corpse, pushing it back with one arm, careful to avoid being bitten or clawed too deeply. "Why do you get to give up so easily?"

If he thought the obstinate man was ignoring him in life, he proved worse in death, ignoring the words and the shove, almost tripping over his intestines, which dragged afoot like a tail stemming from the wrong side of the body. In no hurry, he staggered toward Metzger, keeping his eyes on the prize, baring his teeth to accompany a body that looked to be in complete shambles.

"You lied," Metzger said, thinking back to the comment about slitting throats in the middle of the night. "If *this* was your backup, you really were fucked up."

Having wasted enough time, and feeling emotionally spent after seeing his efforts squandered, Metzger held the sword, pulled it back across his left shoulder, and let it fly through the center of the man's skull. Fragments of bone and hair flew through the air, along with the top half of the cranium, and when it struck the ground the darkening gray brain popped out of the protective skull. The body collapsed in a messy heap as well, and Metzger stayed clear of any projectile fluids.

Only when he was assured of tranquil surroundings did he kneel down to dig for the man's wallet inside his pants, wanting to know a little something about the man. He found it surprising how many people actually kept wallets and cards with them, even though such things held no value. He felt as though people wanted to maintain their identity in case death came for them unexpectedly so they wouldn't be forgotten. Burial in the apocalypse was a luxury few people afforded in death.

"Frank Robertson," Metzger read the man's name aloud as he pulled the driver's license from the wallet.

He stood there feeling somber a moment until he decided to return to the bed and breakfast, wondering if he'd been missed.

***

When Metzger returned to the rural homestead he found only Jillian walking around the driveway as though waiting for him to return. He soon discovered why as Vazquez and Luke cooked some breakfast while Gracine waited beside Sutton's bed to see if he regained consciousness.

"I saw your guest wasn't in the cottage," Jillian revealed before the pair stepped inside. "Did he escape, or did you take him for a ride?"

"Let's just say I know exactly where he is," Metzger answered ambiguously, not wanting to discuss specifics.

Jillian didn't press the issue, but when Metzger walked inside he felt all eyes upon him as though they suspected him of some heinous crime, or conducting some misconduct behind their backs. They would know the truth soon enough, he figured, so he quietly ate some breakfast in the form of cream of chicken soup and walked outside to double-check that everything was packed into the truck. While placing some canned goods he'd found behind the seat he noticed the short sword sticking out of his pack, a few droplets of blood remaining along the tip of the handle.

After pillaging what they could from the three buildings and loading their finds into the vehicles, the group set out to carry Sutton from the bed to the box truck. Metzger felt a bit surprised that no one even mentioned the notion of staying an extra day. The group had numerous options, including splitting up, waiting a day or two, or looking for supplies that might better help with Sutton's condition.

It seemed a foregone conclusion that they were going to inspect the restaurant after enduring such a ferocious battle, and they were going to continue moving south. Metzger didn't know whether the camp was still a possible stop with Sutton's condition, or if they were going straight to the Navy base. If the decision was his, and quite possibly it was, he would take Sutton to the base hoping to get the man true medical attention.

When they loaded Sutton into the passenger's seat of the box truck, they provided several pillows to keep him comfortable, and to prevent him from striking his head on the side window or other unforgiving surfaces. Even in the light of day his face didn't look much better. Swelling and general redness had replaced blood and open wounds, but the most concerning aspect was the fact that he really hadn't regained consciousness for more than a few minutes at a time.

"What's with all the dirty stares I received?" Metzger asked Jillian once they were halfway to the restaurant.

"They think you set him free," Jillian answered rather bluntly.

Metzger immediately understood their legitimate concern, though it disturbed him that they thought he was that much of a softy.

Saying nothing, Metzger waited until they approached the restaurant because he only wanted to relive what little he planned to say about the ordeal once. When the vehicles approached the diner this time they parked a little differently because of the mess in the parking lot and the fact that the scenery had changed. Almost as though she sensed no danger remained, Gracine parked at the edge of the road, slowing to look at the old and fresh carnage before stopping.

"Dare I ask?" she inquired of Metzger once everyone except Sutton stepped from the vehicles.

Even Buster jumped out, immediately turning his head in every direction, attempting to detect any undead in the area.

Metzger narrated the morning's events briefly to the group, skipping over the parts where he tried to connect with the older man before he went on his suicidal mission. The version he spun left a little more mystery because he didn't speculate on the man's motivations, or the depths of his insanity.

Everyone in the group seemed to believe his story, and understood how the man broke his own thumbs to escape the handcuffs, which in itself meant he was crazy or some trained operative for the government, which sounded implausible. Soon enough they cautiously stepped into the building, finding no armed traps awaiting them, leaving Metzger to wonder if the man disarmed them, or there weren't any others beyond the double entrance.

While the others foraged for food and supplies, Metzger located personal items he assumed once belonged to the line of undead bodies outside. Wallets and purses were neatly organized in one corner of the desk inside the manager's office, and as he quickly went through them he wondered if some of the people died inside the diner originally, or if they came seeking shelter later. It took a few minutes, but when he found two identifications inside clutch wallets, he pulled them out for a look.

Terri Robertson.
Brie Robertson.

Indeed the older man's wife and daughter of nineteen died at the diner, likely sending him into a spiraling depression among other undiagnosed conditions. As far as driver's licenses went, they looked like normal, well-adjusted people, but some families hid secrets well. He didn't want to dwell on what might have been, so Metzger reached into his pocket and pulled out a third laminated driver's license.

Metzger had pocketed Frank Robertson's identification earlier, and considered keeping these as well, but ultimately decided he didn't want to drag along any physical or emotional baggage. Placing the identifications together, he stacked them neatly along a clean spot on the desk. There wouldn't be a burial, at least not by him and his companions, but maybe someone else would come along and give the small group of unfortunate souls a proper sendoff.

Wasting little more precious time, Metzger left the office to help the others collect goods from the store. The gift shop held little more than trinkets of local sports teams, T-shirts, and cheap plastic replicas of known Virginia landmarks, including a military ship inside a snow globe. Metzger picked it up, smirking at it before setting it down and grabbing the nearby packets of sunflower seeds, potato chips, and other bagged snacks. Gracine and the others were beyond the kitchen, grabbing what few bulk cans remained of food that the restaurant once planned on serving.

Not much was left, indicating at least some survivors had once made a stand at the diner, but Metzger felt as though none of them lasted nearly as long as Frank Robertson. He wondered when the man's wife and daughter died, and exactly how that altered his mental state. Perhaps the others wanted to put down Terri and Brie for good, but Robertson would have none of it. Maybe he fed the other survivors to them instead, accidentally forming his undead watchdog regime.

By the time the crew readied themselves for longer travel with secured goods in every vehicle, they checked on Sutton one last time, finding him much the same.

"I don't know where his camp is," Gracine revealed to Metzger in front of the others. "If he doesn't wake up soon, I say we continue on to your destination."

Metzger looked to Jillian, recalling that she said her family wasn't far from the military base.

"If we get to Norfolk, I can get to my family," she said.

"If you know the way, feel free to keep the lead," Metzger said.

Gracine nodded.

"I've been up and down these roads a thousand times, honey. We won't be stopping anytime soon unless we have to."

With that settled, the group continued southeast along the highway once they returned to it, making decent time for a while until they needed to stop when Metzger's truck ran out of fuel. Deciding it was easier to switch vehicles, rather than syphon fuel, he and Jillian quickly transferred their goods and belongings to a crew cab truck, deciding they wanted the four-wheel-drive to navigate ditches and uneven roads, rather than fuel economy.

A dark blue color, the truck sat a bit higher off the ground, and appeared newer than the last truck. Metzger wondered why someone abandoned the vehicle, which held a nearly full tank of gas and no undead waiting inside.

He considered both finds bonuses.

Metzger immediately plugged in the sat phone to charge with the vehicle charging cord, because he hadn't done so since the group crashed in Virginia. A sense of nearing his destination, like a kid about to experience a museum or theme park for the first time, spread a sense of anticipation throughout his body. It replaced the feelings of sorrow and foreboding that came with realizing how the Robertson family members met their ends.

Only a few minutes into their journey, Metzger needed to follow Gracine around a line of cars that occupied a lane by driving partly along the side of the road to avoid hitting them. He thought he might have screwed up the phone when plugging it in to charge because it made a strange noise. He gave it a glance, trying to navigate the truck without planting them in a ditch, but Jillian looked from the phone to him with wide eyes.

"It's ringing!" she exclaimed.

Metzger slammed on the brakes, almost causing Luke to rear-end him with the other truck as he scooped the phone from the center console. He stared at it momentarily, thinking of all the bad news that might come over the line, particularly if his brother wasn't the one placing the call.

"Well answer it," Jillian urged, not sensing his internal reluctance, because Metzger couldn't stack any more bad news atop his already growing pile.

"Hello?" he answered reluctantly.

"Hey, little brother," a familiar voice said over the phone. "I've only got a minute, but we need to talk."

Twenty-Two

Jillian jumped out of the truck to spread the news to the others, even before Metzger spoke his first words to Bryce.

Metzger barely saw the look of confusion on Luke's face turn to one of hope, or Gracine jumping from the box truck after stopping to discover the reason for the holdup. He simply held the phone close to his ear and absorbed the words his brother spoke.

"We just got to the base," Bryce revealed. "It's organized chaos here, and the guys are still rounding up family members from the housing areas."

Metzger recalled that most of the housing for enlisted men and women, and even most officers, remained in town, separate from the base.

"Where are you?" Bryce asked.

"In Virginia, but not real close to the base yet."

"You need to get your ass down here."

"Where do I go? How do I locate you when I get there?" Metzger questioned almost frantically, knowing his brother couldn't talk for very long.

"The undead are starting to swarm the fences, so you may have to get creative. I'm not sure how long we'll be at the base."

"What's that supposed to mean?"

"They're working up some kind of plan to deploy some of us to the bigger cities."

Metzger felt his heart sink. If he missed his one opportunity to lay eyes on his brother, they might never find one another.

"Look, I'll stay here as long as I can. They're sending the Marines and the Army guys on these missions first, but there's only so many of them."

"I can't promise when I'll get there. It's slow going along the roads, not to mention dangerous."

Bryce gave a sigh that indicated he understood the hardships, even if he hadn't personally experienced many of them yet.

"Hang in there, and keep your phone handy. We'll meet up and you can tell me all about what you've seen when you get here."

"Okay," Metzger said, thinking of the heartbreaking news he needed to tell his brother.

"I've gotta go. Talk to you later, Dan."

"Bye."

Metzger hung his head as he shut down the phone, finding everyone around him waiting with baited breath for news. Even Buster was released from the box truck by Gracine, though he busied himself with sniffing the area and using the tall grass beside the road for relief of his bowels and bladder.

"Not much news," Metzger said to dispel their looks of anticipation. "My brother's ship arrived in Norfolk, and the government might not be done with him."

"What does that mean for us?" Luke inquired.

"I'm not sure it changes much. They're trying to gather their families and protect them before the soldiers depart for their missions. We get to the base, we get protection, food, and supplies."

Metzger spoke the words, hoping he wasn't misleading the group, because he didn't truly have any assurances. As the brother of a Navy officer, he was certainly blanketed into safe haven, but he wasn't sure if the people left in charge would be willing to stretch their limited provisions for complete strangers.

"It would seem I'm more pressed for time than ever," he revealed the obvious information to the group.

"What about Sutton and his camp?" Jillian asked. "Do we even have time for that pit stop?"

"No one knows where it is," Vazquez said, nodding to Gracine. "Not even her."

"We have to keep going," Luke said, providing Metzger with relief that he wasn't the only one who wanted to avoid additional stops along the way. "We can get Colby medical attention and he can double back to his camp when he gets well."

"*If* he gets well," Vazquez stated. "He's been out a long time."

"He's been in and out of consciousness," Gracine revealed. "But he never stays awake for very long."

"We need to get moving before the undead spot us," Metzger said, feeling even less patient than his traveling companions at the moment.

"We aren't going anywhere except my camp," a voice said from the side of the box truck, causing everyone to look in that direction.

Sutton held a shotgun at his side, his face still battered with remnants of dried blood. Forced to use the truck as a makeshift crutch to support his weight, he moved forward, continually leaning against the sturdy vehicle as he walked. His condition apparently left him too weak or too disoriented to walk upright.

"You're in no condition," Gracine said sternly, taking a step toward him until he held the shotgun in a more upright position.

"We aren't hand-delivering a truck full of food and supplies straight to the military," Sutton replied stubbornly.

Everyone stood perfectly still, looking to one another for answers, knowing Sutton wasn't in any condition to drive, much less defend himself once he reached the camp.

Already losing precious time, Metzger decided he needed to defuse the situation before it got out of hand. Half of the people currently traveling with him wanted to find loved ones somewhere nearby, and he supposed his latest companion wasn't so different. Sutton didn't appear to have all of his faculties after taking so many shots to the skull, so Metzger couldn't rule out violence against his group of normally peaceful people.

"We go to the camp," Metzger decided aloud, looking to Gracine, who gave him a look that indicated if he rethought his decision she was onboard with whatever he wanted to do.

He gave her a negative shake of his head with minimal movement. For now they would appease Sutton, hoping he might slip into unconsciousness again, or that the camp wasn't far out of their way.

***

"Why are you giving in to what he wants?" Jillian asked once they'd been on the road for almost fifteen minutes, weaving around cars as usual. "He's nothing but a bully."

"I don't think he's nearly as bad as he pretends to be," Metzger answered. "He's just doing the same thing we are."

"And what's that?"

Metzger turned to her before he answered.

"Looking for his family."

Jillian looked down to her lap.

"I feel like I'm wasting my time if I look for the rest of my family."

Metzger followed Gracine's lead around a car parked the wrong way in the road, maneuvering slightly into the median before posing his next question.

"You said it's only been a week since you last talked to them," Metzger said. "You can't give up that easily."

"It's not that I'm giving up. After seeing what some of these people do to one another, I worry about what I'm going to find."

From experience, Metzger could relate to the feeling.

"You can't go the rest of your life wondering," he said after a brief pause. "It'll consume you, and if they're still out there, they need to know you're alive."

"I can't believe how many bad people survived this thing," Jillian said almost absently, staring out the side window.

"I'm not sure they were all bad. Maybe what happened changed some of them."

"So if there aren't any rules, or anyone to enforce them, we're all just inherently evil?"

"No. Not all. I think we all have an idea what it's going to take to survive, but some people want to take shortcuts."

Both pondered the world around them silently until Gracine turned onto a county road that Metzger assumed started the part of their journey where they visited the rural camp. He considered it a blessing that gridlocked traffic appeared minimal as stranded vehicles, buildings, and clusters of the undead disappeared, giving way to trees and open fields. Whenever he departed from urban settings,

Metzger felt as though he was experiencing a vacation of sorts, leaving worries and cares behind.

Part of him wanted to divert from the pack and head straight for the military base, but he wasn't going to leave the group in the hands of an unpredictable Sutton. As much as he wanted to see Bryce, Metzger felt a kinship, new as it was, to these people who assisted him, and vice versa, whenever the need arose.

He trusted that Bryce would stall as long as he could, and that answers would be available if his brother needed to leave on a mission. He couldn't imagine the nature of the operations, or what the military hoped to find, but he didn't suspect they'd waste resources on such endeavors when they needed to protect assets, unless they had good reason.

Eventually the convoy took a few more turns, several miles apart, until they made their way onto a gravel road that eventually turned into a dirt road once the vehicles reached a densely wooded area. A grove of trees soon became what Metzger believed might be considered a forest because the only daylight he saw came from the occasional clearing above them, or through branches spaced just far enough apart. When the vehicles reached a small entrance gate in the form of two metal poles and a chain with a "No Trespassing" sign already lying on the ground, they passed with minimal hesitation.

Almost immediately Metzger's sense of impending danger blinked red with blaring alarms inside his mind. He spied undead lumbering through the trees to either side in a spot that should have been barren of living or dead. As if that weren't enough to make him nervous, he smelled smoke, like that of a wood fire, through the top of the window where he'd cracked it for some fresh air.

Perhaps Sutton detected the danger as well, because the box truck sped up, despite the bumpy dirt road. While Gracine might have been driving the vehicle, Sutton certainly asserted his will the last time the group stopped. Nearly a dozen times over the next mile, Metzger and Jillian came close to striking the truck's top with the tops of their heads. Several other dirt roads branched away from their current path, but Gracine continued to go straight, likely in the direction of whatever lake, pond, or river awaited them at the site.

Metzger figured any location within the thick woods provided good hunting, but one needed to be near the water for the added benefit of fishing. For some strange reason the undead didn't thin out in number as the group drove deeper into the woods. Metzger couldn't imagine how the undead population remained so steady, even as they drove closer to the water. Something felt extremely suspicious and out of place to him, as though someone had sabotaged the area or people had flocked there only to experience disastrous results.

A zombie tumbled into the trees from the dirt road ahead when the box truck clipped it, clearing the way without hesitation. Metzger understood Sutton's desire to examine the camp as soon as possible, though he worried the man might accidentally place them all in danger, blindly leading them into the heart of the evident danger surrounding them.

While they traveled too quickly for the undead to reach in and assault them, Metzger dared roll down his window all the way, drawing the intensifying odor of fire into the vehicle. Nothing visible ahead indicated smoke or flames, but Jillian now tensed in the passenger's seat, sensing something the abnormal danger.

"Why can't we ever go somewhere and find peaceful surroundings?" she asked.

"I'm not sure there's a place isolated enough to be peaceful right now," Metzger thought aloud.

A few more zombies fell to the grill of the box truck before the group finally reached a fork in the road. Ahead, the path led directly to what appeared to be a shack and a dock capable of securing about a dozen boats. A few boats remained moored to the anchor points, and two were partly submerged in the shallow water near the shore, giving Metzger an eerie feeling when he spied the wrecks. Another path went to the left with a fairly smooth-looking road, but Metzger knew his luck wouldn't allow such an easy trip as the box truck took the path to the right instead.

Although the road wasn't terrible, several dips ensured the ride wasn't going to be smooth. At the junction the forest had diminished considerably, but this path took them back into the thicket of trees, barely allowing them a view of the lake to their left. More outlet roads appeared to their right, which would take them deeper into the woods, but the group passed all of them until they came to a path that appeared as though it might take them closer to the lake once again.

Metzger took notice as a charred odor returned to the air, and with it, the landscape began to reveal evidence of what happened in the wooded area that housed multiple camps. Trees and shrubs were sometimes partially burned, or reduced to piles of ash, which caused him to believe someone carelessly or intentionally set fire to part of the camp. The further they traveled, the more destruction he saw on either side of the truck, with barely any plant life surviving whatever blaze ripped through the woods.

He suspected that natural firestops in the form of occasional gaps between the wildlife, and the fact that the ground remained somewhat moist from recent rainfall, kept the fire from spreading throughout the entire forest. Strangely, it was the *only* damage they found in the private reserve, and it happened to be in the direction of Sutton's cabin. A knot formed in the pit of his stomach because he couldn't imagine they were about to discover anything positive once they reached the cabin.

For the briefest of moments the landscape to his left opened up, and Metzger was able to see the lake in all of its beauty. It looked like it went on forever, or at least farther than he believed he could swim without needing assistance from a life preserver, before reaching a shore on the opposite side. The water looked clear, and the sun glistened off the top of the tiny crests that lapped inward toward the shore. It reminded him of warm summer days around Lake Erie when he and his brother visited the beach, or his father took him to the old railroad depot that had since been turned into a strip of giant windmills built to produce power.

Lake Erie wasn't always pleasant, sometimes bringing harsh winds inland, which in turn brought heavy snow during the winter months. The picturesque scene before him was enough to remind Metzger of his childhood days for what amounted to a flicker in time before trees obscured his view momentarily. After a few seconds passed, with the burning odor growing stronger than ever, a horrific view replaced the magical moment when trees now reduced to black, charred stumps revealed the camp at last, and a scene that looked like something out of a Hollywood blockbuster in the background.

"Oh my God," Jillian muttered slowly as Metzger brought the truck to a stop.

All three vehicles stopped in what could be considered a driveway of sorts to the cabin that once provided a summer retreat for Sutton and his family. It was literally the end of the road because every other cabin along the lake, or deeper in the woods, required a path they'd already bypassed.

Metzger stepped from the truck, looking at the remains of the cabin, mostly standing a foot or two off the ground in smoldering remains. A stone chimney towered above the blackened remains of the building, and part of the front porch was spared for some reason, but the rest was left utterly destroyed. Every tree, every shrub, and virtually every blade of grass around the camp was scorched. Metzger looked to the woods off to his right, seeing that the destruction continued several hundred yards before it ran out of fuel, tapering off to a smoldering fire.

Everyone in the group, including Sutton, looked in shock at the cabin briefly before their attention fell to the unavoidable carnage in the lake, entirely out of place in the otherwise natural setting. Not even a hundred yards away from the shore, with its front end submerged below the surface of the water like a Styrofoam airplane thrown and lodged halfway into the sand by a child, a jetliner looked more like a museum piece on display than a tragic accident. Metzger recognized the logo on the gigantic passenger jet, figuring this happened soon after the world transformed.

He found it odd that the nose of the jet, buried underwater, presumably in sand and silt, didn't succumb to the weight of the jet, allowing for the remainder of the aircraft to fall to a horizontal position. Even then the aircraft likely would have stuck out of the water in part, keeping it visible. Damage to the jet was easily visible with stress fractures, a few parts of the metal singed by flames, and the rear access hatch open as though some passengers survived and made their way to land.

Metzger took a step forward, finding Sutton completely stunned, his plans of meeting up with his two sons completely shattered and lying in ruins.

"They wouldn't have gotten here yet," Metzger said calmly to the man.

"And now they have nothing to come to," Sutton said in an unusually tranquil manner.

Making matters worse, the group spotted the undead floating along the water in various spots. A few were close to land, and another three were stumbling towards the arriving vehicles and the noise they made during their approach. They all appeared as though they were dressed for business, meaning they once occupied seats in the jet. Metzger wondered if the front hatch was somehow opened, or the windshields of the jet shattered, allowing any unbuckled undead to float out of the aircraft to wherever the current took them.

He briefly questioned how they died, and why they turned, but didn't have time to search for answers as he reached into the truck, drawing his short sword. All three zombies remained at various distances, so Metzger held up a foreboding hand to the others before stepping forward. He sliced the skulls of the first two in half before moving toward the third undead, a businessman wearing the remains of a shredded sport coat and blue tie atop a heavily soiled white shirt. Before Metzger could use his sword, however, a shot rang out and the zombie crumbled to the ground only a few feet from him.

Before he even turned around, he knew Sutton had used whatever firearm he drew from his side. Though he understood the man's frustration and utter sadness at finding his safe haven destroyed, Metzger couldn't bear much more of Sutton putting everyone else in danger. His loose cannon actions had gotten him severely injured, and twice now he had thoughtlessly put everyone else behind him in the pecking order.

Saying nothing, Metzger shot him an angry stare as though to ask Sutton if he was through being irresponsible. Instead of pursuing an angered path that would simply waste time and keep them in danger longer, he approached Sutton.

"What do you want to do?"

"I need to check the cabin," Sutton said gravely, indicating he might not like the end result.

Every member of the group stepped forward, prepared to help with the search, and to gain a closer look at the spectacle dangerously close to the shore. A small wooden pier in the water was a short walk down a slight hill from the cabin's remains. No boat was secured to the pier, but several boat wrecks were now visible in the water to either side of the jet, as though people were foolhardy enough to attempt boarding the aircraft, or collided with it during the blackness of night.

Metzger followed Sutton up to the cabin's front landing, stopping short of entering. The man walked inside, beginning to search the rubble for any surviving items, or human remains. Metzger stepped toward the pier, wondering if the water was contaminated, if the fish were safe to eat, and what goodies remained aboard the plane. He wasn't about to chance a swim, or look for a boat, because more pressing matters awaited him further south.

A few zombies near the pier clumsily attempted to drag themselves ashore, but their lack of motor skills kept them from climbing while downgraded brainpower prevented them from discovering an alternative route. They grumbled and growled upon seeing living people on the shore, and Metzger simply stared back at their yellowed eyes, wondering how they arrived in rural Virginia beyond the obvious conclusion.

One jet in the lake didn't explain so many undead wandering through the woods, and the private campgrounds certainly wouldn't have attracted so many living or dead. He hated to imagine a conspiracy, but perhaps the plane was rigged with the same toxins that blew up within numerous factories and infected people. Some might have survived the initial wave, gotten sick, and turned later on, but many other explanations existed.

When a few straggler undead emerged from the woods, Jillian and Vazquez dealt with them quietly while Sutton finished conducting his search of the ruins. He walked to the edge with an unsettled, perplexed expression, looking to the front landing before locking eyes with Metzger.

"No remains," he reported evenly.

"That's good," Metzger said. "Morbid, but good."

Sutton looked to both sides as though he were lost. Not lost in a directional sense, but rather in life, as though he didn't know where to go from here.

He stared out to the lake, eyeballing the downed jet as though the same questions Metzger silently asked finally entered his mind. Still weakened from the beating and the likely concussion that accompanied it, Sutton shook his head, trying to regroup. It appeared to take every ounce of strength for him to stand, much less walk around and carry out a search.

"You shouldn't be up," Metzger said with concern.

"What should I be doing?"

"You should be making assurances that your boys can find you."

Sutton looked at him with a furrowed eyebrow.

"Staying here doesn't solve a thing," Metzger said. "Leave them a note here, and one at the entrance, letting them know you've headed to the Navy base in Norfolk with a group of good people."

"You're making some assumptions, aren't you?"

"That you'll make the trip to Norfolk?"

"No, that I consider you good people," Sutton said, letting a grin slip. "Look, I'm sorry I've been such an ass."

"I know exactly what you're going through. And while I'd like for you to come with us, I don't want you doing crazy shit that's going to endanger the rest of us."

Sutton appeared torn about the decisions before him, and his recent mistakes.

"I should wait for the boys here," he finally said.

"Sleeping in a burned out hull of a cabin, fighting off the undead on an hourly basis, and hoping your boys make it here in one piece? If they can make it *here*, Colby, they can make it to the base. And don't give me your bullshit about not trusting the government. We're running out of options."

Openly pondering his immediate future, Sutton looked at the box truck before his eyes shifted to the destruction surrounding him. Wisps of smoke occasionally plumed upward from the cabin's remains, indicating the fire may have been more recent than the aircraft's plummet from the sky. Survivors could have set fire to the place for warmth, or to distract the undead while they made an escape into the woods. It seemed highly unlikely Sutton's sons ever made it to the camp, and if they had, they likely weren't coming back.

"I hate to break up this little lover's quarrel," Gracine said as she approached them with Buster at her side, "but we need to make a decision before every maggot farm in the water decides to come visit us."

Sutton smirked.

"She keeps stealing my nicknames for them."

All three stood silently a moment until Metzger spoke again.

"Look, when we get to Norfolk we can hide your truck before proceeding to the base. The way things sound, we may not be staying there long anyway. My brother said something about soldiers getting deployed for missions inland." Sutton formed a face that indicated he was about to say something against the men and women in uniform, but Metzger held up a foreboding finger. "Before you say they're being issued flamethrowers to light up women and newborns, let me assure you my brother isn't that kind of person, and he isn't going to continue to work for the government if they ask him to harm innocents."

"Can you guarantee he'll tell you the truth, no matter what his superiors tell him to say?"

"I'm confident Bryce would never lie to me, and he's not going to put any of us in danger. If he feels the government has lost its way, he'll come with us and we can leave the base in our rearview."

Sutton pondered the situation momentarily, and the remainder of the group joined them around the vehicles. Buster remained on the edge of their uneven circle, watchful with all of his senses for the undead.

"Okay," Sutton agreed. "But we need to make a few signs in case my boys make it here."

"Deal," Metzger said with a nod.

***

Before leaving, the group placed several signs comprised of paint and wood planks or poster boards outside of the cabin, and at the camp entrance. They addressed both sons by first name, telling them the camp wasn't safe and to head to the Norfolk military base. It was agreed that few random people would come across the signs in such an obscure location, so the group members didn't feel in danger of being followed.

Metzger couldn't get the image of the downed aircraft out of his mind, even as the vehicles returned to the highway. He wanted to make better time, though he suspected the closer they got to the military installation, the worse the traffic would be. Many people trusted first responders and the military when things turned bad, but a base was still a secure facility, unable to take in civilians.

Soldiers surely put their own families first, and bases weren't equipped to handle additional people when food and supplies were delivered almost daily before the world fell apart. The military ran like clockwork under normal conditions because deliveries were scheduled and arrived in timely fashion, orders were given and carried out, and soldiers trusted that they were protecting something greater than themselves. With communications mostly wiped out, vehicles gridlocking traffic virtually everywhere, and a majority of the world's population wiped out, who knew how well the hierarchy of the military branches held together?

"Do you think his sons are dead?" Jillian asked once they were on the highway for about ten minutes.

Metzger followed the box truck, which barely navigated around a few stopped vehicles, close to tipping over into the center median that was more like a trench.

"It's quite possible," Metzger answered. "I know from experience that traveling across state lines isn't easy. There's danger around every corner."

"If they learned anything from him about guns and survival, I'd say they have a chance."

"Agreed. And if we don't find a sign of them soon, we might lose Colby. He's not going to stick with us if he thinks there's a chance to find them back at the camp."

Metzger continued driving as the highway's roadblocks thinned in number and the vehicles were able to make better time. Congestion always seemed worst around towns, cities, and exits. The undead were more evenly spread out, as they were virtually always mobile, shuffling from one location to the next in search of living prey.

Thinking they were making good time, Metzger had just grown accustomed to keeping a fairly decent clip of speed once they passed a slightly clustered exit. He took a few seconds to glance out his side window, catching a most peculiar sight along the opposite side of the highway. Glancing back to the road for just a second, he found the box truck's brakes being tapped and the truck coming to a very sudden stop as Gracine or Sutton had obviously noticed the strange occurrence as well.

"What is it?" Jillian asked as the truck behind them nearly collided with their rear bumper.

As what could only be termed a herd of staggering undead made their way in the same direction the group was heading, a lone individual stood in the middle of the pack, staring directly at the three vehicles. Paying no mind to the hazardous undead around him, he stood with his arms at his side, making no secret that he was observing their actions while standing perfectly still. Stranger yet, the undead passed him without giving him a second thought, occasionally blocking their view of him and vice versa. Jillian leaned forward for a better look, locked onto the same bizarre phenomenon that had the rest of the group questioning how such a thing was possible.

Something about the man looked odd, and the distance made it difficult to tell exactly what, but Metzger thought it looked as though the man was wearing a Halloween mask depicting an old man's wrinkled face. He squinted, trying to make out details when a horrible realization reached his mind.

"Holy fuck," he muttered. "That's no mask."

Twenty-Three

Metzger stepped from the vehicle around the same time as everyone else in the group. They all wanted a closer look at the stoic stranger standing across the median in the center of the opposite highway. Upon closer examination it appeared as though the man not only wore a mask consisting of flesh, but it might have been adhered to his neck and arms. He wore dark pants of some kind and a shirt that might have been white or an eggshell color at one time, but stains had taken their toll. Metzger noticed stains along his clothing that looked like blood, along with a few lighter flaky patches that might have also been flesh attached to the cloth. Strangely enough, chunks of animal fur and raw pelts appeared fastened to the clothing as well.

It wasn't until Vazquez started to take a step forward that the stranger finally turned and walked casually in the opposite direction.

Still the undead paid him no mind, even though he didn't walk or act anything like they did.

"Well that was fucking weird," Sutton commented.

"Agreed," Gracine said, still staring across the highway as though she entertained thoughts of following him to discern his immunity to the undead.

"Was he wearing a mask?" Luke inquired to no one in particular, keeping Samantha beside him.

"I don't think that was a mask," Metzger answered. "It looked like real human skin."

"Is that a thing?" Sutton asked with a surprised look through his injured face.

Seldom did he register surprise with the group, often trying to play it cool during even the most hairy of situations.

"I'm saying if you're willing to skin the undead, maybe you can blend in," Gracine answered with a shrug. "But what the fuck was with the animal parts?"

"You noticed that, too?" Sutton asked. "I guess dead is dead to them, no matter what it comes from."

Although his experience was limited between deceased humans that didn't reanimate and dead creatures, Metzger recalled the smells being similar. He wondered if the undead simply used instinct to differentiate between mobile beings with the odor or without it.

With the undead across the highway, and some closer to them beginning to take notice, the group silently decided to jump into their vehicles and continue their journey, knowing they were drawing close to their destination. In the previous norm, they might have reached the military base within a few hours, but there were times where they literally had to move vehicles out of their way, or syphon fuel before continuing south.

Metzger began to feel the monotony of the trip, repeating the same actions over and over again. Only the vision of seeing the military base, albeit surrounded by the undead, and finding his brother propelled him forward. They had only gotten a few miles behind them when the skies turned gloomy, and then ominous. Before the group could even slow down or take evasive actions, the sky cut loose with hard rain and hail the size of peas. Metzger could barely see ten feet in front of him, even with the headlights turned on, so he felt thankful when Gracine found a section along the side of the road for everyone to pull over.

Seconds later the winds began howling and Metzger noticed one undead straggler navigating a few nearby vehicles, succumbing to the gale forces and falling face first onto the concrete. It struggled to regain its footing with the combination of rain, hail, and wind gusts pinning it to the ground. Without the benefit of weather apps, or any kind of weather predication, he wondered if a tornado might be heading their way. Some form of shelter sounded appropriate, but he hadn't seen many buildings near the highway for quite a few miles.

"Have you seen any good leads where we might find shelter?" he asked Jillian.

"Getting worried about this weather?"

"A little."

"That makes two of us."

She thought a few seconds, looking in the side mirror as though it might offer something to jog her memory.

"There were signs for some church up ahead that made it sound like it was right off the road. It looked like kind of a big deal."

Metzger pulled out from their parking spot, stopping beside the box truck. Jillian rolled down her window so he could speak directly to Gracine.

"There's a church a little up the road," he said. "I don't like the look of this weather."

"What are you worried about?" Sutton inquired from the passenger's seat.

"The vehicles are going to get damaged, or we're going to be in the middle of a tornado. It can't be far off the road."

Both Gracine and Sutton looked at him as though he was acting paranoid, but Luke had already pulled up behind the truck, ready to follow the convoy again.

"If it's not close by, we'll just pull over again," Metzger assured them, drawing a shrug from Gracine.

"Fine."

Metzger pulled forward, noticing a stronger surge in the wind that shook every tree around them, tossing debris across the highway like tumbleweeds. A few items the wind often failed to move, like a small cooking pot, and tea kettle, bounced atop the pavement until they struck the truck. Feeling somewhat justified in his decision, Metzger pressed onward, looking for any sign of shelter, or an exit that immediately led to safety.

Within half a mile he spied a sign that pointed off to the right, indicating the church was a quarter of a mile down the road. He made the turn, seeing a paradox in that the sun shined in the distance, but the surrounding winds currently hunted them like prey. At first, a wooded area obscured the property they searched for, but after climbing a small hill with the vehicles, Metzger and Jillian saw a clearing with a church, several outbuildings, and a graveyard.

"Creepy," Jillian said as the wipers cleared the way for them to see through the windshield.

Aside from the church grounds, no other houses, barns, or businesses were visible in the distance. It looked like a safe haven, despite the winds hurling plastic bags and other waste across the property that still looked somewhat manicured. In the foreground the graveyard contained close to a hundred graves, occupying a rolling hill that descended toward the highway behind the drivers. The church, a white building with a steeple, stood out as the most prominent feature on the property, but a small pavilion was located further in from the county road. A small white utility shed could be seen between the church and graveyard, but a larger, almost barn-sized structure painted a slate gray color loomed on the other side of the worship building.

Raindrops hit the windshield sounding like pebbles, and only turning the wipers to their highest speed allowed Metzger to see the grounds. He drove down a slight bank before an equally inclined hill brought him to the gravel driveway of the church. It had a very grassroots feel about it, as though a single preacher presided over a few dozen devoted followers each Sunday, and possibly on Wednesday evenings. Perhaps the churchgoers volunteered their time and money to help maintain the grounds, because the paintjobs looked recent and the grounds didn't look like hayfields.

He half expected to see a zombie staggering through the cemetery to complete the cliché zombie movie setting. Having never seen a case of the already dead being grandfathered in with whatever plague killed the living and turned them, Metzger didn't envision the dead clawing at their coffins, six feet under, trying to free themselves. This particular area appeared too rural to attract the undead, though that didn't mean it was exempted from danger. Driving along the driveway to the side of the larger outbuilding that protected his truck from the elements, Metzger didn't harbor any intentions of stepping out of the vehicle.

Taking notice of skylights or solar panels atop the roof of the larger building, he wondered if it might be an area for recreation, though this didn't appear to be a mega church that lured people in with a gymnasium or a coffee shop. If anything, congregation members likely enjoyed the fact that it wasn't attached to a big city, or surrounded by urban landscape.

During the flight, and later driving south toward Norfolk, Jillian and Metzger transitioned from small talk to conversations about faith, their past lives, and how the world might end up moving forward. Metzger even shared the story about how Sutton claimed to have met Gracine, mostly because he ran out of other things to say. Now Jillian brought up a part of one conversation Metzger hadn't provided details about during an earlier talk.

"Why didn't you ever look for her?"

"Who? My girlfriend?"

"Yeah. I mean I get that she dumped you for no reason, but it just seems a little cold that you never called or looked for her before heading to New York."

"I don't know," Metzger admitted, his tone as neutral as his feelings on the subject. "I suppose in my mind she was with some other dude and they were probably scrambling for their lives, or already chasing the living to munch on them."

"Did she ever call *you*?"

"No," Metzger said as rain continued to pelt the windshield, not yet ready to relent. "We never communicated after the split, and admittedly I was pretty bitter after getting my teaching credentials in Ohio and making the move there. I was planning for marriage and a family, but I guess she had other ideas."

"Why Cincinnati?"

"It was a smaller area outside of Cincinnati, actually, but she had family down there and wanted to be closer to them. So I made the sacrifice."

"That's pretty noble," Jillian said with a bit of admiration. "I wish I could've found a guy who would make that kind of commitment."

Metzger scoffed, unable to believe she found time for anything aside from classes and weekend parties.

"What?" Jillian asked defensively.

"You're barely twenty, and you were still in college," he answered. "I can't believe a steady relationship was even in your wheelhouse."

"You were in college once. Don't tell me you sat in your dorm studying all the time."

"Touché."

"I wasn't a heavy partier or anything, but I didn't sit around the house either."

As though a stark reminder of how they had it in days past, a zombie smacked against Metzger's window, wanting to get at them as it clawed at the glass with a snarl. Rain and wind failed to faze it, though the fact it was able to stand indicated the weather pattern might finally be breaking.

After being startled momentarily, Metzger returned his attention to the conversation.

"So you were going to graduate, get your doctorate in history, and settle down with the perfect husband and raise two perfect children?"

"I hadn't thought that far ahead. I just wanted to unwind on the weekends and occasionally get laid."

Metzger felt certain his face flushed a little, feeling as though one of his high school students had just confessed something naughty to him.

"And now?" he asked as the zombie continued to make noise behind him, refusing to leave now that it found certified living humans.

"Now I'm just looking to survive first and foremost," Jillian answered in such an apathetic way that Metzger questioned how much of her past few statements held true.

In what seemed like an instant the rain and hail ceased and the clouds broke overhead, allowing the sun to stream through for a few seconds. Metzger popped his door open, sending the zombie tumbling to the ground a safe distance from the truck. Pulling the pack containing his swords from the seat behind him, he stepped out and used the shorter blade to slice cleanly through the skull of his dimwitted adversary.

He looked around, finding his colleagues stepping from their vehicles, all immediately struck with the few final raindrops. Taking in a deep breath through his nostrils, Metzger enjoyed the fresh smell the cleansing rains brought through the area. More often than not, the living grew accustomed to body odor and the lingering stench of the undead.

Metzger cleaned the blade of his sword along the flannel shirt the zombie had worn, but no longer needed. Replacing it to the pack where he usually stored it, he heard a snort from the building behind him that caused him to slowly turn. They were parked on one of the narrow sides of the barn, but the double doors were located at the opposite end.

Metzger thought of the gray building as a barn because it didn't truly fit any other description so far as outbuildings went. He tried looking for any holes in the wood slats, or gaps between the seams to look inside, but the building was well put together and didn't offer many flaws. He thought the noise he heard sounded like an animal, and now the others followed him around the longer side of the barn as curiosity got the better of them.

No lock held the double doors shut, but a wooden post was lying across two clasps so the door didn't simply open on its own. Unsure of what to expect, but feeling reasonably certain the creature inside wasn't a zombie, he slowly removed the post and tossed it to the ground, allowing the doors to slowly fall open.

"Wow," he said, finding two pens inside.

One contained a chestnut horse and a smaller brown pony with a mane that appeared a straw color. The other pen held a cow, and none of the animals appeared to be malnourished or desperately in need of food or attention. The barn protected them from the elements, and the undead, but someone obviously made a point to care for the animals.

"What do you make of that?" Luke asked aloud as Samantha perked up around the creatures.

He picked her up, allowing her to stroke the horse along its elongated face since it seemed friendly, even welcoming human affection. For a fleeting moment the world felt a little normal without the weight of having to travel, being attacked by strangers or zombies, or scrounging for food on their minds. The advent of fall colors surrounded them with some leaves beginning to turn, a few lying at their feet, and the grass beginning to turn from a lush green to a softer hue.

An upper level accessible only by a stairway along the right side of the barn might have held feed, supplies, holiday decorations, or any number of other items. Metzger thought about the panels along the roof, wondering if it might be some kind of greenhouse since the barn didn't really need electricity. His mind quickly changed direction to hitting the road and getting to the military base before his brother was deployed on some secret mission. He wasn't about to leave the three animals penned inside the barn unless he knew someone was available to care for them. He felt animals deserved freedom to roam, even if the odds eventually caught up with them.

About to take another deep breath of fresh country air while he could, Metzger heard the sound of footsteps in the leaves on the other side of the open door, so he quickly moved it for a look, all too aware he wasn't readily armed to confront the living. Instead of one of the usual threats, however, he found an older man with a fringe of gray hair holding up his hands defensively.

"Please don't hurt the animals," he immediately pleaded, his left eye wandering toward his left temple.

"Who are you?" Gracine inquired, already clutching a sidearm much to Metzger's surprise.

"I'm the caretaker for the church. My wife and I are all that's left and we live here now."

He suddenly looked regretful over mentioning his wife to strangers, though he looked rather nervous overall. Metzger supposed half a dozen armed people visiting one's property would likely cause anyone some tense moments.

"You look like nice folks, so I'm just going to ask that you don't harm us or the critters."

"We're not the types to harm anyone unless we're defending ourselves," Metzger stated. "We stopped here to escape the weather, and heard your horse."

"What are you doing with the animals if you don't mind me asking?" Sutton inquired.

"At the moment we're trying to preserve the species. In the wild they'd certainly get attacked by those things."

"In a pinch they become food?"

"We hope it doesn't come to that," the older man answered. "I've been building them a pen out back as I find the materials, but we've had issues with people stopping by."

"Where's the rest of your congregation?" Luke asked.

"Some came here, but they didn't make it. A few contacted me after things went bad saying they were going to try and make a run for their families, or out here for safety with others. I think some of them were bitten and never made it."

Metzger wanted to trust the man, and instinct told him this wasn't a dangerous situation, but experience kept nagging at the back of his mind. He hadn't seen a sweet old lady wife yet, and for all he knew she was a rotting corpse seated in a rocking chair that this man talked to, answering himself in a woman's voice as he played both roles.

"We should probably get back on the road," he said, not feeling entirely comfortable lingering around inhabited property.

"Stay a little while and rest if you want to," the man offered, lowering his voice a bit. He spoke the words quickly, almost desperately as his eyes glanced to one side as though testing if anyone noticed his actions. "The wife can put on some tea and your little one can play with the horses if she wants to. We don't get nice folks stopping by here very often."

"You sound as though you've had some bad ones though," Vazquez stated. "We'd hate to impose."

"We've had trouble," the man admitted. "The rotters, animal predators that want to eat these three, and a few people here and there. My name's Tom by the way. Tom Alderson."

"Good to meet you, Tom," Metzger said, shaking the man's hand. "And I hate to be rude, but we really have somewhere to be."

A look of absolute desperation now crossed Alderson's face.

"I can't stay out here long or he'll get suspicious," the man said just above a whisper, immediately drawing Metzger's eyes toward the house. "Don't look! He'll know I said something."

"Who?"

"This lunatic has been keeping my wife and I hostage the past few days. He sent me out here to get rid of all of you, saying he'd kill my wife if I didn't."

Metzger glanced at Sutton, wanting the man to voice his usual stance on such matters.

"Don't look at me," Sutton replied with a shrug.

"I knew I could count on you, Colby."

"You already know this isn't our problem," Sutton said, the sour look on his face not changing one bit.

"This *isn't* our problem," Metzger reiterated, wanting to get back to the highway, sensing this man wasn't telling the whole truth based on his twitchy behavior.

"Please," Alderson pleaded.

"You can't be serious," Jillian said, stepping forward. "We could walk in there and end this now."

"My wife," Alderson said nervously. "He might shoot her."

Everyone remained silent a moment, fearful of taking too long and alerting the potential threat inside the church.

"We could wait until nighttime," Gracine suggested.

Metzger sighed inwardly, knowing the delay would be devastating to his plan of reaching Norfolk by the end of the day or sometime the next day. Sutton shot him a look that indicated complete agreement. Everyone else appeared sympathetic to the caretaker's plight, and even Metzger felt sorry for the man if the tale he told was legitimate. He questioned why an individual would take two people hostage for a few days. A drifter would either take what he wanted and leave, or simply murder the couple if he was truly delusional.

"We need to go," he finally said aloud.

Luke and Jillian started to say something in protest.

"We need to go, or we'll look suspicious," Metzger said firmly, beginning to close the barn doors, much to Samantha's chagrin.

Everyone followed suit, a few even waving goodbye to Alderson to sell their departure to anyone who might be watching.

A few minutes later everyone was loaded into their vehicles and driving down to the highway until they parked to talk strategy. Metzger still wasn't certain he wanted to put lives at risk over someone's tale of woe.

"We aren't going to make it to the base by tonight," Vazquez spoke first, indicating he wanted to stay and help.

"No, but we still have a few hours of good daylight," Metzger countered. "We could get awful damn close."

"How can you be so heartless?" Jillian asked, turning on him a bit suddenly for someone who usually followed his lead.

"I don't trust everything he's selling us."

"Are you sure it's not just for selfish reasons?"

"I'd be lying if I said I wasn't being a little selfish, but my instincts are telling me something's up with this situation. People don't just walk into a church and hold other people hostage for days on end."

All eyes began drifting toward Sutton.

"Why are you putting this on me?" he asked gruffly. "I'm the only logical one here, and you already know I think this entire trip is a waste of time."

"A few of us could stay and handle this before catching up," Gracine suggested, indicating she and Sutton would be the two.

"It's not a good idea to split us up," Metzger said. "Too many things can go wrong on the road, and we have strength in numbers."

Buster had been walking around, sniffing the area since the group exited the vehicles. He suddenly made a noise that indicated he detected danger somewhere nearby. Everyone looked, finding a zombie who appeared covered in mud as though he'd fallen into a dirty puddle during the storm, navigating through some disabled cars.

"Got it," Gracine said, walking over to silently handle the threat.

"We don't *have* to wait until dark," Sutton suggested. "If it's really one guy, we could take him out quickly."

"I'm not comfortable murdering someone if we don't know the whole story," Metzger said. "If we're seriously going to deal with this, we need to observe the situation, decide what's going on, and figure out how to handle it."

"Which would mean staying until dark so we can see inside the church without getting spotted," Jillian stated the obvious.

"I guess it does," Metzger said with a sigh.

***

After a few hours of cautiously rummaging through nearby vehicles and dealing with the few undead that approached them, the group looked and felt exhausted. Following the rain, an intense sun appeared, bringing an unusually muggy fall heat that followed the storm. Sunscreen wasn't readily available, and a few members of the group showed signs of being sunburned. Metzger often thought of items he took for granted back in the day, feeling his own skin irritated by the sun's rays.

Eventually they all drove back to the church, parking out of sight from anywhere on the property. Considering they were all armed, and only a single threat allegedly awaited them inside the church, they didn't approach in covert fashion. Luke stayed behind with Samantha and Buster to watch over the vehicles as the others approached the graveyard, attempting to stay out of direct view of any church windows because they weren't crawling, and they barely bothered crouching as they darted around the tombstones.

A purple hue overtook the sky as the sun slowly disappeared over the horizon, giving the group better cover. Sutton had brought along a conventional sniper rifle, along with a shotgun for closer range. Most everyone else carried pistols, prepared to act as backup or defend themselves if necessary. Not much else had been spoken about anyone's take on Tom Alderson's story, or how much of it they believed. Once it was determined they were sticking around until dark, everyone simply relegated themselves to seeing the truth in person.

Metzger approached the graveyard with Jillian a few paces away. Just under a hundred tombstones lined the hill, and it was easy to distinguish the older stones from the more recent ones. What caught the attention of both Metzger and Jillian, however, was the presence of eight markers consisting of manufactured wood in the form of crucifixes. Each of the markers contained a name, but no additional information, appearing very recently placed.

Thinking perhaps some of the congregation simply died on the grounds, or requested to be placed near their loved ones in death, Metzger passed the markers without much further thought. Most of the group began splitting up, looking for windows in the church or the residential area connected to the building that might offer them a view inside. Metzger, however, grew curious when he looked to the gray building that housed livestock and something upstairs.

Sutton looked at him curiously and Metzger motioned that he wanted to take a look inside the building while they conducted surveillance outside the church. Four of them could easily handle the spy work while he discovered what, if anything, awaited him in the upper floor of the barn.

All the way to the barn he kept looking over his shoulder toward the church, trying to make certain no one stared at his movements. Seeing no lights on inside the sanctuary, he carefully removed the bar and opened the doors to the building, slipping inside to find it almost completely dark in the lower level. The horse grunted a bit upon seeing him, possibly thinking it might get fed. He scratched its head when it drew near, but wasted little time making his way around the pens to the stairs that led upward.

Hearing no screams or gunfire as of yet, he hoped his colleagues were being careful while approaching the church. He trusted Sutton's instincts, and the man tended to err on the side of caution when entering dangerous situations. The incident at the restaurant nearly got Sutton killed, but it wasn't due to anything he personally did wrong. A brilliant, insane man had gotten the better of him for a few seconds, and nearly finished him off before help arrived.

Slowly climbing the stairwell, Metzger craned his neck for a look into the room that awaited him, almost expecting something out of a horror movie like a skinned body, or a collection of permanently dead zombies. Unable to see very well, he pulled his small flashlight from a pocket and switched it on. No foul odors reached his nostrils, however, and when he finally broke the plane of the second level he saw crafted tables holding dozens of plants. Above them, the glass panels allowed all kinds of natural light to enter during the day, and Metzger immediately felt a sense of relief seeing only plant life around him. Although he didn't dare linger long, Metzger wanted to know he'd inspected everything before returning to the group. Due to the caretaker's strange behavior, he felt the need to solve the mystery before determining what actions to take inside the church.

Every instinct told him to move on and leave the man and this strange church behind, but it wasn't truly his nature to turn his back on others, and the group decided they wanted to help.

Metzger hoped they didn't live to regret that decision.

He quickly discovered the upstairs in fact acted as a greenhouse, containing tomatoes, cucumbers, onions, peppers, and a few other vegetables that grew as though the season meant nothing to them. Every plant was arranged in rows along the tables, providing easy navigation as Metzger walked between the rows, not sampling the plants because it would be rude. As he reached the far corner a different set of plants with strange leaves of a purple color and no buds or fruit visible caught his attention. All around the isolated square table that occupied this corner were signs reading "Danger" and "Poison" to warn unsuspecting pickers of the plant's hazards.

A desk near the table contained paperwork about gardening care for the plants within the greenhouse, but a file caught his attention, separate from the other papers. Metzger picked it up, opening it to find a recipe of sorts. Several ingredients were listed, along with the procedure to properly mix them. Certainly no alchemist, Metzger thought the potion created by mixing the ingredients didn't sound very inviting, or healthy. As though to confirm his thoughts on the matter, the title at the top of the paper struck him squarely, particularly considering the fresh graves lining the cemetery.

"Slumber Mix," he read the words aloud, his mind requiring only a few seconds to piece together what might have really happened on the church property after the fall of civilization.

He dropped the file, taking the stairs down two at a time in his rush to prevent another tragedy from transpiring on the grounds. Halfway down, he switched the flashlight off, pocketing it when he reached the solid ground below. Bursting through the barn doors a few seconds later, he found it nearly dark outside, but he could see Sutton and Gracine just outside of the church doors about to force their way inside. If that happened, he could picture any number of disastrous scenarios unfolding.

Unable to yell because he might endanger them, Metzger broke into a dead sprint toward the church, hoping to prevent any new wooden crosses from being placed in the cemetery.

Twenty-Four

Luckily the distance between the barn and the church building wasn't far, so Metzger waited until dashed nearly halfway before giving a stifled yell to Sutton and Gracine.

"Stop!" he cried, fearing that Sutton was about to bust down a door and march inside.

"What is it?" Sutton demanded with a whispered hiss when Metzger finally drew near them, wearing a scowl as though he'd been interrupted before getting to kick some ass.

"I don't think any of this is what it seems."

Metzger glanced at a plaque mounted beside the side entrance of the church that contained a dedication. He didn't have time to read it thoroughly due to the circumstances surrounding him, but he did notice the recent year of the building's dedication.

Gracine looked through the window right beside her with a look of growing concern.

"I think we're about to deal with whatever it is."

Before any of them could truly prepare for the confrontation heading their way the closest door opened and a young man aimed a pistol at none of them in particular. All three of them already had their weapons prepared, however, and pointed them at the young man who wore an expression as though he figured visitors were coming.

In the room behind him within the church, Tom Alderson and a woman sat atop a bench, huddled together, and shivering from fright.

"I see Tom duped you into helping him," the young man said with an unwavering expression, refusing to lower the gun.

"Maybe you should tell us why you're holding him and his wife hostage," Sutton suggested, taking aim at the stranger's forehead.

"We've all had a long day," Metzger said, quickly trying to broker some peace. "Why don't we help you figure this out so we can be on our way."

Before speaking, the man provided an insincere smile.

"Help me figure it out? These two callously murdered my family and you think you have all the answers?"

Sutton was about to say something, likely offensive, so Metzger cut him off and spoke first to enlighten everyone about his find.

"I saw a recipe for some kind of dangerous potion in the greenhouse. Does that have anything to do with what happened here?"

Standing still momentarily, the man's reasonably neutral expression turned to anger as his face reddened.

"There are eight fresh graves out there," he said with seething anger. "These two shitty excuses for human beings are responsible for all eight of them. And the only reason they're still alive is because I haven't decided what's a fitting punishment for them."

Metzger already felt more involved than he cared to be in this situation. He believed they were returning to free the couple from the clutches of some random drifter, and now he needed to rule in some sort of informal court. To decide fairly and impartially, he needed more information, which required additional time he couldn't spare. Still, he inevitably decided to go with the original wishes of the group and stay until a resolution was reached.

"Let's take this one step at a time," Metzger suggested, sensing something wasn't quite right about this young man.

His dark hair was disheveled and he wore an expression of slight uncertainty about him, as though questioning some of his own actions or motivations. He wore clothing too warm for the early fall weather, and nothing even remotely matched between his salmon-colored pants, combat boots, and a dark pea coat that looked as though it had seen better days. While fashion wasn't a priority in the apocalypse, most people dressed in reasonable, conventional, if not comfortable, clothing. Anyone suffering loss, however, might lose all sense of everyday normality, even more so than usual.

Metzger guessed him to be an older teenager, possibly twenty at the oldest.

"What's your name, kid?"

"Graham. Graham Holcomb."

Holcomb took a few steps back, diverting the aim of his gun toward Tom Alderson and his wife, who both cringed at the action.

"Who were your parents?" Metzger further inquired.

"Robert and Julia. They're buried on the hill with the other church members these two murdered."

Vazquez and Jillian joined them momentarily, not presenting themselves visibly at the front of the door when they heard the ongoing conversation.

Metzger stepped aside to Jillian when Holcomb shrunk back into the room where his hostages continued to huddle together.

"Can you check and see if there's a Robert Holcomb or wife Julia in the cemetery?" he asked of her just above a whisper.

"Sure. And it's technically called a graveyard since it's on church property."

"Thanks for the history lesson," Metzger said insincerely.

Jillian flashed him a knowing smile before leaving to check the grave markers.

Metzger decided to try a different tactic to break the ice, and perhaps engage with the hostage couple a little bit.

"What kind of church has animal pens and a greenhouse?" he aimed his question at Alderson and his wife.

"We have," Alderson caught himself using the wrong tense, "*had* members who rode their horses to church from nearby farms."

"Tom, is that young lady your wife?" Metzger asked, possibly trying too hard to involve everyone in the conversation.

His flattering words drew a roll of the eyes from Sutton.

"Her name is Melissa," Alderson said meekly.

Metzger felt as though he was being played from all angles. None of these strangers seemed completely genuine to him, as though each harbored secrets of some kind. He wasn't sure he possessed patience enough to solve the puzzle laid before him because the Atlantic and Norfolk felt so close.

"Tom, can you tell me what the deal is with the poisonous plant upstairs?" Metzger pressed, still not lowering his gun completely from the man creating the hostage situation.

"Isn't it obvious?" Holcomb blurted out. "They killed everyone here."

"That's not what happened," Alderson said vehemently.

Holcomb stepped back, placing his gun dangerously close to the older man's head.

"That's enough!" Sutton barked, obviously fed up with Holcomb's aggressive behavior since the group wasn't proving themselves a threat to anyone present. "Son, it's time for you to put the gun down or you'll be joining your folks out there."

Sutton used his own firearm to point the direction of the graveyard.

Growing irritated again, Holcomb took a step forward before returning to the older couple, waving the gun dangerously near them.

"Graham, let's talk this out," Metzger suggested, trying to be the voice of reason before the church became the site of a shootout. "We aren't here to hurt anyone, or we would've made our move before letting you see us. We just want to sort this out and go on our way to Norfolk."

"Norfolk?" the young man inquired, perking up as though he hadn't a care in the world suddenly. "You mean where the Navy base is?"

"Yes. That Norfolk."

Knowing Sutton wasn't laying down any firearms, Metzger holstered his sidearm when he felt certain Holcomb's eyes were upon him.

"Graham, I'm not going to hurt you. I just want to sort this out, and I can't do that until you show me a little trust."

Although he didn't put his pistol down, Holcomb retreated further into the room with the couple and took a seat in a chair set to the side. Metzger truly stepped inside the building for the first time, but the three people before him sat in a staging room of some sort rather than the main portion of the church where worship once took place. A door to his left led to that part of the church, barely ajar, teasing at the tranquility the other side might offer him. He saw a stream of light from the other side strike the door frame, wondering where such a beam might come from as though it were sent from above.

It flickered momentarily, and he knew the light originated from a candle.

"What's going on here, Graham?" Metzger asked as he took the last available seat inside the room, his back now to the only people he trusted.

"These two," Holcomb said as he shook the gun. "Them and their 'Slumber Mix' killed what few church members remained. I remember coming to this church as a kid with my folks and I never trusted them, even then."

Alderson shook his head, either from disbelief of what Holcomb spoke, or denying that he and his wife had anything to do with sending church members to their deaths.

"What was this place like?" Metzger asked, hearing a grumble from Sutton behind him because the man was ready to move on and leave the church in the rearview mirror.

"It was a church," Alderson answered before he could be denied. "Same as most, I suppose, but we had a lot of people come from the country. And people who were passing through and saw our signs on the highway."

"Not a church that hurt people, or meant any ill will?"

"No."

"Not until you killed my parents," Holcomb finally chimed in. "That was your biggest mistake."

"Why are you torturing them, Graham?" Metzger asked. "You've held them for two days according to Tom and you haven't shot them or let them go. Why hang around?"

"I have nowhere to go. They took everything from me."

"What if we offered to bring you to Norfolk?" Metzger asked, drawing an argumentative throat clearing from Sutton.

"What?" Sutton asked incredulously from behind him a few seconds later.

"I heard Norfolk might be protected since it's right off the water and the Navy brought home all of their ships," Holcomb stated.

"That's right," Metzger said. "All of them."

Metzger studied the contents of the small room, seeing little of value or use. Alderson and his wife continued to shiver in the presence of the young man holding a gun near them. Melissa looked innocent enough with her gray hair cut in short curls and wrinkles etched along her forehead and beneath her eyes. He couldn't imagine the couple simply murdering church members for no reason, particularly if they took the time to bury them in marked graves.

"What is one of your fondest memories of attending this church?" he decided to ask Holcomb with good reason.

"Pastor Townsend spoke a sermon about a family going to fetch the descendants of Jonadab for wine at a gathering. Hope I said that name right. The family declined to drink the wine because they were obedient to their forefather's wishes. I want to obey the wishes of my parents now that they're no longer here."

Metzger didn't exactly consider that a fond memory, per se, but decided to press forward.

"Would your folks wish for you to take hostages and threaten complete strangers in a place of holy worship?"

Holcomb's eyes fell to the ground before they ascended upward, as though looking for an answer.

"Who was Pastor Townsend?" Metzger inquired, directing his question at the couple.

"He was the senior pastor here," Alderson answered quietly. "He's buried in one of the new graves out to the side."

"I want to hear how he died."

"No," Holcomb said firmly. "They don't get to spill their lies on this holy ground."

"Graham, I have to hear both sides of this before I decide what to do."

"What to do?" Holcomb questioned as though Metzger should have automatically been on his side the entire time.

Or he believed Metzger *was* on his side until this very moment.

"These two committed murder and you're going to let them tell untruths to lie their way out of it?"

"Even trials hear both sides of a case, Graham. Unless they made a full confession to you when you stormed in here, I'm not sure you have much of a case. And while you may be holding a gun, you could kill both of them, or me, but my friends will put a dozen holes in you after that and nothing will be accomplished. I'm trying to end this standoff in a civil manner, but I need your cooperation to do that."

Metzger felt amazingly calm as he spoke. Perhaps the routine of constantly being in danger from literally everything around him provided uncanny nerves of steel, but he felt death was a certainty on any given day, and it was simply a way of life now.

"This wasn't a suicide pact, or anything like that," Alderson answered after a few seconds of awkward silence. "Church members filed in a few at a time and we tried to make a go of it. At first, none of us knew exactly what was going on. We came here for strength and unity, but we didn't have the internet or television to keep us informed. We kept seeing these sick people staggering around the church and the countryside, and we wanted to help them. It wasn't until a few members were bitten that we saw them catch the fever and pass within a few days."

"Was the pastor one of those people?" Metzger asked.

"Yes, but not for about a week. By then we knew what was going on. One of our members stopped by to check on us before traveling to Georgia to meet his family at a property they owned. We knew what needed to be done, but it felt like murder because these people, these *things*, were still up and walking."

Holcomb appeared agitated, but Metzger couldn't tell if his unrest stemmed from the maintenance man's words, or the fact that he doubted his own take on the situation. He stood, running a nervous hand through his hair, still clutching the gun in his right hand. Before he could decide how to handle the situation going forward, Jillian whispered something to Sutton before the man stepped forward to speak to Metzger.

"Jillian says the graves are marked like the guy said."

"Okay," Metzger answered.

"There's something else," Sutton said, keeping his voice low. "She heard noise coming from beneath the sod."

Metzger closed his eyes a few seconds, exhaling through his nose as he processed the new information. He decided exactly what needed to be done to bring the situation to a close.

"Can you dig those two graves up without letting whoever's under there loose?"

Sutton returned a skeptical look, as though this wasn't one of Metzger's better ideas.

"Trust me."

Sutton didn't appear convinced, but he left the church in search of a shovel just the same.

"What was that about?" Holcomb asked with irritation.

"My friends verified that Robert and Julia Holcomb were indeed buried in the graveyard."

"Why wouldn't they be?" Holcomb sneered angrily. "Why are you doubting me when clearly these two have wronged eight people?"

When he spoke the words, Holcomb pointed toward the tombstones on the other side of the wall, and Metzger noticed a band around his wrist where the skin wasn't as tan as the rest of his flesh. It could have been from a watch band, but he didn't see a round spot in the area where the watch itself might have rested.

"I don't know you, kid," Metzger said firmly. "I'm still trying to figure out exactly why you're here *now* and why you weren't with your parents when all of this went down."

"We were separated. I couldn't get to them."

"Where were you?" Metzger pressed, leaving anger and distrust out of his tone, realizing he was teetering between a breakthrough and a mass shooting with the young man.

"I was being held somewhere against my will," Holcomb answered simply.

Vazquez approached Metzger from behind, leaning in to speak with him.

"After looking around, I've found photos and information about most of the people who attended this church. There was information about the Holcombs, and even a picture, but nothing about this kid."

"Maybe he wasn't a regular?" Metzger offered.

Vazquez returned a skeptical look.

"The register was pretty thorough."

"What are you two talking about?" Holcomb asked heatedly. "If you're going to doubt me, I might as well off these geezers right now and be done with it."

"Let's settle down a minute, Graham," Metzger said calmly. "You've clearly been patient during these past few days, and I'm guessing you haven't slept very well."

"I haven't," Holcomb confessed after a few seconds with an unclear stare that didn't have a specific direction.

Vazquez slowly backed off to avoid irritating the young man any further. Metzger watched as Holcomb rubbed his face several times with the palm of his hand, the gun waving at more random intervals in the other. For the first time

Metzger truly feared the young man might take sudden aim at Alderson and his wife, murdering them both without regard for his own safety.

"I have to ask," Metzger said, directing his attention at the couple once more, "what's with the slumber mix inside the greenhouse?"

He hoped to draw Holcomb back to his side, or at least a neutral stance, by interrogating the couple a bit further.

"Some of our members knew what they were going to become," Alderson answered. "They didn't want to suffer for days on end once they were bitten, so they opted to simply go to sleep and not wake up."

"You took them out so you could have this place to yourself," Holcomb said as though it was a fact everyone should have known.

He flushed with anger, his tone and expression showing how close he drew to the breaking point as frustrated tears welled in his eyes. Once again he grew highly agitated, putting both hands up to the sides of his head, still clutching the gun.

"Isn't that technically a form of suicide?" Metzger inquired of Alderson. "Don't most Christians consider suicide a one-way ticket to Hades?"

"Is it really suicide if you're on the way out anyway?" Alderson countered. "Only a few of them asked for it, and we had the plants, so we helped them on their way."

Holcomb let out a brief scream that indicated he couldn't hear any more of their tale. Metzger knew he needed to act, but he didn't want to put anyone at risk, if at all possible.

"Graham, I need you to come with me," he said with coaxing, soothing words, as though he genuinely wanted to help the young man. "My friends went to check the graves outside, and they heard some noises below the surface of the ground."

"What kind of noises?" Holcomb inquired, genuinely surprised and hopeful.

"I think these people may have buried your parents alive."

"What?" Holcomb asked, aiming the gun purposefully at Alderson, who shielded his wife with his own body in case bullets flew.

"No!" Metzger said, trying to draw Holcomb back to him. "If your folks are alive, you should be the first person they see. One of my friends has started digging to get them out of there."

Holcomb stood in awe for a moment, possibly trying to assess the validity of such a ludicrous notion that anyone buried in the ground might still be fighting for life. In truth, Metzger suspected exactly what happened with the eight people buried in the graveyard, but he needed the young man away from the couple if at all possible. He also needed to verify one last thing before he carried out the heinous plan swimming around in his mind.

Unwilling to simply trust Metzger at his word, Holcomb snatched Melissa from beside her husband, holding her hostage with a gun to her head.

"Lead the way," Holcomb urged, using the older woman as leverage to make everyone else walk in front of him toward the graveyard.

Most of the others had already started the walk to side of the church, and Metzger made certain to give Holcomb a wide berth as he exited the church, ushering Alderson to him. Alderson appeared fearful of what might happen to Melissa, turning every so often to ensure that the young man didn't harm her. Halfway to the graveyard, Metzger leaned into ask Alderson a question, wondering if he should have simply put a bullet in Holcomb and been done with it.

"Why didn't you keep them from coming back after they died?"

"At first we didn't know," Alderson said, his eyes indicating shame for having participated in any of part of killing someone, even if it was a mercy killing they requested. "Even after we found out, it still felt like murder to shoot or stab them, so we just buried them quickly."

"Less chatter," Holcomb demanded, even though most everyone around him still held firearms, and could easily overtake him at any given second.

Metzger's morals still didn't permit him to carry out cold-blooded murder, even though the incident at the school edged him closer to that line he didn't want to cross. He worried about having to inform his brother about the death of his parents, thinking he might want to omit the part about the cafeteria skirmish that left one of Xavier's people dead. Bryce tended to think analytically, rather calculating and detached sometimes. It made him a better warrior like the military wanted, but it left him lacking as a brother one could confide in sometimes.

"You said you remember coming here as a kid," Metzger commented to Holcomb. "Do you have any good memories about coming here with your parents?"

"I remember walking up to the place every week," Holcomb commented. "On rare occasions it would snow and I remember feeling sheltered inside like nothing could ever touch me. I couldn't wait to get out of youth group to go home and make snow angels or build a snowman."

In his own mind, Metzger couldn't determine what Holcomb had created through fantasy or psychosis, and what truly occurred during his childhood. He did know holes existed in the young man's story, and while Tom and Melissa Alderson may have been guilty of some version of a crime in the old world, they simply assisted their fellow church members and tried leading a quiet existence until Holcomb, or whatever his real name was, came along.

Metzger needed to test one last thing before sentencing the young man to whatever fate he deserved, and as they came upon Sutton digging up a shallow grave, everyone froze where they stood. Due to the unforeseen circumstances, Sutton hadn't started on the second grave yet, lacking time to properly finish unearthing the first body.

"Mom?" Holcomb asked, a despondent look crossing his face as he spied the dirt mound beside the grave.

Metzger circled around, finding that Holcomb indeed knew the right grave. He seemed focused on certain aspects intently, while overlooking details that most people might automatically provide when prompted.

Sutton stopped and stared at the group momentarily. Realizing they were waiting for him to finish, he continued carefully plunging the shovel into the ground, trying to avoid stabbing into the body. A moment later he discovered minimal surface area of what looked like a canvas sack. He used the shovel to carefully remove the dirt from the top of the covering until most of it was revealed and the sack moved within the hole like an insect larva squirming along the ground. On instinct alone he took a step back and prepared to crash the shovel down upon the zombie thrashing and hissing within the sack.

"No," Metzger said, holding up his palm toward Sutton.

Sutton complied, allowing Metzger to draw the knife from his side and kneel down beside the recovered body.

"I have one last question for you," he said to Holcomb before taking the tip of the knife to the canvas, delaying the freedom of the zombie below him.

Holcomb stared anxiously as though his mother was indeed alive and Metzger endangered her by keeping her inside that canvas sack. His reaction alone told Metzger he couldn't be allowed to continue to roam the earth as a danger to himself and other living people when so few good people existed.

"What is it?" Holcomb virtually pleaded, releasing Melissa whether he intended to or not.

"Do you swear to me that you attended *that* church, that *very building* as it stands, since you were a child?"

"Of course I have," Holcomb said as though the question was preposterous.

Metzger stared at the ground, feeling defeated because no other choice lie before him as he cut the first slit into the canvas sack. He motioned for Holcomb to come over to the hole, handing him the blade as he stepped a safe distance back. Part of him felt guilty for encouraging the delusion in the man's head, but the other half of him wanted to give Holcomb every last millisecond to come to his senses and realize the truth surrounding him. Whether the man had gone his entire life with an undiagnosed mental illness, or ran out of medication in the weeks following the apocalypse, didn't matter. There simply wasn't a good place for him in this world if he couldn't function properly on his own, or with others.

"I'm here, Mom," he mumbled, carefully taking the knife and cutting the sack open.

While everyone else recoiled in horror at the sight of a decomposing zombie more dirty than most, with her hair a mix of blond strands and earthworms, Holcomb drew a relieved smile. Metzger couldn't imagine what distorted visage the young man saw, because everyone else saw a menacing, hideous, and revolting being rising from the grave. Metzger audibly sighed with relief, only because his suspicions were proven correct and his conscience wiped clean.

Perhaps Holcomb saw a loving mother smiling back at him, or she appeared relieved for him rescuing her from the evil couple who buried her alive. Regardless of what he saw in his mind, it was fictional and completely opposite of what everyone else staring downward viewed.

The young man maintained his skewed version of events until the zombie lurched forward and chomped into his throat, ripping pieces of flesh and ligaments away from his body. Blood spewed all over both of them, coating the dead woman's already filthy dress with the crimson liquid and existing dirt. Holcomb immediately went into shock, not realizing what was happening to him, or the grievous error he made due to his impaired judgment.

Sounds of slurping and crunching that sounded like a dog chowing down on a mix of meat and tendons on a bone reached the group's ears and a few of them turned away. Holcomb faded quickly, his throat and upper torso immediately torn into by the zombie's mouth. Sutton simply pulled his sidearm and angled his shot to enter through Holcomb's skull and exit through the zombie's, saving ammunition. He fired, bringing the bloody mess and the grotesque sounds to a sudden end as the shot echoed through the nearby fields.

"How did you know?" Alderson asked, still openly numb from the series of events that unfolded.

"I didn't know much except that he wasn't who he claimed to be," Metzger answered. "I also noticed your church had some kind of dedication way too recent to extend back to his childhood."

"The original building burned about five years ago," Alderson said as though the destruction still plagued him. "We built this one and the barn with the insurance money."

Alderson's wife stumbled over to him and they finally embraced with the danger out of the way. She cried openly as tears ran down her cheeks, indicating the couple hadn't dealt much with the horrors of the apocalypse in regards to dangerous living people.

"You might want to take those roadside signs down," Vazquez said, half-joking with the couple.

Nodding, they forced understanding grins, knowing the signs served no purpose except to attract trouble.

"I'm sorry this happened to you," Metzger said. "It's just terrible luck."

"If you people hadn't come along who knows what he would have done," Melissa stated, wiping a tear from her cheek.

"What will you do now?" Jillian asked her.

"We'll survive somehow. We've made the church our home while we've waited for any of our flock to return."

Metzger walked over to the now fully deceased young man, tugging a wallet from his back pocket. He opened it, finding an identification that revealed his name to be Graham Owens, twenty years of age, from North Carolina.

"Well, he kept half of his name true," he muttered.

Staring at the wrist and its strange tan line, Metzger figured he was correct in assuming a band had occupied the man's wrist for a few weeks before falling off or getting slit. Graham Owens likely left a mental institution or a hospital psych ward shortly after things went bad, possibly overtaking a guard, or maybe getting released by a sympathetic staff who didn't want to see him starve in captivity as they abandoned their posts.

"If we miss your brother," Sutton said as he walked by, stabbing the shovel into the ground, "it's completely on you."

Sutton continued walking, and Metzger knew he was right. By doing the moral and correct thing, he put them further behind schedule. If he had chosen to go with his initial choice, the group would have inevitably followed and gotten over his decision in time. In the scheme of things, saving the older couple was the right thing to do, but no one knew if Owens would have killed them, or if they would have overpowered him in his sleep at some point. Every decision felt as though it held life or death consequences in the modern world, and one slip sometimes meant joining the undead.

"I'll get them," Alderson said, drawing near Metzger as he clasped the shovel, looking to the bodies.

"I think it can wait until morning," Metzger said. "You need to start thinking more clearly about whom you can trust and what to do with the undead."

Alderson gave a thin smirk.

"It's a little late in life for me to start changing my ways. We trusted that boy, even though we didn't recognize him from the church. He gave us some sob story about being lost until we brought him inside. Only then did he claim to be the son of Robert and Julia, and we didn't know if a single word he spoke was true after that."

"Did they even have a son?"

"No," Alderson said solemnly, shaking his head. "We figured he snooped around the graveyard and the barn, creating this elaborate story in his mind about what happened. Once he took us hostage, he firmly believed his parents were murdered by us."

Everyone took a final glance at the two bodies lying atop the open grave before heading up the hill toward the church. In his mind, Metzger knew hitting the road after dark wasn't safe, but he didn't want to linger around the church much longer. The group needed to make up for lost time, and Norfolk felt extremely close.

"What can we do to repay you?" Melissa asked no one in particular as they neared the main building. "Can we put you up for the night, or give you some supplies for your trouble?"

"We don't want anything," Metzger assured her. "We pulled in here to get shelter from the storm, and that's enough."

"Are you certain? We don't have much, but we want you to have something in case you don't make it back this way."

Metzger was about to ask what she meant, but he recalled saying something to the imposter about heading to Norfolk.

"Thank you, but no. Maybe we'll bring *you* something if we make it there and back."

Saying goodbye to the older couple felt somewhat awkward to Metzger and the entire group, except for Sutton. He had already started trudging down the hill toward their vehicles while everyone else exchanged quick hugs with the care-takers. Metzger felt less regret for assisting them after seeing how thankful they appeared. Their future likely consisted of taking in a few stray refugees, hope-fully with additional screening, and burying the occasional soul down the hill. He wasn't certain how long they'd make it, but he knew they weren't foes in the new world.

Everyone kept the same driving arrangements as before once they made their way down to the vehicles, Samantha choosing to squeeze in between Luke and Vazquez rather than spend more time around Gracine. Metzger believed the girl might be intimidated by Sutton, influencing her decision. Jillian said little as the three vehicles pulled onto the highway, waiting a few miles before speaking to Metzger.

"Do you regret helping them?"

"No," Metzger answered. "It was the right thing to do."

"Even though you could miss your brother?"

"Just knowing he's alive is enough for now," Metzger said with a nod. "I know we'll see each other again someday."

Metzger began noticing signs for Suffolk, knowing they were drawing close to the Hampton Roads area where multiple cities and counties comprised the natural harbor and metropolitan with Norfolk, acting as a hub of sorts. He knew travel was destined to become much worse because he wasn't fortunate enough to have all of the zombies tumble into the local bays and rivers like lemmings. The same barricades that once protected the living now kept the undead safe from similar hazards.

Thoughts of finding somewhere to settle in for the night crossed his mind, but Metzger wanted to spot a landmark first, to *know* he was close to his destination. They soon found themselves on Bridge Road, which was still technically Route 17, crossing nearly a mile over water to reach Suffolk on the other side. A two-lane road that provided one of several methods to cross into the Hampton Roads from the mainland, it didn't provide any issues at first. Only a few cars were abandoned in this area, and getting around them didn't prove problematic. Metzger knew gridlock anywhere along this lengthy bridge might prove dangerous for the group.

Headlights and nothing else illuminated their way along the bridge. Clouds continued to obscure the moon and any stars in the sky, making it difficult to know what lie ahead. Eventually they reached the city limits of Suffolk, finding rather nice housing to their left as the road began to split into two sections comprised of two lanes each. They began passing businesses in the form of fast food restaurants, an occasional church, and some insurance agencies set within small plazas. Barely any undead occupied either side of the highway, likely attracted to the houses and local businesses with so few cars passing through. When Metzger saw a sign for a popular hotel chain ahead he flashed his bright lights to indicate he wanted to speak with Sutton.

"What's up?" Sutton asked when they pulled beside one another after Jillian rolled down her window for them to converse.

"That hotel sounds like as good a place as any to crash for the night."

"What's with the lack of rotters?" Gracine asked.

"I'm not sure," Metzger answered. "It's kind of unnerving."

He looked down the road, not seeing much beyond the reach of their headlights.

"I don't think the hotel is much further," Metzger added. "If we're lucky they'll have some fresh towels and hot water."

Sutton caught the joke, providing a rare smirk.

"Hopefully the pool and hot tub are still open."

Metzger pulled ahead and took the lead, pulling into the hotel parking lot less than a mile down the road. It sat across the street from a rather large church on the same side of the highway, and the group finally spotted their first few undead stragglers milling around the area of both properties. A few abandoned vehicles remained in the parking lot, along with a large trash bin that indicated the hotel might have been in the midst of a remodel when things turned bad. The area showed no indications of lights or electricity, and any natural light from above remained suffocated by cloud cover as spatters of rain began dotting the windshield of the truck.

Everyone parked in the center of the parking lot, prepared to examine the area before hiding the vehicles and settling in for the evening. As the group emerged from the trucks, they stretched while Buster walked to the edge of the parking lot to relieve himself in the closest grassy patch. Several turned on flashlights because natural lighting was absent on the dark, cloudy evening as clouds continued to pass overhead. Everyone grabbed their weapons and supplies before sauntering toward the entrance doors of the hotel, finding them intact from a distance. Metzger had nearly reached the glass doors when he heard a vocal groan from behind him, and then another. Within a second of the sound, Buster began growling to indicate danger wasn't far away.

Turning, he saw nothing in the black of night until Jillian shined her flashlight beam towards the open parking lot and the field beyond it. There, dangerously close to them, the group saw what had to be fifty pairs of yellowed eyes staring back at them, now fully aware that seven warm-blooded meals were within reach. A virtual wall of the undead stood motionless until the moment a light illuminated the way for them.

"Shit," Metzger muttered, knowing he'd made a mistake pulling into the lot and not sweeping beyond it with his headlights before parking.

Exhaustion sometimes left people careless, even when their lives depended upon the utmost caution.

With the vehicles too far away, he knew they'd get swarmed if they attempted to return to the trucks. The group's only hope was to get inside the building, and fast, or the undead would dine well within a few minutes.

Twenty-Five

"We need to get inside," Metzger stated the obvious. "Now!"

Not since the Cessna's impending crash had Metzger felt such an intense sensation of panic. From a glance behind him he detected everyone else in the group shared the sentiment, because most of them hadn't seen a group of undead gathered like this in quite some time, or possibly ever.

He and Vazquez motioned for everyone to head for the entrance door, hoping the doors weren't locked, or worse, more danger awaited them inside. Luke scooped up Samantha while Jillian and Gracine ran ahead to test the doors. Sutton left his sidearm holstered, opting to take aim with the AR-15 he'd grabbed from the box truck. Since every single zombie was trudging their way the three men took aim and downed a few of them immediately, not concerned about drawing additional undead to their location at the moment.

"The doors are locked!" Jillian proclaimed behind them.

Due to the sheer number of zombies approaching them, the group needed to find cover. With their vehicles cut off by the herd, and only one way to run, they headed for the side of the building that faced the highway. Metzger waited as everyone darted for cover behind him, still taking aim at the incoming zombies with his .357, knowing he had two shots left. Vazquez took a final shot with his semi-automatic before falling back with the others, and Sutton continued to take aim with his rifle, thinning the herd slightly.

"Go," Sutton said calmly between shots, even as the undead closed within ten feet of them. "Buster!" he called during the brief silence, drawing the canine over to the group.

Metzger warily looked around as he followed the others around the hotel, thinking what a nightmare it would be if they couldn't access the building or get back to their vehicles. Surrounded by darkness except for flashlights held by Jillian and Luke, the group made their way along the doors, finding them all closed. A rogue zombie emerged from the darkness, groping at Luke and Samantha with a groan. Luke had his hands full holding a flashlight and Samantha, and the girl let out a shrill scream that pierced the calm night, likely heard for miles.

Sutton was still behind the others, fighting off the undead as best he could, so Metzger took aim, blasting the zombie in the skull. Left with one bullet and no chance to reload his gun, he drew closer to the others, hoping for a safe exit soon.

Given time to ponder the situation, he might have considered it similar to being in a staged haunted house around Halloween. It was almost completely dark, with no distinct path to follow, and a chance that someone might grab them in the darkness any given second. Only being grabbed in this scenario meant almost certain death because there wasn't time to react when teeth were already diving toward exposed flesh.

Only one flashlight remained lit for fear that the undead might follow the light, and thus, the group, wherever they went. Metzger held onto a sleeve from someone one second, and the next he found himself completely separated from his friends, the hotel, and any sense of shelter. He froze, knelt down on the ground, listening for the throaty growls of the undead or salvation in the form of a sign from the others. Touching the front right pocket of his blue jeans, Metzger felt the tiny flashlight he kept in there for emergencies. It wasn't very reliable, often blinking or going out temporarily from any bump that rattled its cheap innards.

Whether or not zombies possessed a better sense of smell than the living still eluded Metzger, but he figured it wasn't good enough to detect him in the dark like a tracking dog.

He heard panicked, muffled cries from the individuals traveling with him, knowing they dared not call out to him, or reveal their location because a few dozen undead were also waiting for a sign. Feeling around the ground for something useful, Metzger managed to grab a rock about the size of his fist in the darkness. Hurling it in the direction of the parking lot, he hoped it would make some noise and distract the zombies long enough for everyone to find cover.

Skipping a few times, cracking against the concrete, the rock finally made a clanking sound as it likely struck a hubcap. Metzger listened as the zombies, easily distracted creatures, turned toward the noise as their groans slowly grew more distant. With every passing second, however, he felt more and more isolated and alone, trying to keep from breathing because he feared a zombie might hear him in the dark and chomp into his shoulder, or his arm, before he even knew it was upon him.

Not breathing felt incredibly difficult as his heart pounded what seemed like a hundred beats a minute as his adrenaline kept him focused on his surroundings, even if he couldn't see them at the moment.

Somewhat reassured the undead were reaching the edge of the parking lot, a safe distance away, he reached for his flashlight to use sparingly just to locate the hotel. He couldn't believe how pitch black the night remained as clouds obscured everything in the sky. How so much cloud cover shut out the stars and moon without pouring down rain eluded him. Taking hold of the flashlight, Metzger was about to click it on for only a second when something brushed his shoulder.

Giving an involuntary yelp, he jumped to one side, but the hand that found his shoulder wasn't cold or coarse like one covered in dirt and blood.

"Come on," Jillian whispered, not letting go of his shoulder as she used her own flashlight sparingly to lead them back to the hotel.

Between blinks of the flashlight beam he could see the hotel walls, and then a set of stairs that led to the second level, safely tucked between two solid walls. The undead didn't manage stairs particularly well, and considering these turned directions twice before coming out on the balcony of the second level, none were able to track the group's movements to follow in the dark.

"Well this is fucking awesome," Sutton said sarcastically, staring at a door that required an electronic keycard.

And electricity.

"Can we kick it in?" Luke asked from nearby.

At this point only Luke kept his flashlight on, with Samantha only a few steps away from him.

"Fat chance," Sutton replied. "These door frames will have metal in them. We'll need a pry bar or something heavy enough to ram it through."

"Or we could break the windows," Gracine suggested, holding up a small tool less than two inches in length.

"What's that?" Jillian asked, still looking behind her and Metzger as though a zombie might make it up the stairs any second to attack them.

"It's a window punch," Gracine answered. "Firefighters use them to get trapped people out of cars. In my line of work I always carried one because it also has a seatbelt cutter on it."

"Didn't you drive a truck?" Luke asked.

"I seen some crazy shit on the road, mister."

Luke shrugged.

"If we don't mess up the whole window, maybe we can put Samantha through there to unlock the door," he suggested.

"And put her in danger?" Jillian asked with surprise.

"If they don't come when we knock on a door or bust a window, they ain't coming, honey," Gracine answered for Luke.

Metzger thought a bed sounded like heaven after their long day on the road, and at the church, but nothing ever came easily. It required several minutes for Gracine to decide the best place to break the glass to avoid maximum damage but leave enough space for Samantha to fit through. She finally took out a lower corner, small enough for a child, but not for adults or the undead. The group swept a flashlight beam inside seeing no danger, and Sutton even reached inside to knock on the wall a few times, but nothing emerged from the bathroom area. He tried reaching the door's lock, discovering it was too far away for his fingers to reach.

Luke handed Samantha a flashlight and gave her simple, straightforward instructions about how to climb inside and turn the lock. He didn't mention the door guard bar because it seemed unlikely someone locked themselves into the room, and it couldn't be locked otherwise. Samantha didn't seem to mind, and Luke played it off like a quick adventure for her. Metzger assumed Luke and Albert kept it light for Samantha, trying to play games and adventures with her when possible to keep her mind off the deadly world just outside their beautiful home.

Samantha navigated the door with minimal trouble, and Sutton allowed Luke to reach inside and grab her before sweeping the room for hidden dangers.

He checked the bathroom and beneath the bed, finding no issues, so he opened the door along the wall to the adjoining room, quickly clearing it as well.

Everyone else stood watch along the balcony. The clouds parted momentarily, allowing them to see the undead milling around the parking lot below. None of them had spotted the group above them, fortunately, so everyone tried to remain quiet.

"We need one more set of rooms if we want a comfortable stay," Sutton suggested when he returned to the group.

"We're safer together," Gracine suggested emphatically, almost as though she expected Sutton to bolt in the middle of the night.

Metzger could have cared less if they slept stacked atop one another at the moment. His eyelids felt droopy, and he fought to keep vigilant watch over the nearby danger. Once the adrenaline surge from being alone in the dark passed, his body felt spent. Being in the cool, fresh air only added to the factors making him sleepy and ready for a good night's sleep. Besides, the sooner he rested up, the sooner morning came, along with the possibility of finding Bryce.

Sutton didn't give in to Gracine's wishes, and as the two held a debate in whispers on the balcony, Metzger checked inside the first room. He sighed in relief, finding the room pristine, almost as though it was made the morning everything fell apart and left that way. Part of him wondered why the hotel hadn't been ransacked, but he supposed lots of other options were available, and people were either heading toward the Navy base with hopes of rescue, or getting the hell out of town.

Growing tired of arguing, Gracine gave in first, and carefully punched a hole in the window two doors down from the first to get the group two more adjoining rooms. Again they looked inside and banged on the wall before sending Samantha inside, and again she came through, opening the door and allowing the adults inside to clear two more rooms for immediate use.

So far as Metzger could tell, Gracine stayed with Sutton, possibly to monitor him, Luke shared a room with Samantha, and Vazquez got a room to himself because Jillian opted to stay with Metzger. After setting his gear on the floor beside the bed, Metzger looked between the single king-size bed and Jillian.

"I can sleep on the floor," he offered.

Jillian tilted her head slightly as though surprised at him.

"I was thinking we could share the bed," she said.

In part due to his grogginess, Metzger didn't immediately catch her drift, but when she walked over and grabbed both sides of his head to plant a long kiss on his lips, he moaned slightly, catching on. She released him after about five seconds, and Metzger could already feel the infant stages of an erection within his pants. He grabbed her, running a hand through her hair before pulling her in for another long kiss, knowing both of them needed this release, even if it was simply a one-night stand.

"Wait," he said when their lips parted, diving down into the pack he'd brought that contained his swords and some other items.

He dug through the pack until he found his wallet, pulling it out and flipping it open to reveal the object of his search. Jillian smiled when he pulled a wrapped condom from inside the wallet.

"And they say chivalry is dead," she said, shaking her head.

"I was keeping it in case a situation ever arose," he revealed, kissing her once again as they began removing one another's clothing.

Assured the door was closed, and Vazquez wouldn't come barging in from next door, they tried to keep their foreplay quiet, leading into a brief night that neither would forget for quite some time.

*****

Metzger found himself back in his classroom in Ohio in his next conscious thought. Daylight streamed through the windows, the floor and desks looked spotless from the custodial staff's overnight work, and Metzger sat behind his desk during his prep period doing paperwork. He referred to his break from the students as a prep period, but they were actually in physical education class for the better part of an hour. For some reason the hallways were dead quiet, and he sat alone in his classroom while the students romped about elsewhere.

He sometimes ate lunch in the cafeteria, but often brought in his own food to save money, and to assure he could eat something he liked. Looking down at some quizzes he needed to grade before the students returned, he found several errors on the math paper, realizing he needed to be a jack of all trades as an elementary school teacher while teachers in secondary education got to focus on one or two studies. Granted, he didn't need to be an expert in English, math, social studies, or science, but he needed to know enough about each to educate youngsters.

For the first time in over a month Metzger didn't feel the itch that sometimes accompanied his beard. As a teacher he typically grew a beard or full goatee during the colder months, sometimes keeping a clean face during the spring and summer months.

Complete silence surrounded him a few more minutes while he graded quizzes, and when he finally looked up, Timmy Fuller stared back at him with a mop-like haircut that hung over his ears and forehead. His brown hair matched the color of the numerous freckles dotting his face, and the child's hazel eyes looked at his teacher as though needing to ask something. Timmy was always asking to go to the bathroom, or saying he felt ill to visit the nurse or get out of the classroom for a few minutes. Metzger never got to the bottom of the student's need to escape the classroom, whether bullies taunted him, or he simply preferred time alone.

Perhaps Timmy Fuller was a future serial killer.

"What is it, Timmy?" Metzger asked patiently as he held a pen, looking at the student and away from the quizzes.

"I don't feel good. Can I go to the bathroom?"

"Sure," Metzger said, handing him a hall pass from atop the desk.

Watching the child turn for the door only a few seconds, Metzger returned to grading the papers, sensing a presence lingering nearby almost immediately.

He looked up, finding Timmy standing in the center of the room with his back to the chalkboard and Metzger's desk.

"Everything okay?" Metzger inquired, ready to return to his paperwork without waiting for an answer.

When Timmy didn't answer, or move, however, Metzger shoved his office chair back and stood, slowly maneuvering around the desk and into the center aisle of neatly arranged student desks. Odors of cleaning products and disinfectants lingered in the air from the overnight sanitation of the classroom as Metzger walked toward his student, who stood frozen in place. Metzger always felt compassion for his students, but this time, in the back of his mind, he sensed some form of danger that he shouldn't have felt in a normal, conventional world.

As he drew closer, Metzger noticed the child beginning to teeter between both feet as though ready to move, but lacking a destination, simply bobbing back and forth on each foot. Strangely, a thumping sound accompanied each shift of his weight on each foot, though Metzger thought little of it at the moment. When he stepped within a few feet of the student, Metzger placed his hand on Timmy's shoulder, causing the child to turn around with a gruesome, bloody face that contained no skin along the lower half of his face, providing a full view of gums and gnarled teeth, ready to bite in his sudden zombie form. The eyes were already yellowed, despite an apparently immediate transformation, and Metzger was about to take a step back when Timmy snapped at him with those awful bloody teeth.

Metzger awoke with a flinch, finding a warm body beside him in bed, quickly taking in the hotel room surroundings as the light of dawn peered around the closed window shades. He draped one arm around Jillian, feeling the rhythmic ins and outs of her breathing as he closed his eyes, smiling to himself. He felt relieved to have found comfort in someone else after being alone for the better part of a month. The thumping sound from his dreams continued in reality as he heard several rhythmic thuds from the room adjacent to them. It almost sounded like a robotic mechanism repeatedly running into the wall every five to ten seconds, but getting nowhere.

Figuring Vazquez was suffering through a similarly strange dream and kicking or punching the wall, Metzger slowly opened his eyes to find Jillian studying his face, as though questioning where they went from here.

"I can't believe we did that," Metzger commented, staring at the wall directly ahead of him that held a painting of some country cottage beside a river that looked dreamy compared to anything in the apocalypse.

In truth their love making was animalistic, fierce and almost desperate as though neither felt certain they'd ever find the opportunity to have sex with another living being again. Jillian didn't seem experienced, but Metzger wasn't a great judge of bedroom performance, having only slept with two women previously. Before, he wondered if each might be his last, tending to stay committed in relationships, ready to live out the American Dream of having a job, a family, and a house in the suburbs.

Now he believed staying in a hotel without power or hot water felt luxurious.

"What's so hard to believe?" Jillian asked. "It's not like we're strangers. We've been riding together for days now."

"It just feels a little weird. Before, we never would have been on the same wavelength. I had a career, and you were probably out with a fake ID, hanging out with frat boys."

"Don't sound so high and mighty," Jillian objected playfully. "You know me well enough to know I was into my studies, and not partying, and you're not exactly old enough to be my dad, Daniel."

"I know it's just the mentality from the old world talking, but it feels a little wrong," he said, prompting her to draw him into a long kiss until the thumping noise from next door distracted both of them.

"How long has that been going on?" Metzger inquired, rolling his eyes at the annoyance.

"At least an hour now," Jillian answered. "It kept waking me up."

Now Metzger felt alarmed, sitting up in bed. He sprung from the bed and began replacing his clothes, making certain he had at least a few of his weapons handy before leaving the room.

"What are you doing?" Jillian asked when he walked to the exit door.

"I've heard that kind of sound before," Metzger answered, keeping his voice low. "They sometimes bump into walls repeatedly when they hear something on the other side, or don't know where to go next."

"*They?*"

Metzger nodded affirmatively, so both knew he was speaking of the undead.

"You can't go out there alone," Jillian said quickly, tossing aside the sheets and revealing her nude form for the briefest of moments before she snagged her clothing and began getting dressed.

For his part, Metzger started to turn away, trying to be honorable before remembering that he had seen virtually every part of her the previous evening by the thin beam of a flashlight. He wasn't quite sure how to act around Jillian now, because they weren't exactly an item, or familiar in every way with one another. Part of him wanted to maintain that safe emotional distance until they decided where to take their relationship.

"There aren't that many out there," he informed her, peering through the side of the blinds, able to see some of the ground level below.

"Still, you shouldn't go alone."

Metzger pulled the .357 from its holster, realizing he hadn't taken time to reload it after getting safely into the hotel room. He also had a semi-automatic pistol with him if he required firepower, but he certainly preferred the survival knife or the short sword for dispatching zombies if necessary. Stuffing the .357 in the back of his belt, Metzger held the other pistol in a ready position, his free hand capable of snatching the knife from his belt, or the sword from the pack he slung around his back in an instant.

Not waiting for Jillian to finish getting dressed, he slipped out the door, using the security tab to keep it from shutting completely. He immediately walked to the front of the adjacent room, preparing to look inside, hoping to spy the cause of the disturbance when a face suddenly appeared at the busted portion of the window. The face of a child, scratched and bloodied with streaks of crimson running through her blond hair pressed between the edges of the glass, further ripping the flesh from the tendons and bones beneath as her undead form attempted to get at Metzger.

Startled, he stepped back as the small arm reached for him, wondering how the undead child got into the room at all. More importantly, he wondered what happened to Vazquez, or if the man remained in some form of jeopardy, bitten and dying, or trapped inside the bathroom without the benefit of a weapon.

Metzger drew the knife, hesitating momentarily as thoughts of his odd dream swirled within his mind. Though he had never seen any of his students transformed into little monsters, he thought back to them whenever he found a miniature zombie that wanted to take a bite out of him. Although he didn't substitute the zombie in front of him for one of his students, he wondered if somewhere a parent, or a teacher, gave thought to this particular young one.

Perhaps they shared a similar fate and simply craved human flesh as well.

Shaking emotional ties from his mind, he quickly stabbed the child zombie in the skull during the midst of its growl. She fell back, allowing him to stick his head closer to the window for an examination of the hotel room's interior.

"Juan?" he called out softly, trying to avoid attracting more trouble to the second story.

No answer.

He tried the door, finding it firmly secured, knowing he couldn't personally fit through the window. Studying the opening momentarily, he also thought it doubtful a zombie, however small it might be, possessed dexterity enough to climb up and through the opening. Just barely past dawn, with zombies milling around below, and the others likely sleeping in, he didn't want to make a ruckus. If Vazquez was bitten, there was no helping him at this point, and if he was trapped in the bathroom, he was now safe whenever he emerged.

Jillian finally entered the balcony from the room, so Metzger turned to make certain she secured the door open behind her. She let the door bar catch against the frame, taking his side for a peek inside the room. It required only a few seconds for her to find the deceased little girl on the floor, explaining the bumping noise they heard next door.

"Juan?" she asked quietly.

Metzger shrugged.

"Haven't seen him yet. I'm going to start eliminating some of these things since we're up."

Jillian followed him down the winding stairwell to the ground level, finding the undead rather scattered in the early light of day. Most of them probably couldn't scale the stairs upward, or lost interest once their prey disappeared from sight. They often followed the most recent sight or sound that caught their attention, requiring stimulation to keep them occupied. Reaching the ground level, Metzger immediately had to plunge the knife into a female zombie's skull, downing her instantly. Pulling the knife and the blood droplets that followed from the zombie's head, he noticed several nearby stragglers had taken notice of his actions.

Not waiting for a signal, Jillian used a hatchet she had picked up somewhere along her adventurous path to chop one of them in the side of the skull, putting it down. Metzger made certain she was able to retrieve it from the bone and flesh before moving over to the vehicles, taking down a black zombie with a local baseball jersey that wasn't worth selling in a yard sale for a quarter with all sorts of bodily fluids now staining its formerly white surface.

A few more undead took notice and headed their way, but the total within their line of vision was half a dozen. Metzger was about to wipe out any local danger when a loud thumping noise reached his ears from one side, causing him to spin and look. Inside the smaller of the two trucks he found Vazquez pounding his fists against one of the windows.

"Juan?" he questioned, walking over to the passenger side of the vehicle. "Get out of there, man."

"I can't," Vazquez answered through the window since he couldn't likely roll it down without the keys.

Metzger looked over the window, finding the man wearing only underwear inside the vehicle.

"This is no time for modesty," Metzger said, reassessing the danger closing in on his position. "Get out here and help us."

"I need pants," Vazquez insisted.

Rolling his eyes, Metzger took a few steps forward, striking another zombie in the skull with the knife, rendering it motionless once it slumped to the ground. Jillian managed to finish off another one with two strikes from the hatchet. The four remaining zombies were some distance away, leaving him time to converse with Vazquez again.

"What the hell happened?"

"I heard a thump against the door after you two kept me up half the night," Vazquez began, implying that Metzger and Jillian weren't as subtle as they originally thought with their bedroom activities. "So I went to answer it and this kid zombie came charging inside. I barely got the fuck out of there with my life, and they were still down in the parking lot, so I jumped in here to stay safe."

"No pants, and no weapons, eh?"

"Funny."

"What's his deal?" Jillian called over, still on guard in case additional undead drew near.

"He doesn't want you seeing him naked."

Jillian shook her head as though she could care less.

"I'll keep my back turned if you want to run him up through our room to his," she offered a solution.

Metzger shrugged, seeing no flaws with the plan.

Once Jillian remained turned around, Vazquez opened the door and began following Metzger up the stairs.

"Don't be tackling all of those on your own," Metzger insisted to Jillian. "Everyone else will be up soon and we can deal with them then."

"Don't worry about me," Jillian said without turning around.

Metzger led the way up the stairs and through the room, unlocking the adjoining door to Vazquez's room.

"Were we really that loud?" he asked before Vazquez could step through the threshold.

"I was dead tired and you two kept me up during your romp in the sack. I drifted off eventually and lost track of time, which is part of the reason that zombie caught me off-guard."

"Sorry about that," Metzger said for both the noisy sex and the zombie intruder, feeling his face flush from embarrassment.

"At least someone around here is getting some," Vazquez said with a shrug before entering his room and finding the motionless zombie child beside the door.

He picked up the corpse, opened the door, and hurled it over the guard railing to the ground below where it made a squishy splat noise with several bones breaking against the hard surface. Turning around, he snatched some of his clothing from beside the bed, prepared to get dressed and start his day.

"You could sleep in," Metzger suggested, feeling somewhat guilty.

"I slept in the truck. Besides, the others will be up soon. We might as well clear the way so we can get moving when they're ready."

Metzger walked out the door and down the stairs, finding Jillian dealing with another member of the undead group. She lodged the hatchet along the side of its skull, dropping it, but having some trouble pulling the weapon away.

"You're too strong for your own good," Metzger said, stepping on the top of the skull, which allowed her to free the blade.

"I just wish there was an end to these things," she said, shaking the hatchet violently toward the ground in one swift motion to free the blade of the blood and brain matter clogging the business end of the tool.

By the time the duo finished executing the last of the zombies for the final time, the rest of the group reached the ground level, prepared to start their morning and head for the military base. Metzger didn't know what to expect when they arrived, thinking Bryce's superior officers might not allow the group into the base, or Bryce might already be gone. Metzger understood the risks associated with rolling straight up to the facility, but he banked on military men not being cold-blooded enough to shoot civilians on sight without at least speaking to them or providing fair warning.

While some of the others packed belongings and relieved themselves in the hotel rooms, Luke took a few minutes to further educate Samantha on the use of firearms. He went over some of the pointers Albert had taught her, letting her aim a pistol outward, making certain she looked through the iron sights accurately. Luke also reviewed her stance before showing her how to drop the magazine from the gun and place a new one inside. He didn't show her how to rack the slide to ready the gun, because that was likely a lesson for another day.

Being in the open world had opened his eyes up to how the living and the dead threatened their group, so he made certain she stood a fighting chance against any threat.

"When are we going to shoot?" she inquired.

"When we find a place where the creatures aren't around," Luke promised. "I'll show you how to load it, shoot it, and everything."

"Promise?"

"Promise," Luke said, holding out his pinky so they could pinky swear and make a pact.

In the meantime, Metzger and Jillian tried playing it cool regarding their evening events, but both realized quickly the others were eyeballing them suspiciously. Vazquez didn't say a word, but he, too, acted strangely in their eyes as everyone silently loaded their gear into the three vehicles.

"What the hell is wrong with you three?" Sutton finally asked bluntly.

"Nothing," all three answered simultaneously.

Sutton made a face that indicated he knew better, but also suspected he might not want to hear what recent secrets they harbored. Even Buster wore a strange expression, as though having heard something his ears weren't accustomed to the previous evening.

A few minutes later the group left the minefield of zombie corpses along the hotel property, heading east through the remainder of Suffolk and into Portsmouth. Metzger asked Jillian to drive this time so he could study the routes and decide the best course of action. He looked at the maps available to him, finding the group could drive directly north toward a body of water almost directly across from the base, but if boats weren't available they'd have to double back. Thinking very few, if any, recreational boats remained in the area, because people were desperate to get off land, Metzger decided to take the land route to the base.

A Coast Guard base was located just south of the Navy installation, but again it would waste time if they arrived to find no watercraft, or guns pointed in their faces. No, he decided, they needed to head directly for the base on land and hope for the best. Before they reached Portsmouth, the small convoy passed through Chesapeake, finding the highway impeded on occasion, but certainly not impassible. Roadside businesses such as a credit union and workout facility looked uninviting with smashed windows, parking lots containing the undead and abandoned vehicles, and the occasional scavenging animal darting off when the noise of the trucks reached its ears.

Much of the area was comprised of the towns and small cities that simply bordered one another, all tied into the waterways surrounding them. Everywhere around them, the group found signs of death and decay, stark reminders of how quickly the world faded and fell apart in just over a month's time. None of the lights looming over the highway provided guidance during the early morning hours, and all of the businesses remained dark, as though their owners simply threw in the towel one day and never came to work.

Eventually the group drew near a major intersection where Highway 17 met up with Interstate 264 in a spaghetti knot of roads and exits. It was time for them to leave the state highway because the interstate led to several more direct paths if one wanted to reach the shipyard. Once the group safely traveled northeast on the wider roadway, Metzger buried his nose in the map, trying to decide the best route to Naval Station Norfolk, and some emergency secondary paths, when the vehicle began to slow.

"What's wrong?" he asked Jillian, looking up from the paperwork to see several abandoned cars immediately in front of them, and something potentially far more dangerous down the road.

Three military vehicles were parked along both lanes of the road, completely blocking the path of any would be travelers. Two looked like armored Humvees, much like the military used in the Middle East, but the third was a larger transport vehicle with plating, and half a dozen soldiers seated in the open rear. Metzger couldn't see much detail so far away, but it looked as though the soldiers had certainly taken notice of the small convoy heading toward the only base left in the area. Although there were a few alternate routes to the base, Metzger knew all too well the military might have them sealed off as well.

"What do we do?" Jillian asked, keeping the truck stopped in the center of the road.

Metzger saw little alternative. He didn't want to waste more time, and if the military had designs of murdering seven civilians and a dog it was going to happen either way. Pulling the door handle, he decided to step out of the truck and see what fate awaited him down the road.

Twenty-Six

Before he walked down the road, Metzger decided to bring the others up to speed on his plan, if it could even be called a plan.

"I'm going to talk to them," he said once everyone stepped from the vehicles. "If things go badly, turn around and run for the hills."

Sutton clutched a sniper rifle in his right hand, looking angrily at the vehicles ahead. Metzger suspected he was enduring flashbacks about saving Gracine from some National Guardsmen who'd gone bad in the chaos of the apocalypse. Personally, he still believed a great majority of any police and military members left alive were still solid, law-abiding citizens who retained their compassion for others.

For her part, Gracine tried to appear unconcerned, but the twitches in her cheeks spoke a different story to Metzger. She couldn't trust soldiers at this point, likely thinking of them as bullies with guns, willing to impose their wills upon those who couldn't fight back.

Huddled almost like football players, the group had certainly attracted the attention of the soldiers dressed in their camouflage fatigues down the highway. Metzger wanted to exercise caution, but also didn't want the soldiers to believe his friends were aggressive and open fire on them.

"No one aim a gun their way or provoke them, please," he said. "I'm going to try and get information and see if they'll let us pass."

"And if they won't give you either?" Sutton questioned with a growl.

"We'll figure out something. But I'm not going to know until I get down there."

"Let me go with you," Jillian said, which Metzger initially took as concern for his well-being.

"Too dangerous," he said, shaking his head.

"It'll be less dangerous," she insisted, "if they think we're a couple trying to reach a destination. They won't see us as a threat."

Metzger ushered her aside from the others.

"I don't think the power couple play is a good move," he said. "Walk halfway with me and be visible. These guys could shoot me full of holes in a second and they could get you just as fast if you're that close."

Drawing close to Jillian, Metzger reached behind him to grab the semi-automatic from his belt. He could have kissed her, but neither was ready to reveal their secret to anyone beyond Vazquez, so he thrust the gun into her hand instead. In life before the apocalypse he might have breathed in her perfume, overwhelmed by a need to be physical with her a second time. Perfume and cologne weren't items the survivors typically sought out when raiding homes and stores, and body odor didn't quite capture the allure of artificially smelling good.

"Just have my back and I'll try not to get killed," he said.

"Deal."

Metzger met the gaze of the others in the group, noticing their varying degrees of concern for him and their own lives. Removing his pack with the sword, the holster with the .357, and the sheath containing the knife, he set them on the ground. Having his weapons stolen or used against him didn't sound like a good end result, and he wasn't going to battle trained soldiers by himself, so leaving them behind sounded better. He sighed, took a deep breath, and finally turned to walk the distance between his allies and the soldiers.

Walking along the highway, he dodged several stranded cars and trucks, noticing the clouds forming overhead were thickening and turning various shades of gray. More rain was incoming, and the breeze began to pick up. Being so close to larger bodies of water, the wind was a constant factor in the area anyway, and Metzger could now smell the clear air that came from being near the ocean, overcoming any odors of the undead in the area.

Bodies in varying degrees of decomposition became visible in the road, under vehicles, and near the medians. Metzger didn't stop to study them, but he noticed a few had very precise head wounds that looked like bullets entered through the forehead. He guessed the military had used the undead, and hopefully *only* the undead, for target practice.

Metzger felt unusually nervous about his trek across the highway. He couldn't truly tell if the knots in his stomach emanated from knowing the fate of his group depended on his interaction with the National Guardsmen, or how close he felt to seeing his brother for the first time in months. Unlike Sutton, he hadn't dealt with the military in person. Several times in the early days of the apocalypse he saw them assisting with checkpoints where medical personnel examined travelers for illness, or in towns trying to impose a form of martial law so they could eliminate the undead while uninfected residents remained indoors.

Neither of those actions lasted very long, and evidently some factions of the National Guard went rogue. Metzger found six sets of eyes staring at him intently, not blinking whatsoever, when he finally drew close to the three vehicles. He suspected more of them were hidden inside the vehicles, or taking cover elsewhere, to snipe him if he posed a threat to them. They all held weapons in a ready position, looking between him and the group he left down the road, scanning the entire area for any kinds of tricks or traps.

As he drew close enough to speak with them, he put his hands halfway in the air to indicate he meant no harm, and a man atop the personnel carrier pointed in his general direction, prompting one of the lower-ranked men to jump down and intercept Metzger. Saying nothing, the man stopped Metzger's progress by placing a hand against his chest before frisking him from his feet to his shoulders.

"Clear," the soldier reported to the officer, who certainly didn't appear to be a haggard, old veteran by any stretch of the imagination.

He might have been a few years older than Metzger, and the others ranged from their early to late twenties. Perhaps by design, their ranks couldn't be easily deciphered in their fatigues unless a person drew close enough to read the insignias on their collars. Metzger wasn't a scholar on military ranks, though he knew a few when he saw them from visits to police and fire stations with his students.

"What brings you this way?" the officer asked Metzger, maintaining his position in the transport so Metzger was forced to look up at him, as though he were a king atop his throne.

"I'm looking for my brother."

"The last of the survivors were ordered out of town a week ago. Our people personally assisted about a hundred to safety."

Metzger wondered where the hell any safety existed, because he certainly hadn't witnessed any such thing in his travels.

"My brother isn't a civilian," Metzger clarified. "He's on the *Ross*, and they should have docked at Naval Station Norfolk by now."

Some of the soldiers, who had been scouring the area with their eyes like hawks, glanced in his direction as though wondering how a civilian survived such a perilous journey.

"It's too dangerous for you to go this way," the man said, finally hopping down from the transport vehicle. "This entire area from here to the base belongs to the dead now."

"Belongs to the dead?" Metzger questioned. "You guys have guns and armament. Can't the area be cleared out?"

He was answered with a crooked grin and a negative shake of the officer's head.

"We have our orders. We stop anything else from coming in and they deal with the walking corpses along their fence line."

"Dan Metzger," Metzger introduced himself as he shook hands with the officer.

"Lieutenant Gabe Keppler," the man replied. "You say your brother is on *Ross*?"

Keppler used the traditional method of referring to any ship without the *USS* designation in front of it by leaving out the 'the' when calling it by name.

"He's the XO."

Metzger was finally able to see the single bar on each side of the man's collar. He, like his men, remained clean-shaven and groomed, not reeking from body odor or unwashed clothing like regular people. Apparently the military enjoyed a few benefits, possibly from the hazardous work they put in while securing critical areas.

Although the lieutenant wore a helmet, Metzger could see some of his light brown hair just above a weathered face that indicated the man spent significant time in the sun. Perhaps the tanned skin resulted from recent outdoor activities, but Keppler looked like a man who worked on the water, or in a field somewhere, perhaps on a tractor. His hand felt like a fine grit sandpaper when Metzger shook it, and he possessed a laid back country easiness about him as though wearing a uniform and carrying out orders still wasn't natural for him.

Even so, he led youngsters barely out of high school against a legion of the undead while dealing with survivors desperate for some form of shelter and hope.

"Communications haven't exactly been stable for weeks," Keppler noted. "How have you been in contact with your brother?"

"Sat phone," Metzger said, deciding not to dance around the answer.

Keppler gave a cagy grin.

"Clever. That's one way around the phone issues."

"We have our father to thank for that. He believed in preparing for every disaster. So, what exactly is the deal here?"

"What do you mean?" Keppler asked. "Did you think the federal government would leave one of their largest military installations unguarded and overrun by the infected?"

"You make it sound like it still *is* overrun by the infected. How do I get to the base to find my brother?"

"You don't. At least not this way."

"How do you and your men get around then?"

"We have our vehicles, but we also have the Coast Guard to get us across the water when necessary. We've been able to keep much of the infrastructure intact around here."

Metzger started to question why the Coast Guard wasn't an option for him or his group, but Keppler cut him off.

"We aren't a ferry service for everyone wanting to get to the base. Our resources won't hold out forever, and we have our orders."

"Are there any boats anywhere along the shore?"

"None that aren't heavily guarded or under lock and key. I haven't looked recently, but most people took to the water when they saw what happened on land."

"I'm not asking for a handout, and I don't need protection. Just tell me the best way to get there and I'll give it my best shot."

"You and your posse back there?"

Metzger looked back, seeing his group waiting patiently beside the vehicles.

"Isn't there someone you can call?" he asked.

"I don't have direct contact with the Navy," Keppler said. "Our orders are on different wavelengths, and they have half a dozen ships docked right now. We're basically their security detail and they have better things to do than talk to us."

Turning so his back faced the soldiers, Metzger was able to get the lieutenant to follow suit. He needed a word with the man away from prying eyes and ears.

"I'm not asking for the world here," he stated. "If we get in there and don't make it, that's just another seven animated corpses you deal with later."

"Dan, I can't even begin to describe how dense Norfolk, and the area leading up to it, is with the infected. It's suicide to go near that base, and I can't have your death on my conscience if I could have prevented it."

Keppler spoke the words, but his face didn't register profound concern.

"Sir, I'll swim across that channel if I have to," Metzger said, glancing in the direction of the Coast Guard station. "They're about to deploy my brother on some new mission and this is my one and only chance to see him. I know you think I could be making this up, and that I'm just trying to weasel my way to some safe haven, but I believe you when you say the city is dangerous. I've had a taste of the infected, as you call them, and I know they're everywhere. So if I'm going to die at their hands, I want it to be while I'm trying to do something worthwhile and not on the road, or while I'm sleeping."

Keppler twisted his face in thought momentarily, wrestling with how to best assist Metzger, or let him down easy. He looked back at Metzger's group with a poker face, not indicating what he thought of the people one way or another. When Metzger tried following his gaze, he wondered if it wasn't on the vehicles rather than the six people, because they weren't all in plain sight.

"We don't have a shift change for a few more hours," the lieutenant revealed. "If he's willing to go, I'll send my scout in with you to show the best way to the base. He won't go all the way with you, and you'll have to get creative just to make it to the fence. Chances are you'll get overtaken by the infected before you get the Navy's attention or convince them to let you inside. I'm not trying to scare you off, or paint some picture of certain death, but I want you to know what awaits you before you agree to cross this line."

"It's appreciated," Metzger said with a nod, "but I'll take my chances just the same."

"I'm going to recommend you condense to one vehicle. Along with the roamers, the stalled vehicles get thick the further in you get."

"Okay," Metzger said with a nod. "I need a few minutes to get things together and we'll be ready to head that way. Your scout really doesn't need to risk his life for us if he doesn't want to."

"Oh, he won't be," Keppler said assuredly. "Like I said, he'll only take you to the edge of the safe zone before you part ways."

"Fair enough."

Metzger returned to his friends, still wondering if the offer was too good to be true. For a few minutes he didn't think the lieutenant was going to let him pass at all, but some persistence eventually got the man to agree. Sutton didn't like the idea of leaving his box truck behind, but he reasoned that it made more sense to hide it for the time being. The group found a non-military Hummer, black in color, that held six adults, one child, and a large dog with a little bit of work. They stowed what weapons they could easily store, a few supplies, and little else before driving the vehicle up to the blockade.

"There's something I need to tell you all before we do this," Metzger confessed once everything was loaded and ready to go. "The lieutenant says the closer we get to the base, the denser the population of the undead will be. It sounds like a lot of people made a run for military protection and it didn't work out very well for most of them."

"And you really think we can trust him?" Sutton questioned, outwardly indicating his personal doubts.

"He tried to stray me away from this several times over. Look, this is my quest, and none of you should feel obligated to come along if you don't feel safe. God only knows what we're going to find in there once we get close to the base. So, if anyone wants out, there won't be any hard feelings."

No one moved an inch.

"Okay. We should be safe inside this vehicle, and if things get hairy we can always back out of there and look for another way, or leave the area."

A few minutes later the group stood at the military border forbidding entrance further into the Hampton Roads unless permission was granted.

"Do you really have every highway and interstate covered?" Metzger asked of Keppler.

"We really do. Of course living and dead can slip by if they avoid the main roads, but bad things await them further down the road."

Drops of rain fell from the sky, pelting the soldiers and the weary travelers who wanted to get beyond the new border.

"This is Corporal Martinez," Keppler said, introducing a young soldier to Metzger. "I'm loaning him a vehicle and I expect you to ride with him while the rest of your group follows."

Metzger fought back the urge to question the decision, but didn't want to jeopardize his opportunity for a guided tour into the undead warzone. He simply turned to the others, who hadn't stepped very far from the black Hummer.

"Just stay close," he said to Sutton with a nod, knowing the man was going to do the driving for the others.

"I have a feeling this will be the last time I'll see you," Keppler said, offering his hand, "so good luck to you."

Metzger shook his hand, forcing a smile.

"Do you mean to say the last time you'll see me with a pulse?"

"No," Keppler said firmly, as though incapable of showing any glimpse of humor.

Metzger didn't like the negative vibe from the lieutenant, and couldn't imagine what horrors awaited him closer to the base. He looked to Jillian, who wore a look of concern about the change in situation. Metzger tried providing a reassuring look in return, but all positivity had long since been drained from him.

Keppler turned away without so much as a goodbye, returning to his duties, leaving Metzger to the young corporal who looked rather Caucasian for having a Hispanic name, though he possessed black hair and slightly olive skin.

"This way," Martinez said, leading Metzger to a gray Nissan car that looked as though it had seen better days.

Perhaps it was expendable compared to the other utility vehicles the military had seized during their occupation of the area. Metzger jumped into the driver's seat when the soldier headed for the other side, taking a last look back at the soldiers who seemed to have a slump to their gaits. Either they thought seven civilians were about to become zombie chow, or they didn't like something their officers had commanded of them.

Almost immediately the blockade moved out of their way and Metzger was able to drive through. He wasn't exactly certain why Martinez wanted him to drive the car when the corporal obviously knew the way better.

"If it's so important to protect the shipyard, why are all of you stationed to keep people out, rather than exterminate the remainder of the undead?" Metzger questioned.

"You've got to understand that the military works like any other business, so to speak," Martinez answered, his eyes never leaving the road ahead as though scanning for impending danger. "When the explosions occurred and the plague began spreading, the government foresaw all of this and tried to stockpile what supplies and ammunition they could, but it still wasn't enough."

Metzger thought the corporal was being a bit more forthcoming than expected, almost as though he knew such secrets would never leave the car. He began questioning the integrity of the soldiers altogether, wondering if Sutton might have good reason for his abrasive side.

"But the infrastructure of the government is still intact, isn't it?" he asked.

"Well, yes, all of the branches are intact to some extent, and many government officials were whisked to safety, but a lot of our resources were isolated from us, and the channels used to bring us supplies previously were cut off when the undead began outnumbering the living."

"You seem to have some inside knowledge about what really happened out there."

"Yes."

Based on the succinct answer, Metzger realized he wasn't going to get full disclosure from the young soldier after all.

He weaved around some unsteady zombies, since any remaining vehicles already appeared to be driven to the side of the road. At this point the undead didn't appear to be very dense in population, but it was a highway not easily accessed by them compared to the streets of the surrounding communities.

"You can tell me what happened," Metzger said as the car clipped one of the zombies in the outer thigh, knocking him to the ground. "Either I'm about to die at the hands of hundreds of undead, or my brother is going to tell me when I meet up with him."

"I doubt you'll be meeting him," Martinez said steadily, almost emphatically, as though being skeptical instead of issuing a threat.

"Why would you say that? My entire last month has been spent trying to locate the last of my family despite the slimmest hope any of them are alive."

"I hope you find your brother," Martinez said, showing emotion for the first time since they'd met. "But I know the government has their own agenda, and I know they aren't going to let him go anywhere with you."

"But they saved his wife and son."

"Of course they did. I'm guessing they lived on the base, or damn close to it, so of course they're going to keep their people happy by securing their families. They leave the undead around their gates as a security measure in addition to conserving ammunition. The people in charge aren't interested in saving people a few at a time so much as they are the whole."

Metzger understood the grim words. It likely took every last strand of humanity for the soldiers not to shoot anything that came their way. People could lie about being infected, or manufacture stories to get supplies or protection. There were even people who wanted items the military possessed, who wouldn't hesitate to create a distraction and take out the soldiers for their goods. He also understood that not everyone could be saved, but it seemed dangerous to leave the undead lingering outside any gate while activities occurred within eyeshot of the bloodthirsty creatures.

"You don't sound entirely sold on the mission," he noted aloud.

"They didn't save *my* family," Martinez answered, trying to curb the bitterness in his voice. "And they certainly didn't want to cut me loose to check on them. I'm just waiting for the day I make it back to Houston so I can find out what happened to them. Maybe they're huddled together with my aunts and uncles somewhere, or maybe I'll see them roaming the streets like some of these unlucky souls."

"Did you get to talk to them after everything happened?"

"Once," Martinez answered, fighting to hold back the emotions that accompanied not knowing the fate of one's closest loved ones.

Metzger fully understood. No words, however, could convey his sympathies to the young soldier for his possible, and likely permanent, losses.

"I know you have questions," Martinez said. "They don't let us know every-thing, but the news trickles down to us in time. There are only so many people left in the world, and it's hard for even our leaders to keep secrets to themselves for very long."

Sensing they were growing close to Norfolk and the base, Metzger glanced into the rearview mirror, seeing Sutton driving the black Hummer behind him. The next bridge was actually the Downtown Tunnel that took Interstate 264 across into the city of Norfolk. Once a toll road, the tunnel immediately grew dark, forcing Metzger to switch on the vehicle's headlights after a brief search for the switch. The entrance was completely clear of undead and vehicles, and any vehicles left inside were parked along the right side of the bridge, near a narrow walkway.

Strangely, the undead population hadn't increased much at all. Perhaps some of them fell into the surrounding water, forever polluting it, or they migrated to-ward sights and sounds that could only come from so many factories, businesses, and a military presence.

"What caused it?" Metzger asked, assuming the corporal wanted him to ask his questions.

"We know it was an act of terrorism," Martinez replied. "Of sorts."

"Of sorts?"

"We know the explosions were intentional all over the country. All over the world, from what I've heard. What we don't know is if this was the intention, or if the perpetrator had something else in mind."

"How could explosions cause all of this?"

"The explosions were just the catalyst. They projected dust particles into the air that infected everyone with whatever the canisters in those trucks were carrying."

"I remember the news talking about it."

"What the news didn't tell you was that everyone who breathed in even one speck of the stuff was infected. It somehow bonds with your system, and a dose that small won't get you sick right away and kill you, but when you die, you'll turn."

"That explains a few things," Metzger commented, knowing not everyone who died necessarily reanimated.

People who were bitten were guaranteed to turn, from every bit of evidence he'd seen.

"They had us wearing masks for a week or so after the event," Martinez revealed. "When they first summoned us they gave us the impression the illness could be contained and things get back to normal. That was just propaganda to get us onboard before they laid the heavy stuff on us. Who were we to question orders? We were saving the world. They said we were the start of putting things back together."

"But?"

"But there isn't going to be a normal, ever again. There is no cure for being dead. And that's what they are."

"Do scientists know exactly how that works?"

"No, not that they've told us, but they assure us they're working on it in case there's a chance to get our loved ones back."

"Of course," Metzger said sourly, understanding the government's need for control even amidst the chaos.

He worried that his brother might be far too loyal to a government that didn't truly give two shits about him as an individual. The same government obviously dropped the ball when it came to preventing the largest single terrorist act in the history of mankind, so Metzger didn't feel exceptionally patriotic at the moment.

In less than a minute, the two vehicles crossed over to the opposite side of the tunnel and into a new area. At last they were officially in Norfolk, drawing very close to the military base, but the scenery began to change. Not only were the fall colors prominently in bloom within what few trees dotted the business district, but the numbers of undead also seemed to pick up. They walked in small groups, almost like hunting packs, afraid to go after prey alone. Metzger knew their logic only extended so far, but perhaps some human element remained within them that drove them to seek minimal companionship.

"We're almost to the point where I have to leave you," Martinez said as a matter of fact. "If you have any final questions, you should ask them now."

"We saw a large military plane, like a transport, fly overhead a few days back," Metzger stated. "Where would the military be sending people, and why?"

"That's a question for your brother," Martinez replied. "They're dispatching specialized groups to some of the major cities. That's all I know."

"Are there any other checkpoints between here and the base?"

"No. We set up shop along all of the major highways to keep civilians from entering and becoming more casualties, and to keep the undead population from growing inside the city."

"What is your lieutenant up to?" Metzger decided to ask pointblank since they were on a roll with questions and answers.

Martinez hesitated momentarily, possibly to frame the answer correctly, or perhaps think of the most thorough answer. He didn't seem the least bit reluctant about answering the question as he'd been straightforward thus far.

"He doesn't think you or the others will make it back," the corporal answered bluntly. "He may not even give it the day before he goes down the road, finds your box truck, and raids it for everything he can get."

"Are you that hard up for supplies?"

"Times are tough, and they're getting tougher," Martinez replied. "No one is bringing supplies to these bases, and we've had to scavenge just to keep ample supplies. We've been no better off than you folks on the road. The only difference is we're tethered to a city that holds a base with a lot of mouths to feed. Their shoestring lies are about to come back and bite them in the asses."

Metzger wasn't quite certain how to respond, because Martinez obviously felt embittered towards the people who once covered his paycheck. Perhaps promises, particularly empty ones, only carried loyal soldiers so far before they began to think independently. At this point he wondered how the corporal intended to part with the group, and what he might demand before giving the group any final directions or advice.

"Let me ask you a question," Martinez said, breaking the awkward silence. "If you don't mind."

"Shoot."

"What's driving you to find your brother from God knows what part of the country?"

Metzger diverted his attention from the road for just a few seconds, already knowing the answer in his heart.

"He's the only person I definitely have left."

"The rest of your family?" the corporal inquired.

"I just assumed my grandparents wouldn't have survived, and my cousins, aunts, and uncles are scattered. Bryce has been a familiar voice on the phone promising to meet me if I could make it this far."

"Did you expect him to break away from his ship once you found him?"

"In my mind I expected him to grab his family and for all of us to make a run for it wherever we thought the safest place might be," Metzger confessed. "But after our last conversation I feel like he's putting duty above his family."

"There's certainly an allure to their promises," Martinez said. "There's food and shelter, and strength in numbers, but there isn't a paycheck, and there's a certain emptiness that comes with knowing the only family you have left might be the guy in uniform right beside you."

Metzger managed to navigate around several undead that heard the vehicles coming and turned to see if the noise might provide them with fresh meals.

"Take a left up here," Martinez instructed, and Metzger assumed they might be taking some lesser-used streets to the base's entrance.

He followed a few more instructions, finding the undead population grew less and less with each turn. Thus far the promise of zombies as thick as trees in a grove hadn't exactly come true, but he assumed the corporal wouldn't take them into the most populated area. After all, his life depended on not getting swarmed and devoured by the undead as well.

Slowing down around a curve, Metzger laid eyes upon a mammoth ship as it materialized around the turn. For a moment he felt certain the ship was coming at him, possibly running aground due to some tragic maritime disaster. He quickly realized the vessel was sitting perfectly still in the water, and he remembered that the *USS Wisconsin* was decommissioned for use as a permanently loaned museum in Norfolk. He noticed Martinez measuring his reactions, possibly having experienced the same emotions his first few times traveling through the city after arriving with his unit.

"Rumor is they thought about recommissioning her in case we needed her at sea," the corporal stated. "But I think they realized she could serve the same purpose docked right here."

"What purpose is that?"

"Sanctuary for government officials and soldiers onboard. Countries aren't at war with one another these days, so there isn't much need for another weaponized ship. Cannons and air defense missiles aren't much help against millions of reanimated corpses. Not that she has the latter anyway."

Metzger pulled the vehicle to a complete stop, enamored by the magnificent size of the ship right beside a residential street. It felt as though he could throw a ladder against the side of the old vessel and climb aboard if ladders or gang planks were readily available. He glanced to his right at long last, seeing Martinez holding a gun, though it wasn't aimed his way and it wasn't a traditional firearm.

"This is where I have to leave you," the corporal said, offering Metzger the orange flare gun. "I need the car, but I have this and something else for you."

Metzger nodded, understanding from the start that this was a limited partnership.

"You're not going back to them, are you?" he asked.

"You've found some answers, and you're about to find a few more. I envy you for that, but it's time I found some answers of my own. They'll label me a deserter, but the chances of them ever finding me are slim."

Metzger grinned.

"Why would they do that? If anyone asks me, you were overtaken by the undead while trying to lead us to the base."

Martinez returned a smile at the sentiment.

"I appreciate it, but they're going to hold a grudge either way. And it definitely wouldn't be best for you or your people to interact with Keppler and the other soldiers again. He certainly doesn't want to see any of you return, because then he won't get to loot your stash. I'm not sure he'd shoot you on sight or anything like that, but best not to take any chances."

"Understood," Metzger said. "The car is all yours," he added, reaching for the handle to open the door, noticing there weren't any undead stragglers nearby.

"You'll want this," Martinez said, stuffing a crumpled map into Metzger's right hand. "I've been through these streets a dozen times or more and mapped out the best ways to get around. You won't have much trouble getting to the base, but when you get there expect resistance from the infected and the living. The flare gun may save you, or get you killed. You really need to find a way to let your brother know you're here if you can."

"Thank you," Metzger said earnestly. "I hope you make it to Houston and find some good news."

"That may be pushing it," Martinez surmised, "but miracles can happen."

The two quickly shook hands before Metzger exited the car, seeing lingering signs of chaos all around him as Martinez drove away. While parts of the highways and interstates were cleared of the undead, with vehicles moved to the side, the town of Norfolk appeared to have been neglected of such treatment. Abandoned vehicles were parked every which way, and the undead began rounding the block ahead of the group, having heard the two incoming vehicles. Metzger glanced at the map, seeing he still had a few miles to cover along a mix of residential streets and business districts before reaching the edge of the base.

Holding the map in one hand, and the flare gun in the other, he stared into the eyes of the half dozen undead who wanted to make him their midday lunch. He turned to see the questioning stares of his colleagues in the Hummer momentarily before trudging their way to join them. At long last he neared the end of his journey, but his stomach tightened at the thought of what he might find, much like it had when he entered the house of his parents.

He needed to find his brother, regardless of the personal cost, but he didn't like the idea of risking their lives to complete his quest. A few difficult decisions awaited all of them during the next few miles of their journey, but for now Metzger felt glad to have their companionship as he climbed into the large vehicle.

"Where to?" Sutton asked when Metzger settled into the seat behind him.

"North," Metzger answered, pointing out the direction. "Let's see how many of these motherfuckers the military left wandering around the city."

Twenty-Seven

etzger possessed the tools necessary to contact his brother, and other items that might alert the Navy to his presence prematurely and get him shot.

Due to their hasty transfer to a single vehicle, certain items were left behind, so the six adults and Samantha were forced to survive on limited ammunition and handheld weapons. Metzger managed to maintain items important to him, including the .357, his two swords, a semi-automatic pistol, the sat phone, and a set of keys, complete with fob, to a car that held some of his last remaining sentimental family memories near Buffalo.

He also maintained the family photo he managed to snag before leaving his old stomping grounds, although it hadn't remained in mint condition. So much of his journey from Blue Ash to Buffalo felt like a tedious, dangerous month of his life, filled with worry about his own life and the lives of his family members. After his arrival the following events felt more like a roller coaster, meeting people left and right, finally trusting select people for the first time since the apocalypse, and arriving in Virginia far sooner than he ever expected.

Jillian sat in the middle of the bench seats, and Vazquez sat on the other side of her. Luke and Samantha were crammed in the back, neither complaining one bit because it was likely the safest place inside the Hummer. Buster sat back there with them, letting Samantha scratch the top of his head, occasionally letting out a delighted moan as he soaked in the affection. Neither Metzger or Jillian felt obligated to reveal the previous evening's events to everyone, particularly considering they were about to enter hostile territory, but every so often Jillian would clutch one of his fingers with one of hers, and he returned the finger squeeze. Knowing someone cared helped remove some of the butterflies inside his stomach, but he suspected the group still had quite a fight ahead of them.

"There's something I need to tell all of you," Metzger announced after about half a mile of avoiding the undead, which seemed to be aimlessly walking throughout the streets.

"You can start by explaining why soldier boy took us only so far before bailing on us," Sutton complained.

"I think he has some personal plans in mind," Metzger answered neutrally, avoiding the subject of the box truck for the moment.

"What's your announcement?" Luke asked from behind him.

"The corporal told me the undead are indeed thicker around the base," Metzger began. "But there's also a danger from the Navy personnel. They could mistake us for the undead, they could think we're looters, or any number of things could go wrong. I don't want any of you going into this with blinders on. It might be smarter if I get my own vehicle at some point and approach the base alone."

"If they aren't bothering to thin the undead numbers, why would they attack the living?" Gracine said, providing a counterpoint of sorts.

Metzger had provided the group with a brief summary of what Keppler told him when they loaded up the Hummer with supplies.

"I'm just giving full disclosure here," Metzger said. "I don't want anyone getting hurt on my account."

"We'll know more when we get there," Sutton said confidently. "First we need to get through the brain deads."

Metzger navigated for Sutton, reading the map while stealing glances of the defunct businesses they passed. Restaurants, banks, churches, and workout centers went by in a blur, all victims of the collapse of society. Weeds popped up in random places, and the grass was often knee-high where it could be found, because no one remained to tend to such affairs. The local streets, including walls and windows, appeared to have a dusty coating on them. Metzger knew dust was mainly comprised of dead skin cells, so it only made sense that an area densely populated with the undead would contain so much of it. He also knew the find didn't bode well for their immediate future.

Some of the streets parallel to their route teemed with the undead, leaving him assured that Martinez definitely provided him with the safest path to the base. For that he was thankful, and genuinely hoped the young soldier made it to Texas and found some answers regarding his family's fate. He couldn't imagine sacrificing so very much to guard others, and possibly set the world right, that soldiers were asked to forego knowing about their loved ones.

He imagined the military permitted them to attempt contact as long as communications held up. Bryce even indicated as much, which explained why he couldn't call very often, and was crunched for time when he did.

"What's that?" Samantha inquired upon spying the flare gun.

"It's a flare gun," Metzger answered. "It shoots a firework into the air to signal other people."

Luke provided a strained smile because he obviously harbored concerns for the safety of Samantha and the others. Light-hearted moments came few and far between during the apocalypse, and Metzger supposed each of them longed for days of peace and solitude in a safe haven.

Sutton stopped at a four-way intersection, taking in the disturbing view of buildings and their unlit windows, like creepy haunted houses within a movie. Occasionally a zombie pressed itself against a window, serving only to add to the grim reality that surrounded the group. Sutton waited only a few seconds before driving forward once again, drawing the attention of more undead inhabitants along the streets. For any number of blocks they had passed only a handful of zombies at a time, and suddenly the number seemed to multiply. Metzger understood that the undead certainly weren't stationary at all times, particularly when something, even distant, drew their attention. Some of them had obviously migrated since the military last scouted the streets of Norfolk, forcing Sutton to either dodge them or push them out of the way with the vehicle. Ramming them at a faster speed would likely dent the grill and the hood, allowing body parts and guts to strike the running engine and compromise it.

Most of the zombies were halfway limp anyway, barely turning to see the Hummer before it knocked them to the ground. Their muscles never seemed to tense, and even when they groped at potential victims their arms came up slowly as though great effort was required to move faster than their usual pace.

Metzger looked ahead, but also glanced out each side of the vehicle to observe the landscape. Having metal and glass between him and the undead did little to smother any fears he felt for the safety of himself and those surrounding him. The deeper into the city they drove, the more danger surrounded them with each passing block. He took notice of the various clothing the undead were wearing in various states of decay. In addition to everyday people who might have been working at a construction site or white-collar businesses, he spied nurses, doctors, and police officers who probably tried to hold the line and assist the living. He also noticed a few zombie wearing military uniforms like the men they just passed.

No one was exempt from death, of course, and it appeared that even the best-prepared could still fall prey to the plague and the undead army it created.

A large railyard became visible along the left as the group traveled parallel to Highway 337 on their right. Apartments, houses, and a few parks slowly passed, but the freshly-painted houses, multiple story apartments, and changing trees didn't provide the same inviting tourism brochure appearance with zombies in the foreground.

With the variety of clothing and uniforms lining the streets, it might have been a picture of Americana worthy of coffee table books if the people wearing the clothes were alive. Now they looked more like some frightening videogame cover with their empty eyes, gnashing teeth, and wounds with dried, clotted blood.

"You'll have to get on 337 to cross the bridge," Metzger said, pointing the way as he looked between the street they were on and the map.

"This is getting deep," Sutton commented as they drew closer to another bridge, this one providing six lanes total with a thin concrete barricade in the center.

Metal rails on either side acted as pens to keep the undead who wandered onto the bridge contained there unless they fell over or crossed to the other side. Some vehicles were moved to the right side, meaning Sutton needed only navigate around the zombies most of the time. They crossed, finding a string of two-story apartment buildings on either side. Metzger guessed the neighborhood was named Meadowbrook because the first apartments they passed were named that and a street sign beside a church had Norfolk printed above the name Meadow-brook once again.

"I wonder if some of this is military housing," he questioned aloud. "A lot of the families don't live on the base."

"A lot of them probably didn't make it to safety," Gracine said grimly as a higher number of female and underage undead stumbled into the highway from the sidewalks.

Metzger looked back to Samantha briefly, wondering how any child could survive the current circumstances without a small army to protect them.

Very little changed as they approached a campus surrounded by green fencing and imposing gates. It appeared to serve one or more military branches, but school was definitely out as the yard within the gates appeared neglected. It may have been free from any undead, as none of them wandered aimlessly within, but the complete lack of activity indicated someone might have sought shelter within the buildings or fought to defend the campus.

"Anyone hungry?" Sutton asked when they reached the business district.

Packed with restaurants, auto parts stores, and convenience stores long since looted, the area might have been worth exploring were they not pressured to reach the base as soon as possible. Much of the area looked like any other small city between the coasts, but the streets and storefronts indicated the town thrived due to the tax base when the government was functioning. The sky ahead of them remained a strange gray-blue shade that seemed to go on forever, indicative of towns off the water.

It felt foreign to Metzger not seeing a skyline or trees blocking the sky. Buildings and storefronts technically impeded the view, but just barely, like a distant horizon appearing low to the ground.

"A drive-thru sounds awful damn good right now," Gracine commented, staring longingly at the unlit signs of familiar eateries.

"We have to earn everything we eat these days," Vazquez said in a shallow voice, as though his mind was wandering back to some distant memory.

Nothing inside the fast food restaurants would still be edible after so long, short of mustard and ketchup packets. Metzger felt reasonably certain they too would have been raided shortly after people realized all consequences went out the window with manners and accountability.

"Can you call your brother on the sat phone?" Gracine inquired, turning around to look at Metzger.

"I can call the number, but it sounds like it's kept in a designated area. If Bryce isn't there I have no idea who I might reach."

"It may get to a place where we don't have a choice," Sutton chimed in.

"I'm aware," Metzger said. "It has to be a last resort if we don't see any other way into the base, or we can't establish contact with the Navy folks."

Drawing close to the southern edge of the base, and near the end of the business district, Sutton pulled into a hardware store parking lot. Through the long since smashed display window Metzger could see the place was looted, but Sutton obviously felt the need to check for something, or a few items, within the old store. In a sea of household name chains, this was a mom and pop store with a white sign overhead and red lettering that proudly stated Williams Hardware was in business.

Even if it wasn't.

"I'll be right back," Sutton said as he grabbed the door handle.

"Sure you don't want an extra pair of eyes?" Metzger asked.

Sutton hesitated a second before answering.

"Come on."

Metzger jumped out of the Hummer, immediately drawing the attention of a few zombies across the street. With the knife sheathed at his side, he didn't worry about dealing with them unless they drew much closer. He didn't want the others getting out of the vehicle, risking the possibility of separation, so he quickly followed Sutton through the large opening into the store.

"The base is going to have defenses," Sutton said assuredly. "I'm guessing they prepared primarily for attack from air or sea, leaving their ground defenses in the hands of armed guards. We may have to deal with a fence or two to get where we need to go. I suspect the Navy didn't leave too many access points for stragglers to wander inside their compound. Look for anything we can use."

Metzger found empty hooks along the walls, very few containing any items. The floors were a mess, littered with discarded items civilians and the military alike probably rejected during their searches. Feeling the stop was a waste of time, he helped rummage through the items just the same, following Sutton's lead.

Sutton ducked behind the counter, not finding anything useful, so he switched on a flashlight before going through a swinging door to search the stockroom. Metzger continued looking along the floor, locating a few lighters and flashlights he swiped up. Heat and light sources always seemed to be lacking, so he always took what he could find. He discovered a cordless rotary tool that might have enough charge to carry out some light cutting, so he snatched the box from the floor as Sutton emerged from the stockroom.

Sporting a rare smile, Sutton held a pair of bolt cutters in one hand and a crow bar in the other.

"Let's roll."

Metzger followed him back to the Hummer, not bothering to deal with the zombies, even though they were within striking distance of the vehicle. Both slid inside and closed the doors as three members of the undead laid hands upon the Hummer. Growling and fussing, they pawed the vehicle even as it backed into the road and headed north toward the base.

Sutton had handed off the equipment to Gracine as soon as he slid into the driver's seat, and Metzger honestly had no idea whether they would need to sneak into the base, or if a military presence remained to meet them. Time for details hadn't exactly worked its way into the few conversations Metzger held with his brother. Cutting the fence was an absolute last resort in his mind because he expected to be met by some military presence, and he didn't want to leave a gaping hole in the base's defenses for the undead to stumble through.

Daring to roll down the window halfway, Metzger put his nose to the edge of it, breathing in the fresh air that came from the ocean mingling with the local lakes and rivers. The wind picked up due to the large bodies of water, but he felt the tradeoff was worth leaving the stench of the undead behind him. With so much of the population dead, whether walking around or left to rot on the ground, urban areas were comparable to strolling through a landfill. The only creatures capable of scavenging the bodies in the streets were insects and worms, and that process took an eternity by comparison. Any mammals attempting such a feat were either chased off or consumed by the undead.

Metzger felt a strange mix of freedom and excitement, hoping to finally see his brother and provide some sanctuary for the six people who survived the journey. The words of the soldiers returned to his mind, however, as he wondered where the massive herd of undead they spoke of might be roaming. Not the least bit stealthy, or capable of lying in wait, the zombies had likely migrated to an area that drew them, and he worried it might be exactly where the black Hummer was heading.

"We're getting close," Sutton noted as they passed the last few buildings in the town before open fields appeared on the right and the outskirts of what Metzger assumed was part of the base emerged on the left.

Buildings, trees, and decorative shrubs blocked the view on the left side, and it wasn't until they reached a checkpoint gate with a blue sign that Metzger knew they had reached the base. Strangely, no guard stood watch at the gate, and no crowd of the undead was visible. Several stragglers moped around the highway and the sidewalks, but the situation wasn't anything the group couldn't deal with rather quickly.

As though expecting an ambush, Sutton pulled up beside the guard shack, stopping beside it for a look inside, and around the surrounding area. Everyone stepped from the Hummer, observing and listening for any unusual activity. Metzger questioned whether or not they had gone far enough to reach the base because he only heard a low murmur of groans from the nearby undead.

While everyone took a step forward, Buster stayed near the vehicle, sniffing the air and making a sneer with his face as though something undesirable wasn't far away. Metzger looked back, seeing the dog's actions, chalking it up to the few undead wandering nearby. He emitted a quiet growl from his throat, taking half a step back as the others continued to inspect the area.

Peering inside the guard shack, Metzger half expected to find blood smearing the glass surface that comprised much of the tiny structure. He noticed a clipboard sitting atop a desk as though the guard had stepped away for a smoke break rather than abandoned his post. A helmet hung on one hook, and a few other papers tacked to the wall blew with the light breeze that passed through the shack.

Metzger didn't let the haunting visual faze him for very long as he stepped forward, past the broken bar that once forbade traffic to pass through until authorized. A few concrete barriers like those set in the center of highways to divert traffic during construction, blocked the path ahead. No vehicle larger than a motorcycle or four-wheeler could possibly pass through, and it became apparent the Navy took steps to keep out the living more so than the undead rather early in the apocalypse. The concrete road only went a little bit further until it reached a mesh wire fence that tied in with the more concealed security barrier surrounding the base. Metzger guessed this fence was added rather hastily as an added security measure when it was decided the base would act as a stronghold.

Metzger realized the guard shacks acted as checkpoints from the roads because parts of the base appeared to simply blend into the regular community. All of the essential portions of the base were separated by the checkpoints, and Metzger suspected crossing them without permission didn't end well for those who tried. The mesh wire fences were likely to impede the progress of the living to enter the base, and certainly to keep the undead from wandering inside an otherwise clean perimeter.

Much of the fence around the base was concealed with giant trees and shrubs, partially for decorative purposes, but also to keep prying eyes from learning about the defenses within. Tracing the road with his eyes, Metzger quickly noticed an issue with the fence, namely in the fact that he couldn't see much of its lower half.

"Oh, no," he muttered, realizing in horror that the dark band along the bottom of the fence was actually a mix of colors worn by various zombies that lined the fence, trying to get inside.

In some areas the undead were three or four deep pushing against the same area of the fence, and the line of undead seemed to stretch as far as the eye could see in either direction. Metzger felt his heart sink, wondering how anyone could possibly get past the accidental, yet threatening, security system set up along the outskirts of the base.

By now the others had reached his side, seeing the same exact terrifying sight, knowing thousands of undead were lurking just outside of the place they desperately wanted to enter.

"We have to go," Sutton said quietly as several of the zombies turned, spying the group standing there in lieu of whatever drew them to the fence in the first place.

A dozen, and then several hundred dead eyes turned to see them as they backed away toward the Hummer. No one in the group wanted to open fire and draw all of the undead their way, so they hastily made their way into the vehicle as the undead stumbled around the concrete barricades, a few even falling headfirst onto the hard surface. Barely closing the door before scores of hands pressed against the metal and glass, all seven survivors took some deep breaths, trying to collect their wits. Including Buster, the group found themselves randomly piled into the rear seats of the vehicle, trying to separate and adjust for some sense of comfort.

Sutton threw the vehicle into reverse, ramming a few of the zombies as he pulled away, driving down the road in search of a different way into the base.

Metzger counted himself fortunate none of the undead had groped inside his partially open window and clawed at him. Freeing his arms and legs from the pile of people stacked in the same seat with him, he quickly rolled the window up, shutting out the delightful odors of the ocean. Still catching his breath from the momentary brush with death, he stared out the window, seeing the protective buildings and shrubs along the road occasionally give way, allowing glimpses at non-essential portions of the base. The base felt a million miles away because the line of undead pawing at the fences didn't seem to have an end.

Sutton passed a checkpoint gate because the undead were visible just inside along the fence. The base's acreage stretched on for miles, and the Hummer drove past the third gate after the group found similar results. Closer to the fourth gate the number seemed to thin significantly, so Sutton slowed down for a closer look. He started to make the turn, finding the guard shack empty and just a few zombies milling around the fences ahead.

"We could try making entry here," he said, turning to Metzger with one hand still on the steering wheel.

"It doesn't feel right that they'd leave every single gate unmanned," Metzger replied. "There can't be more than one or two gates left, and I don't want to bust their defenses unless it's absolutely necessary."

"Maybe your brother wasn't fully informed of the situation," Jillian suggested. "If the base was compromised, they could have walked into a trap."

"The undead aren't getting through the fences," Luke pointed out. "The base isn't compromised."

Sutton backed away from the gate, driving a bit more slowly down the road to examine the condition of the fences, when visible, and the number of the undead. The further they went, the fewer zombies they spied, which boded well for the fifth and possibly final gate when they spotted it from a distance. Metzger drew a deep breath, wondering if he was about to break into a federal government facility to see his brother, or if the federal government even truly remained in existence.

Metzger's heart sank when they finally pulled to the last gate and found no activity. Tumbleweeds could have blown past to accentuate the moment as they found the gate empty and the fence beyond it devoid of any undead.

Once again the area between the gate and the fence, which contained a sliding gate constructed from similar mesh wire, was dotted with concrete barricades to keep a vehicle from getting through and crashing through the fence. Metzger supposed it might have also slowed the undead, making them easier targets, but they didn't appear to have any interest in such a desolate area of the base.

Prepared to do whatever was required to see his brother, Metzger stepped from the Hummer first, and the others followed a bit more slowly this time after the mob nearly tackled them and ate them as a late lunch at the first gate. Looking all around him, Metzger saw several buildings across the road that weren't important enough to be located within the main security fence. He peered inside the guard shack, seeing a few clipboards and a small desk, but no indication of life, and no blood to indicate previous violence occurred within the enclosure.

Buster jumped from the vehicle sniffing the air, taking a much calmer stance this time without growling or backing away from the gate in retreat. Sutton walked over to him, scratching the top of his head, which caused the pit bull to wag his tail. Metzger turned from his fellow travelers and the Hummer to navigate past the guard shack and the concrete barriers, walking up to the fence. He could see some buildings that looked like hangars ahead, but he wasn't certain. The base appeared to go on forever, which made it difficult to gauge the distance inside.

Secured by several additional chains and locks in addition to what once protected it, the gate was sealed to prevent anything from getting inside. Metzger examined the gate and the fences leading up to it on either side, deciding one of the locks was too high to cut without the benefit of a ladder, so he would need to cut through the fence itself.

Walking almost casually back to the Hummer, Metzger reached inside to grab the bolt cutters as the others stood watch or explored the area surrounding the base. He supposed if he possessed a ladder he could simply climb to the top of the fence and jump over, though the risks of injury or being stuck inside might deter such a brazen move.

"If I didn't know any better, I'd say this place is abandoned," Vazquez commented as Metzger navigated his way past the guard shack and the concrete barriers again. "If that airfield had any aircraft, we could go anywhere we wanted."

He spoke the last words almost dreamily, as though he knew of somewhere specific he wouldn't mind flying.

"I just want somewhere to sleep in for a few days without worries of zombies or douchebags busting down the doors to get me," Metzger confessed.

He opened the bolt cutters as he drew near the fence, prepared to make the first cut when he heard a clicking noise at his feet followed by the sound of a rifle firing. Metzger looked down at his feet, seeing the mark where a bullet struck the concrete and skipped away like some high-velocity rock on a pond.

Dropping the bolt cutters to the ground, Metzger drew closer to the fence, attempting to see where the shot might have originated. He couldn't see anyone, surely by design, figuring the military had snipers posted to watch each of the gates to ensure their base wasn't compromised. Knowing he was lucky they didn't make an example of him by shooting him in the head, he still decided to push his luck by raising his arms over his head and waving them back and forth to attract their attention and let him know he wasn't some malicious intruder.

Or so he hoped.

After a minute or so he quit waving his arms and simply stood at the gate waiting for some kind of response. The others walked forward, taking his side as though to say they weren't going anywhere without some answers. Even Buster walked forward, standing by Samantha as they all stared forward, into the base, until a topless utility vehicle drove their way, creating a trail of dust as it drew closer.

When it finally came to a stop about forty feet short of the fence, four soldiers dressed in fatigues stepped down, each holding an assault rifle. All of them were tall and imposing, and they walked rigidly toward the fence, looking around as though expecting an ambush.

"You're trespassing," one of them said, approaching Metzger directly while the other three held back to survey the area.

"I'm on this side of the fence," Metzger replied. "And I'm under orders to be here."

For a split-second the soldier appeared perplexed at such an answer from a civilian.

"I don't have time for jokes."

"Neither do I," Metzger pushed. "My brother is the XO aboard the *Ross* and he told me to get my ass here because he was about to receive new orders."

Now the soldier looked concerned because he obviously knew at least a little something about the lieutenant commander.

"What's your brother's name?" he asked.

"Metzger. Bryce Metzger."

Standing stiffly, the soldier inhaled the fresh air through his nose as though delaying to speak the words he needed to say.

"He's about to get deployed," the soldier finally said.

"Can I see him?" Metzger asked anxiously.

"He made arrangements for you to stay here at the base or travel with him."

Metzger couldn't imagine that the military would allow a civilian, even in such strange new times, to tag along on a mission.

"What about my friends?" he inquired, concerned for their safety after they traveled so far with him.

It openly pained the soldier to speak his next words, but orders dictated that he do so.

"Family members only are allowed inside. I'm sorry, but we're already stretched thin protecting and feeding everyone."

Metzger felt devastated. He wasn't prepared to choose between his brother and the people he now considered family. He couldn't simply abandon them to fend for themselves after they accompanied him, hoping for sanctuary at the end of the journey. Slowly, Metzger turned to them. For a fleeting moment he thought about saying Jillian was his wife, or at least his girlfriend, to get her asylum from the elements, but it wasn't fair to any of his friends to lie for her. It denied the rest of them the protection provided by the military, but also denied her the opportunity to discover the fate of her loved ones as Metzger had done.

Expecting to see anger, or perhaps disappointment, in their faces, he found them glad for him instead, providing comforting smiles because they understood the situation.

Looking between them and the soldiers he realized he needed to make a life-altering decision within the next minute or two. He felt irritated at his brother for not finding a way to escape the stranglehold the military used to keep him in line. Protecting one's wife and son within a secure compound sounded like incentive to remain a good soldier, but even the military wasn't going to hold out forever without food and supplies being delivered. Metzger envisioned desperate times ahead for them, like the rest of the world, so letting his group move on might be the safer bet for them.

"I hate to be pushy, but your brother's plane leaves in about ten minutes," the soldier said.

"Plane?"

"Plane. I can't say much, but he's flying out on a mission that may make the difference in us winning or losing this war with the infected."

Metzger looked from the soldier to his companions, forced to decide between accompanying his brother on a likely dangerous mission, staying at the base with his sister-in-law and nephew, or continuing in the open world with his new friends.

"Well, fuck," he muttered aloud.

Twenty-eight

Jillian took hold of his hand, looking him in the eye.

"You have to go in there. We'll be fine."

"But I feel like a selfish asshole," Metzger replied, forcing a smirk. He turned to the soldier beyond the gate.

"Are you sure you can't add extended family to the list?"

"No," the soldier said firmly, shaking his head negatively. "The list is final."

Jillian reached up, touching Metzger's cheek to get him to look her in the eyes.

"We knew there weren't any guarantees when we asked to come along," she said. "You've gotten us this far. We'll find our families and make the best of it."

Metzger purposely clasped both of her shoulders, continuing to look her in the eyes.

"Stay alive no matter what occurs," he said. "I *will* find you."

Sutton and Vazquez both snickered, realizing what Metzger had just said, and where it originated, and for a second he believed Jillian had no idea, but she had a habit of proving him wrong.

She sighed through her nose, giving him a mock disapproving, almost scolding look, in response.

"Did you seriously just quote *The Last of the Mohicans* as my sendoff?"

"I really didn't think you'd catch it," he said, handing her the sat phone. "The charger is in the truck that we left beside the box truck."

"You're avoiding my question."

"And because you knew where that came from I think you may be the coolest woman on the planet."

"There are a lot fewer of us," she said, pulling him into a hug.

The soldier on the other side of the fence grumbled, clearing his throat as one of the other soldiers undid the locks for Metzger to cross inside.

"Do you have any issue with me bringing my belongings and weapons?" he asked the soldier who appeared to be in charge of the situation.

"No. You'll probably need them where you're going."

Not sure he liked the sound of that, Metzger walked over to the Hummer, grabbing what few weapons and supplies he could carry. Figuring the military possessed far better firearms than he could bring, he left those for the others, only taking the .357 and one of the semi-automatic pistols. He also took his personal belongings, and the two swords he had definitely fallen in love with during the course of his travels.

Metzger quickly gave everyone in the group a hug and a few hopeful words, whispering to Gracine that the soldiers on the highway might be after the box truck. She was the only one capable of keeping Sutton in check in case he considered engaging the soldiers in a firefight. No box truck was worth risking lives to recover if the military had indeed confiscated it for their inventory.

"I'll take care of it," she said.

Metzger stood in front of Sutton last, but the man wanted nothing to do with a hug. Instead he offered a handshake, which Metzger accepted, clasping the top of the man's hand with his free hand. He wanted Sutton to know that he, like the others, meant more to him than any regular traveling companion just trying to survive the apocalypse as long as possible.

"You're going to have to stop being such a hard-ass one of these days," Metzger told him when they shook hands.

"I'm not making any promises," Sutton replied, unwilling to change his ways. "You're leaving me with this group of Yayhoos, so I can't afford to go soft."

Metzger's grin faded a bit as he made his last comment to the best gun in the group.

"Take care of them."

"I'll do my best. We'd better see you again."

"God willing," Metzger said, backing away from the group, raising his hand for a final wave before crossing the threshold.

He dared not look back again until he neared the utility vehicle with the soldiers, finding that his traveling companions felt the same way about goodbyes, because they had begun to disperse. Only Samantha turned around for one last wave as Luke scooped her from the ground, and Metzger choked up a bit as his eyes felt a little misty. He truly hoped to see them again, but so many things could happen along the road, and he didn't have much of an idea what kind of mission he was about to embark upon as an untrained civilian.

Fighting back any emotions, he jumped into the utility vehicle with the soldiers, crammed into the middle of the rear seat, trying to keep his weapons from poking either of the men. He felt a little intimidated because although he was nearly six feet in height and very capable of taking care of himself, these men were in peak physical condition.

"You're about the last of the holdouts," the soldier in charge commented from the front passenger seat.

"Holdouts?" Metzger asked in return.

"We rounded up most of our local relatives within the first week of the attacks. We've had a few families trickle in here and there, and we've kept a list of who to expect. Your brother kept insisting you'd get here, but a lot of us had our doubts. Buffalo is a long way off."

Metzger wondered how Bryce kept in touch with the mainland if he was on a ship, but he supposed they possessed advanced methods of communication compared to the poor saps trying to survive on their own.

He wanted to inquire about the attacks, but he figured his brother could fill him in more thoroughly when time permitted. The thought of someone deliberately transforming the world into its current state felt preposterous, but Metzger wasn't certain if he'd torture the person or people responsible, or just shoot them outright. He felt anger from his personal losses, and the fact that he was one of the lucky few survivors didn't mean the responsible party would be granted any mercy if he ever caught up to them.

"If you don't mind me asking, were you able to drive all the way here?"

"I drove, rode, and walked from Cincinnati to Buffalo," Metzger answered. "I got lucky and caught a flight out of Buffalo to somewhere in the middle of

Virginia. One of the people in my party was a pilot and knew where to find a Cessna."

"How the hell did you find an open airstrip to land?"

"We didn't. Crash landed in a pumpkin patch of all places."

For the first time all of the soldiers chuckled, showing a human side to their gruff appearances.

"If you don't mind me asking, why are all of the dead huddled on one side of the base?" Metzger inquired.

"They're attracted to the noise around the ships. We're often outside, walking or driving through the area."

"Why don't you clear them?"

"We eliminate a certain number of them per day so they don't bust down the fences, but they've actually become a part of our defense perimeter."

Metzger took in part of his surroundings, finding the base looked somewhat like the industrial area of virtually any city. Some buildings were little more than pole barns near the airstrip, while others maintained a purposeful appearance as though important meetings once transpired within their walls. Roads and parking lots segmented the base, and each building was identified with a sign outside, likely to help new sailors and visitors learn their way around when the base functioned fully.

To these soldiers driving through the base was old hat because they barely looked off to either side, not even in a guarded sense, looking for threats. Metzger couldn't help himself as buildings blurred by without a single person standing outside.

"Why aren't we seeing anyone outside?" he asked.

"We've cordoned off parts of the base beyond the outer perimeter to keep everyone safe. Some of the families are allowed to stay on the ships, and we've set up shelters within the buildings closest to the docks for everyone else."

When they drew closer to the docks he discovered children playing outside a few of the buildings, providing him with a sense of relief. For a minute he wondered if only a handful of families survived to see the inside of the base, but he noticed mothers hanging clothes, children throwing large rubber balls back and forth, and a few husbands grilling out for the new extended family.

He assumed the men were married to military women because he saw no one here in uniform, as everyone remained busy with daytime chores. While the outside world fell into chaos, the military seemed to function about as normally as ever. The picture painted around him was a far different story than what Martinez told him during the car ride. He supposed the Navy conducted things with more discipline at their own base, and people knew their survival hinged on doing their part. The National Guard soldiers might have been treated like lesser citizens, and likely traveled miles, perhaps even many state lines, away from their families when the apocalypse broke out.

Deciding he couldn't feel sorry for everyone, Metzger discovered a greater number of people enjoying the outdoor climate when he stared out the window again. A minute or two later he discovered people in uniforms, and not just Navy uniforms, working closer to the docks where several ships loomed much like the *Wisconsin* had earlier. Metzger couldn't pinpoint the awe that came with seeing a ship so close to land. Perhaps it was because they stood as tall as downtown buildings, with lengths that exceeded football stadiums, or because he couldn't fathom how something so solid and imposing floated.

He felt incredibly safe and secure among so many trained, armed, men and women, tucked behind fences so tall and unyielding that the undead couldn't even be seen. Shrubs and trees merely kept the issue from sight, but he knew the zombies were pushing against one another, lunging into the base's defenses without rest, day after day. Eventually even nature and steel would bend to their persistence if the military forces didn't keep them cleared away.

Vehicles were apparently allowed only so close to the docks because the driver stopped some distance back from a ship Metzger recognized from online research and items Bryce sent to him shortly after he received his most recent assignment. Feeling almost like he'd come home, Metzger stared out the window at the destroyer, wondering how his brother felt serving upon such a capable watercraft. A few sailors milled about on the deck, looking much like ants on a bird feeder by comparison. Although destroyers weren't among the largest of Navy ships, they were still an imposing sight to anyone standing below their decks.

"Stay here while we get things sorted out," the soldier in charge said.

Metzger stepped from the vehicle to stretch his legs as three of the four soldiers headed for the dock where the ship sat like an immovable stone extending from the inlet. He took notice of how everyone, not just the soldiers, appeared clean, likely smelling far better than him because he hadn't seen deodorant in a few weeks. The rare shower came with cold water in a house that wasn't his own, and baths were often in some pond, a lake, or a pool with a green tint from a lack of chemical application.

He didn't want to feel self-conscious, but couldn't help himself. These people appeared civilized and adjusted while he felt something like a caveman visiting an industrialized civilization for the first time. With new information coming at him so quickly he hadn't found time to process his immediate future, and suddenly he needed to vacate his bladder in the worst way. Perhaps nervousness from the thought of finally laying eyes on his brother got the better of him, but he literally hadn't answered the call of nature in hours.

"So every branch is here?" he asked the soldier who stayed behind just to pass the time, and keep his mind from thinking about how badly he needed to piss.

"A lot of us were ordered here or San Diego when it started," the young man answered, obviously considering Metzger part of the fold because everyone else trusted the brother of a lieutenant commander.

It made sense to bring the military branches together at two of the largest Navy bases in the country, but he wondered if other bases were still operational, and how long even sat phones and advanced communications would hold out.

"Why exactly *is* everyone here?" he asked.

"What do you mean?"

"Well, is there a plan or objective, or is everyone simply surviving day by day?"

"A little of both. Some of us go on runs to get food and supplies, while others go on missions that aren't public knowledge. And some of us watch for intruders about to cut chain link fences that let the infected inside behind them."

"I didn't really want to cut it," Metzger said somewhat sheepishly. "Truth be told, I thought there'd be someone at one of the gates to meet us."

Staring forward at the *Ross*, the soldier shook his head.

"It got too dangerous early on. We tried staying out there and picking them off, clearing the bodies when it thinned out a little, but more of them kept coming. Eventually the National Guard was used as a perimeter defense to keep people from getting close to the base and getting killed. Some of those guys bugged out early on, or never came in the first place, so they ended up bringing some guardsmen in from the lower states."

Metzger thought back to Martinez, who desperately wanted to get back to Texas. Perhaps many of the reserve soldiers thought they were serving their country and returning to their families in short order, like every other time.

"What about you?" he asked the soldier. "Did they get your family to safety?"

"I'm not married," the man confessed. "My folks, aunts, uncles, cousins, all live in California. I lost touch with them after the fourth day, so I'm not holding out hope that they survived." He looked somewhat despondent, as though thoughts of his family plagued him regularly. "And there's no way I'm getting there any time soon. Either way, this is my family now."

Metzger felt California was an unrealistic trip on the survival rate scale. Even flying there wouldn't be easy, because no small plane could make the journey without refueling at least a few times.

"If they have any assignments out that way I might volunteer," the man said. "They've been sending people to places familiar to them to make the missions go more smoothly. I think that's why they chose your brother to head up the operation in Buffalo. And it's probably how he got permission to bring you along."

Metzger wasn't particularly thrilled about returning to his home area so soon after leaving, but he looked forward to seeing Bryce. He found it odd they were sending a Navy man on a mission obviously meant to be carried out on land, but Bryce was a natural-born leader. Metzger couldn't hold a candle to his brother's abilities, though he somehow managed to safely bring a group from New York to Virginia on what few survival skills he honed.

"How do you know about the mission?" Metzger inquired, thinking the missions were supposed to be secretive.

"Word gets around. We don't have the use of radios, printers, and emails like before, so people overhear things. Supposedly, they're investigating one of the factories where the explosions happened to see if they can trace it back to someone."

"That won't be particularly easy without technology," Metzger thought aloud. "My brother isn't a Navy SEAL, or a detective, so why would they ask him to head this up?"

"They probably wanted him for his familiarity with the area. They're going to send specialists with him to keep the group safe, and investigate. We have a pretty good return rate so far of the people we've sent out."

Metzger didn't necessarily consider the soldier's words reassuring. He didn't want to be a liability needing protection from the military, and he didn't want to be viewed as some kind of civilian tagalong who was only there due to nepotism.

"They were waiting for your brother to get to port," the soldier said, making certain no one except Metzger heard his words. "I think this mission is really important to the brass. Don't know why, but they're kind of putting a lot of their good eggs in this basket if you know what I mean."

Metzger nodded, not daring to utter a response. Lots of major cities across the country were rocked by explosions that fateful day that proved far worse than 9/11 in so many ways. At least in 2001, in both Metzger's mind and the history books, they knew the culprit responsible for almost 3,000 deaths almost immediately. In this scenario, the death toll reached the millions worldwide, and at least partly by default the people left in charge seemed to know nothing.

Seeing the other three soldiers return from the direction of the *Ross*, Metzger immediately read the concerned, grim expressions on their faces and wondered why Bryce wasn't accompanying them. The leader drew near Metzger and pointed for everyone to climb back into the utility vehicle.

"We need to go," he said to Metzger directly. "Your brother is minutes away from leaving for his mission."

Everyone climbed inside the vehicle and the driver immediately sped them back in the direction they had just come from a few minutes prior. Metzger guessed they were heading for the airfield, because the military wasn't going to ask their people to drive and risk life and limb if the mission was truly vital to the future of mankind.

His need to urinate subsided while he was standing on solid ground, but now in a moving vehicle he felt certain an embarrassing stain would cross his crotch if he didn't see a restroom soon.

Once again feeling the whirlwind of his new surroundings, wondering if he truly would ever get to see his brother, Metzger began wondering if leaving his comrades behind was the correct decision after all.

***

Jillian contemplated how much she missed Metzger just minutes after their departure from the base, and more importantly, *why* she wanted him around. Granted, their relationship had gotten physical at the hotel, which satisfied her needs in that department, but she immediately missed his voice of reason when Gracine and Sutton started arguing in the front seat. Metzger was the glue that held six strangers traveling in a black Hummer together, whether he knew it or not.

Now they were more like a haphazard group of six people with no real plan and no real connection with one another. She barely knew Vazquez, felt acquainted with Luke and Samantha even less, and wasn't even certain she trusted Sutton and Gracine. At least Gracine appeared capable of stopping Sutton from carrying out impulsive acts that placed the group in peril most of the time.

She numbly thought about losing Metzger at the base, ignoring the first few minutes of conversation around her. Not until she noticed Sutton taking a much different route back to their vehicles did she begin registering their conversation. If she remembered correctly from the map, there wasn't a way back, at least not an easy one, that didn't require them crossing at least one bridge to leave the Hampton Roads region. Luckily most of the military posts were set up along the major highways prior to reaching such bridges, so she understood Sutton's notion.

Of course they couldn't afford to get spotted by the military if they wanted to recover their belongings without incident.

"The chances of them grabbing the truck, while you still possess the keys, is highly unlikely this soon," Gracine said. "We've been gone, what, an hour?"

"Those sons of bitches were eyeballing that truck," Sutton argued. "They sent us in there hoping we wouldn't make it back."

"If we don't slip past them it won't make a difference. You're driving like you *want* us to be spotted."

"Maybe I do! We could take those weekend warriors if we needed to."

"Oh," Gracine countered, holding up a foreboding finger. "You're willing to risk our lives, even the life of an eight-year-old child, because you don't want to lose a few motherfucking supplies."

Deciding she'd heard enough already, Jillian reached down, pulling out the set of maps the group had used to navigate through Virginia, thumbing through the pages to find the Norfolk area near the end of the pages.

"Enough!" she exclaimed, getting them both to set aside their quarreling temporarily. "I've got the map right here and I think I can get us through their blockades without them spotting us."

"It better not take much longer," Sutton warned, trying to maintain what little control he could over the situation.

His hands may have been gripping the steering wheel, but he certainly wasn't allowed to run rogue with Gracine questioning his every move.

"Even if they somehow nabbed the truck, we can't go confronting the military," Vazquez muttered just above a whisper.

"Can't we?" Sutton questioned. "Take down one or two and the rest would scurry like cockroaches."

Gracine shot him a fiery look.

"We aren't those kind of people," she said with an even temper, but a hint of anger in her voice. "We don't stoop to their level, and we don't murder in cold blood, even if they *have* wronged us."

"I'm a little surprised to hear you of all people say that," Sutton said in the calmest voice he'd used all day.

Jillian wasn't certain what Sutton's words meant at first, but she recalled Metzger saying something about Sutton rescuing Gracine from some unsavory soldiers not far from the farm. Gracine didn't say a word as she settled into the passenger's seat, staring directly out the front window. Evidently the words were meant to hurt, because Gracine couldn't muster a response to them for some reason. Although Jillian didn't like seeing them at odds, the silence provided her an opportunity to guide Sutton along some side roads that wouldn't take them near the highways and interstates where the soldiers might be looking for deserters from the military, or civilians not welcome near one of the few remaining strongholds in the country.

"Won't they hear the vehicle?" Luke asked from the rear compartment where he and Samantha sat with Buster.

"Probably, if they haven't already," Sutton answered.

"They're going to have equipment that can spot us and hear us coming," Jillian surmised, looking to the map.

She wasn't certain any method of bypassing the main roads kept them safe from detection, so perhaps speeding through the area was a smarter alternative.

"Surely they wouldn't open fire on us," Luke stated, trying to keep his words from frightening Samantha, who seemed to perpetually tune out adult conversations because they were seldom positive.

"Who's going to stop them?" Sutton raised the question that no one dared audibly counter because his words rang with truth.

Knowing where the outpost they passed through the first time was located, Jillian directed Sutton to some roads south of the area, hoping they didn't draw too close to another of the National Guard checkpoints on a different highway. If they encountered a different set of soldiers their vehicle might be viewed as one that soldiers would drive off the base, but they still couldn't chance stopping.

Whether they stopped or not, any group deviating from the main roads was sure to raise suspicions from any guardsmen who took notice.

Although it required about fifteen extra minutes to go around the outpost they originally passed through, the group managed to avoid detection so far as they knew by using some side roads. More rundown businesses and undead made for bleak scenery, but Sutton managed to circumvent the original checkpoint enough that Jillian doubted they were seen or heard. Sutton also took a different route to the parking area where the three trucks were parked, but when they pulled around the side of the building they surprised two uniformed men who turned as though expecting more of their own people to arrive.

Their smiles quickly dissolved into frowns when they spotted the black Hummer approaching, and before they could jump down from inside the open box truck to grab their weapons, Sutton jumped out of the Hummer and aimed the M-16 he'd been keeping close to him in their direction.

"I wouldn't advise it," Sutton warned as the others jumped out to take his side, each of them holding their own weapons with the exception of Samantha.

Keppler looked down at the weapons propped against the bumper with a sneer, knowing blood and pain awaited him if he made a move to arm himself.

"You were supposed to keep watch," Keppler angrily reprimanded the younger soldier who slowly jumped down from the box truck, a look of shame and disappointment crossing his face.

"Something tells me you were thinking of keeping my supplies all to yourselves and not telling the others in your unit," Sutton deduced aloud, prompting the lieutenant to step forward, using his last ditch effort to assert himself.

"This is an abandoned vehicle," Keppler said, walking rigidly as though he still controlled the situation. "It's been commandeered by the United States Government for use as we see fit. If you try and take it back, you're making a big fucking mistake."

Sutton allowed the officer to draw a few steps closer before thrusting the butt of the weapon into the man's stomach, sending him to one knee with a pained groan while the younger soldier stared in shock. Jillian doubted the man had ever seen anyone stand up to the military before, much less the lieutenant who displayed fearless demeanor in any situation. Sutton quickly removed the sidearm from Keppler's right hip, handing it to Gracine.

"Stay the fuck down," Sutton issued an order of his own. "You didn't waste any fucking time running to my truck, did you?"

"You're going to regret that," Keppler said, drawing breaths in pained heaves from the blow to his stomach.

"Not as much as you're going to regret sending us into a hazardous situation with no forewarning so you could steal my truck."

"You seem to have made it out just fine," Keppler said, attempting to stand at last.

Sutton put a hand on the lieutenant's shoulder, pressing down with enough pressure to keep the man in a kneeling position. He wasn't ready to let him up quite yet.

"You should probably collect yourself a moment."

Sutton walked over to the truck, grabbing a bagged item just inside the open door, motioning for the younger soldier to stand beside the lieutenant. He hadn't dared move after seeing Keppler floored by the M-16, but now he slowly walked over to the officer, holding his hands meekly just above his shoulders.

"Luke, get his sidearm," Sutton requested.

Anxious to prove himself as an asset, Luke left Samantha beside Gracine while he walked up and removed the sidearm from the soldier's side. He spent a few extra seconds working around the holster's safety mechanism intended to prevent theft from terrorists and attackers, but he got the gun free. Holding on to the firearm personally, he returned to his position near Samantha, waiting to see what fate Sutton had in mind for the would-be thieves.

Removing two zip ties from the bag, Sutton forced both of the soldiers to lie with their stomachs on the ground at gunpoint. Jillian noticed Keppler seething with anger, but the lieutenant dared not rebel against Sutton because Sutton wasn't the reasonable, kind-hearted man who dealt with him earlier. She wondered briefly what the commanding officer did as a day job before the apocalypse, because he seemed to be a bully of sorts without much concern for others when it came to supplies for his unit.

Sutton appeared to take some pleasure in disabling the soldiers and leaving them behind to the elements. He checked them over to make certain they had no additional knives or weapons on them before collecting their automatic rifles and placing them inside the box truck's cab. Jillian grew concerned that more armed soldiers were likely on the way, because these two weren't concerned about the sound of a vehicle approaching until they turned around. Sutton secured the back of the truck as best he could with no lock available.

No immediate danger threatened the soldiers as everyone climbed into the trucks and took one last look back at the restrained men.

"You're going to regret this," Keppler called as loud as he dared, trying to avoid summoning the undead his way.

Sutton, who had stepped halfway into the driver's seat of the box truck, stopped to look back at the lieutenant.

"You were in the wrong," he said. "Suck it up and stop harassing innocent civilians, or next time you might lose more than your guns."

Keppler glared at him, saying nothing. Jillian saw the saga unfold from the driver's seat of the truck she and Metzger had driven throughout most of Virginia. Now Vazquez sat beside her, looking anxious to get back on the road and leave the dangerous military sector behind them. Jillian felt certain Sutton was asking for trouble by antagonizing the soldiers further, and in Sutton's mind she supposed he was trying to justify his actions and warn the soldiers about the dangers of pursuing the group.

About a mile down the road, Sutton stopped the box truck to hop out for an impromptu group meeting. Jillian wouldn't have been shocked if he requested they go their separate ways now that Metzger had parted from their collective, but he stepped from the truck all business, perhaps even protective of those around him.

"I need to go back to my camp to see if my boys have checked in," Sutton said without hesitation. "If you're all willing to stick by me one last time, I'm willing to help you see if your families made it or not."

Everyone appeared to breathe a sigh of relief that he didn't say something smart or arrogant, finally showing indications he might be at least somewhat of a team player. Perhaps he knew other groups weren't so amicable or willing to bend to his tantrums, so he'd be taking a risk by leaving them for other people, or striking out alone.

Being truthful, Jillian wanted him along because he knew how to use firearms proficiently, and Buster provided an element of security by detecting the undead. Sutton wasn't remotely predictable, but he'd proven to be loyal, backing up his words and protecting the group, even when they didn't know he was acting as their guardian.

She liked the idea of searching for her family with others along for support. Each day held no guarantees of safety, finding necessary items, or even survival, so Jillian planned on waking up each morning with a plan that might come to fruition or end in complete failure. She trusted the people around her, and though they might not have been the most skilled survival group, they didn't scare easily.

Feeling the sat phone in her pocket, she knew the rest of the essential items she needed were in a small satchel beside her. All else could be left behind in an emergency, but if she ever wanted to hear from Metzger again, she needed that phone and the means to charge it. Looking around, she saw no one openly opposed to Sutton's offer, and everyone seemed to be in agreement that they wanted to stick together.

"We've still got daylight," Sutton said. "Let's get moving before the dead start stalking us."

Jillian took one last look at the crossroads behind them, wondering if she would see Metzger again, or if he would survive whatever the military had planned. She no longer believed the government possessed *all* of the answers. Surely they possessed inside information, some shared openly, some not so much, but they also harbored an agenda that quite possibly didn't put the safety of civilians first and foremost.

She couldn't focus on people who weren't with her at the moment. Distractions got a person killed when the undead roamed nearby, so as the group broke from their huddle, she assumed the driver's seat while Vazquez, still trying to heal from the recent gunshot wound, went around the truck. He knew she still had family in the area, and his sister might have been north in the nation's capital, or safely tucked away with political figures. So much uncertainty existed without the benefits of the internet and cell phones.

"Once we check on Sutton's boys, where do we go from there?" Vazquez asked, apparently questioning whose situation took priority.

"I guess we'll go where the roads and the undead allow us," Jillian answered. "We've got nothing but time at this point."

Twenty-Nine

etzger felt like a basketball getting bounced all around the base, and *still* not seeing any proof his brother was even within the secure compound.

As the military vehicle crossed the base with a sense of urgency, Metzger looked to the south, hoping to catch a fleeting glance of his allies if they had lingered. They hadn't, and for the first time since he arrived just outside of Buffalo he felt truly alone again. The idea of leaving the security of others, only to join his brother in some mission that would take them God only knew where, bothered him.

Being inside the base reminded him of the normal world for a moment. The military appeared to carry out their daily regiment with the same rigor as he imagined they did before the collapse of civilization. Soldiers walked with a purpose, carried out their orders, and showed no fear of the world just beyond their fences.

Any barriers between the base and the airfield were no longer guarded, and Metzger spied a transport plane at the closer end of the runway. Swallowing hard, he wasn't sure he wanted to fly again after the Cessna crashed in a Virginia pumpkin field. Beside the plane he noticed half a dozen soldiers dressed in fatigues, and civilians whom he guessed were there to say goodbyes. He still didn't see his brother, but he finally did recognize a few familiar faces slowly stepping back from the aircraft.

His sister-in-law and nephew.

A few seconds later the vehicle came to a stop and as Metzger squeezed out beside the four soldiers who escorted him, they each offered to shake hands with him. He quickly responded to each, and they wished him well, because his civilian status offered him no special treatment in the war against the undead.

"Take care," he said to them as a group before walking toward some of the few family members left in his life.

Because their eyes never left the plane, Metzger caught Isabella and Nathan off-guard when he drew close enough to make them turn and look at him.

"Uncle Dan!" Nathan exclaimed with a wide smile, despite the tears welling up in his eyes from the idea of his father leaving the base on a mission.

Metzger dropped down to give his nephew an embrace while Isabella looked on with equal surprise.

Nathan inherited his father's eyes and chin, but the red hair came entirely from his mother's side of the family. Somewhere close to a month away from his tenth birthday, the boy seemed to grow six inches taller between Metzger's visits. Metzger sometimes tried to envision his nephew as an adult, wondering which traits he might take from the family line, but now he struggled to imagine Nathan reaching adulthood with so much danger everywhere.

"Izzy," he said when he stood, calling his sister-in-law by her nickname.

Her strawberry blonde hair normally reached her shoulders but she had it pinned up today, as though getting ready for battle herself. She wore blue jeans and a buttoned checkered shirt of tan and green coloration. The green accented her eyes of the same color, and Metzger wondered how his brother managed to marry up. She came from a family that did fine with their own precision metal shop that crafted objects for factories and the government. He had no idea how they fared in the apocalypse, but he recalled her brother and folks being rather rugged people who probably owned their share of weapons.

"Dan," she replied warmly. "Glad you could make it."

"Just barely," he replied, glancing at the plane as a few of the soldiers began breaking away from their families. "Half of me is tempted to stay here with you guys, but I haven't seen Bryce yet."

Isabella drew a concerned expression.

"Keep him safe, and bring him back."

"I'll do my best, but I'm a novice compared to these guys."

"He *trusts* you," she said with an implication that Bryce wasn't entirely sold on the military's game plan. "He said you'd make it down here."

"I wasn't so sure for a while."

Isabella looked concerned.

"They wanted him for his knowledge of the Buffalo area," she admitted. "It's also how he got them to bring you along."

"We know it well," Metzger said more confidently than he felt. "And I've been there *very* recently."

"Your folks?" she inquired.

Metzger shook his head negatively. Further elaboration could wait until he made it back from the mission to Buffalo, if he survived.

"Your family?" he asked in return, kneeling to open his pack to retrieve an object from within.

"Last I knew, they were making a stand on their property," Isabella replied. "My father was prepared for about anything, so I have little doubt they're doing just fine."

"That's good to hear," Metzger said, pulling out a gold-colored coin with an embossed train engine on the front, and a caboose on the flip side.

He handed the coin to Nathan, who looked at it with a puzzled expression.

"That belongs to Grandpa," Metzger explained, careful to not use the past tense when referring to his father. "He received it for his service on the railroad. It's one of the few things I have that belonged to him, so I want you to take care of it. Can you do that?"

Nathan nodded affirmatively, and Metzger recalled his father always taking a shine to his only grandchild, and vice versa.

"Good. Looks like I'd better get going."

He quickly hugged Nathan again, and stood to pull Isabella in for a longer embrace so he could speak words only she would hear.

"I'll bring Bryce back," he promised. "You be careful. Things can go bad here as quickly as they can anywhere."

"I'm aware," she said as though having already assessed the hazards.

Isabella was intelligent and tough, far more independent than most officer wives, who enjoyed the privilege of the Navy hierarchy. She was a stronger person with Bryce around, but certainly didn't need him to make every decision for her, or pamper her. Isabella would require mental fortitude for the dangers that accompanied the apocalypse, particularly where the scheming survivors were concerned.

Metzger finally pulled away from them, prepared to board the aircraft with the last of the soldiers who had finished their goodbyes and walked aboard with rigid posture. They appeared to have purpose in their steps, as though they still believed the mission they were undertaking held significance. Wondering what his brother thought about the military's stance, Metzger decided to ask him in person.

"Bye," he said to Isabella and Nathan before turning to walk up the open ramp where the soldiers had entered.

Upon entering the rear of the plane, he found two Humvees strapped down, obviously for use once the aircraft landed. The military spared no expense in their missions, deeming them worthy of whatever resources could be spared. An odor that he found similar to the industrial smell inside a factory reached his nose, either from the plane or the equipment stored within. Walking ahead, Metzger found seats on either side of the plane where soldiers checked or cleaned their weapons, inventoried their supplies, or talked about things other than the task at hand to preoccupy themselves from what lie ahead.

A few glanced his way, but they basically paid no attention to him as though he was entirely expected to tag along on the mission. He glanced at faces, not finding his brother among either row, counting roughly a dozen soldiers as he passed them, all wearing camouflage fatigues that contained various shades of tan and green. In cities that all began to look like sepia photos from the Old West, Metzger supposed no degree of urban concealment would be entirely effective.

He felt like a kid walking into school with generic versions of everything a student was supposed to have on the first day. These men carried automatic weapons, explosives, and body armor while he brought along a few handguns, two swords, and some trinkets from his previous life. Under no circumstances did he want these men to protect him, but he also felt rather impotent comparatively. Such firepower might prove effective against the living and the undead, but it also drew swarms of the undead. One simple bite that drew blood was enough to infect a living person, and Metzger had seen how quickly an individual could be overtaken by several zombies.

Reaching the end of the line, Metzger began to wonder if his brother truly *was* on the plane when he spied a man up front talking to one of the pilots, going over some kind of checklist. He recognized the authoritative voice immediately, and studied Bryce, who also wore fatigues, appearing prepared to carry out his orders despite what Isabella stated.

Perhaps an inch taller than Metzger, Bryce was every bit as strong as his younger brother, and he knew multiple ways with which to defend himself. He kept his brown hair parted to one side, and appeared to have recently shaved, save the thick mustache he'd grown when he first became an officer in the Navy. Perhaps he wanted to separate himself from the younger enlisted men, or simply liked its appearance after he grew it in, but Bryce hadn't shaved it off in years, and apparently wasn't about to.

When he looked up from the list, the lieutenant commander looked stunned for a fleeting second. His grim countenance quickly transformed into a smile as he recognized his brother, excusing himself from the pilot before briskly walking over to give Metzger a stiff hug.

"I knew you'd make it," Bryce said before letting his brother free from the grip.

"I cut it a little close."

"Mom and Dad?" Bryce inquired with concern.

"No," Metzger said, fighting back the sadness that pained the pit of his stomach. "I'll tell you about it later."

"Okay," Bryce replied, openly disheartened, though not shocked, by the fact his parents hadn't survived the end of the world. "I hope you're ready for this, little brother."

"What are we doing exactly?"

"We intend to find the son-of-a-bitch responsible for all of this and get some answers. And if I have my way, we're going to cut off his dick and feed it to him."

Metzger removed his pack by slinging the strap over his shoulder, setting it on the ground. Prepared to settle in for the long haul, he would follow his brother to the ends of the Earth, much like he did when they were kids. The concept of following Bryce to such lengths felt more literal in the present, but he trusted his brother to do right by others, and the planet, only following orders so long as they met his moral standards.

"I'm glad you're here, Dan," Bryce said.

"*I'm* glad I'm here."

Bryce smirked.

"Let me straighten out a few things with the pilot and we'll be on our way. If this goes well, we may be able to set things back to the way they were. It won't be easy, but they seem to think it can be done."

Metzger watched his brother turn to deal with preparations, wondering who 'they' were exactly. He suspected they were government officials who knew more than they revealed, or the same people who would puppeteer soldiers to do their bidding with false promises. Metzger assumed some great scientific minds were hard at work, trying to figure out the science behind the deadly virus that came with a nasty side effect.

While Bryce might have been the ranking officer aboard the plane, Metzger suspected the mission lie in the hands of the capable men surrounding him. Most likely members of the Special Forces, SEALs, or both, they would ensure nothing about the mission went sideways.

He heard the plane's engines roar to life as everyone began securing their belongings before latching their seatbelts. Metzger followed suit, finding an empty seat, keeping what little he owned with him. As the rear door rose from the ground, the view of daylight and the handful of people still standing outside disappeared, giving way to the plane's dim interior. Metzger couldn't believe he had traveled all the way from Buffalo to Virginia simply to turn around and commute back to his hometown within a matter of days. Only heartbreak and terrible recent memories awaited him there, but at least this time he would face any adversaries with his brother and the might of the United States military.

Metzger hoped that was enough as he watched his brother strap on a seatbelt beside him, looking every bit as stout and confident as Metzger recalled. Looking for answers certainly meant walking into the belly of the beast, more specifically the point of origin, where the explosion in Buffalo took place.

Ground zero.

Metzger couldn't imagine what they might find there, questioning if the site was even safe for human habitation yet. He suspected the military wouldn't send some of its best people on a suicide mission, but he planned to remain vigilant just the same.

Shaking his head, he prayed for his brother to make continued good choices, because countless lives depended on it. He trusted Bryce implicitly, feeling absolutely no regrets about joining up with his brother, though he already missed his other comrades after forming a bond with them. He wished them well with their travels, hoping they found resolutions with their family members, good or bad, as he'd done.

Thinking about Jillian in particular, he wanted to see her again, though he expected the coming days and weeks would shape them into somewhat different people. She helped him reconnect with people after a month of isolation, and he wouldn't forget that. He wasn't going to lose himself in the memories of their time together, because the mission ahead required him to remain focused.

Something in the reaches of his mind tugged at his reasoning, letting him know the world was about to grow more dangerous and complicated in the coming days. He suspected the terrible events he'd experienced since leaving Blue Ash before Labor Day were just the tip of the iceberg.

A sound similar to a boiling tea kettle reached Metzger's ears once the plane finished taxiing around the runway to a suitable takeoff point and the engines whined once the pilot revved them up. Soon the noise was replaced by a constant, steady roar that Metzger dulled by putting on the wired headphones beside him.

Feeling a slight vibration from the large plane as it began moving down the runway, Metzger glanced at his brother. Bryce kept busy, checking over his assigned weapons and inventory as though he were sitting at the foot of his bed instead of heading into the deadliest situation of his life. Metzger felt the g-forces at work as the plane gathered momentum and took off, angling slightly upward. He wasn't even certain at which point they left the ground with such a smooth ascent, and he silently praised the pilot for being so incredibly good at his occupation.

Feeling assured his tax dollars were spent wisely when it came to training military pilots, Metzger closed his eyes, trying to envision Buffalo and its suburbs during better times.

Strangely, he couldn't shake images of the dusty wasteland, complete with ravaged streets and staggering zombies, from his thoughts.

Epilogue

Keppler managed to find some jagged metal along a car door, not far from where he and Corporal Caleb Jones were bound by the strangers who owned the box truck. Although enraged by the fact that they returned to get the truck, disarming and binding him in the process, he felt a certain particular seething anger towards the young corporal. Given one job, and one job only, Jones failed to keep adequate lookout while Keppler rummaged through the truck for useful supplies.

"Corporal, you are a disgrace," Keppler announced as he moved his hands up and down, allowing the jagged metal to cut through the plastic restraint.

"I'm sorry, sir," Jones said, still trying to remove his zip tie with pieces of large debris on the ground.

He fared badly compared to Keppler, who wasn't about to share in his find just yet. He wanted Jones to suffer a bit before setting him free.

Not accustomed to failure, the lieutenant rather enjoyed his position in the new world. He gave orders at his previous job as well, keeping people under his thumb at a factory that produced creamer and chocolate milk mix. Some called it micromanaging, but he referred to his technique as getting desired results. He didn't like it when people crossed him, countered his opinions, or tried to usurp his authority, because his methods and opinions were often proven correct.

Jones had already made reference to the fact that Keppler shouldn't have let the civilians cross their barricades, at least not without obtaining permission first. In carefully crafted words, the corporal had also suggested that Keppler let the group inside with the hopes of them not returning, either through the cruel hand of fate, or the military bringing them inside the fold.

All of the soldiers were weary, and some of them had come from other states at the very beginning. There really wasn't pay in the traditional sense, and most of them stayed for food, lodging, and the security that fellow men and guns provided. Some of them wanted to check on their families or return home, but the chances of crossing numerous states and surviving the undead and marauders looked bleak at best.

"I'm sure that punk Martinez bugged out on us," Keppler sneered as he felt the final strand of the plastic begin to give way, careful not to cut his flesh. "That's why I sent him, basically to test him."

Keppler hadn't waited to see if the corporal returned before he went to search for the box truck, leaving another of the men temporarily in charge. Martinez occasionally spoke of home, subtly hinting that he wished to return there. The lieutenant often sized up the people working for him, assessing their strengths and weaknesses, often playing human chess with them to get what he wanted. He usually sought information, and he learned to play some of the soldiers against one another to draw a select few to his side as spies. Jones wasn't one of those people, partly because he didn't have much to offer in the way of information or useful allies.

"You going to bug out on me, too?" Keppler asked the young soldier, who continued to battle the plastic strand binding his wrists.

"No, sir. I don't really have anywhere to go."

Keppler watched him struggle with the zip tie only a few seconds more before verbally intervening.

"Stop," he ordered. "You're going to hurt yourself and I don't want to be cleaning up blood, or bandaging wounds."

"Yes, sir."

Feeling the final strand of plastic break free from his own wrists, Keppler stood, momentarily massaging his wrists before looking into nearby vehicles for something more practical than jagged metal to free Jones. He found a small car off to the side of the road that held a backpack in the back seat. Wondering why his soldiers hadn't gone through the vehicles more thoroughly for potential supplies during their free time, or while moving the vehicles to the side of the road, he realized they didn't share his work ethic.

Barely better than the entitled teens and young adults that couldn't be bothered to look for work before the end of the world, they simply stood by, waiting for orders.

Keppler rummaged through the backpack, finding several sealed bottles of water, some individually wrapped food items, and a sturdy utility knife with a retractable blade. He pulled out the knife, still feeling some heft to the bag, so he dug a little further, finding a semi-automatic Smith & Wesson at the bottom that the car's driver obviously never got to use when it counted the most.

Quickly checking it for ammunition, and to make certain a round was readied in the chamber, Keppler tucked it along the back of his belt. He took up the other supplies, prepared to cut Jones free and begin the next chapter of his life in the apocalypse. Tired of obeying orders from a government that treated him like a secondhand citizen, only to have asshole civilians get the better of him thanks to his inept subordinates, he finally found something worth his time.

Revenge.

"I don't know about you, but I'm ready to find those dickheads who took that box truck and left us for dead," he informed Jones as he walked over to the soldier, who remained seated atop the concrete parking lot.

He reminded the lieutenant of an upended turtle, unable to fend for himself.

"Sir?" Jones asked, looking up at him, squinting because the lieutenant stood with the sun at his back, temporarily blinding the young soldier.

"We're getting the boys together and we're going after these assholes, corporal."

Jones looked hesitant, and helpless, still restrained and seated on the ground.

"Sir, we can't just abandon our post."

"What has the government done for us?" Keppler asked, irritated that his soldier, *his soldier*, would question his orders and even momentarily put the government's commands ahead of his lieutenant's.

"Have I not taken care of you since the beginning of this thing?" Keppler asked with a bark in his voice.

"You have, sir."

"We haven't experienced a single casualty as a unit, have we?"

"No, sir."

Keppler stood above the corporal, momentarily saying nothing, continuing to weigh his options. He needed to convince his men to abandon their post, an act worthy of court-martial, a dishonorable discharge, and prison time when a system remained in place to carry out such sentences. Now, living in a virtually lawless land, Keppler saw nothing stopping him from doing whatever he wanted, but he needed some followers, because individual unregulated people were like minnows that the larger lawless fish sought to devour.

"The government isn't doing us any favors," Keppler said, trying to reason with the soldier. "We're going to run out of supplies, water, and food with so many people staying in this area. The military is a business, Jones, and without that convoy of goods coming this way, things are going to dry up. Shit, I'm surprised they haven't already. They leave us out here like guard dogs, throwing us scraps of food, and expect us to salute and say 'Yes, sir!' whenever they come around. It's bullshit, and it's time we stopped putting up with it."

Jones eyeballed him momentarily, unable to disguise his tentative feelings about packing up and leaving a secured area. Perhaps he thought the lieutenant was testing him, because he appeared uncertain of what to say next.

"Sir, we have numbers here. We have shelter, food, water, and we work eight hour shifts. It isn't that bad."

"Isn't that bad? Well, it's going to be."

"Permission to speak freely, sir?"

"I thought we already had been, Jones."

Jones twisted his face in thought, trying to frame his words carefully, and Keppler already had countermeasures working within the depths of his mind.

"Sir, are you just wanting revenge on these people for getting the better of us?"

"Getting the better of *you*, Jones."

"Sorry, sir."

"You should be, son."

Keppler knew the other soldiers would be joining them shortly, once their shift concluded. Even taking himself and Jones out of the rotation to check the box truck was against orders, and the last thing he needed was more trouble. At this moment, he needed loyal soldiers to help him track the box truck and the individuals responsible for causing him embarrassment. Perhaps his soldiers would return to the base if they tracked down the civilians quickly and dealt with them, but more than likely the soldiers would strike out on their own and build a new life for themselves, once free of governmental restraints.

"Sir, can I get free now?" Jones asked hesitantly.

Keppler held the knife in front of him, looking between it and Jones momentarily.

"Just answer me one more question, son."

"Shoot."

"Do you think the boys will back me if we go after these douchebags who took what could amount to a month's worth of supplies?"

"That's asking a lot, sir. This place is a lot to leave behind right now."

"I suppose it is," Keppler said, dropping the knife beside Jones, watching as the soldier turned his body and wriggled his fingers to reach the object of his freedom. "I suppose they just need some motivation."

With that said, the lieutenant reached behind him, pulling the gun and firing a round into the surprised corporal's forehead before he could even utter a plea. Dropping dead like a sack of potatoes atop the concrete, Jones remained perfectly still because there was no chance of his corpse reanimating. Blood slowly oozed from his forehead, creating a small pool atop the concrete while his open eyes stared into a void, perhaps even the afterworld, painting a perfect picture for the scenario Keppler had cooked up.

Knowing the gunfire would draw his people that much quicker, Keppler cut the zip tie free from Jones's hands. He then placed the knife near the body, providing the method with which the plastic tie was severed, even wiping it off with his uniform out of habit to leave no fingerprints. Forensics weren't likely to be utilized again for years to come, but he wasn't taking any chances that someone might be a police officer in their civilian life and know how to use forensic tools.

With the gun, he took a little more time and care, burying it in a mulch mound beside one of the local businesses. No one would suspect once he weaved his woeful tale to his soldiers, rallying their support for his cause. The government often used propaganda and deception to get what they wanted from their soldiers, so Keppler saw no reason not to use the same tactics.

He knelt beside the body, looking down at the wide-open eyes once again as the smell similar to copper reached his nostrils. Wafting it upward so he could take in the unusual odor from the blood, he heard the sound of vehicles approaching. He made one more motion with his hand for a final sniff, putting on his game face before turning to face his squad that came running to his aid within minutes of the gunfire.

"What happened?" one of them inquired as they jumped out of the vehicles, armed to the teeth, shocked looks crossing their faces at the sight of a comrade dead in the middle of a parking lot.

Most of them hadn't experienced the death of a relative or close friend in person, so this likely came as a shock to see one of their own murdered.

"Boys, those assholes with the box truck doubled back and got the jump on us," Keppler stated without falter.

He hesitated momentarily, playing out the charade. Acting somber momentarily, he ran a frustrated hand through his hair before letting them see his angry side with a flushed red face. He wasn't going to cry, or even pretend to, because he would never let his soldiers see him in a weakened state.

"They tied us up," he continued, struggling to maintain his composure by all appearances with a fallen soldier at his feet, "and when Jones tried to break free, they killed him for it."

"Dear God," one of the soldiers muttered as the fable was taken hook, line, and sinker by the entire squad.

"Who knows why they let me live, but the cowards loaded up and took off when they knew you were coming," Keppler continued with the deception, feeling satisfied with every word, because the looks of the soldiers indicated each detail brought them closer to his side. "They took all of our weapons, and every scrap of food and water stored inside that truck. Supplies that would have gotten us through another month or more without worry. They didn't have to murder Jones, but they did."

"We need to find them," one of the soldiers finally said, relieving Keppler's worry that *he* would actually have to present the idea after spinning his tale of woe.

He needed them to think it was *their* idea, and a good one at that, to abandon their post and hunt down the civilians who left in such a hurry.

"Boys, we can go find those sons-of-bitches, but it may not be easy, and it may not be quick. If we leave now, we can catch up with them that much sooner, but we're going to get labeled deserters if we do. I don't think we'd make it back in time for our next shift."

"Fuck the government, lieutenant," one of the men said, his finger near the trigger of his tethered firearm. "What have they done for us?"

Keppler couldn't have agreed with the sentiment more, and he saw no dissension among any of the soldiers. Figuring the other military forces around them weren't keeping much of a headcount, he needed to get the corporal's body out of sight before questions arose.

"Boys, a few of us are going to stay here and give Jones a proper burial, because the government can't know what we're doing, and this man deserves that much. The rest of us are going back to the base to grab a few things we need, and then we're hunting these motherfuckers down," Keppler said with resolve, displaying anger for Jones's murder that he actually felt for being bested by a ragtag group of civilians. "We're going to hunt these fuckers down and kill every last one of them if it's the last thing we do."

End Volume 1.